A THOUSAND LIES

By

SHARON SALA

Book cover: Kim Killion of HotDAMN Designs
www.hotdamndesigns.com

ISBN:9780989628600

Dedication

Knowing whom the people in your life are either gives you the impetus to make them proud, or in some cases, to get as far away from them as you can get.

I have been blessed in my life to come from good, hardworking people who took pride in a job well done and never minded if their hands got dirty in the process.

But there are just as many people in the world who spend their lives trying to live down the circumstances of their birth and raising.

I'm dedicating this book to those who found the strength to walk away——to shed the mantle of public shame and scrutiny with both dignity and grace.

Whatever it took for you to take that leap of faith, you have forever blessed the generations of your people yet to come.

Chapter One

Wisteria Hill wasn't on a hill at all, but in the Louisiana lowlands outside of New Orleans. Jason Poe had it built for his Irish bride, LilyAnn, in 1859, and in its time, it was as lovely as anything on the Mississippi. It had survived the Civil War, carpetbaggers, hurricanes, births and deaths enough to fill a book and, in later years, more financial crises than the New York Stock Exchange.

But after one hundred and fifty-plus years of wear and tear, the grand lady had become as down-at-the-heels ragged as an old hooker plying her trade from the shadows of an alley on Beale Street.

The current heir and resident of Wisteria Hill was Anson Poe. Like his ancestors before him, he was black-Irish, handsome verging on beautiful with hair the color of midnight, clear blue eyes, and a face reminiscent of a Ralph Lauren clothing advertisement. He had everything going for him but a conscience. It was as if all of the good traits had been used up in the preceding generations and bequeathed Anson nothing but the crumbs of self-respect. Behind the knockout looks was a man incapable of compassion and fair-to-bursting with greed. He filled his physical needs for drugs and sex on a whim while his narcissistic, Napoleonic need to rule kept his family in constant turmoil. The only things he could not control were the encroaching rot of Wisteria Hill and the heat of a Louisiana summer.

****

Sweat rolled out of LaDelle Poe's hairline, then down the back of her neck and points south as she stirred the crawfish gumbo she'd been making since daybreak. Once the hour hand on the clock passed 10:00 a.m., the kitchen usually closed due to heat and Delle's disposition.

Anson stood in the doorway watching the way his wife's body moved beneath her loose blue shift and wondered what the odds were of getting a blow job before breakfast. When she caught his look and glared, he eyed the bruise he'd put on her cheekbone the night before and moved to the coffee pot instead. Caffeine was second best to the adrenaline rush of sex, and from the look on her face, he'd best not put his dick anywhere near her teeth.

"Is that breakfast or lunch?" he asked.

"It's whatever you want it to be," Delle muttered, still mad at her husband for what he'd done to her face last night.

Anson frowned. "A man doesn't like to eat the same damn thing all day long."

Delle swung a filet knife toward his tight, flat belly. "And a woman doesn't like to stand over a hot stove and cook for a man who hurts her. You want to live better? Well so do I, Anson Poe, and for starters, you can air-condition this money trap. God knows you can afford it."

Anson smiled.

Breath caught in the back of Delle's throat. She'd seen that look before. Before the day was over, she'd pay for talking back.

"There's bread for toast if you're too hungry to wait," she said, pointing at the bread on the kitchen counter.

He popped in a couple of pieces, then continued to watch her as he sipped his coffee. Even after four children, she had held her figure. Except for a faint grey streak at her left temple, her hair was still the same shade of auburn she'd been born with. He didn't even mind the small laugh lines at the corners of her eyes, although he suspected they were there more from squinting against the sun than smiling. She didn't have much of a sense of humor when it came to him.

"Where's Linny?" he asked.

"Outside playing."

He moved to the screen door to look out, but didn't see her anywhere.

"I don't see her."

Delle shrugged. "That's probably because she doesn't want to be seen. She's fine."

Anson thought of his daughter with the curiosity of a stranger. She was their only girl and had come along seventeen years after Brendan, the youngest of their three sons. She was tall for her age, and it was already obvious what a beauty she'd be. The girl definitely had his looks, and he immediately wondered if there was a way to cash in on that. Other than money, the girl meant nothing to him and he focused on the old stable at the far end of the grounds, instead.

His great-grandmother had loved the Orient and at one time had an Asian garden on the grounds she had enclosed with a stand of bamboo. Over the years, the garden went to weeds and eventually died. Everything had long since disappeared except for that stand of bamboo. It took over the back of the property, spread into the trees, and like kudzu, became the pest that wouldn't go away.

Anson went through the last of the family's money within a year of getting married and immediately turned to farming. Unfortunately, the crops he began growing were illegal. Needing a cover crop to hide the fact he was growing and selling marijuana, he turned the old stable into a work shed and began cutting, rooting, and potting the rampant stands of bamboo, then sold them to landscapers and florist shops. When the bamboo business became successful, it gave him the cachet of a legal businessman, although his other, more profitable, business was a poorly concealed fact.

Anson shifted his stance, frowning as sweat ran down the middle of his back. Delle was right. It was hot in here, but if he had to work outside in the heat, then she could work in the heat, too.

He glanced at his watch, wondering where the hell Sam and Chance were. He had a big shipment of weed going out today and needed his sons on site.

****

The baby cottonmouth slithered out from beneath some kudzu vines and into the still, green waters without leaving a ripple. Belinda Poe—Linny to the family—watched from her post on a nearby rock until it disappeared before she opted to come down. Water moccasins were lethal no matter their size, and Mama would have herself a fit if she knew where Linny was playing, but she loved the swamp. It was her private jungle. Down here, she was Queen Belinda and ruled over everything residing within.

Linny was as long and lean as a newborn foal with slender arms and legs, bare and brown. Her jeans shorts were nearly white from countless washing. Her tank top was yellow, a good contrast to her smooth, brown skin. Today the shirt was stuck fast to her body from the heat. The black hair she'd inherited from her daddy hung nearly to her waist and had been pulled up in a ponytail. She'd woven a crown from the kudzu vines and wore it as elegantly as if it were made of gold.

Standing tall for a nine-year-old, the jade green diadem on her head added inches to her height, and in the sunlight at the edge of the bayou, she almost pulled off the queenly look. The final touch was her scepter, a repurposed walking stick she'd found in the attic.

She was poking about in the underbrush looking for frogs when something rustled the grass behind her. Fearing it was the enemy, she leaped back up on her throne. Then she saw an old snapper crawl out of the woods and pointed the queenly scepter to announce the knight's slow arrival.

"Behold, Sir Snapper has entered the royal chamber! What have you to say for yourself?"

The snapper wasn't fazed in the least by her presence and continued toward the murky waters just as the little water moccasin had done. As the turtle pushed off from solid ground into the water with a loud splash, Linny raised her arm in a gesture of farewell.

"Godspeed, Sir Snapper... O faithful servant of few words."

A bead of sweat ran down the middle of her back as she glanced at the sky. The sun was higher now. All manner of critters would soon be coming up to the water's edge, which meant it was time for her to go home. She still had the shade of the live oaks to play under and would do anything she could, for as long as possible, to avoid being inside with Daddy.

He was mean to Mama, which Linny didn't understand because Mama was as sweet as the day was long. If he could be mean to Mama, then he would be mean to anybody, and Linny wasn't in the mood to get a whipping just because Daddy was in a pissy mood.

"Pissy," she said, giggling as she jumped off the rock. "Pissy, pissy, pissy."

Saying bad words when no one could hear was an adrenaline rush, the same as playing in the swamp. Belinda Poe was only nine, and to her daddy's way of thinking, nothing but a useless girl. But she had the same fire in her blood as all of Anson Poe's offspring had, and strode through the woods toward home without fear still in queen mode with the scepter in her hand and the crown on her head, unaware she was the current topic of conversation at home.

****

Delle eyed Anson's on-guard stance, mistaking his interest as concern.

"I told you. Linny is fine. She'll come home when she's ready."

Anson didn't bother acknowledging her comment, mostly because he didn't like her tone of voice.

Delle shrugged to herself and went back to check on her gumbo, but she was uneasy about the way Anson looked at Linny these days—like he was eyeing a hunting dog for bloodline. She was measuring up rice when she heard an approaching car.

"Who's coming?" Anson's eyes narrowed.

"Brendan."

Unlike his older sons, Anson didn't get along with his youngest and resented that Brendan was Delle and Linny's favorite.

Then he saw a flash of yellow down at the end of the yard. It was his daughter, running out of the woods and across the clearing toward Brendan's SUV. She had a bunch of leaves wrapped around her head and a cane in her hand, and he wondered what the hell she'd been doing. When he saw Bren get out of the SUV and wave at her, the space between his shoulder blades began to itch. He needed to hit something—or someone—to make it better.

"Your toast is getting cold," Delle said.

He turned away from the doorway in sudden anger, grabbed the toast, and refilled his coffee cup. He walked past Delle and without missing a beat, flung the hot coffee on her bare feet, then watched the hot dark liquid run between her toes and down into the cracks of the old linoleum flooring with unhidden glee.

Delle screamed as she danced backward from the

puddle beneath her feet, but it was too late. The damage had already been done.

Anson grabbed a towel from the counter and threw it at her.

"Sorry about that," he drawled.

Delle knew he'd done it on purpose, but she was in too much pain to fight. Moments later, she heard footsteps running up on the back porch and knew things were going to get worse. Tears flowed down her cheeks. Her hands trembled as she looked up at the man who shared her bed.

"Why, Anson? What worm is in your brain that makes you so goddamned crazy?"

Anson arched an eyebrow and smiled.

****

Brendan Poe was a carbon copy of his father in looks, but that was where similarity ended. He hated the bastard in more ways than he could count, and he only came back to Wisteria Hill on a regular basis because of his mother and sister. He loved them with a passion and still wrestled with the guilt of moving out after he turned nineteen, knowing he was leaving them behind to his father's mania.

When he turned off the main road and started down the driveway, the knot in his belly grew tighter. The first sight of the old Antebellum mansion was always one of unease. It would have been magnificent in its day, and although he'd been born in that house, he'd always been overwhelmed by the impending decay of both his family and the structure.

The mansion was in need of more than a coat or two of paint. One shutter from a front window was hanging by a hinge and another completely gone. The bottom step at the front of the verandah was also gone, which was why everyone used the kitchen door around back. Shingles were missing on the west eaves of the roof, and the grounds were as dejected as Brendan's mood. The Spanish moss hanging from the trees made them look as ragged as the house. The only spots of color were the vast assortment of birds flying about and the purple wisteria that had been allowed to grow wild, overtaking anything that would hold the climbing vines.

Although it was a little past 9:00 a.m., the day was already sweltering. Brendan circled the house and pulled up to park in the shade beneath one of the trees. He heard someone call out his name as he got out and turned to see his little sister running out of the woods. The knot in his belly eased. Belinda was the light of his life. He couldn't love her more if she'd been his own child. He waved and then waited in the shade for her to arrive.

"Brendan! Brendan! I didn't know you were coming!" she shouted as she jumped into his arms.

He was laughing as he hugged her, a little stunned by how long her legs were getting as the toes of her shoes bumped against his knees.

"You are growing like a weed, little sister. And speaking of weeds, what is that on your head?"

Linny wiggled to be put down, which he did. Then she straightened her crown, stabbed her scepter into the dirt, and lifted her chin.

"I am Belinda, Queen of the Bayou! This is my crown."

Brendan laughed and tweaked the leaves. "Looks more like the Kudzu Queen to me."

She ignored him. "A queen is a queen, and you are Sir Brendan, my good and faithful knight!"

Another twinge of guilt shot through him. He wasn't all that faithful or he wouldn't have left them alone with Anson Poe. All of a sudden, they heard a high-pitched shriek come from inside the house.

"Mama," Linny whispered. The crown fell from her head as she turned to run, but Brendan was already ahead of her.

He was the first to see his mother on the floor and

Anson standing over her with an empty coffee cup dangling from his fingers. Rage blossomed as he dropped to his knees beside her. He saw the bruise on her cheek, the tears on her face, and the skin on the tops of her feet already beginning to blister. His voice was calm, belying the hate in his gut.

"Mama, what happened?"

When his little sister dropped down beside them and started to cry, he heard a soft chuckle. Anson was actually laughing.

He needed to get Linny out of the room.

"Sugar, I need you to go get that bottle of aloe vera gel out of the back bathroom for me."

"Mama, your feet. Your poor feet." Linny sobbed.

Brendan patted the top of her head. "Go on, honey."

She jumped up and ran.

Brendan doubled his fists.

Delle grabbed his wrist.

"It was my fault, Bren. I bumped his arm and—"

"Really, Mama? And what exactly did you bump to get that bruise on your cheek?"

She blushed under her youngest son's stare and then looked away.

Brendan stood up, turned the fire out from under the gumbo, and then hit his father so fast Anson never saw it coming.

Anson fell backward with a resounding thud, and when he opened his eyes, the water stain on the ceiling was going in and out of focus. His head still buzzed as he dragged himself from the floor, too stunned to make a remark.

"Sorry about that. I was aiming for that fly," Brendan drawled and swung his mother up into his arms.

She didn't weigh nearly enough, which made him wonder what else she was enduring as he sat her on the counter, and swung her feet into the sink.

"Oh God, dear God." She kept moaning and gritted her teeth to keep from screaming.

When Brendan turned on the cold water, she shrieked. She rocked back and forth as Linny appeared in the doorway, a look of terror on her face.

"It's okay, sugar," Brendan said. "We're just putting cold water on Mama's burns."

Linny saw the blood running from her father's lip, and she took a deep breath. As long as Bren was here, nothing bad could happen.

"Did you find the aloe?" Brendan asked.

She handed it to him and then slipped beneath her mother's arm.

"I'm okay, baby. The coffee was hot. It was just an accident," Delle said.

Anson picked up the toast he'd dropped and tossed it in the trash, swiped the blood off his lip with the back of his hand, and pointed at his daughter.

"Make me some more toast, girl."

Linny flinched.

Delle tightened her grip on Linny's shoulders.

"Make it your damn self," Delle said.

Linny spun out from under her mother's grasp, grabbed the other piece of toast from the toaster, and thrust it into her father's hand.

He grabbed her by her ponytail, yanking her head back just enough that she was forced to look at his face.

"You don't feed your daddy leftovers," he snapped.

Linny knew Daddy burned Mama. Her anger made her brave.

"It's not leftover, Daddy. I never took a bite," she said calmly.

"Turn loose of her now," Brendan said.

Anson looked up. Brendan's hand was only inches from the knife-filled butcher block. It was time to deflate this before it got dirty. He laughed and released his grasp.

"Son-of-a-bitch, ya'll. Calm down. Everything's cool. Like your mama said, it was an accident."

He winked at Belinda and then took a great big bite out of the middle of the toast, chewing loudly as he left the kitchen.

Brendan spun to face his mother.

"Why do you stay with that bastard?"

Delle's voice was just above a whisper.

"He's my husband. I took a vow to—"

"He took the same vows and he's broken every one of them, which damn sure nullifies yours," Brendan snapped. "You and Linny can come live with me. I have plenty of room and the apartment is air-conditioned."

Delle's shoulders slumped. "If we did, he wouldn't let it go. None of us would ever know peace. He wouldn't leave you alone until he hurt you, son."

Linny was shaking as she slipped back beneath her mother's arm.

"I'll watch out for her, Bren," she said.

"You're supposed to be playing and being a happy little girl, not standing guard against Anson Poe."

Delle frowned. "Hush, Brendan. Do not bad-mouth your father in front of me."

"I'm twenty-six years old, LaDelle, not twelve, and Anson might have supplied the sperm that made me, but he is not, nor ever has been, any kind of father. Now stop talking, get your feet out of the sink, and let me have a look."

"Do not call me LaDelle," she muttered. "I am your Mama."

"It got your attention now, didn't it? Let me see your feet, please."

She moaned as he turned off the water. He began patting her feet dry and frowned. Water-filled blisters were already forming.

He upended the bottle of aloe and carefully squeezed

the cool gel on both of her feet, then wrapped them in the oldest, softest dishtowels he could find.

"That's the best I can do," Brendan said. "Linny, go get Mama's purse."

"What for?" Delle asked as Linny ran out of the room.

"You're going to the hospital."

She panicked. "No, no, I can't go. I'm making gumbo."

"It can finish cooking on the back of the stove," Brendan muttered.

"But Anson—"

Brendan's eyes narrowed sharply, and in that moment, Delle shut her mouth. One Poe could be as hard as another.

Linny came back with the purse, only steps ahead of her father.

"What the fuck do you all think you're doing?" he yelled, as he strode into the kitchen.

Brendan pulled the cloth back from one of Delle's feet.

The sight actually left him speechless.

Brendan wrapped it back up and picked his mother up in his arms.

"Linny, get the door," he said.

Anson reached for his daughter. "She stays with me."

"Like hell. Linny, get the door," Brendan repeated, then turned his back on Anson.

Anson was furious. "Boy, you overstep your bounds! That's my wife and my daughter and this is my house. You don't—"

Brendan pulled the door shut behind him and all but ran toward the SUV, half expecting to hear gunshots.

He heard vehicles approaching as he was loading Delle into the backseat and looked up. His brothers had just arrived. They pulled in beside him and parked.

Samuel Poe had just turned thirty and was Anson's firstborn. Chance was twenty-eight, only two years older than Brendan.

"What's going on?" Sam asked as he got out.

Chance tugged at Linny's ponytail just hard enough to make her squeal, then tweaked her nose.

"Anson poured hot coffee on Mama's feet," Brendan said.

Sam frowned. "The hell you say." He saw the pain on her face and the wrappings on her feet. He flushed a dark, angry red. "I'm sorry, Mama."

Delle was scared of what was going to happen to her when no one else was around and kept trying to smooth it over.

"It's okay, Sam. I'll—"

"It's not okay, Mama. It'll never be okay," Brendan snapped.

Chance leaned in to give his mother a quick kiss on the cheek.

"Sorry, Mama."

Delle's fingers were trembling from the pain as she patted his cheek.

"Linny! Get in the car," Brendan said.

"Where are you taking her?" Sam asked.

"To the hospital and then to my place to get well. After that, it's Mama's call what she does. If she wants to come back, I'll bring her myself. If she doesn't, that's fine, too. Just know that I'll put a gun to his head and shoot him myself before this happens again. I'm done with him. He's a mad dog someone needs to put down."

"Are you taking Linny, too? He won't like that," Sam said.

Brendan looked at his brother in disbelief. "So, your suggestion would be to leave her here alone with him? Seriously?"

Sam looked away.

Brendan got in the car and drove away.

They stood watching him go, somewhat in awe of his

defiance. They had less trouble with Anson than most people, only because they never balked or argued. All their lives it had been Brendan, the little brother, who would not bend to Anson's will.

"Boy, he's done it this time," Sam muttered and glanced at his brother for confirmation.

Chance shrugged. The war between Brendan and their father was nothing new.

They heard the screen door squeak.

Anson strode out of the house, slamming the door shut behind him.

They saw his swollen, bloody lip and could tell by the length of his stride that he was pissed. Since neither of them was ready to die, they looked away.

"What do you need us to do first?" Sam asked.

Anson pointed toward the packing shed. "Start weighing up Riordan's order. He's coming in early to get ahead of the weather."

"How much time do we have?" Chance asked.

"He'll be here by 2:00 p.m."

"Then we better get busy," Sam said and headed for the shed.

There was a secret room beneath the floor of the old stable that had once been a stop on the Underground Railroad. Back then, they'd hidden runaway slaves. Now, it was where they stashed the dried and bundled pot.

Satisfied his two older sons were on board, Anson looked up the driveway at the slowly settling dust. There would come a time when he and Brendan would come face to face on a subject that couldn't be ignored. When that happened, one of them would wind up dead, and he didn't plan on it being him.

****

LaDelle cried all the way to New Orleans. Her skin was cold and clammy and she couldn't stop shaking. Shock had set in.

Linny was in the front seat sobbing in concert. Witnessing her mother's misery was more than she could bear.

Brendan drove as fast as he dared until he hit the city limits, then was forced to slow down. By the time he wheeled up to the emergency room entrance at the Touro Infirmary on Foucher Street, Delle was shaking so hard she couldn't speak.

Brendan slid to a stop.

"We're here, Mama. Hang on."

He jumped out, lifted her out of the back seat, and carried her inside.

"I need help," Brendan said. "My mother has been burned."

An orderly appeared with a wheelchair, but Brendan shook his head.

"I'll carry her. Just tell me where to go."

The orderly led the way through double doors into ER, then into an empty room. Two nurses followed them in as Brendan laid Delle down on the bed.

"Oh my God, oh Jesus," Delle moaned, as the nurses began to unwrap the white cloths from around her feet.

Brendan's hand was on her shoulder. He was angry and so sick at heart he wanted to weep, but he had to stay calm, both for her and for his sister.

"Her name is LaDelle Poe. She's allergic to codeine. All I did was run cold water on the burns. That's aloe gel on her skin and the cloths were clean."

"Good job," the nurse said.

Brendan grabbed his little sister by the hand.

"Linny, stay right here with Mama," he said. "I have to go move the car."

The little girl was wide-eyed and tearless as she moved up to stand beside the bed. She laid her hand on her mother's arm to let her know she was there.

"Brendan, don't go," Delle cried.

"I'm not leaving you. I'll be right back," he said and left with a hasty stride.

He parked the car in the first empty space he came to and ran all the way back. He could hear her screaming as he entered the building, but upon entering her room, he was relieved by the progress being made.

They already had an IV in her arm and were now cautiously cleaning her feet. He slid a hand across his sister's shoulder and gave it a squeeze to let her know he was back.

The doctor working on Delle glanced up.

"Are you family?"

"Her son."

"How did this happen?" the doctor asked.

"Hot coffee spill," Brendan said.

"These are second-degree burns on the tops of her feet and between her toes and first-degree burns on the bottoms."

"What happens next?" he asked.

"After we clean them properly, we'll apply antibiotic ointment and wrap them lightly. I recommended hospitalization for a day or two, but she has refused. I'll give you instructions on how to care for her at home, including pain meds. She'll need to see a doctor regularly to have the burns tended and rewrapped, and she'll need to stay off her feet."

Brendan frowned. "Mama, if he thinks you need to stay, maybe you should—"

"I won't stay," she said.

He recognized that tone of voice and said no more.

"Will she be alone?" the doctor asked.

Even though she was overwhelmed by the sight of her mother in so much pain, Linny stepped up.

"I'll be there," she said.

The doctor smiled at her. "Good girl."

"You're both staying with me," Brendan said.

Linny slumped from the relief of knowing she wouldn't have to face her father alone.

A nurse walked into the room and caught Brendan's eye.

"Sir, they need you to fill out some papers at the reception desk. If you'll get that done, we'll have her ready to go by the time you get back."

Chapter Two

It was nearly noon by the time Brendan got to his apartment. They rode the elevator up with Delle in his arms. Her hair was damp and stuck to the side of her face from the heat, and the fabric of her little blue shift was as limp as a rag. Her cheek rested against the side of his chest, her face streaked from the tears she'd shed.

Linny ran ahead with the key and had the door wide open as he carried her inside.

For Delle, everything was something of a blur. The painkillers they'd given her were momentarily easing the pain, but the adrenaline crash had left her weak. When the cool air from the air conditioning inside the apartment hit her, she sighed with relief.

"Oh my, but that cool air feels good. I wish we had air conditioning at home."

"I wish you did, too, Mama," Brendan said softly and kissed her forehead as he carried her to the spare bedroom.

Her sigh was loud and heartfelt as he laid her on the bed.

"This feels so good," she whispered, and within moments, she drifted off to sleep, clutching an edge of the comforter as her anchor.

Brendan put a light cover over her legs, and then he slipped out of the room with his sister at his heels.

There was still a bit of kudzu vine caught in her hair

and a smudge on her tank top. Her eyes were brimming with unshed tears, her chin quivering. Now that the drama was over, she was left with hard facts. Daddy had hurt Mama bad enough this time to send her to the doctor. He'd never done that before. She didn't know how it would impact her fate, but she sensed it wasn't good.

Still, she took comfort in the sight of her brother's broad, strong back as he walked down the hall in front of her. Sir Brendan, her knight in shining armor had rescued them both today, but he didn't live with them anymore. She shivered. What would happen to them when they went back?

Unaware of Linny's panic, he led the way into the kitchen and then the pantry, revealing cans of tuna, soup, vegetables, and boxes of quick-fix foods.

"I have stuff for sandwiches and cans of soup. You pick out the soup, and I'll make sandwiches, okay?"

She leaned against the wall, watching as he began lining the counter with lunchmeat, bread, and mayo. His long fingers were like Mama's, she thought, able to do hold big loads and able to do lots of stuff at once. Daddy's hands were stubby. He had a pretty face but ugly hands. She wondered if Daddy knew that. Maybe that's what made him so mean. It must take ugly hands to do ugly things to people.

"Do you have to go to work later?" Linny asked.

"I don't work until dark, remember?" Brendan said.

"Yes. You're the bumper at The Black Garter bar."

He grinned. "I'm the bouncer, not the bumper, but sometimes it's all the same thing."

She turned to the business of picking out soup, then a short while later began setting the table, coveting the rooster and hen salt and pepper shakers and wishing they had a set like that at home.

She could smell the vegetable beef soup heating on the

stove and thought of the crawfish gumbo Mama had been making. Her gumbo would have been better, but nothing was better than being with Brendan.

The calm ended with a knock at the door.

Linny gave her brother a frantic look.

"Is that Daddy?"

"It better not be," Brendan muttered and wiped his hands as he headed for the door.

It wasn't Anson.

The blonde barely came up to the third button down on his shirt, but despite her fragile appearance, she was very strong and agile. He knew because she'd stripped him more than once of all his clothes while he stood motionless beneath her gaze. It was his Juliette of the sexy smile and dark brown eyes, who just happened to be his neighbor two doors down.

"Hey, Bren. I smelled soup and knew you weren't sleep—" When a little girl walked into her line of vision, she took a step back. "I'm so sorry. I didn't know your family was—"

He looked over his shoulder and saw the confusion on his sister's face.

"Come in, Julie. It's time you met them," he said and took her by the hand. "Linny, come meet my neighbor. Her name is Juliette March, but you can call her Julie. Julie, this is my favorite sister, Belinda Poe, but we call her Linny. As you'll notice, she's almost as tall as you are and she's only nine."

Linny wasn't sure if she liked knowing there was another girl in her brother's life and frowned.

"I have to be your favorite 'cause I'm your only sister, Bren."

Julie could tell the little girl didn't like the competition and quickly put her at ease.

"Men! Can't live with them. Can't live without them," she said and rolled her eyes as she offered to shake Linny's hand.

Linny smiled in spite of herself. "That's what Mama says, too."

"Hey. No fair. I can't have all my favorite women ganging up on me now," Brendan said.

Linny got the message. Brendan had a girlfriend.

"Mama got burned," Linny said.

"Oh no! Is she in the hospital?" Julie asked.

"She's here," Brendan said. "They're both staying here for a while. At least until she's better."

"What happened?"

When Linny sidled up beside Brendan and then ducked under his arm to lean against him, Julie guessed it was something traumatic, and she'd heard enough from Brendan to know his father was bad news.

"Anson poured hot coffee on Mama's bare feet," he said.

"Oh my God! Why? No, wait, I shouldn't have—"

"He doesn't need a reason," Brendan muttered. "Linny, go see if Mama is awake. The food is ready."

She ran out of the room.

Julie shook her head. "I'm sorry. I didn't mean to—"

"Let it go," Brendan said and pulled her into his arms. "I'll just say this day hasn't started off well, and I've come to the realization that one day I'll have to fucking kill my worthless father."

Julie wrapped her arms around his waist and buried her face against his chest.

"No. No, you won't, Brendan Poe. You might want to, but you won't."

He fisted his hands in her hair, thankful for the comfort of her presence.

"Stay and eat with us," he said. "Mama will want to meet you."

"I don't know... Meeting strangers when you're sick or in pain is never good. Are you sure?"

"I'm sure. Check the soup for me, will you? Oh, and get another bowl and plate. I'll go see if she's up to eating."

"Can she walk?"

"No."

"So, bring her into the living room where she can stretch out on the sofa, and we'll eat in here with her."

He smiled. Behind the pixie face and tiny body beat the heart of a really big woman.

"That's a good idea, sugar," he said, and Julie promptly began rearranging pillows.

Linny was sitting on the bed with her head on her mother's shoulder when Brendan walked in.

"I made sandwiches and soup, Mama. Can you eat?"

Delle frowned. "I hurt too much to be hungry, but if I keep taking these pain meds, I'm going to have to eat or they'll make me sick."

"I'll carry you to the bathroom. When you're done, yell at me and I'll carry you to the living room. There's someone I want you to meet."

Delle managed a shaky smile.

"Linny said you have a girlfriend. I didn't know."

He shrugged. "I didn't want to scare her off by meeting the family until she was stuck enough on me not to run."

Delle frowned. "I'm sorry."

"Not your fault your husband is an ass," Brendan said. "Scoot, Linny. I need to carry Mama into the bathroom. You can stay in there and help her then yell at me when you're ready to go."

Linny stood up on the bed and then threw her arms around her brother's neck before he could move.

He felt the tension in her body and knew today had rattled her greatly.

"You're gonna be fine," he said, as he hugged her tight. "Now let's get this show on the road."

A few minutes later, he carried Delle into the living room to the mini-bed Julie made on the sofa. There was a blanket over the cushions, throw pillows at one end to prop her upright, and the coffee table next to the sofa with eating utensils within reach.

"Looks like Julie has you all fixed up," he said, then eased his mother down onto the sofa. He pulled the afghan up to her lap, leaving her feet uncovered so the weight of the cover wouldn't hurt her.

"I hate to be a bother," Delle said.

Brendan stepped back with a grin. "After all the trouble my brothers and I gave you growing up, I think you're due a little TLC."

She caught a glimpse of the tiny blonde coming out of the kitchen and self-consciously smoothed a hand over her hair.

Brendan knew she was curious and a little anxious.

"You're beautiful, Mother. Stop fussing," Brendan whispered.

Breath caught in the back of Delle's throat. If it was a sin to favor one son over the other, then she was going to hell. Brendan had what his father was missing, a beautiful soul.

"Mama, this is Julie March. Julie is short for Juliette, who, as you can see, is as short as the nickname."

Delle frowned. "Brendan Wade, you shouldn't make fun—"

Julie was laughing. "Everyone says that, Mrs. Poe. It's how I was introduced to him, so he didn't come up with that on his own."

Brendan grinned.

"Julie, this is my mother, LaDelle Poe, but everyone calls her Delle... for short."

They laughed, which broke the ice.

"Nice to meet you," they said in unison, then laughed again for echoing each other.

Linny slid in beneath her brother's arm again.

He looked down at her and winked.

Linny felt good inside. Sir Brendan made all the women in court happy. A bad day was turning into a good one.

"Soup is ready. Can you eat a little?" Julie asked.

"Yes, thank you," Delle said.

"Great. Be right back. Linny, come help me," Julie said and headed for the kitchen with Linny skipping along behind her.

"She's adorable, Bren, but she looks like a kid. Is she legal age?"

He smiled. "She's twenty-five, legal *and* lethal."

"Do you love her?"

He sighed. "Yep."

"Good. Treat her right."

"You know I will."

A shadow passed over Delle's face. "Brendan?"

"Yeah?"

"Keep her away from Anson."

The skin crawled on the back of his neck. "I'm already on that. It's why you didn't know about her."

Moments later, Linny and Juliette came back, carrying the food and giggling as if they'd just shared a secret.

Brendan watched the three females interacting, wondering at the quixotic nature of fate. He'd made a point of keeping the women he loved most apart, and now this unexpected crisis had brought them together.

As they ate, Delle could see why Brendan was so taken

with Julie. She was funny, charming, and as sweet as could be. And they worked together. A match made in heaven.

"So, how long have you been bartending at The Black Garter?" Delle asked.

Julie put her plate aside, anxious to get to know his mother better.

"Since I turned twenty-one, and in spite of my mother's displeasure, I've been in and out the back door of that place all my life."

"Her daddy owns it. She's Grayson March's one and only," Brendan said.

Everyone in and around New Orleans knew of Grayson March and the March family. They were old money and could trace their roots back a good two hundred years in New Orleans. Delle was impressed her son was dating someone like her.

She listened intently as Julie talked and every so often caught a glimpse of the changing expressions on her youngest son's face. He was definitely in love. At last, one of her boys was showing signs of settling down.

"I'll bet your daddy had a small fit when you moved out of the house," Delle said.

Julie rolled her eyes. "No, ma'am. Daddy didn't like it, but it was Mama who pitched the fit."

"Please, call me Delle."

"Thank you," Julie said and suddenly noticed Brendan's little sister was looking a bit forlorn. On a whim, she dropped a piece of cracker into Linny's soup bowl.

Linny looked up.

Julie dropped another one.

"What was that for?" Linny asked.

"You looked like you wanted to bite on something and I was afraid it would be me. I gave you some of my crackers, instead."

Linny giggled, then scooped up the crackers in her spoon and popped them into her mouth, making a big deal out of the crunching sound.

Brendan sat quietly, watching the interaction between the women, and knew his instinct about Julie had been spot on. She fit into the family. If Anson didn't exist, life would be pretty close to perfect.

After they'd finished eating, Julie took Linny into the kitchen to help clean up, leaving Brendan alone with his mother.

"If we stay here, we're going to need some things from home," Delle said.

"I know. I'll take Belinda with me to help get what you need."

Delle frowned. "I don't want her to go back there without me. I'm afraid your daddy will take his anger out on her."

Brendan leaned forward. "Mama. Look at me."

Delle lifted her gaze.

"I'm bigger than Dad. I'm stronger than Dad. And I will take a gun. Does that ease your concerns?"

She leaned back against the pillows and closed her eyes, staying silent for several long moments. When she finally looked up, there were tears in her eyes.

"I am so sorry."

Brendan frowned. "*You* have nothing to be sorry about. I'll get some paper. Make a list of what you want us to get. Sam and Chance will most likely still be there. They wouldn't let Anson pull any shit, okay?"

"Yes. Okay."

"Get my phone while you're there," she added. "It's just inside the cabinet door next to the sink."

Brendan laughed. "That's a weird place to keep a phone, Mama."

She shrugged. "I don't have a pocket in this dress and I like to keep it close by while I work."

Brendan thought that was odd and looked up, but when she wouldn't meet his gaze, it took him a few moments to realize she was afraid of her own husband. He didn't know what to think. His parents had always fought, but he'd never thought of his mother being afraid.

"Do you have a gun in the house, too?" he asked.

"No. Your daddy keeps all the guns."

He frowned. "I'll go get that paper and pen."

Delle said a quick prayer. Her precariously balanced world was finally coming undone.

****

Julie offered to stay at the apartment until they got back. Linny was as scared of going back as her mother was for her to leave. She sat in the front seat as they drove away, her knees pulled up beneath her chin, trying to make herself as small as possible.

Brendan knew it was a defense mechanism for staying out of trouble. The smaller you are, the less likely it is that anyone will see you. He wondered how often she did that at home.

She hadn't said two words since they left New Orleans and was staring out the window at the passing scenery while picking at her cuticles in quiet agitation. She finally broke the silence, Brendan got why she'd been so quiet.

"Will Daddy still be mad?"

"Honey, Anson is always mad about something, remember?"

Linny sighed. "You're right. He is, isn't he?" She got quiet all over again, and then she cast a sideways glance at her brother. "If I tell you something, you won't tell Daddy, will you?"

"I haven't told him anything but 'Go to hell' in so long that we have nothing to talk about. Of course I won't tell."

She unfolded her legs and put her feet down in the floorboard as if bracing herself to confess.

"I have a secret place in the swamp where I play. When I'm there, I am Queen Belinda and my subjects are the critters who live there. I call you Sir Brendan. Mama is Lady Delle, and Daddy is the Evil Overlord."

Brendan grinned. "You got that last part right."

She giggled again. "Don't tell. He would be really mad."

"I cross my heart and hope to die," Brendan said solemnly and made the sign of a cross over his heart.

She nodded, satisfied with the pledge.

"What do you call Sam and Chance?" he asked.

"Big Samuel, the blacksmith, makes the armor you wear, and Chance is the court jester."

He was a little surprised at how she had segregated the members of her own family into these odd caricatures of themselves and how spot-on she was with her perceptions. He watched the changing expressions on her face with a mixture of curiosity and regret. They'd all been born into a tough family, but somehow it seemed worse for a girl.

"Are you lonesome, Linny?"

She frowned. "What do you mean?"

"You never get to play with other little girls. You don't have sleepovers or best friends, or anything like that, do you?"

She shrugged. "Mama says it wouldn't be safe."

"I'm sorry."

"Sometimes I'm sorry, too," she said, then sank back into the seat. She pulled her knees up beneath her chin again, an unintentional "tell" of the urge to hide.

Brendan frowned. "Life will get better for you. I'll make sure of that."

She reached across the seat and patted his arm. "I sure do love you, Bren."

"I love you, too, baby girl," Brendan said and swallowed past the lump in his throat.

A few minutes later, he turned off the road into the driveway, bracing himself for the confrontation that was bound to come. When they parked at the house, he got his handgun out of the console and loaded it.

Linny's eyes widened. "What's that for?"

"Just in case. Let's go," he said and tucked it into the waistband at the back of his jeans.

Their exit from an air-conditioned vehicle into the Louisiana heat was palpable. Brendan paused, eyeing the house in which he'd grown up and the land around it.

Except for that massive grove of bamboo, it was typical Louisiana low country, a density of growth thick enough to hide anything living or dead, and water in abundance almost anywhere within walking distance. Even the ground on which he was standing held water as close to the surface as a mother holds her babe to her bosom. It was an old place, full of centuries of secrets and betrayals— deaths and lies.

He couldn't help but wonder how many thousands of lies had been told under the roof of that house. Some of no consequence, surely—while others were vile enough to change the course of a man's life. One thing was for certain, the man of this house was nothing but a liar, capable of a thousand lies all on his own.

"Is everything okay, Bren?"

He shook off the weight of the centuries and reached for her hand. "Everything is fine, sugar. Let's get this over with and get back to your mama."

****

The clear sky that had come with daybreak was swiftly disappearing behind the building storm clouds as Sam and Chance continued loading the bales of pot into Wes Riordan's motor home. From the outside, the motor home looked like a retiree's dream straight off of a KOA campground. Riordan had even gone so far as to have a bike rack mounted on the back with dual bicycles chained in place. The driver, a man named Marty, looked like someone's grandfather in a floral Hawaiian shirt, cotton shorts, and a little golf hat covering his bald head.

But the motor home was no retiree dream. It was gutted down to the floor and walls, and the windows were darkly tinted. He added packing straps and rubberized treading to keep pallets of marijuana from sliding; leaving just enough room for Wes and Thorpe, his hired gun, to ride guard inside.

Riordan was a tall man with a non-descript face. While he could do nothing about his height, he dressed down to stay under the radar of normal curiosity. Not a lot of people even knew he existed, which was intentional.

Anson Poe was one of the few he did business with personally. So far, their association worked. Poe grew good stuff in large quantity, but today was the first time Wes had come to pick up a load in daylight, and Riordan was more than a little antsy. He stepped outside to check the weather, then glanced down at his watch. It was nearly 2:30. He needed to be out of here before the storm front blew in, or he'd miss his connection farther down the line.

"Hurry the hell up, you two!" Wes snapped, aiming his complaints at Sam and Chance.

Anson frowned at his sons. He needed to keep his best customer happy and added his voice to the urgency.

"Get a move on, damn it! The sky's about to unload and he should've been gone ten minutes ago."

"Yes, Daddy," Sam said, as he and Chance kept carrying bale after bale of marijuana up from the room beneath the shed.

Thunder rumbled in the distance.

"Damn it! Someone's coming and it better not be the cops," Wes muttered, as the rumble of an engine was suddenly heard over the dissipating thunder.

Anson glanced out and recognized the car.

"I pay plenty to make sure I am not bothered by the parish police. Besides, that's my youngest son's car. He and my girl took my old lady to the doctor this morning. She spilled hot coffee on her bare feet. They're probably just bringing her home."

"I didn't know you had another son," Wes said.

"Well, I do. We don't like each other much, but he's mine."

"What about all this?" Wes asked, gesturing toward the bales of pot.

"What about it? He knows what I grow."

"Well, alright then," Wes said. Wes watched them pull up to the house, then glanced over his shoulder. Only a couple more minutes and he'd be out of here. He looked back, eyeing the tall, dark-haired man and the young girl who got out, then gave the girl a second look. Watching her walk was like watching silk blowing in a breeze—all smooth and fluid, without a jerk to her step.

"That is one fine-looking girl you've got there," he said softly.

Anson looked up toward the house, his eyes narrowing thoughtfully.

"Yeah, she takes after me."

Wes's eyes narrowed as he watched her disappear inside.

"Damn shame she's your kin. She'd bring a good hundred thousand on the open market."

Anson didn't know whether to be pissed the man had pretty much offered to buy his daughter or stunned at the money she was worth.

"She's only nine."

"The ones I know like 'em young."

Anson turned around and pointed a finger under Wes's nose. "We're done talking about this now."

Wes backed off and held up his hands. "No offense meant. Just talking about stuff I know, that's all."

"We're done here, Daddy," Sam said.

"About time," Wes muttered, eyeing the sweat-stained shirt and the size of Samuel Poe's chest. He was one big son of a bitch. "Say, boy, if you ever want to move up in the world, there's a place for you in my crew."

Sam looked up. "Are you talking to me?"

Wes nodded.

Still pissed by what he'd overheard Riordan say about Linny, Sam answered shortly. "Not interested," he said and walked out of the packing shed with Chance right behind him.

Anson was more concerned that Wes had offered Sam a job than he had been by his half-hearted comment about buying Belinda.

"Damn it, Riordan. First, you eyeball my girl, and now you try to steal my son out from under me. It's time for you to get the hell on down the road."

Wes grinned as he handed over the money. "Nice doing business with you, Poe. We'll be in touch."

The trio climbed inside the motor home and drove away as Anson settled his hat down on his head, grabbed the grocery sack full of hundred dollar bills, and headed toward the house.

****

Brendan pulled an old duffle bag from the closet and, with Linny's help, began gathering up the clothes on Delle's list.

"Where does Mama keep her underwear?"

"In there," she said, pointing to a dresser near the closet.

"Count out eight of each and put them in the bag, okay?"

She was counting them out into her arms when they both heard footsteps coming up the stairs.

"It's Daddy!" she whispered and threw the underwear in the bag, then stood behind Brendan.

"It's okay, honey. I hear your brothers talking. They're here, too."

She shivered. "He's gonna be mad."

"Well, he's gonna have to just get himself glad because he only has himself to blame."

She ran back to the dresser and scooted down between it and the corner wall.

Brendan was stunned. He had no idea she was this afraid. "Damn it, Belinda, I won't let him hurt you."

"I know," she whispered. "I just don't want to see his face. His mean face scares me."

Before he could say more, his brothers walked in.

Sam looked toward the bed, expecting to see his mother there. "Hey, Bren, where's Mama and Linny?"

He pointed in the corner. "There's your baby sister, hiding in a corner, scared to death of her own damned father. Mama is at my place, and they're both staying with me until she can walk again."

Sam went to the corner. "Come here, little girl. Daddy's not gonna hurt you," he said softly. He pulled Linny out from behind the dresser, sat down on the bed, and plopped her down beside him.

Chance was still trying to process what Brendan just said. "She can't walk? Why the hell not?"

"First-degree burns on the bottoms of her feet. Second-degree burns on the tops and between her toes."

"Bren carried Mama to the bathroom," Linny said softly.

Sam frowned. "This didn't need to happen."

"But it did, and we all know why," Brendan said.

Another set of footsteps was coming up the stairs. Anson was on the way.

"He's not gonna like this," Sam said as Linny positioned herself behind him.

"As if I give a fuck," Brendan said and then he pointed at Linny. "Mama wants her pink nightgown. Can you find that?"

Linny ducked into the closet just as Anson walked into the room.

Like the boys, he'd expected to see Delle laid out on the bed, not a half-packed duffle bag. He eyed his sons' expressions, and he knew they were pissed at him, but he didn't care. It wasn't the first time, and it most likely wouldn't be the last. At six feet two inches, he was an imposing sight, especially when he was mad, and right now, he was furious.

"Where's Delle? Where's my wife?"

"She's staying with me," Brendan said. "And so's Linny."

Anson eyed Sam and Chance's expressions. Brendan had just usurped his power, not only by defying him, but taking his wife and daughter away. It was time to remind them all he was still boss.

"Like hell," Anson said softly and started toward Brendan with his fists doubled.

"Oh, we've already been down that route," Brendan said and pulled a handgun from the back of his belt and aimed it straight at Anson's face. "The urge to pull this trigger is so strong I can taste it," he said softly. "You burned her bad, you son of a bitch! It'll be weeks before she will be able to wear a shoe, and several days before she can walk. For a human being, you are a worthless piece of shit."

Anson grunted. "You boys gonna stand there and let him point that gun at me?"

Sam looked at Brendan but didn't speak.

Chance glared. "You shouldn't have done that, Daddy. Mama is a good woman and didn't deserve that."

Anson's eyes narrowed as a cold smile spread across his face. "I'll remember this."

Sam looked up. "So will we."

Anson caught movement from the corner of his eye and saw Linny standing in the shadows of the closet like a mouse, watching to see what the tomcat did next. Still convinced he could handle this situation, he pointed.

"Fine, but she stays with me."

With the gun still aimed, Brendan moved between them. "No. She's a little girl who needs her mama. And right now, Mama needs her, too. She's gonna have to be Mama's feet until she heals. If you don't like it, suck it up. You brought this down on yourself, Anson."

Anson doubled up his fists. "I am your father, goddamnit! You do not call me Anson."

"I have no father," Brendan snapped.

Enraged, Anson started to lunge.

Brendan pulled the trigger. The hat on Anson's head went flying as Anson froze mid-step.

"You tried to kill me," he whispered.

"If I wanted you dead, we wouldn't be talking. Now stand back."

Anson was in shock. Brendan has just as good as castrated him in front of his children. He thought about going for a gun, but from the temperature in the room, he knew he'd have to kill them all to walk away, and he wasn't ready for that. He lifted his chin, staring Brendan straight in the face.

"You'll pay for this," he said softly.

Brendan didn't flinch. "Linny, what's next on the list?"

"Mama's nightgown."

"Right. Maybe you better get a couple, and her robe, too."

Linny stepped out of the closet, slipping past Brendan with her head down, she began gathering up the rest of her mother's clothes.

Anson turned and walked out.

"We'll keep an eye on him," Chance said, as he and Sam followed. "Just hurry."

Brendan went back to the business of getting what they'd come for. "So, little sister, did we get all of Mama's stuff?"

She nodded.

"Then let's get your things and we'll be done."

"I'll get my clothes and Rabbit. I don't want to forget Rabbit."

Brendan followed her out, kicking Anson's hat aside as they went down the hall to her bedroom.

When she began gathering her things at a frantic pace, he couldn't blame her. What just happened was a hell of a thing for a kid to see.

She threw her stuff inside the bag without folding it, anxious to be gone. The old stuffed rabbit she slept with was still sitting on her bed, so faded the pink fur almost looked white.

"Don't forget Rabbit," he said.

"I won't," she said, tossing in clean socks and underwear, a hairbrush and some bands for her ponytail, and then she grabbed Rabbit. "I'm ready, Bren."

"So am I. Let's blow this joint."

She giggled, then put a hand over her mouth as if she'd just committed a social faux pas.

"Just stay beside me," he said.

She hooked a finger through his belt loop as they left the room. Hugging Rabbit a little tighter, she eyed the pistol in the waistband of his jeans and lengthened her stride to stay up with his step.

Instead of another confrontation, Anson was nowhere in sight, which elated Linny. Brendan stopped in the kitchen to get Delle's cell phone and found it in the cabinet beside a stack of plates.

When they got outside, he noticed his brothers' trucks were gone, as was Anson's. All of a sudden, he thought of the women in his apartment on their own.

"Hop in the car and buckle up, honey."

Linny got in the SUV as he loaded the bag in the back. He paused for a better look, hoping to see Anson's truck parked down near the shed or catch a glimpse of it disappearing in the trees on his way to one of his grow patches, but it was nowhere in sight. In fact, the whole place was too quiet. Not even a bird was calling. The world was holding its breath, waiting to see what happened next.

He reached for his phone.

Chapter Three

Julie was in the living room watching television when her cell phone rang. When she saw it was Brendan, she smiled.

She'd never been in love like this before. The simple act of watching him walk into a room made her weak in the knees.

"Hi, Brendan, is everything okay?"

"It is now. Are you two all right?"

"We're fine. Your mother is a sweetheart. She's been asleep almost ever since you left."

"Don't open the door to anyone but me."

The warning was unexpected and frightening.

"What's wrong?"

"Anson didn't take well to the news that Mama and Linny would be staying with me."

"But didn't you tell him how badly she was hurt?"

"He doesn't care, Julie. He's the one who burned her in the first place. For him, it's all about control."

"Why did you tell me not to answer the door?"

"Because I just found out he's not here and we did not part amicably."

"What happened?"

"I put a gun in his face."

She staggered, then backed up to the wall to keep from falling. "Oh, Brendan."

"It was that or fight until one of us was dead. We're on our way. Be there in about fifteen minutes."

"Okay. We'll be fine and I won't go to the door."

"If he shows up before I get there, just call the police."

"Oh my God."

Brendan heard the fear in her voice and was immediately ashamed. "I'm sorry. I'm so sorry I put you in this position."

"No. I'm fine with that. I just can't imagine being afraid of my parents."

"It happens. You're one of the lucky ones. I gotta go. See you soon."

"I love you, Brendan." But she'd said it too late. He'd already hung up.

Now she was uneasy. She hurried to the front door to make sure the deadbolt was on, then fastened the security chain as well. Now she needed to find something that would serve as a deterrent should the need arise.

She dug through the coat closet until she found a baseball bat and took it with her to the sofa. She leaned back to continue watching her show when she realized if the sound was up, she might not hear danger until it was too late. So she left it on mute and sat in the quiet, clutching the bat with her gaze fixed on the door.

****

Anson drove without caution. All he could think about was that gun going off in his face. He couldn't wrap his head around the fact he'd fathered a child who just tried to kill him. It had shaken his confidence. The analogy of a younger bull challenging the old bull was not lost upon him. He kept thinking of a thousand ways in which he would make Brendan pay. He just needed to bide his time and do it right.

By the time he hit the city limits of New Orleans, he was on an adrenaline high. He was determined to get Delle and bring her home. It didn't matter that she wouldn't be able to care for herself, and he had no intentions of doing it for her. It was just a knee-jerk reaction to having someone else make a decision for him.

He'd never been inside Brendan's apartment, but he knew where he lived. He made it a point to know everything there was to know about all of his kids. Never knew when some information would prove important in swaying them to his side of a situation.

He pulled up in the parking lot and got out with his fists doubled and his head down. He would have Delle home before they knew what was happening.

****

Julie was watching the clock and trying not to panic when she began to hear footsteps coming down the hall at a hasty pace. Her heart began to pound as she tightened her grip on the bat.

To her relief, the footsteps passed. Moments later, she heard someone knocking at a door down the hall, and then a familiar voice was calling her name.

"Julie! Juliette! Are you there? It's Dad."

She quickly unlocked the door and leaned out. "Daddy! Daddy! I'm here."

When Grayson saw where she was, he frowned, well aware of who lived in that apartment.

"Come in," Julie said, and then she put a finger to her lips. "Brendan's mother is here and she's asleep." She closed and locked the door behind him.

He would've thought nothing of the fact that she'd locked the door until he saw she was also holding a bat.

"What the hell is going on here?"

"If you'll talk to me in a normal tone of voice, I'll be happy to share," she said shortly.

He glared and sat down at one end of the sofa as Julie sat at the other. She knew him so well. He did not look a day over forty, even though he'd turned fifty last year. Well-groomed hair as blonde as hers was a perfect foil for his tan skin and beach-boy good looks. She knew he didn't like her choice of apartments, or her friends, and this was going to make it worse.

"As I was about to say, Brendan's mother is here. She suffered bad burns on her feet this morning, and after he took her to the hospital, he brought her and his little sister here to stay while she recovers."

Grayson had the grace to be ashamed. "That's too bad. I'm really sorry to hear that."

"She's very sweet, Daddy, and a really beautiful woman."

He shrugged. "I know what LaDelle looks like. We were all in school at the same time. She was one of those girls every guy wanted to date, but she only had eyes for Anson Poe and his pretty face."

Julie frowned. "I didn't know you knew them personally."

"It's because I know him personally that I do not approve of your association with his son."

"You raised me to be honest and fair-minded, and blaming a wife and children for one man's sins does not seem to fall into either category for me."

He ignored her and pointed at the bat. "It still doesn't explain that."

When his daughter lifted her chin defiantly, he knew he wasn't going to like the answer.

"The burns on Delle's feet didn't happen by accident. Anson poured hot coffee on her bare feet on purpose. And she has an older bruise on her face. I don't know what hell she's going through, living in that house, but Brendan is sick at heart and wants them with him, which is what's going to happen for the time being until she's healed enough to walk again."

Grayson paled. "The burns are so bad she can't walk?"

Julie nodded. "She has first-degree burns on the bottoms of her feet and second-degree burns on the tops." Julie's eyes filled with tears. "Oh, Daddy, she's in so much pain and she's being so brave. And she has the sweetest little girl. She's only nine and quite a beauty, although she seems older."

"Probably seen too damn much of the hard side of life," Grayson muttered. "So where are Brendan and the girl?"

"They went back to Wisteria Hill to get clothes for their stay."

"I still don't know why you have the bat."

"Brendan called me. He said he and his father had a big fight about them staying here, and as they left the house, he realized his father was gone. He just told me not to open the door to anyone until they got back."

His cheeks flushed red with sudden anger. "I can't believe he left you here on your own and put you in danger."

"He didn't leave me in danger. I volunteered to stay with Delle in case she woke up. He had no way of knowing how all this would unfold, and he's already on his way back. He's already apologized profusely to me over the phone, and that's all I'm going to say to you about it."

Grayson glared.

Julie glared back.

And in the middle of the angry silence, they heard a thud and then a shriek of pain.

Julie was up and running before her father could move. She rushed into the room to find Delle sprawled on the floor. She dropped to her knees and cradled Delle's head in her lap.

"Oh, honey! What happened?"

Delle moaned. "I dreamed I was running away."

Then she looked up past Julie's head and saw a man in a tan linen suit standing in the doorway. By the time she realized who it was, she was already embarrassed to tears and trying to cover up her bare legs.

"I'm sorry to intrude," Grayson said gently. "I was just visiting my daughter when we heard you cry out." He walked into the room and then squatted down next to Delle and lifted a lock of hair from her eyes. "It's been a long time, LaDelle. I'd ask how you are, but it seems obvious you're in considerable pain."

"Grayson."

He smiled. "Yes, ma'am, in the flesh. Now, I'd like to continue this conversation, but how about we get you back in bed first? May I?"

She nodded.

He slid his arms beneath her body and lifted her back up on the bed, then carefully pulled the covers back over her legs.

"Thank you," Delle said. "I'm embarrassed for anyone to see me like this."

His eyes narrowed angrily. "And I'm sorry for your suffering."

All of a sudden, there was a loud shout out in the hall, and then someone pounded on the front door.

Delle's face lost all hint of color. "Oh my God, it's Anson."

Julie pivoted to get the bat when Grayson stopped her with a look.

"I've got this," he said. "You stay here with LaDelle. This won't take long."

Delle was shaking. "Anson will hurt him. You have to

stop him. I'm sorry. I'm so sorry. I should never have come here."

Julie sat down on the bed beside her and reached for her hand. "It'll be fine. Just listen and you'll see."

Grayson grabbed the ball bat on his way to the door. Anson was still shouting and pounding when Grayson opened it.

Anson froze, his fist in mid-air.

"Uh—"

Grayson rolled the bat in his hand, just like he used to do in high school before he stepped up to the plate, then jabbed it in Anson's belly just sharp enough to back him out into the hall, then followed him out, shutting the door behind him.

"What the fuck's your problem?" Grayson snapped.

Anson knew Grayson March. He didn't like what was happening, but wasn't stupid enough to mess with one of the most powerful men in the state of Louisiana. He eyed the fine linen suit and the shine on his shoes and immediately hated March's guts for being everything he wasn't.

"I must have the wrong apartment," Anson said. "Sorry."

Grayson rolled the ball bat again and then he held it across his body, like he was getting ready to swing.

"If you were looking for your son, then you had the right apartment. He's just not here at the moment. Can I take a message?"

Anson's mouth dropped. It took him a few seconds to remember that Brendan worked for this man. Although why he'd be in Brendan's apartment when he wasn't there was still a mystery. Then, he realized his wife *was* inside, and Grayson March was in there, too, and saw red.

"What the fuck have you been doing in that apartment with *my* wife?"

Grayson's eyes widened in disbelief. The man was truly mad.

"I'm doing nothing with your wife. I was visiting with my daughter, who happens to be sitting with LaDelle, and after seeing the condition that *your wife* is in, I'm stunned that's where your goddamned mind just went. You're one sorry motherfucker for what you did to her, and you've got about five seconds to get out of my sight before I call the police. At the least you'll be arrested for physical abuse and disturbing the peace, and with a few choice words in the right ear, we might tack on some drug charges as well."

It was the drug charges that got his attention. Anson was whipped and he knew it. Still, he couldn't leave without throwing out a threat of his own.

"You'll be sorry you interfered," he said softly. "I know where you live, and I know who you love."

Grayson jabbed the ball bat in Anson's balls so fast he never saw it coming.

He dropped to his knees, clutching himself from the shock of the pain.

Grayson tapped Anson's head with the bat just enough to get his attention.

"Know this, Anson Poe. From this moment on, you better live your life looking over your shoulder, or you'll never see what's coming."

Anson shuddered. He'd said too much to the wrong person.

"I didn't mean that," he mumbled as he dragged himself to his feet. "I was just mad. I didn't mean that."

"Well I did," Grayson whispered.

Anson staggered as he took the first step, and then walked toward the elevator. He threw up just outside the entrance to the apartment, and then threw up again just before he got in his truck. Without knowing it, he drove out one side of the parking lot as Brendan and Linny drove in the other.

Grayson watched until the elevator doors close then went back inside, locking the door behind him. He tossed the bat on the sofa and went back to reassure Delle that she was safe.

The women were sitting side by side on the bed, wide-eyed and fearful when he walked in, and he could tell by the look in LaDelle's eyes that she was in agony.

"He's gone," Grayson said.

Delle wilted. "Oh my God. I don't know what to—"

"LaDelle, we go back a long ways and I'd like to think that we're friends. You do not apologize to a friend for helping you out. Now I'm going to go out to the living room and give you some privacy. I won't leave until your son arrives, so never fear. Julie, I came by to remind you about your Nonny's 89th birthday party this Sunday. We dine at 7:00 p.m. and don't be late. You know how your mother gets about late arrivals."

He bowed as he would to any of the finest of ladies before backing out of the room and closing the door.

Delle moaned and then doubled over with pain. "Lord, lord, my feet. They feel like they're on fire."

Julie glanced at the clock. "It's time you can take a pain pill. I'll get some water."

Delle rolled over onto her side, gritting her teeth to keep from screaming.

"I'll be right back," Julie said, and hurried out of the room.

Grayson heard her coming and got up.

She waved him away. "I'm getting water. Delle needs to take a pain pill," she said, but before she got out of the room, there was another knock at the door.

"Julie! It's me. Linny and I are back."

She backtracked and ran to open it.

Linny entered first, ducked her head, and ran for her mother, ignoring the stranger in the room.

Brendan took one look at Julie's face, saw his boss standing behind the sofa and the ball bat on the cushions, and knew something had happened.

"What did I miss?"

Grayson eyed his daughter. "Go on and get the water for LaDelle. I need to talk to Brendan."

Brendan's stomach rolled. His boss was most likely mad, probably because he'd inadvertently gotten Julie mixed up in the family mess. Everything went through his mind from being forbidden to see Julie again to being fired.

He set the duffle bag down on the floor and closed the door.

Grayson didn't give Brendan time to get defensive. "I came to see Juliette this afternoon. She heard me knocking on her door and invited me here. I apologize for invading your space, and hope you are not upset with me for involving myself in your personal business. Suffice it to say, your father was here."

Brendan groaned. "I was afraid—I'm so sorry... Did he threaten Julie? Was she—?"

"Julie's fine. I got here first, walked in to find her brandishing a ball bat, which, now that I think about it, turned out to be a mighty fine weapon against the son of a bitch Anson Poe has become."

Brendan sat down with a thump. Just thinking about Julie sitting here on her own, preparing to defend herself and his mother with a damned ball bat made him sick.

"Oh my god," he mumbled.

"No, no, you mistake my point," Grayson said, and sat down opposite him.

"Yes, your father was here, pounding on the door and shouting. I took him and the bat out into the hall and reminded him that disturbing the peace and threatening people was against the law. I punctuated my warning by jamming his balls back up his ass. Far enough I hope that he is constipated for a month."

Brendan had always liked his boss, but was reminded that Grayson March hadn't become the man he was just because he inherited the March name and money that went with it. It would appear that he knew how to turn a screw when the need arose.

"You should know he threatened your safety and that of my family as well, so you need to be wary," Grayson added.

"I've been wary all my life. I don't know any other way to live," Brendan said. "I'm sorry he involved your family."

"Believe me, so is he," Grayson said. "From this day forward, I'll have someone watching him, and I told him as much. I do this to protect me and mine, not to get him in further trouble. If the law in this parish chooses to turn a blind eye to his industries, I'm not the crusader to take him down. However, I have no problem taking him out if the need arises."

"Fair enough, and thanks for the warning," Brendan said. "Is Mama okay? I mean, he didn't get close enough to—"

"His arrival scared her, but he didn't set foot over the threshold. We took our conversation into the hall."

Brendan lifted his chin, refusing to accept the shame his father had put on their name. "I am grateful for what you did."

Grayson shrugged. He wasn't happy, but he couldn't find a way to place any blame on Brendan other than the circumstances of his birth.

"You're the bouncer at my club. It seems only fair I return the favor when the need arises."

Juliet walked into the conversation, which ended it. It didn't matter. They'd said what needed to be said.

She eyed them anxiously, afraid that her father had been critical. "Is everything all right?"

"We're fine," Brendan said briefly. "Now, if you two will excuse me for a bit, I need to go reassure my mama that I'm still in one piece."

He picked up the duffle bag as he left the room.

Julie crossed her arms across her chest and waited for her father to speak.

He read the defensive gesture for what it was and decided not to push the issue. "I need to be going. I trust I'll see you Sunday. Wear something pretty. Your mother is going all out as usual."

"I will," she said.

"You work tonight I assume?"

"Yes, but I'm not sure about Brendan's plans. He can't go off and leave his mother and Linny here by themselves."

Grayson frowned. "I'm putting some men on Anson Poe's ass. Where he goes, they'll go, although I'd bet my favorite horse that Anson Poe never comes near here again. If Brendan is comfortable with leaving her alone, she'll be fine. If he wants the name of some reputable home health caregivers, I can help. He can give me a call. Now I really need to go. Come lock up behind me."

Julie followed him to the door, turned the deadbolt and put on the safety chain. When she turned around, Brendan was coming toward her.

She walked into his arms.

Brendan was sick for what she'd endured. "I'm so sorry you were afraid. This should've never happened. The bad part is that I can't promise it won't happen again."

Julie looked up. Brendan towered above her, but right now, he looked like a scared little boy. "We can handle anything when we do it together."

He swung her up into his arms, kissing her hard and fast. "I love you madly, Juliette."

"I love you, too, Brendan Poe. Not despite who you are, but because of it, and let this be the last time you ever apologize to me about your family."

He buried his face against the curve of her neck without comment. Even though she'd gotten a taste of what Anson was like, she didn't have a clue as to the depths of his depravity, and he prayed to God she never found out.

Chapter Four

Anson was in so much pain it hurt to breathe. He drove all the way home with his thoughts in free fall. Twice in one day he'd been challenged, and both times he'd lost—first, by a whelp of his own, and second, by a man with more power than God. He couldn't touch March without signing his own death warrant, but he could make Brendan pay, and he would, of that, there was no doubt. It had to be something irrevocable. Something Brendan couldn't fix. Something he would have to live with for the rest of his life and know he was the reason it had happened.

By the time Anson got home, a notion was stirring. It would take some maneuvering, but he was a patient man. Lord knows he regretted the fuck that caused Brendan Poe to be born. Before he was through, he would make sure Brendan was just as sorry, too. Now all he had to do was get LaDelle to come home, and he knew just how to do it.

****

Julie went back to her apartment to get some sleep before her shift later this evening.

Normally Brendan would have done the same, but not today. It wouldn't be the first time he'd gone to work short on rest. He was hanging up Delle's clothes after taking her to the bathroom, when she startled him by coming out on her own, wincing with every step.

"Mama, why didn't you call me?" he said as he picked her up and carried her back to the bed.

Delle went limp against Brendan's broad shoulder, trembling from the pain. "I need to get well as fast as I can. The sooner I'm home, the quicker your life gets back to normal."

"My life will never be normal as long as Anson draws a breath," he muttered. "Here's your cell phone."

She didn't chide him for the comment, which was telling. But watching her tuck the phone under her pillow was just as startling as seeing Linny hide behind the dresser. He wondered how many times she'd done that before Anson got in bed. It was further evidence of the increased stress in her life since he and his brothers moved out.

"I have to say this air-conditioning is wonderful," she said as she smoothed wisps of hair away from her face. "What's Linny doing?"

"She's in the living room playing a game on my Xbox."

She frowned. "I hope it's not one of those violent war games."

"It's not. It's actually a game about castles and wizards and dragons. She likes stuff like that, and it's okay for her to play. How about I carry you into my bedroom so you can watch TV in there this evening?"

"Oh, I'm fine here, honey. Besides, I don't get much time to watch TV."

"Well you have time now if you want to. Do you want something to read? I have books."

"You can bring me something if you want, but I feel like I'm probably going to sleep again. I don't know what's wrong with me."

"The pain pills are making you sleepy. Are you in much pain?" he asked.

"Not anything I can't stand. I'm used to—" The moment it came out of her mouth, she knew it was a mistake when she saw a muscle jerk at the side of his mouth.

"You're used to hurting?"

LaDelle sighed. "Go find me that book, son, and stop worrying."

He started to leave and then stopped. "Mama, what does he say to you? What does he do to you to turn you into a willing victim?"

She shrugged. "Just go get my book, Brendan."

She watched him leave with a heavy heart. It hurt knowing he thought less of her for being a doormat, but what he didn't know—what none of her children knew—was that every harsh word, every blow, every indignity she suffered was so that he didn't do it to them.

They had a deal, she and Anson. She was his wife forever unless he touched one of her children. After that, it was all bets off. She cooked his food. She watched him sleep. She knew a multitude of ways to make a man suffer long and hard before he died, and she'd made sure he knew it. It was an odd relationship, but she considered her suffering God's punishment for marrying a man because he was pretty, and not because he was good.

By the time Brendan came back with the book, she was asleep. He laid it down beside the lamp and walked out.

He knew March was putting guards on Anson, but he couldn't go to work tonight and leave these two on their own, no matter how many guards were on Anson's tail. He needed someone inside who was strong enough to carry Delle to the bathroom when she needed to go, and someone Anson wouldn't want to challenge. After a brief glance at his little sister, who was still playing in the living room, he went into the kitchen to use the phone. The number he called wasn't in the book, but he knew it by heart, and it was entirely because of the woman he was about to call that he was still alive. She'd saved him from snakebite the summer he turned sixteen, and they'd shared a bond ever since.

The call rang four times, and just when he thought it was going to go to voicemail, he heard a click, then a breathless, raspy voice.

"*Bonjour.*"

"Mama Lou, it's me, Brendan Poe."

There was a brief moment of silence and then a shuffling of papers. "Something is wrong in your family."

It was a statement, not a question, which didn't surprise him. Whether her knowledge came from the voodoo she practiced, or the fact that she had an ear to everything that went on in the city, it didn't matter. What she knew, she knew.

"That's the understatement of the day. I have a need."

"Who do you want to die?"

It was daunting to know she wasn't kidding.

"My father, but if and when that ever happens, I'll do it myself. Today I have a different kind of need."

Another moment of silence, then a soft moan.

"Ahhh, the pain. LaDelle Duveau has been burned."

He wondered why she used his mother's maiden name instead of Poe, but didn't ask about it.

"Yes, ma'am, she has, and she and my little sister are in a fair amount of danger. I need to go to work and can't leave them alone. Do you know of someone strong enough to carry about a hundred and five pounds' worth of woman back and forth to the bathroom, the good sense to call the police, and the backbone to stand up to Anson Poe if the need arises? I'll pay a fair wage and will need her to come every day by 11:00 a.m. and stay until after 3:00 a.m.

every night but Sunday. It would be at least two weeks' worth of work."

"Yes, I know of this person. She will be at your door by 5:00 today. You can give her instructions and rest assured your family will be protected."

"Thank you, Mama Lou."

"Au revoir."

The line went dead in his ear. He didn't have to know who was coming to know he could breathe easy now. He glanced at the clock. It was almost 4:00 p.m. It felt like a lifetime since he'd driven out to Wisteria Hill, and there was still so much to do before he left for the night.

He got a package of hamburger meat from the fridge and dropped it in a skillet, stirred in some seasonings and covered it with a lid. It wouldn't be as good as the food his mama made, but it was cheaper and better than take-out. By the time 5:00 o'clock rolled around, he had his version of goulash ready to eat, and a salad in the refrigerator. Linny knew where he kept ice cream and cookies, so dessert was taken care of, and he'd written down the instructions his helper would need to take care of his mother's meds.

When the knock sounded at the door, Linny bolted up from the sofa and came running into the kitchen.

"Brendan, someone's at the door. Is it the babysitter? I've never had a babysitter before. Lucia, from my class, has a babysitter every Saturday night. Her mama and daddy have date night. Why don't Mama and Daddy have date night? Maybe if they did, Daddy wouldn't be so mean."

He shook his head. "Date night won't fix what's wrong with Anson. Go in the bedroom with Mama. I need to talk to the lady first."

Linny waved her hand into the air in a gesture of

queenly approval. "Yes, of course. You should have the first audience with the new handmaiden, Sir Brendan. I will be with Lady Delle."

He grinned as she flew out of the room; her long ponytail flying out behind her like Superman's cape. It seems that Xbox game she'd been playing segued into her own game of make-believe quite nicely.

When he opened the front door, it took everything he had not to back up. The woman standing just outside the threshold was so tall she was looking him square in the eyes. She was dressed more like an islander than a native of New Orleans, and for a moment, wondered if this was who Mama Lou sent. Before he could ask, she answered for him.

"I am Claudette. You are Brendan Poe?"

"Yes. Please come in," he said and stepped aside as she strode in.

He tried not to stare, but it was nearly impossible. She was at least six feet tall and wearing a long, multi-colored dress that hung loosely on her body. With her smooth, tan skin and fine features, she could've passed for a young woman, but her hair was completely grey and in dreadlocks hanging down past her shoulders.

"Show me what I am to do."

He took her to the kitchen, showed her the food and the list with his contact numbers. "Nothing is off limits to any of you. If you want it, it is yours, understand?"

She lifted the lid from the skillet, eyeing the dish of hamburger meat, sweet peppers and pasta and then replaced it gently.

"You cooked this."

"Yes, it's not the best but—"

She put a finger to her lips. "Never apologize for doing a good thing," she said softly. Then she put a hand in the middle of his chest and briefly closed her eyes. "You are a good man, Brendan Poe. Be watchful."

"Thank you, I will. Now come meet my mother and sister," he said, and led the way into the spare bedroom.

When they walked in, Delle was sitting up, and Linny was brushing her hair.

The moment they entered, Linny froze. Her lips parted, but nothing came out of her mouth.

LaDelle was another story. Her eyes widened, and then a big grin spread across her face as she leaned forward about to lunge from the bed.

"Claudette?"

The woman flashed a wide, happy smile.

Brendan stared. "You two know each other?"

Delle was laughing as Claudette slid onto the side of the bed. "Yes, Lord yes, we know each other," Delle said, clutching Claudette's hands. "We are within twelve hours of being the exact same age, and we slept in the same bed until Claudette got so big Mama had to get her a bed of her own."

Claudette was laughing. "For which I was most grateful since you continued to wet the bed until you were almost four."

Linny grinned. "Mama wet the bed?"

Claudette smiled and beckoned for her to come close. As soon as she could reach her, she pulled Linny into her lap.

"Every child wets the bed at least once, is this not so?"

Linny nodded, fascinated by the woman's manner and looks.

"Okay, Mama, I'm still waiting for an explanation," Brendan said.

"Claudette is my half-sister, Brendan. Daddy had two families, which no one knew about until Claudette's mama died. She was barely a year old when Daddy brought her home. Mama put Daddy out of her bed for a whole year, but she took Claudette in her arms like she was one of her own."

Brendan grinned. "I have an aunt?"

Claudette stood. "Yes. Yes, you do, Brendan Poe. If it is not to your liking, I—"

She never got to finish what she was saying.

Brendan threw his arms around her, kissed her on both cheeks, and then hugged her again.

"Finally! Family I can be proud of," he said.

Delle felt shame, but at the same time a relief. This day was long overdue. Her marriage to Anson Poe had separated her from everyone she'd known and loved, and if Anson knew Claudette was here, he'd be livid. The thought made her smile.

Brendan shook his head. "Okay, so now I owe Mama Lou even more than my life. She's given me back family as well, and she's never gonna let me forget it."

Claudette lifted her chin, ready to take charge.

"Go to your job, Brendan Poe, and rest assured I can handle any and everything that might possibly occur."

He left with a smile on his face and a bounce in his step.

****

The Black Garter was in the middle of a block on Rampart Street. The entrance was painted black, and there were no windows to see what was going on inside, partly because of the semi-nudity of the dancers, and partly because the people who were inside had privacy issues of their own.

The décor skirted gaudy, hinted at macabre, and bordered on just enough reality to be interesting. The undertones of a drumbeat played in the background beneath a constant loop of Cajun music. The cocktail waitresses wore black slacks and black lace camisoles with barely there red bras peeking through the naughty lace. It was meant to keep emotions hot, while the constantly circulating air conditioning kept bodies cool.

There was a raised stage behind a half-circle bar where a nearly naked dancer twisted and writhed to a wild jungle drumbeat. The fact a python, white as the dancer was dark, dangled around her neck was almost noticed after the fact.

The two other bartenders who usually worked Juliette's shift were Toni and Wynn, and they all worked within the open arc between the bar and the stage.

There were two bouncers on every shift, three if it was a weekend or a convention was in town. Tonight, Brendan was on duty with Deuce, an ex-pro football player who'd grown up in the area.

Brendan stood near a wall in the middle of the room that gave him free access to watch the people on the floor as well as people at the bar. There was no access to the stage from the front of the house, but it didn't stop the occasional customer from trying to climb the bar to get to the woman and her snake.

Deuce was in the process of removing a very drunk customer from the premises for putting his hand down a waitress's bra when Brendan saw a heavy-set man come inside and head for the bar. He reminded Brendan of a hairless ape: long arms, short legs, and a bald head jammed onto shoulders too big for his body.

It was the same man who'd been coming in every night for a month and making a point to take a seat at the end of the bar where Juliette worked. He wouldn't look at her, or anybody else, until he'd had at least one drink. After that, he stared at her for hours on end, watching her like a mongoose watches a cobra, waiting for the right moment to strike.

Brendan knew the man made Juliette uneasy, but he'd never said or done anything that would get him removed from the premises. And, until he did, he had free range to come and go and look all he wanted.

****

Julie saw the man approaching and shuddered inwardly. The moment he sat down at the bar, she looked for Brendan across the crowd. Once she caught his eye and realized he'd seen the man come in, too. She relaxed.

The man she privately referred to as "the troll" tapped the bar loudly to get her attention.

She turned, her voice cool and business-like. "What'll it be?"

"The same," he said softly without looking at her face.

Julie sensed he liked knowing she was familiar with his tastes, and detected a small glint of satisfaction when she put the first gin and tonic down in front of him. Even though she quickly moved on to the next customer, trading wit and quips with her regulars, the silence between her and the troll grew ominous by the absence of conversation.

Sometimes she would get busy and forget he was there, then hear that sharp *tap, tap,* as he rapped the bottom of his empty glass against the bar for a refill. But it was the second drink he ordered that got to her, because once the first was gone, he watched her non-stop.

He always stayed until fifteen minutes before closing, at which time he paid his tab plus a ten-dollar tip, and walked out without a stumble, even with five drinks and a bowl of pretzels in his belly.

What Julie didn't know, and Brendan had yet to find out was that, when Chub Walton left the bar, he stood in the shadows of a nearby alley, waiting to see her come out. He also knew where she lived and followed her home every night. He knew she had a thing with the big, dark-haired bouncer, but that didn't bother him. He didn't want her forever. He just wanted her once. Women didn't last beyond that. Growing up, his mama had always accused him of being hard on his shoes. She's had no idea he would be hard on his women as well.

For now, Chub was satisfied to anticipate. It was part of the game, which made it better for the main event, and this night was no different. When closing time drew near, he paid up, left, then went to the alley to wait.

A short while later, the big bouncer and the little blonde walked out hand-in-hand to where their cars were parked. After a quick kiss, the guy got in his SUV and followed behind her all the way home.

Chub followed a distance behind them, cruising past only after they went inside, and then made his way home.

****

Two days later

Anson was doing a walk-through of Wisteria Hill with a pad and pen, making notes of things that needed to be fixed or replaced. He hadn't looked at the place like this in years and it had long since lost the connotation of home. It was just the place where he ate, slept, and fucked. He'd left the child rearing and the house to Delle, and made sure the money he gave her was barely enough to clothe and feed them. But if he was going to get her back, this had to be done. She had to come home on her own to make the rest of his plan work.

When he finally sat down to a solitary supper, it was to the last of Delle's gumbo. After this, he was going to have to cook his own food, or buy it in town. Once he finished eating, he began making phone calls, wasting no time in getting started.

Within two days, he had a crew repairing the roof, another repairing the exterior in preparation for a paint job, while a third crew was tearing out the old kitchen flooring to install new tile. The last crew was prepping the interior walls of the house, readying them to be painted as well. Once all that was completed, he had a local interior designer on standby to hang new curtains and drapes. His family and neighbors would view it as a much-needed renovation, but to Anson, it was nothing more than a very expensive trap.

****

When Sam and Chance showed up for work that morning and saw what was taking place, they were in shock. They stood on the threshold in the kitchen, staring in disbelief.

"What's going on?" Sam asked.

"What's it look like?" Anson asked as he circled the work crew and headed for the door.

"You're fixing the floor?" Chance said.

"Good observation, but it's not just the floor. It's the whole damn place," Anson said. "Let's go outside to talk."

They followed him out and then into the yard.

"What the hell, Dad?" Sam asked.

Anson shrugged. "I'm fixing the place like Delle wanted, and putting in some air conditioners, too. It's damn hot inside."

"It's been hot for as long as I've been alive," Sam muttered, still pissed at Anson for what he'd done.

Anson looked up, his eyes narrowing in a warning Sam recognized. "Don't challenge me," Anson said softly.

Sam stared back until, to his shame, he was the first to look away.

Anson shifted his focus to Chance, but he refused to meet his father's gaze. He grinned, knowing they'd been properly cowed.

"Well, now. Let's talk about what's up today. Chance, I want you to check the grow sites up north. Sam, you take the ones to the East. If either of you see anything off, let me know. Last time I was up north, I swore someone had been there. It could be some Cajun up the bayou decided to snag a little weed thinking it wouldn't be missed, but I'm not running a charity. Pay attention. When you come back, there's a shipment of bamboo to get ready. The invoices are on the clipboard in the shed."

The brothers glanced at each other and then walked away.

As soon as everyone was otherwise occupied, Anson got a flashlight and headed for the attic. When he opened the door, the movement sent dust motes swirling. The heat in the highest floor of the old mansion was basically unbearable, but he didn't intend to linger. Sweat beaded almost instantly on his upper lip, and soon ran out of his hairline and down the middle of his back, as well. He wiped his face with a handkerchief as he moved farther inside, wrinkling his nose as he went.

The musty smell came from the accumulation of centuries: old furniture, dressmaker's dummies from at least three different eras, a half-dozen chests, Christmas decorations from the family before them, boxes and boxes of crap, and a multitude of old paintings from his long-dead ancestors.

He caught a glimpse of movement that made his heart

skip a beat before he realized he was looking at himself in a full-length mirror. He stared, then frowned and looked away from the signs of visible aging on his face.

The single window facing the East was covered in grime, leaving the room and contents in a sepia-colored half-light. He walked the length of the attic and back, ducking a birdhouse hanging from the low ceiling, and what looked like a handmade wind chime. He hadn't been up here in years, but he seemed to remember playing in a small storage space his mother had called a cubbyhole. After pushing a few chests and boxes around, he finally found it and got down on his knees to open it only to find that it was stuck. He pulled harder on the little knob, then harder again until it finally opened up with a loud squeak.

As he peered into the darkness, he thought again about what he was planning and for a few seconds contemplated the idea of relenting on revenge. But then, he heard a loud bang as one of the workers dropped something downstairs, remembered the gun going off in his face, and shifted focus.

Hell no. I won't let this go.

He aimed a flashlight into the darkness, saw even more boxes inside, and began pulling out everything he could reach until he'd cleared away a large space. Satisfied, he pushed the door shut, shoved a chest back in front of it, and headed downstairs to check the progress in the kitchen.

The workers were down to the subflooring.

"Hey, how much longer in here?" he asked.

The foreman stood up, wiping sweat off his face as he eyed the room.

"We'll lay all the new wood tomorrow, then your tile the day after. I picked it up before I came out this morning. It's in the hall if you want to make sure it's what you ordered."

Anson liked playing lord of the manor almost as much as he liked being drug boss. He strode back into the hall, opened a box, and pulled out a tile, running his hands over the smooth surface as he admired the pattern. *Fleur de lis* was a damn fancy design for a kitchen floor, but that's why he'd picked it.

"Yeah! It's the one," he yelled and then went out the front door, pausing on the verandah to assess the grounds.

He hadn't looked at Wisteria Hill from this vantage point in years, but it was a reminder of the prestigious family into which he'd been born. It looked rough now, but it could and would look good again.

He glanced at his watch and made a mental note to have Chance put that belly mower on the little tractor and knock down some of this grass.

It was nearly noon. He was hungry, but not in the mood to eat alone. As soon as the workers stopped for lunch, he got in his truck, drove into New Orleans through the old part of the city, then down a narrow one-way alley, and parked behind a certain two–story brick building. The back stairs creaked at every step as he ascended. He knocked twice and waited.

The door opened, revealing a tall, thin woman wearing a long, yellow sundress. She had a black patch over one eye and wore her very curly hair cut close to her scalp. He eyed the stiletto knife in a scabbard at her waist, but frowned when she barred the doorway.

"What do you want here, Anson Poe?"

He didn't like being challenged like this, but was well aware she knew how to use that knife, so he took a roll of money out of his pocket and flashed it openly.

"The same thing any man wants here, Lisette."

Lisette Branscum lifted her chin defiantly. "Last time you were here, I told you never come back."

He stood his ground. "Last time I was here, I made a mistake in judgment. I was hoping we could get past that."

"Last time you were here, you put one of my girls in the hospital. You're no good for my business."

"Like I said, it was a mistake. A man can reform."

She stared at him without comment.

He tried again.

"I had a hankering for one of Jean-Luc's shrimp po-boys, and for dessert, a blow job compliments of your pretty Corinna."

"You can go downstairs and order your food in Frenchie's like everyone else, but you are no longer welcome upstairs."

Anger rolled through him, flushing his already sweaty face. This challenge felt too much like the shot that knocked the hat off his head. He wasn't going back to the little café she ran on the floor below. He wanted the special treatment she gave to the second-floor guests. He put the money back in his pocket and spit on the step between them.

Her eyes narrowed. She took a step back and swung the door shut in his face.

Inside, he was seething, but he knew she'd gotten the insult loud and clear. He stomped back down the stairs to his truck and drove out of the alley. Yet one more person who'd crossed him and was going to wish she hadn't.

He picked up some barbeque instead from a local diner, and just for the hell of it, he drove by Brendan's apartment on his way out of town. When he saw the SUV parked in the usual spot, he pictured them all happy and cozy inside the fancy air-conditioned apartment, eating and laughing, maybe laughing at him.

He took the next turn and headed home, eating as he drove. But when he got to the turn-off leading to Wisteria

Hill, he drove past and farther up the road. The workers would go on without him for a while. He had more pressing matters to which he needed to attend.

****

Voltaire LeDeux lived as far off the beaten path as a man could live, which was just far enough for strangers to get their asses lost and suffer the consequences. He was, for all intents and purposes, anonymous. He had no birth certificate, because his mama had birthed him all by herself in the bed in which he now slept. He'd never been to a public school in his life, and the one time someone had come to insist his mother was breaking the law by keeping him at home, she'd run him off the property with a shotgun. He got the message he weren't welcome and never went back.

As a result, he'd never been listed on a census. He didn't have a social security number because he'd never worked. He existed entirely from the food he hunted or grew.

His clothes came in trade for his services, and while there wasn't a woman living who'd been willing to live such a meager existence, Voltaire did not do without sex when he wanted it. He did favors for people who did favors for him. That's how it worked. And that's why, when he saw Anson Poe pull up in his yard, he got up from the bench on what passed for his porch, and waited for his approach.

"Hey, Voltaire, long time-no see," Anson said and handed him a small package. "For when you're in the mood."

Voltaire took the marijuana, laid it on the bench and then walked over to a small bucket sitting in the shade.

"You got a bucket in that truck?" Voltaire asked.

Anson went back to the truck, got a small plastic bucket out of the truck bed and handed it to Voltaire, who dumped the contents into Anson's bucket.

"Crawfish. I thank you, Voltaire. That'll be good eating."

Voltaire nodded and only then pocketed his weed. He would accept a gift, but he had to give one in return. He lived his life by never being beholden to another man.

"I have business," Anson said, carefully eyeing the leather-faced man with the small, black eyes.

Although Voltaire looked innocent enough, he knew the man was always armed, most usually a hunting knife he used for skinning gators.

"Take a seat," Voltaire said, indicating the bench he'd just vacated.

Anson set his bucket aside and pulled out the wad of cash he was carrying. "What I need will require payment to others to make it happen."

Voltaire leaned back and folded his arms across his chest. He knew all there was and more about Anson Poe. He didn't want him for an enemy, but he wasn't afraid of him either.

"Tell me what you need, and I will tell you how much it will cost," he said.

"Payback," Anson said.

Voltaire nodded once. "Revenge is costly. Kindly elaborate."

"I want two fires set."

"Name the places."

"Frenchie's."

Voltaire's eyes widened slightly. It was his only reaction to setting fire to what his mama had called a house of ill repute.

"And the other?"

"The Black Garter on a Saturday night."

Voltaire stood. "Entering into a war with Grayson March will end badly."

Anson unfolded his six-foot plus height as a muscle jerked at the corner of one eye. "Do you want the job or not?"

"This will cost much money."

Anson opened his fist, revealing the wad of one hundred dollar bills. "There's five thousand dollars here. If you need more, I'll get it."

"It will suffice," Voltaire said, and held out his hand.

"Within the week," Anson added.

Voltaire nodded once, then went into his house and shut the door.

Anson picked up his crawfish, got back in his truck, and headed home. Back on the main road, he caught a glimpse of a vehicle he didn't recognize parked back up in the woods. Grayson March thought he was smart, having Anson tailed, but they couldn't put one over on him. Not out here. This was his milieu, and there was more than one way to skin a fat cat like March.

****

Three days later

The endless days and nights of living two separate lives was finally wearing Brendan down. By the time he got off work, it was almost 3:00 a.m. He fell into bed and slept until Linny woke him up, usually sometime between 8:00 and 9:00 a.m. After that, he was up for the day, making breakfast for the three of them while planning what needed to be done before Claudette's arrival.

Delle's feet were at a painful stage of healing. The

burned skin was beginning to slough off, and Brendan had to take her back to the doctor. The removal of dead skin and fresh bandages was a painful process that left Delle shaking and in tears.

On this particular morning, they had just returned from the hospital when Claudette met them in the parking lot. She was carrying a large tote bag, which she quickly slung over her shoulder and grabbed the sack of groceries from the SUV.

Brendan carried his mother into the apartment with Claudette at his heels and Linny tagging along behind all of them. They rode the elevator up together, and once inside his apartment, he settled Delle in bed while Claudette and Linny began putting away groceries. He gave his mother a pain pill, which she took gratefully, chasing it with a drink of cool water.

Once it was down, Delle fell back against the pillows. Despite the cool air inside the bedroom, there was a bead of sweat on her upper lip.

"Mama, I'm so sorry," Brendan said softly.

She grabbed his hand, holding it against her heart. "You have nothing to apologize for, son. I just need to rest for a bit."

He pulled a light cover up to her waist and then waited for her to fall asleep. As he sat, he thought of his brothers. Although they called daily for updates, they had yet to come see her. They were stuck in the middle of their father's illegal trade, but aligned with their mother's plight.

When she suddenly cried out in her sleep, he touched her arm and she stilled. It was eerie, looking at her like this, like looking at a body in a casket. Had it not been for the soft rise and fall of her breasts, she could have been mistaken for dead. Anson had beaten the life out of her, and the body had yet to acknowledge the death.

Linny slipped into the room and whispered in his ear.

"Aunt Claudette wants to talk to you."

He tweaked her nose as she darted away and went to the kitchen where Claudette was preparing lunch.

"What's up, Auntie?"

Claudette loved the title he had bestowed upon her and made no attempt to hide her affection for her sisters' children.

"We will talk about your father," she said and pointed to a chair. "Please sit. Linny is going to go play with the doll I brought for her today."

Linny had just been dismissed and knew it. She skipped out of the room, anxious to give the doll and the small chest of doll clothes a closer look.

Claudette sat down to face him. Today she wore another loose dress, this time of green fabric with large white flowers in the design and had her dreadlocks tied back with a long black ribbon. She was a magnificent woman, and he knew she knew it.

He frowned. "Why do I feel like I'm going to get the third degree, and what about Anson?"

"Mama Lou sends a message. Your father's heart is very dark. He has a plan of which you should beware. He wants revenge for something you have done to him and will go to extremes to get it."

Brendan's gut knotted. "I expected as much."

"What did you do to him?" Claudette asked.

"Enough," Brendan said.

Claudette shrugged. "Just beware. It won't be just you who suffers when he strikes."

"It never is," Brendan said, thinking of the three women in his life, and knowing he would never be able to keep them safe as long as Anson Poe was alive.

"So, I have delivered the message. Now I will make lunch," Claudette said.

Brendan glanced at his watch. "Nothing for me. I have a couple of errands to run, and I want to go check on Julie before I leave."

Claudette moved to the refrigerator and took down a small stack of crockery from the top. "Then, please, give these to Juliette for me, and thank her very much for the food. When you are hungry, there will be enough leftovers for you to eat."

"Will do, and tell Mama Lou thank you for the warning."

"I will do that," Claudette said, and went back to her tasks.

Brendan paused in the living room to watch his little sister, then set the dishes down and walked closer.

The doll Claudette brought her was beautiful, and obviously old. Linny had the clothes laid out along the back of the sofa and was talking to the doll as if she were real, while Rabbit sat at the other end of the sofa, observing.

He smiled. "So is Rabbit on guard today?"

Linny looked up. "Rabbit is always on guard. He keeps me safe at night."

Brendan frowned. "Are you afraid sleeping here, honey?"

"I'm always afraid. Something's going to happen to me. I don't know when or what, but it will. I need Rabbit to stand guard."

His frown deepened. "Why would you say that, baby? I won't let anything happen to you."

She shrugged. "It just will. I've always known it."

A sudden chill shot through him. "I won't let Anson hurt you," he said, and sat down beside her.

She wrapped her arms around his neck and buried her face in the space beneath his chin. "I love you most of all my brothers," she whispered.

"And I love you more," he said, his voice suddenly shaking. "I have to go run some errands, but tomorrow is Sunday. It's my day off. If Mama feels like it, we can take a ride out to the Crab Shack on the bayou to eat dinner."

"And could I get a beignet? I love them so much, and Mama doesn't make them anymore since you moved away."

Yet another surge of guilt swept through him. "Yes, you can have all the beignets you want. We'll even get some to bring home."

"Yay! That will be fun, Sir Brendan."

He smiled. "I live to serve the good Queen Belinda."

As soon as he got up, she went right back to playing.

"Come turn the deadbolt after I leave," he said and picked up the dishes.

She followed him to the door and waved good-bye.

He stood out in the hall until he heard the deadbolt click and then headed for Juliette's apartment.

Chapter Five

Julie was hanging up the clothes she'd picked up from the cleaners. Tomorrow was Nonny's birthday dinner and all she had left to do was wrap her grandmother's present and she was good to go. She noticed a business card on the bedside table as she started to leave and picked it up.

It was from a lawyer. She recognized the name but not how it had come to be in her bedroom, and guessed it had fallen out of Brendan's wallet the last time they'd made love. Just the thought of being with him was enough to curl her toes.

Then a faint ding from another room caught her attention. It was the bell on her kitchen timer reminding her the food she'd put in the oven was done. She set the card aside, gathered up the plastic bags from the cleaners to put in the garbage, and headed for the kitchen.

A few minutes later, she was dishing up seafood casserole when she heard a knock at the door.

"Well darn it," she muttered, set her plate of food into the microwave, then made a run for the living room.

"Who is it?" she asked, her hand on the knob.

"The big bad wolf."

She swung the door inward. "Brendan! Just in time!"

He handed her the dishes then followed her to the kitchen. The moment she put them down, he swept her off her feet.

She laughed out loud. "What do you think you're doing?"

"Wolfish things," he growled, and nipped at the lobe of her ear.

Julie moaned and melted into him. Casserole be damned. This was food for her soul.

"Do you have time for this?" he asked.

"I always have time for this," she whispered.

He carried her into her bedroom, then laid her down on the bed and began kicking off his boots.

Juliette came out of her clothes without delay, and was ready and waiting when he crawled between her legs.

"Foreplay is highly overrated," she drawled, eyeing his most remarkable erection.

"That's not what I hear," he said and proceeded to prove it.

She was riding the first wave of a climax when he slid between her legs and took his pleasure.

Time ceased.

A cop car flew past the apartment building with sirens screaming, and for a moment, she thought the scream had come out of her mouth. He made her crazy in the best possible way, and she was still savoring the aftershocks when Brendan let out a low groan.

"Dear Lord," he said, as he rolled off her onto his back.

She turned toward him to rise up on one elbow. "If you were praying for mercy, it's too late."

He laughed as he kissed her.

"I have food," she said, when he finally let her go.

"I can smell it."

"Do you want some?"

"Food?"

She doubled up her fist and popped him on the shoulder. "Be serious."

"Hark, what light by yonder... no... yon window

breaks? Is it the Juliette of my dreams creating magic in the kitchen?"

Now she was laughing. "Romeo, oh Romeo, that's not quite how Shakespeare wrote it, and the magic has already been created." She rolled out of bed, grabbing her clothes as she went. "Just let me get dressed and we can eat."

She noticed the card again, and pointed. "I think that's yours. It must have fallen out of your wallet."

He saw it and put it back in his wallet.

"Yes, it's mine, in case Mama ever considers leaving Anson."

Instead of putting on clothes, he watched her dress, wondering how anyone so small could hold someone his size in the palm of her hand.

When she hurried out of the room, the thought of food finally made him move. He got up and dressed, then followed the enticing aroma to her kitchen.

"What smells so good?"

"Seafood casserole. Enjoy," she said, and handed him a plate with a very generous serving. "Dig in, Bren. I'm right behind you."

He sat down and took a big bite, rolling his eyes in appreciation. "She's smart and beautiful, makes love like a goddess, and she can cook. I am such a lucky man."

She took her plate to the table then quickly took a big bite. Making love definitely agreed with her because she was suddenly starving.

"How's Delle? Didn't you take her to the doctor this morning?" she asked.

"Yes, I did. She's healing and still in pain, but convinced she needs to hurry up and get well so she can go home."

Julie frowned. "Oh no. I'm so sorry. I thought—"

He shrugged. "So did I. I don't understand their relationship at all. She lets him hurt her."

Julie heard a slight shake in his voice and knew he was troubled. "Did he beat you boys when you were growing up?"

Brendan frowned. "Not like you mean, although there were countless times when I thought we'd catch hell for sure. But the minute he amped up, Mama stepped in and—"

Brendan paused in midsentence.

Julie saw an odd expression cross his face.

"What's wrong?"

"I never thought of our life quite like that before. We were all afraid of him and pretty much hated his guts."

"And?"

"And I'm wondering now if Mama purposefully took the brunt of his anger for us."

Julie leaned forward. "So maybe that explains why she stayed. As long as she's there, he leaves her children alone."

It was the first time Brendan had thought of his mother's behavior in that light, but knowing his father, it made a twisted sort of sense.

Julie topped off the iced tea in their glasses. Brendan raised his in a toast, determined to change the subject to something more pleasant.

"To women," he said.

Julie smiled. "I'll drink to that."

So they did.

****

Saturday night at The Black Garter was always noisy, and tonight was no exception. Brendan and a part-time bouncer named Marco had just broken up a fight, and were escorting the responsible parties out of the bar. As they came back into the club, Marco moved toward the far end of the room, while Brendan returned to the stage at the front. It wasn't until he paused that he realized Julie's troll was already seated at the bar nursing a drink. He caught the look in her eyes and frowned. She was uneasy, which made him wonder what he'd missed, and when she lifted her chin, motioning him over, he didn't hesitate.

****

The room was packed with people crowding up around the bar, jostling the customers already sitting there. A couple of customers were already three sheets to the wind, which made serving them difficult. Julie stopped serving one man at the bar when she realized he was so drunk he kept falling off his stool. She looked around for Brendan or Marco to come get him, but they were nowhere in sight.

But the larger issue for her was the troll. She was rattled and trying not to show it, but the man had broken his routine. Instead of tapping his empty glass on the bar for a refill, he was loudly calling her by name.

The change in behavior was disconcerting, and when she finally saw Brendan moving back toward the bar, she signaled for help. He came quickly

"What's up, Julie?"

"The troll's talking to me. In fact, he hasn't stopped."

Brendan knew this was aberrant behavior, which was worrisome, but when he turned to look at him, the man appeared to be watching the dancers on the stage behind the bar.

"I'll keep an eye on him, honey."

"Okay," she said, then pointed at the drunk at the far end of the bar. "He needs a ride home."

He spotted the guy, hit speed dial on his phone, and called a cab, then headed toward the other end of the bar.

Julie watched him maneuver the drunk off the stool, and then walk him to the front.

"Hey, Julie! Julie!"

She winced. The troll had just finished his third drink. Normally, he would have still been nursing the second. What the heck was going on?

****

Chub Walton was high on anticipation. Come hell or high water, tonight he was making his move. She was due for a break within the hour, and when she headed back to the bathroom, he was going to be right behind her. He'd seen the exit plenty of times in the back. He also knew there were security cameras, but he was off the radar as far as the police were concerned. Even if he stood in front of the cameras and waved, they still wouldn't know his name.

He slid the glass toward her, knowing she would have to catch it to keep it from sliding off the bar. When her fingers curled around the glass, he got a hard-on just thinking about putting his mouth where her hand had been.

When she set it back in front of him, he purposefully licked the outside of the glass where her hand had been and then grunted—slightly salty with a hint of lime.

****

Anson's footsteps echoed within the house as he walked across the new kitchen floor on his way out the door. The house was shaping up nicely, and he had a field ready to harvest. He liked setting goals, and liked it even better when they were accomplished. He was close—so close—to seeing this one through, but tonight he was in the mood to mingle, and dressed fit to the task.

He locked the door as he left for dinner and drove into New Orleans with a destination already in mind. It was almost 9:30 p.m., which meant he'd be on a wait list for a table, but he had nothing better to do. Considering the threat Grayson March had given him, he had to assume the guards were behind him, but as long as they didn't bother him, he'd deal with it.

By the time he finally found a place to park, it was almost 10:00 p.m. He locked the truck and headed up the street, confident he was a man to be admired. He'd taken pains with his clothing. Even though it was summer, Anson favored black and was wearing a suit more suited for fall. His dark hair was as shiny as the dress shoes he was wearing, and he was sporting his grandfather's gold pinkie ring and his daddy's Rolex, well aware that if he hadn't gotten into the business of growing weed, they would have long since been pawned.

He was working the look and the strut, savoring the attention he was getting as he walked the eleven blocks to his restaurant of choice. When he entered, the aromas reminded him of why he'd come. He approached the smiling hostess with a swagger.

"Good evening, sir. Welcome to Adelaine's. How many will there be in your party?"

"Just one," he said, flashing a quick smile that never reached his eyes.

Her reaction was somewhere between a giggle and a sigh, and he allowed himself a moment to picture her beneath him, begging for mercy.

"Your name?" she asked.

"Poe."

She giggled. "As in Edgar Allen?"

"No darlin'. As in Anson."

The smile froze on her face and then she blinked, which told him she was a local or she wouldn't have recognized the name.

"There will be a thirty-minute wait."

"I'll be in the bar," he said, then winked and walked away.

****

Anson had been right on target about Grayson March's guards. Parker and Roberts, the two who'd been assigned to keep tabs on him, were on his tail the moment he drove away from Wisteria Hill. When he parked, they parked too and followed him on foot, one man behind him, and the other on the opposite side of the street. From the way Poe was dressed, it seemed apparent he was up for some fine dining, and when he entered Adelaine's, they knew their assumptions had been right. They met up at the street corner.

"You take the back entrance," Parker said. "I'll watch the street."

Roberts disappeared within the foot traffic as Parker stepped into the shadows of the alley behind him, making sure he had a clear view of the front entrance before he made a call.

"Boss, it's me, Parker. You told us to let you know when he came into the city, and he's here."

Grayson frowned. "Where?"

"He just went into Adelaine's, dressed to kill."

"Poor choice of words," Grayson said. "Don't lose him."

"Yes, sir. We have eyes on both exits."

"Fine. Carry on."

When the line went dead in Parker's ear, he glanced over his shoulder to make sure he was alone. A few moments later, he got a text from Roberts telling him he was in place. He texted back "OK" and settled in to wait.

****

Anson sauntered up to the bar and raised his hand. The bartender caught his gaze.

"Whiskey, neat," Anson said, watching as the bartender poured his shot.

When he slid a ten-dollar bill across the bar and walked away with his drink, the extravagance was not missed by the people around him. It was exactly what he intended. He took a quick sip as he strolled through the crowd.

A few people nodded as he passed, but no one struck up a conversation, which was fine. He wasn't here to visit. He was here to remind New Orleans of his place in society. He'd been born with a very tarnished, but very silver spoon in his mouth, and it didn't hurt to remind them of that now and then. After five minutes or so of mingling, he set his empty glass on the tray of a passing waitress and headed for the men's room.

****

It was Saturday night, which meant business in Frenchie's was brisk. Besides the front entrance where most of Lisette's customers entered for the Cajun food that she served, there was the side entrance in the alley where her more important clientele came and went without being observed. These were judges and councilmen, businessmen and ship captains who'd made prior appointments, the men who paid big money for her best girls.

Anson thought about what was going on there as he took a piss and was once again reminded of Lisette's insult. He didn't know for sure when it would happen, but it only seemed fair that the big shots who fucked the same women he'd fucked got smoked out with her.

When he got back to the bar, he ordered another drink, and was still sipping it when his name was called. He returned to the front of the house and followed a waiter to his table. After the amenities were passed, he continued to nurse his drink while quietly surveying the other diners.

It wasn't long before they began to hear sirens. Moments later, someone's cell phone rang, and then another, and another, and all of a sudden there was a roomful of people taking calls and checking messages.

When someone suddenly shouted, "Frenchie's is on fire!" he stifled a grin.

****

Lisette Branscum's entire life was wrapped up in Frenchie's. She lived on the premises, ran the deli-style café on the ground floor like she was feeding people out of her own home, knew most of her customers by their first names, and didn't have a moment's regret that she ran a discreet brothel/invitation-only poker game on the second floor. The fact that prostitution was illegal didn't worry her because most of her customers were the movers and shakers who ran the city.

Downstairs, the café was packed with a waiting line out the door. Saturday night was always busy, but tonight her servers were running to keep up—just the way she liked it.

She was at the front of her restaurant, critically eyeing the blades on the ceiling fans and wondering when they'd last been dusted, when one of the kitchen staff darted into the room.

Lisette saw the look on the girl's face and her gut knotted.

"Patty! What's wrong?"

"Ma'am! Ma'am! The basement is on fire. Chef said to tell you the back stairs are impassable."

"Have you called 911?"

"Chef called. He's the one who found it."

"Then go tell the kitchen staff to exit the premises now."

The reaction was instantaneous.

The waiting customers who'd been standing nearby bolted. The seated diners noticed the exodus, and it didn't take long for the reason why to spread, although Lisette had already taken charge and was making the announcement.

"Ladies and gentlemen, we have a small fire on the premises. Please make your way carefully out the exit. Forget your tab. It's on the house."

The diners reacted far better than those waiting in line had done, but they were getting their cue from Lisette, and not a panicked waitress.

However, the occupants of her upstairs rooms caused her the most concern. Not only did she need to get them out safely, but it would behoove her to do it as inauspiciously as possible, or the cash cow side of her business would certainly be over.

She grabbed two of her waiters and began issuing orders. "Charlie, see that the customers all get out safely. Tommy, make sure the bathrooms are empty and then both of you leave. I'm going upstairs."

The skirt she was wearing was a long red and black print. She thought it was classy, but class was the last thing on her mind as she hitched it up above her knees and ran up the back stairs in an all-out dash. She hadn't been this scared since the night one of her johns pulled a knife and put out her eye. The moment she reached the second floor, she began hammering on doors.

"Fire! Fire! Get out! Get out!"

Within seconds, doors began opening and half-naked men were running out with their shoes and shirts in their hands, heading for the back stairs.

"No! No! The back stairs are impassable," she cried and grabbed one of her girls. "Carly, take them through my apartment. There is a fire escape on the outside of my bedroom window. The rest of you girls go out the front door downstairs with everyone else. At best we can claim there was a private poker game in progress if the men are seen, but it would be a damn good idea if everyone was dressed before you go down that ladder or the story will never fly."

"*Mon Dieu*," someone moaned, while another man chose a more colorful epithet.

"I am so fucked."

Lisette sighed. Even if she got everyone out without incident, she might not recover from this after all.

****

Julie was getting ready to take a ten-minute bathroom break when people began getting phone calls and texts about the fire. After that, the news spread swiftly through the bar. The Black Garter was too close to Frenchie's to ignore what was happening. She darted out from behind the counter and headed for the manager's office. Jack needed to know.

Jack Michaels was a short, sixty-something man with a

thick head of hair he kept black on the assumption that hair dye was defeating the aging process. He had been the manager at The Black Garter for over twenty-three years, and the only real physical danger the bar had ever faced was Hurricane Katrina, but that might be about to change.

She knocked once then strode in without waiting for an invitation. "Jack! Frenchie's is on fire. Do you want to evacuate the premises?"

"Oh hell," Jack said and headed for the back entrance.

He smelled smoke the moment he opened the door. When he looked up over the rooftops and saw the orange flames against the night sky, the hair stood on up on the back of his neck. He'd watched his grandfather's home burn to the ground when he was ten. It was a horror he'd never forgotten.

"Lord have mercy," he whispered, then turned around. Julie was right behind him. "Get the guys to start emptying the place. I'm calling Grayson."

Julie ran back into the bar, but the place was already a melee. She reached for her phone, but before she could call Brendan, he called her.

"Julie! Where the hell are you?"

"I was with Jack. He said evacuate now."

"On it. I'll tell the others."

She started to tell him she'd meet him out front, but he'd already hung up. Ever her father's daughter, she headed for the bar to empty the registers, and was almost there when someone grabbed her arm. She turned, saw nothing but the fist coming at her, and then everything went black.

Chapter Six

Brendan and Marco were in the street answering questions and directing customers to safety, while Deuce was checking through the bathrooms to make sure every room was vacant.

Toni and Wynn, the other two bartenders, were frantically emptying the registers as Jack came running into the room.

"Just put everything in here," he said, as he slid the deposit bag down the counter, then began eyeing the dirty tables and scattered chairs with a heavy heart. It took him a moment to realize Julie was gone.

"Hey, Wynn, where's Juliette?"

The bartender shrugged. "I haven't seen her since she left to tell you what was happening."

Jack frowned. "I sent her back here to tell the guys to empty the place. Maybe she's with Brendan. Where is he?"

Deuce overheard Jack's comment as he came in from the back. "It's all clear in the back. Brendan and Marco are still outside. I'll see if she's with them."

He left at a jog, but within moments Brendan came running back inside, a panicked expression on his face. "What do you mean Julie's missing?"

Jack frowned. "I didn't say she was missing, I just wondered where she was."

"She didn't come out the front. I thought she was in here," Brendan said. "Maybe she's in the bathroom. Did anyone—?"

"I already cleared them," Deuce said.

Brendan felt sick. All of the weeks he'd been so careful to keep an eye on the man at the bar, and the moment he looked away, this happened. He wouldn't let himself finish the thought and headed for her co-workers.

"Toni, Wynn, did either one of you see her crazy stalker leave the bar?"

Jack frowned. "What crazy stalker?"

Brendan was already on the phone calling her number as he answered.

"She called him the troll. He was one of her regulars, but a real weird customer. She was already spooked tonight because she said he was acting strange. We need to check the security cameras."

Jack was starting to worry. "Damn it! Who else knew about this?"

Toni shrugged. "We all knew. He wouldn't let anyone take his order but Julie. He doesn't talk to her, just stares at her all the time. It freaks her out."

Now panic was setting in. "Why am I just now hearing about this?" Jack asked.

Brendan heard his call go to voice mail. "Damn it! No answer. Please, Jack. We need to check the security cameras."

Jack waved at the bartenders as they handed him the deposit bags. "Toni, you and Wynn go home. We've got this."

Toni's voice was shaking. "I sure hope she's okay."

"Come on, kid, I'll walk you out," Wynn said and escorted her from the bar as Brendan and the other two bouncers followed Jack back into the office.

"Deuce, keep an eye on that fire for me," Jack said.

Deuce did a U-turn and headed for the back door.

Jack had already shut down the computer system and had to reboot it. Waiting for it to come back online was torture.

"Have you called Grayson?" Brendan asked.

"About the fire, but not this. He's on his way down," Jack muttered. "Okay, we're up and running. Give me a couple of seconds…"

His voice trailed off as he began accessing the cameras and, one by one the individual screens went live.

"Now we need to go back on the timeline and see what we have," Jack muttered.

"You won't need to go back more than fifteen minutes because that's about how long it's been since I talked to her," Brendan said.

"Got it," Jack said, and a few moments later, he began to point at the screens. "Okay, everything looks normal here. Customers are still in their seats. Oh look, this must be where the news begins to spread because everyone begins answering phones and sending texts."

Brendan was focused on the camera aimed at the bar and the stage behind it. The dancers were still performing when he caught a glimpse of Julie's head moving back and forth among the customers. She was so small he could barely see her, but she was there, so he began watching for the footage for a glimpse of the man in question.

"There, that's the guy," Brendan said, pointing at the broad back and bald head.

"Can't see his face from this angle," Jack said and began looking at the other cameras.

"There goes Julie!" Marco said, pointing to a different screen showing Julie suddenly running out from behind the bar.

Brendan saw the bald-headed man throw money on the counter and take off after her.

"There! Look! The son-of-a-bitch is following her!"

They saw her move out of view, then picked her up on a different camera as she went into Jack's office, then again as she and Jack went down the back hall. Another camera picked her up she came running back into the bar.

When they saw her take out her phone, Brendan pointed.

"That's when I called her. She told us Jack said to clear the bar, and that's the last time I talked to her.

"Oh! Oh, son of a- bitch!" Jack moaned as he pointed at a different screen. They were witnessing her abduction.

There was a momentary look of shock on Julie's face before the man hit her. He caught her before she fell, threw her over his shoulder, and went out the back door while everyone else was running for the front.

Brendan was in shock. The act was so brazen he could hardly believe it was real.

"I'm calling the police. Pull up the shots on the back exit," he said, and then the 911 dispatcher answered and he began giving her the information while trying not to panic. Time was still on their side, but this was a nightmare. He couldn't believe they'd let this happen.

Jack scanned the footage, groaning again as the camera caught the abductor walking out with Julie slung over his shoulder like it was of no concern.

Jack pointed. "There he goes... down the back alley."

Brendan pocketed his phone.

"The cops are on the way." He pointed at a frontal shot of the man's face frozen on another screen. "He's been coming in here for over a month, leaves about fifteen minutes before we close, and I've tried more than once to see where he goes, but he always disappears in the crowds. I'm going out the back door to see if anyone's in the alley. Maybe they saw something."

All of a sudden, they heard footsteps coming down the hall, and before Brendan could leave, Grayson March strode into the office. It was obvious by his mode of dress that he'd been at some formal affair.

"What's the plan? Have you talked to anyone at the fire department? Do we know if the fire has jumped buildings yet?"

When no one answered, he realized something else was happening. "What? Talk, damnit! I'm not a mind reader!"

"Juliette was kidnapped," Jack said.

Grayson gasped, reached for the edge of the desk to steady himself and then all of a sudden turned on Brendan.

"God damn you!" he said softly.

Brendan blinked. The first thing he thought was *what the hell?* And then it hit him. Anson. *He thinks Anson did it and her association with me is to blame.* He felt the accusation as surely as if the words had been spoken.

"You don't understand," Brendan began,

Grayson pointed a finger in Brendan's face.

"Don't fucking talk to me," he whispered, grabbed his cell phone and make a quick call.

Jack frowned. "What the hell's wrong with you, Grayson? Bren didn't—"

But Grayson held up a hand for silence, waiting for his call to be answered.

"This is Parker."

"It's me. Where the fuck is Anson Poe?"

Parker was still standing across the street from the restaurant. "He's still inside Adelaine's."

"I need his whereabouts verified. Go into Adelaine's and get eyes on him now! Call me back as soon as you know."

Brendan was stunned. He had feared all along

something would happen that would turn Grayson March against their relationship, but nothing like this. And he was also pissed. Julie was missing, and the window of opportunity to stop this before it was too late was very brief. As far as he was concerned, they were wasting valuable time. He pointed at Marco.

"Go out front to wait for the police. I'm checking the alley."

Grayson grabbed him by the arm. "You go nowhere until I—"

It was all Brendan could do not to hit him. Once again, he had been judged and found guilty because of his father's name.

"Take your hand off of me," he said softly. "We already know who took Julie. It's on the fucking security camera," he said and ran out of the office.

Shock swept across Grayson's face, but before he could answer, his phone rang.

"What?"

Parker spoke quickly, sensing the urgency without understanding the need.

"Roberts said the back was clear. No one's been in or out but kitchen help dumping garbage. Poe is inside at his table eating his meal."

"Someone kidnapped Juliette. Don't lose him," Grayson said and disconnected.

Jack was staring at him as if he'd lost his mind.

"What the hell did you just do? Brendan didn't deserve any of that."

Grayson wouldn't admit he'd been wrong. He was in too much of a panic about what had happened. "Show me the security footage," he said shortly and watched all the way through from the moment of panic in the bar, to the actual attack. When he saw the man knock his daughter out and carry her out of the bar in front of everyone, he was so frantic he was shouting.

"Why the hell didn't someone stop him?"

"Because the place was in obvious panic as you can see, and I had the men evacuating the bar," Jack yelled back. "You want to blame me for this now, too? Damn it, Grayson. I thought you were better than this. You owe Brendan Poe an apology."

"You still don't know that!" Grayson roared, and then began to pace. "We need a name. He could be someone Anson Poe hired. If this man has been in here so much, wouldn't one of the bartenders know who he is?"

"I don't know. I'll call them."

His first call was to Wynn, who knew nothing.

He made the second call to Toni, praying she would know more. She picked up on the third ring.

"Hello?"

"Toni, it's Jack."

"Please tell me you found Julie."

"No. The bald-headed guy who always sat at the end of the bar kidnapped her. We caught it on camera. Do you know his name?"

"Oh my God!" Toni cried. "No, no, I don't. He didn't talk. He paid cash. He ordered the same thing every time he came in. I don't think Julie even knew his name. She just called him the troll."

Jack's heart sank. "Okay, but if you think of anything, call me."

"I will."

He could hear her crying as he disconnected.

"Well?" Grayson asked.

Jack shook his head. "She didn't know anything but that Julie called him the troll."

"God Almighty," Grayson said. He felt like throwing up

as he shoved shaky hands through his hair. "Where the hell are the police? Did anyone call the police?"

"Brendan did and sent Marco outside to wait for them."

Grayson staggered toward a chair.

"Look," Jack said. "I know this is a shock, and we're all scared out of our minds here, but blaming a good man because his father is an ass is beneath you."

At that point, Deuce came running.

"Boss, the fire has jumped a building. Now there's only two between us and the fire."

Jack spun, grabbed a box out of storage and began filling it with computer discs, then pulled the CDs from the security cameras and began boxing them up, too.

"What are you doing?" Grayson yelled. "The police need to see this, as soon as possible."

"Tell me something, Grayson. If it burns up before they get a chance to see it, how the hell is that going to help Julie?"

Grayson nodded. "You're right. I'm sorry. I can't think. I can't think. My baby! Oh my God, my baby! This is a nightmare and Lana doesn't even know it's happened. How do I tell my wife her daughter's been kidnapped? Where the hell are the police?"

****

Brendan's mind was racing as he went out the back door to where Deuce was standing watch. Earlier in the evening, the promise of a thunderstorm had been evident by the building clouds and distant flashes of lightning. But now, all he could see was smoke.

"Deuce, did you see anyone in the alley? Anybody dumpster diving or taking a shortcut?"

"No, man, I'm sorry."

Brendan took off through the alley, heading for the

street ahead. It had been a little over thirty minutes now since she disappeared and he was so scared he couldn't think. Where the hell had they gone?

The acrid scent of smoke added to the misery of sweltering heat, and coupled with the constant blast of sirens, it was more than unnerving. Brendan ran, marking off the length of the alley by the number of dumpsters and the piles of overflowing trash he passed. About halfway down, a black cat ran out in front of him and disappeared through a hole in the fence, but the bad luck omen had come too late. Disaster had already struck.

When he ran out into the street, he paused to scan the area. Tourists were scattering like quail while the local vendors were pulling in their street wares and locking up their stores. They couldn't protect their property from going up in smoke, but they didn't want to be with it if it happened.

Then he saw movement in a window of a store across the street and ran toward The Candy Basket just in time to catch the owner coming out.

"Michelle!"

The middle-aged redhead turned and then frowned. "Brendan! You should be getting out of the Quarter."

"I can't. Juliette March has been kidnapped."

"Oh dear lord!" she cried and then looked down the street as a half-dozen police cars went flying past. "Is that for her?"

"Yes. I need to ask you something. By any chance did you notice a bald, heavy-set, middle-aged guy come out of the alley carrying something? He would have been wearing jeans and a navy, short-sleeved knit shirt."

"No! Oh lord! I'm so sorry. Oh, wait! I saw Count LeGrande walking the beat out here earlier. If you can find him, he might have seen something."

Brendan grabbed her arm. "Thank you! Thank you, Michelle."

He scanned both sides of the block then took off up the street at a jog, keeping an eye out for the Count as he went.

Everyone in the French Quarter knew the Count. He hung out on the street corners every night in a dusty black frock coat, an old, black top hat, and white spats on his shoes, claiming ancestors who'd been connected to French royalty and posing for pictures with tourists.

Brendan was about to cross an intersection when he saw a street musician named Eugene on the other corner, packing up his guitar. He cut across the street, dodging another cop car heading toward the fire.

"Hey, Eugene!"

The elderly black man looked up. He'd been trying to get his guitar in the case, but his hands were trembling so much he couldn't fasten the clips.

"Let me help you," Brendan said and fastened it for him.

"Thank you, Bren! You're a good boy! Not like your daddy, for sure."

"Yeah, thanks, Eugene. Listen. I need help. Someone kidnapped Juliette March," he said and repeated the description.

Eugene's eyes were already watering from the gathering smoke, but they filled anew when he heard the news.

"I'm sorry to hear this. Her daddy is like yours, but on the other side of the law. Both of them got their own brand of enemies. As for seeing that man you're talking about, I sure didn't, although I wish I had. She is a fine little lady."

"Yes, she is. By any chance have you seen the Count?"

"Yes, I saw him about ten minutes ago heading to the

riverfront. He's got himself a little place down there somewhere."

"Thanks, Eugene. I owe you," Brendan said and began to backtrack. Now all he could do was pray he found him, and that the old man had seen something—anything that would help them identify who had taken her.

He paused at another intersection as a pair of mounted police rode past on horseback, and as he did, he suddenly remembered Claudette's warning about his father planning revenge. What if Grayson's suspicions had been justified? What if Anson had orchestrated this? His gut knotted. If this turned out to be true, he would never be able to live with himself.

****

Adelaine's restaurant was far enough away from the fire that management had not ordered an evacuation, although a good number of their patrons left once the news began to spread. But Anson was not one of them. Instead, he sat at his table, waiting for the food he ordered while savoring a wine his father had always favored.

He hadn't known the first fire would be set tonight, but since it was happening while he was in town, he needed an airtight alibi. They would, most likely, rule the fire as arson, and after the way he and Lisette had parted company, she might name him as a suspect. He needed to make sure the wait staff here would vouch for his presence.

He was buttering a piece of bread and about to take a bite when he caught sight of one of March's men in the doorway and stifled a smile. And there was his second witness to an alibi.

Damn, but he loved it when a plan came together.

****

Lisette stood on the far side of the parking lot in shock, watching her world burning down. Everything inside the building had been incinerated. Not only was her means of making a living gone, but so was her home. The only positive aspect was that everyone had gotten out alive, including her upstairs clients.

When the old brick walls began to collapse inward, she moaned right along with the crowd behind her, but when she heard another loud, collective shriek, she peered through the smoke and saw the reason.

The fire had just jumped the alley.

Another building was on fire.

Mon Dieu! What else was going to burn?

"Lisette! Lisette Branscum!"

She recognized a reporter from one of the newspapers heading toward her.

And so it begins.

****

Chub Walton was so elated by the unexpected turn of events that he kept giggling, although he was concerned for the little blonde slumped over in the seat beside him, surprised she was still unconscious. He hadn't hit her any harder than he had his other victims, but she was undoubtedly the smallest one physically, which might be the reason.

He had done other women unconscious before, but they didn't pass out until after the third or fourth time he'd had them. He hadn't intended to break this one's neck, but his mother had always said he didn't know his own strength. It was going to be disappointing if the woman never woke up.

He began hearing sirens, and caught a glimpse of flashing lights in his rearview mirror as he braked for a red light. His heart beat a little faster, but he relaxed when they sped on through the intersection. Now all he had to do was get out of the city. As soon as the light turned green, he hit the gas.

****

Brendan was choking on smoke and gasping for breath by the time he reached the riverfront. He paused briefly, looking up and down the long, cobbled street for a tall, dusty man in a top hat, but had no such luck.

His eyes were burning from both the heat and smoke, and he kept blinking them in an effort to clear his vision. It appeared things were getting worse.

The smoke was beginning to gather down on the river's edge, held close to the ground by the damp night air. Even more disturbing, there were so many people down here now, that it would have been impossible to pick LeGrande out of the crowd.

Julie had now been missing almost forty-five minutes. He was not only scared for her welfare, but still reeling from the verbal attack from his boss. He was going to be late getting home and needed to let Claudette know.

"God help me," he whispered and called home.

Claudette answered. "Hello?"

"Auntie, it's me, Brendan. Something terrible has happened and I can't come home."

He heard her gasp. "The fire! Is it the fire? It's all over the news. Have you been burned?"

"No, no, but during the confusion of evacuating the bar, Juliette was kidnapped by a man who's been stalking her. We have the abduction on the security cameras, but no idea of who he is. I'm down on the riverfront looking for the Count. It's possible he could have seen something that would help us. I'm trying to find him now, but everything's in such a mess. People are leaving in droves because of the fire. It's already spread to a second building."

"I can help! I know where LeGrande lives. Look for a very small antique shop between a restaurant and a coffee bar. It's called Time after Time. There will be a stairway in the alley behind those buildings. It leads to a small apartment above the antique shop. That is where he lives."

Brendan choked on a sob. "God bless you, Auntie. This is the first good news I've had all night. Can you stay with Mama and Linny? I don't know when I'll get back."

"Of course I can. We are family. Go find your girl."

She disconnected, leaving Brendan shaking. She might not be his girl much longer if her father had anything to say about it, but the only thing on his mind was finding her. He took off down the street at a lope.

****

Police were all over The Black Garter, but not for long. The fire had taken the second building down far faster than it had burned through the first and jumped to the third rooftop, bringing it even closer to the bar. The entire area was being evacuated.

Jack had wasted no time turning over the security footage to the detectives and was now on his way down to police headquarters to give his statement.

Grayson March was still fixated on Brendan, viewing his absence from the scene as suspicious, and had commented as much to the police after filling them in on the altercation he'd had with Anson Poe. Now he was on his way to the police station as well.

When the bouncers headed up the street to where their

vehicles were parked, Marco realized both Julie's car and Brendan's SUV were still on the street, which meant Brendan was still on foot somewhere in the Quarter.

Sparks were flying upward, forced by the chimney-like force of the fire's inferno. They were in danger of getting their clothes on fire and needed to get out, but Marco's thoughts were of his friend.

"Hold up, Deuce," he said, and made a quick call to Brendan.

Brendan answered on the first ring. "Marco! Any news?"

"No. Where are you, man? We're all heading to the P.D. to give our statements. The bar is going to burn if they don't get this fire stopped. It's already moved to the third building just across the alley from us."

"Jesus," Brendan said. "Look, I'm down at the riverfront. Michelle from The Candy Basket said that Count LeGrande was out on the street about the same time as the abduction, and might have seen something. I'm trying to track him down."

A loud explosion went off behind them, causing Marco and Deuce to duck.

"What was that?" Brendan asked.

"Transformer blew, I think," Marco said. "Julie's car is going to burn, and you're going to lose your truck, too, if I don't move it. Do you still keep that spare key under the left wheel well?"

"Yes."

"Okay. Here's the deal. Since Deuce rode to work with me, he can take my car on to the P.D. and I'll drive yours. At least we can keep one of them from burning."

"Thanks, man, I owe you big time. Tell Jack I'll get to the police station as fast as I can, but if this area goes up in flames, everyone down here will be displaced. God only knows where they might go after that and I don't want to lose this lead."

"You got it. We're out of here. The heat and smoke is bad. You be careful, and don't get yourself caught with no way out."

"I'm always careful," Brendan muttered. "I gotta go."

The call ended abruptly.

Marco found the extra key to Brendan's truck, and followed Deuce out of the parking lot. They were heading toward the police station on Royal Street just as another fire truck pulled up on the premises.

Hell had descended upon the Quarter.

****

An hour later, Marco and Deuce were still waiting at the police department, as were Jack and Grayson. Wynn and Tony were going through mug shots in an effort to identify the perp and everyone was impatiently waiting for news.

When the door suddenly opened and a detective walked into the room, Grayson stood up.

"Mr. March, I'm Detective Carson. I'll be handling your daughter's case."

"Is there news?" Grayson asked.

"Nothing new. I just need to clarify some statements you made to the officers who were first on the scene."

"Ask away."

The detective opened his notebook. "I've seen the security footage, so we know Anson Poe did not physically kidnap your daughter, but am I to understand you are accusing him of orchestrating it?"

Grayson lifted his chin. "What I said was, that it's possible he was behind it because of a recent altercation we had."

Carson nodded. "And what about your accusation regarding Brendan Poe, Anson Poe's youngest son? Are you stating that he could have had knowledge of this beforehand?"

Jack stood up, unable to listen to this any longer. "Hell no, he's not behind this, and if Grayson wasn't so emotionally wrought, he would not insinuate such crap."

Carson frowned at the interruption. "And you are?"

"Jack Michaels, manager at The Black Garter. Brendan Poe has worked for me for the past five years and is a fine, upstanding young man. He is not responsible for his father's sins, and is in love with Juliette. He would do nothing to harm her."

"Does she return the feelings?"

Jack frowned. "Answer him, Grayson. You're the one who pointed an angry finger at an innocent man. Now it's time to do the right thing and acknowledge it was your prejudice talking and not the facts."

When Grayson and Jack did nothing but glare at each other, the detective spoke up. "Somebody start talking," Carson said.

Grayson was mad at Jack, but when it came down to it, he couldn't bring himself to lie. "Yes, Brendan and Juliette have a romantic relationship. It's true I'm not happy about it, but I have no reason to assume he has anything to do with my daughter's abduction."

"Where is Brendan Poe?" Carson asked. "Did he come down with the rest of you?"

Grayson's voice rose in anger all over again. "No, and that's why I was suspicious when—"

At that point, Marco and Deuce began interrupting, and then Marco spoke up.

"We know where Brendan is. He was running down a

lead at the riverfront when I called him. He said someone told him that Count LeGrande was in the vicinity when the kidnapping took place, and he might have seen something. He was afraid the fire would scatter all the locals and if they became displaced, he might lose the chance to talk to him."

Jack glared at Grayson. "I told you he wouldn't run away."

Grayson glared back.

Marco kept talking. "I drove his truck down here for safe keeping. He said to tell Jack he'd meet you all here after he found LeGrande."

"Does anyone know the whereabouts of Anson Poe? Would he be with his son?" Carson asked.

"Brendan hates his father," Deuce said.

"They have no relationship," Jack added.

"I know where Anson Poe is," Grayson muttered. "I've had my men on him ever since he threatened my family. He's at Adelaine's eating dinner. They've been on him all night."

"So your own men have just given the man you accused an air-tight alibi," Carson said.

Grayson frowned. "That doesn't mean he didn't hire it out."

"Do you have any information that would substantiate this accusation?"

"No, but—"

Carson held up his hand. "I understand your feelings, but we operate on facts, and right now we have nothing to implicate Poe. With your business holdings, you must have other enemies. Is there anyone you can think of? Someone you have recently fired or anything like that?"

"No!" Grayson snapped. "I don't personally run my

business interests. I have managers for that. I'm sure dozens of people are hired and fired every day somewhere."

"Then I suggest you start checking with your managers and see if anyone has recently uttered any threats against you or your company."

"Hells bells," he mumbled, pulled out his phone, and moved to the far end of the room to make the calls.

Chapter Seven

The fire sweeping through the French Quarter was a nightmare to those who lived on the streets. They were spilling out of alleys and hidey-holes, running down to the riverfront like rats from a burning ship. It made movement even more difficult for Brendan as he pushed through them, desperate to find the location Claudette had given him.

When he finally located the antique shop and saw an apartment above it, he began looking for an alley to get to the stairs, and was once again deterred. The buildings were connected, one to the other, like little shops in an open-air mall. He was still moving when someone in the crowd cried out, "The Black Garter is on fire."

The fire was getting closer and he was running out of time.

He began to run, dodging and pushing through the crowd until he finally found an open alley and ducked through it. He came out on the backside of the buildings and then began running back the way he'd come, looking for the stairs. When he finally saw them, the gathering smoke shrouded them. He was halfway up them when he heard a door open above him, and then the sound of someone coughing.

He looked up just as LeGrande was coming down. Brendan caught a look of surprise, then fear on the old man's face and quickly called out.

"Count LeGrande! It's me, Brendan Poe!"

LeGrande came down, coughing and choking as they quickly descended. "What do you want, boy?"

"I need to speak with you, but we need to get out of this smoke first."

The old man was staggering. "My home is going to burn. I'm not ready to die."

A loud rumble of thunder rolled above the rooftops. From the sound, it appeared that the predicted storm front had finally arrived.

"Praise the Lord," the Count said, then let himself be led back out of the alley and closer to the river.

As soon as they reached an area where it was easier to breathe, Brendan found a place for the old man to sit, then waited for him to catch his breath.

The Count's chest was heaving, which only added to the stoop of his bony shoulders. He'd never noticed how white LeGrande's hair and beard were up close, almost as white as his paper-thin skin. He looked much smaller without the frock coat and top hat.

As they sat, a wind began to rise, an ill wind for the firemen trying to put out the fires.

"Are you okay, sir?" Brendan asked.

He nodded. "Now what is it you wanted to ask?"

"Juliette March was kidnapped tonight."

The expression of horror on LeGrande's face was real. "Oh no! I hadn't heard. I'm shocked, but how does that pertain to me?"

"Michelle at The Candy Basket said you were still on the streets when it happened. I was hoping you might've seen something. We know the abductor took her out of the back of the bar and up the alley toward the main drag."

"I don't think I saw anything like that, but then the crowd was in constant motion at that time. Everyone was already concerned about trying to get away from the smoke and fire."

Brendan's heart sank, but he kept on talking, hoping something would ring a bell.

"The abductor is bald, heavy-set, and middle-aged with long arms and short legs. He was wearing jeans and a navy blue knit shirt. Julie was wearing black slacks and a white shirt like all the bartenders. He would have been carrying her either over his shoulder or in his arms, because he'd knocked her out."

LeGrande gasped, and then suddenly leaned forward. "Is he a regular customer at the bar?"

Brendan's heart skipped a beat. "Yes, every night for the past month or so. Why?"

"I didn't see him tonight, but I think I know the man you mean. He leaves just before closing every night and then stands in the shadows of a nearby alley, watching as employees leave the bar. I always thought that was strange."

Brendan grabbed Count's arm. "Yes, yes! That's the man. Do you know his name?"

"No, but I know something about him."

"What? Tell me, quick! Her life depends on it."

"I know that he drives a late-model Chevrolet Tahoe, either black or dark blue."

"That's great, but are you sure you've never heard anyone call him by name?"

"I'm sure, but I can help you find him just the same. Do you have a piece of paper and a pen?"

"Why?" Brendan asked.

"Because I know the number of his car tag." Then LeGrande shrugged. "It is a thing I do... memorizing numbers."

Brendan's hands began to tremble as he reached for

his phone. "Give me a second," he said, and pulled up the Notes section.

LeGrande watched. "Amazing things, the phones they have these days."

"Yes, sir, yes they are," Brendan said. "Okay, I'm ready."

The Count rattled off the numbers. "Oh. One other thing about the SUV."

"What's that?" Brendan asked.

"The vehicle is always quite dusty, or when it rains, it's always muddy."

"Meaning he most likely lives somewhere outside of the city," Brendan said.

The Count nodded.

Brendan jumped up and then shook LeGrande's hand. "I've got to call the police with this information. You may have just saved Juliette March's life."

"I'm happy to have been of service," he said.

Another clap of thunder rattled the windows in the nearby buildings, and then it was as if the sound tore a hole in heaven. Rain came down in a sudden sheet, flattening the Count's beard to his neck and their clothes to their bodies.

"Come with me," Brendan said. "You need to get out of the rain."

"No. There's no need to seek other shelter now. Now that it appears my home won't burn, I'll go back. Go rescue your lady love and give her my regards."

Brendan threw his arms around the old man's shoulders, thumping him soundly on the back.

"Thank you, sir! Thank you! I'll be in touch."

He took off running, anxious to get out of the rain to make the call, leaving the old man on his own. LeGrande made no attempt to run as he started back to his apartment. He was already as wet as he could possibly be.

****

Toni and Wynn were still looking at mug shots in another area of the P.D. when the thunderstorm hit.

Grayson March's wife, Lana, had arrived only a few minutes earlier. As soon as he ran to comfort her, she quickly rebuffed him. It was obvious from the expression on her face and the sharp words they were trading, she was not only distraught about her daughter's disappearance, but blaming her husband because he'd let Juliette work in such an unseemly place.

When Jack's phone began to ring and he saw caller ID, his gut knotted.

"Brendan! Are you all right?"

"Yes. I have a lead. I need to talk to someone in charge."

"Just a moment," Jack said, then yelled out at the detective who was out in the hall talking to an officer.

"Detective Carson! Brendan Poe is on the phone. He needs to talk to you!"

Grayson was already on his feet when Carson entered the room and took the phone out of Jack's hand.

"This is Detective Carson."

"Detective, this is Brendan Poe. I have a tag number. It belongs to the car the kidnapper drives. If you run the tag, you should have a name and address, and if God is good, the bastard will have taken Julie to his home instead of somewhere else, and this nightmare might soon be over."

Carson grabbed the notebook out of his pocket. "Go ahead and give it to me," he said.

Brendan repeated the number, and then added, "The

witness said the car was a late-model Chevy Tahoe, black or dark blue, and that it was nearly always dusty or muddy, which means he probably has a place outside of the city."

"Good job, Poe. If this pans out, I know some people who are going to be very grateful to you."

He handed the phone back to Jack and left the room running.

"What is it? What's happening?" Grayson shouted, and tried to grab the phone, but Jack pushed his hand away.

"Brendan? You still there?"

"Yes, I'm here. I'm coming to the police station as soon as I can catch a ride, but between the fire and the thunderstorm, it will take a while. Cabs are few and far between."

"Where are you, son? We'll come get you."

Marco spoke up. "Tell him I'll come get him in his SUV."

Jack gave Marco a thumbs-up to indicate he'd heard.

"Marco said he'll come get you in your SUV. Where are you?"

Brendan was beginning to shiver.

"I'm still down on the riverfront. I think the police and fire department have everything blocked off for at least a dozen blocks in every direction. Tell him I'll be walking North on Canal Street toward Royal, and to watch for me."

"Will do, Bren."

"Hey, Jack. I need to tell you something."

"What's that?"

"The bar is gone. If it hadn't been for the storm moving in and this blessed downpour, it would've burned all the way to the river."

Jack's shoulders slumped.

"Well hell. I was afraid of that."

"Yeah. If March is there, I figured he'd want to know."

"Yes, he's here. Do you want to talk to him about—?"

"I don't have anything to say to him. I'll see you in a few."

The line went dead in Jack's ear. He gave Brendan's directions to Marco, and he and Deuce both left.

Grayson was still standing, impatiently waiting for answers.

"Well! What did he say? Does he know anything?"

"I didn't ask, but I'm gathering from the way Carson ran out of here he had some kind of information to pass on. What he did say, was that the bar was gone."

Lana March had walked up beside her husband while the conversation was in progress, and when she heard the news, her features contorted into a mixture of rage and glee.

"Good! I'm glad it's gone! It was a disgrace that our family was even involved in something so unsavory. God only knows what went on in there."

The moment she said it, she realized she'd just insulted the manager standing five feet away.

Jack dropped his phone in his pocket and walked out of the room.

Grayson gritted his teeth. It was one of those rare times he understood Juliette's resentment toward her mother. There was a muscle jerking at the corner of his eye as he turned on her, his voice low and obviously angry.

"My dear Lana, my great-great-granddaddy made *his* fortune as a rum-runner. Great-granddaddy March added to the fortune by being one of the biggest bookies and gamblers in the state. Granddaddy had his day making and selling bootleg liquor. When my daddy took over the operations, he opened The Black Garter. It was the first honest business in the family in three generations, and during the extent of our marriage, you have been living high on the hog from the largest of three generations of unsavory profits. It would behoove you to remember that the next time you feel the need to parade your proper, high-stepping self about in front of those you refer to as 'the hired help.'"

He watched the color come and go from his wife's face and knew he'd pay for it later, but right now, he didn't give a good damn. He walked out of the room without looking back. He needed to find Jack and apologize.

****

LaDelle woke abruptly when the first clap of thunder rattled the windows in her bedroom. Linny was asleep on a pallet in the floor by her mother's bed, but woke up as well.

"Mama?"

Delle pushed herself into a sitting position and then patted the bed beside her. "It's just a thunderstorm, sugar. Come lie in bed with me. It'll be all right."

Linny stood up clutching Rabbit, but hesitated. "What if I hurt your feet?"

"You can be on top of the covers, and I'll be under. It'll be okay. Come here. I have need of a hug."

She didn't have to ask twice. Linny crawled up onto the bed beside her mother and snuggled under her arm.

For a few moments, they were silent. Just when Delle thought Linny was falling back asleep, lulled by the sound of rain against the windows, her daughter's small voice broke the silence.

"What's gonna happen to us, Mama?"

Delle's heart hurt for the anxiety she heard in her baby's voice. "What do you mean, honey?"

"Are we going back home to Wisteria Hill?"

Delle sighed. "I think we have to, don't you?"

Linny nodded.

"Will you be sad to leave Brendan?"

"Yes, but I miss the bayou. Sir Snapper and all my royal subjects must be wondering where I've gone."

LaDelle pulled her closer. "I never knew when I gave birth to you that I was birthing a queen."

"I guess life is like that sometimes, right, Mama?"

Delle chuckled at the innocence of the remark. Right now, her daughter firmly believed she could become a queen just by naming herself as one.

"Yes, My Queen, life can be a constant surprise."

Linny snuggled closer against her mother and pulled Rabbit beneath her chin.

Within a few minutes, Delle heard the steady sound of her daughter's breathing and knew she'd fallen asleep.

In the other room, a phone began to ring. That meant Brendan was calling. She looked anxiously toward the door, knowing if it were an emergency, Claudette would tell her. When she heard Claudette coming down the hall moments later, her heart sank. She was facing the door when it opened.

"What's wrong?" she whispered.

Claudette came to the other side of the bed and eased down so that she was close to her sister's ear.

"The Quarter is on fire and Juliette has been kidnapped. They are all out looking for her, and Brendan said he will not be coming home just yet. He is running down a lead someone gave him."

LaDelle covered her mouth to smother her gasp of

surprise. She glanced down at her daughter, then back at her sister.

"Do you think Anson had anything to do with her disappearance?"

Claudette shrugged. "Mama Lou said he would seek revenge. She did not say how."

Delle shook her head and then covered her face.

Claudette saw tears coming down between the fingers and pulled her hand away from her face. "Do not hide your tears, sister. It is not your shame."

"It's all my shame. I married him, even when Mama said no and when you said no. I wouldn't hear anything I didn't want to hear."

Claudette smoothed the hair away from Delle's forehead. "That is because you were listening with your heart. It is not your fault you fell in love with a bad man."

"But it's my fault I stayed."

Claudette shrugged. "Life takes us down our path. All we can do is follow to see where it leads."

"Thank you for coming to my aide," Delle said. "I don't know what we'd do without you."

"We are family, Delle. I would have it no other way. Are you in pain?"

Delle nodded.

"I will bring your medicine."

"Are you staying here with us until Brendan returns?"

"Yes," Claudette said and then quickly left the room.

LaDelle glanced toward the windows. Even though the curtains were closed, she could see flashes of lightning and hear the rain pounding against the glass. They were safely sheltered here, in Brendan's home, but they would never really be safe as long as her husband was alive.

****

Chub Walton was out of New Orleans and headed home when the first clap of thunder ripped across the sky, followed by a bright shaft of lightning off to the West. He'd gotten out of the city just in time.

He gave his too-silent passenger a nervous glance. Either the bitch was still unconscious or playing him and waiting for a chance to escape. He should have duct taped her hands and feet, but he'd been in such a hurry to get away he hadn't taken the time. He thought about pulling over and taking the precaution, but he wanted to be inside before the storm hit, so he kept driving. It didn't matter if she did wake up. She was so small he could restrain her easily with one hand behind his back.

He wondered about the fire and how much of the French Quarter would go up in flames before they put it out. He didn't have a personal connection one way or the other with the city, and once he did the little blonde, he was considering moving on. He'd been here in New Orleans for almost a year—through two other abductions. It felt like it was stretching his luck if he stayed after this. He liked being around the water and had always wanted to see Galveston. Maybe Texas would be next on his list.

Even though he thought he'd gotten away clean, he kept glancing up in his rearview mirror for flashing lights. Thunder rumbled again, and the closer he got to home, the faster he drove. He was coming around a curve when he caught movement from the corner of his eye. All of a sudden, there was a cow standing in the middle of the road, staring blindly at his oncoming headlights.

He stomped the brakes and swerved, which sent the SUV into a skid. It was as if everything began to happen in slow motion. He could hear the sound of squalling tires and smelled the acrid scent of burning rubber. He was moving past the cow now, coming so close he could see the wild look in her eyes. If the window had been down, he could have reached out and touched her black nose. When he finally came to a stop, his back wheels were in the ditch and the cow was nowhere in sight. The only sign he had that she'd ever been there was a fresh pile of steaming cow manure.

"Scared the shit out of me, too," he muttered, then realized the girl was no longer in the seat beside him.

He saw her crumpled up in the floorboard, still unconscious. He grabbed her by the back of her collar, hauled her up onto the seat to feel for a pulse, and when he felt the steady thump beneath his fingers, he relaxed. The party wasn't over yet.

He put the SUV in gear, eased out of the ditch and back onto the blacktop, and headed for home, this time paying more attention to where he was going. By the time he took the turn-off onto the dirt road, he was breathing easy.

He had just pulled up into the yard when the storm front hit. The rain was so loud and sudden it made him jump. The keys fell from his hand into the floorboard and he wasted another minute fumbling around until he found them. It was raining so hard he couldn't see the front porch, but he knew it was there. He opened the door and jumped out. He grabbed the girl beneath her arms and dragged her out on her back, then threw her over his shoulder and made a run for the house. It was only a few steps to the porch, but it didn't matter. They were already soaked to the skin. His hands trembled from anticipation as he unlocked the door and went in. He locked it behind him and turned on the lights.

****

The rain woke her. Julie thought she had fallen in the

river because there was water on her face and up her nose. Just when she was about to choke, the water went from her face to the back of her head. She didn't know she was hanging upside down until the a sudden burst of light. She saw a man's butt and legs, smelled cold coffee, burned toast, and the stench of wet clothes on an unwashed body. That's when she remembered the fist coming at her and the glimpse of the man behind it.

Her first instinct was fight and the second was flight. She screamed, grabbed the back of his belt with a sudden yank, and pulled herself up and over his shoulders, going headfirst toward the floor.

Chub was so startled by the sound and the unexpected motion that it took him a few seconds to realize she was no longer in his grasp. By the time he turned around, she was on her feet and staggering.

"Well, well, the little princess finally woke up," he said and lurched toward her.

Julie dodged his hand, slapping it sideways with a karate chop at his arm, followed by one at his throat, which sent him reeling, and then he made a run for the door.

She heard a roar of rage, and then his hand was in her hair, pulling her backward.

"Nooooo!" she screamed, still kicking and fighting until he grabbed her by the throat and shut off her air.

He kept slapping her and shaking her while telling her in no uncertain terms what he was going to do to her, and she was getting light-headed. Any moment she was going to pass out and then she would be at his mercy.

God, please take me now. I don't want to be alive when this happens, and then everything went black.

****

Brendan followed Marco and Deuce into the station, dripping water as he went. He was numb, too afraid to let himself think what Julie might be enduring. He walked into the waiting area and noticed Grayson and his wife, Lana, were sitting apart from the others. Brendan gave them a cursory glance, trying to judge the temperature of the room before going farther, unaware he'd just sent Lana March into emotional rewind.

When Lana saw him walk in, soaking wet with clothes stuck to him like a second skin, her reaction was visceral. She knew who it had to be. All of a sudden, she was in high school again, behind the bus barn at a high school football game having crazy-mad sex with Anson Poe while the crowd was going wild for her boyfriend, Grayson's, athletic prowess.

Oh, fuck. That has to be Brendan Poe. No wonder Juliette is attracted to him. He's even more beautiful than his father ever was.

She was so rattled she grabbed a tissue and covered her face, as if weeping for her daughter's plight.

Brendan's gaze went from her to the other bartenders, but when he realized Toni was crying, his legs nearly went out from under him. What did they know that he didn't?

"Jack? Is there news?"

Jack looked up, then jumped to his feet and ran to him, thumping him heartily on the back.

"Good work, son. Good work! They have a name and address, and are on their way to the location as we speak."

Brendan staggered, then backed into the hall and turned away. He didn't want them to see him cry.

Jack followed, standing beside Brendan as he wept, unaware Grayson had walked out into the hall behind them.

"I knew the man was bad news," Brendan said. "I should've been there."

"You were doing what I sent you to do, and then did what no one else thought to do. You chased after them. It was timing, Bren, timing."

Grayson walked up behind the pair, curious to what they were saying. "What did you see? Did you find a witness?"

Grayson March was the last person Brendan wanted to talk to, and yet he turned to face him, tears mingling with the water running out of his hair onto face.

"I found friends on the street and started asking questions. Michelle from The Candy Basket said Count LeGrande was out during that time. I went looking for him and found an old blues man who plays guitar on the corner. He told me he saw LeGrande going toward the riverfront right after we shut down the bar. My aunt Claudette, who's taking care of my mother and sister, knew where he lived. I found LeGrande because of all of them."

Grayson was impressed in spite of himself.

"So LeGrande saw it happen?"

"No. It wasn't that easy, but I kept pushing, talking to him about everything he might have seen, and when I described the abductor, that's when it clicked. LeGrande didn't know his name, but said he saw a man fitting that description go into the bar every night, and come out right before closing. He said the man always stood in a nearby alley and watched us leaving the bar. He knew what he drove and he knew the tag number. That's what I gave the cops."

The knot of guilt in Grayson's gut was getting tighter. He had to apologize.

"Look, Brendan, I owe you an apology. What I said before... it was just in the heat of the moment. You understand."

Brendan's expression was emotionless.

Grayson kept talking. "I know the bar is gone, but I'll build it back and your job will be—"

Brendan took a step back, but not in fear. It was a subconscious move to put more distance between them.

"You keep your fucking job and I'll save you the trouble of firing me, because I quit. You said you spoke in the heat of anger, but it was your truth. I cannot make the fact of my birth go away. You've made it painfully clear you don't want me anywhere near your gold-plated world. Point taken. And in the spirit of fair play, you leave me and mine the hell alone, too."

He walked back into the room, leaving Grayson and Jack in the hall.

Jack's shoulders slumped. "I don't feel so good about you, myself. All this time I had it in my head that you were my friend, but it's been brought to my attention tonight that it's not so. I think it's time I walked away from the job, too. My heart's not in it anymore."

Jack followed Brendan back into the room, leaving March to stew on his guilt alone, and the worst of it was March still didn't know if he was losing Julie, too.

Chapter Eight

Julie came to, tied spread-eagle and naked on a bed. The troll was standing at the foot of it watching her while slapping the side of his leg with a cat-o'-nine-tails.

Whap. Whap. Whap.

There were beads of sweat on his upper lip, and a flush of sexual anticipation on his face as kept up the rhythm.

Whap. Whap. Whap.

"So, you're finally awake."

Her stomach lurched, but it wasn't from being naked in front of a dangerous pervert or that he was obviously getting ready to use that whip on her. The worst part of it was that she was still alive.

Whap. Whap. Whap.

She thought about begging or offering him any amount of money if he'd just let her go. But she didn't. It took every ounce of courage she had to stay silent, watching him grin as he circled the bed, his black eyes narrowing as he moved closer, wanting her to get the full of effect of the slap of leather against denim.

Whap. Whap. Whap.

In spite of her determination to remain stoic, with the first sweep of the whip toward her face, she whimpered like a dog with a butt full of buckshot.

As soon as he saw the fear on her face, he began hitting himself harder.

WHAP. WHAP. WHAP.

Chub frowned. He liked it better when they screamed. Maybe he needed to give her something to cry about, enough to make it hurt, but not enough to break the skin. He raised the cat-o'-nine-tails over his head and brought it down across her inner thigh.

Her scream was as sharp as the radiating pain in her body, and then it faded to a guttural moan. A faint streak of blood was rising just beneath her skin. She heard him giggle as he did an antsy two-step then slapped himself a little more.

Whap. Whap. Whap.

The smell of his sweat, mingling with the stale air in the house, was as sickening to her as the stench of her own fear. The coppery taste of fresh blood was in her mouth as she realized she'd bitten her tongue. His face was a blur now, but she knew where he was from the repetitive slap of the whip against his thigh. Never in a million years had she imagined this was how she would die.

"Not so tough now, are you, bitch?"

WHAP. WHAP. WHAP.

She blinked past the tears until she could see him again. He was rocking back and forth on the balls of his feet, slapping the cat-o'-nine-tails harder and harder against his leg, breathing deeper and heavier, moaning now between blows.

His excitement was building. It was only a matter of time before he began raping her and he wouldn't be gentle. It would hurt her far worse than the whip. When he began trading lashes from the whip—one for him, one for her— she lost her mind, screaming for mercy, writhing away from the snaky strips of leather and pulling so hard against the ties that bound her to the bed that her wrists and ankles began to bleed.

She shrieked. "Bastard!"

He hit her. *WHAP.*

And then himself. *WHAP.*

Harsh, choking sobs burned the back of her throat as she cursed him yet again.

"Sick, perverted son-of-a-bitch!"

WHAP.

The next blow of the whip was across her face, which finally sent her into blessed oblivion.

She came to again, choking and gasping for air when he threw water in her face. This time he was naked. She wouldn't look at his erection because she couldn't bring herself to face what would come next.

"Got nothing more to say?" he asked and brought the cat-o'-nine-tails down hard on the mounds of both breasts. Bloody welts rose within seconds, although, yet again, he had not broken the skin.

She moaned, trying desperately to form words, but her lips were too swollen to move.

He raised the whip just as another clap of thunder shattered the silence and he brought the whip down across her face.

"Hell of a night to die, ain't it, bitch?"

****

Detective Carson was riding shotgun with a Parish police officer and cursing the weather. Once they'd turned off the blacktop, the dirt road had turned into a thick, mucky gumbo.

"Can't you go any faster?" he asked, thinking of the time that had elapsed since Juliette March had been taken.

"Not without going in a ditch."

"Just don't get us stuck," Carson muttered.

"It's four-wheel drive, sir. We aren't going to get stuck," the officer countered.

Carson glanced in the side-view mirror at the phalanx of parish and police cars behind them. They were running without lights and sirens so as not to alert him to their arrival.

"How much farther?" Carson asked, trying to see through the rainfall and the constant swipe of windshield wipers.

"We're almost there," the officer said, and then all of a sudden, he slammed on the brakes. "I take that back. We're there," and came to a sliding stop directly behind a black SUV.

Their headlights caught on the muddy license tag as Carson peered at it through the pouring rain.

"That's the car!" he shouted as the other cruisers began pulling up. They cut the headlights and killed their engines in unison.

Carson jumped out on the run with a search warrant in his pocket and a gun in his hand, while the others began circling the property.

There was a light on in the living room and another one at the far end of the house. A deputy had already moved to that light source, hoping for a glimpse inside the room. All of a sudden the deputy spun away and started running toward Carson. Even in the downpour, it would have been impossible to wash away the look of horror on his face.

"She's in there, sir! Bloody as hell, tied spread-eagle to a bed."

"Take it down!" Carson ordered and stepped back as a pair of officers took a battering ram to the front door.

It went down with the first blow and suddenly the house was full of police, all running toward the light at the back of the house.

****

Chub heard the thud as his front door hit the floor, but was too excited to focus on the fact the noise wasn't part of the storm. By the time he heard the thunder of running feet, it was too late. He spun toward the bedroom door just as it flew back against the wall. Police swarmed the room— yelling at him to put his hands behind his head and screaming for him to get down.

When two officers tackled him, he lost his erection and the cat-o'-nine-tails at the same time. He hit the floor screaming obscenities while they rolled him onto his belly, handcuffed his hands behind his back, and dragged him backward from the room. He had one last glimpse of the bloody woman on his bed and then he was gone.

Carson had seen plenty in his twenty-plus years on the force, but was shocked by what Chub Walton had done. As horrific as Juliette's wounds appeared, the irony of the moment was Carson's subconscious need to hide her naked body, as if the worst that had happened to her was the nudity, itself.

"Cut her free and cover her up!" he ordered, then pointed at one of the officers. "Go tell the paramedics the scene is clear and get them in here, STAT."

"Yes, sir," he said and ran out of the room.

Julie's eyes were swollen shut and her lips were so painful she could hardly speak, but she knew enough to know she'd been saved and kept trying to talk.

"Who... here? Call Brendan."

Carson already knew the relationship between the victim and Brendan Poe. He wanted her to know who the real hero was.

"You can thank your Brendan for finding the lead that got us here so fast."

She started to shake as they began removing the bindings from her wrists and ankles.

"Bren? Here? I want Bren. Get Bren."

"No, ma'am, not here, but I'm sure he'll be waiting for you at the hospital."

"Waiting," she mumbled and passed out.

Carson glanced at the EMT. "Can you tell the extent of her injuries? It's obvious he whipped her all to hell, but can you tell if she's been raped?"

The EMT frowned. "At first glance, I would say no, but we can't be sure until they do a rape kit. However, at this point, it almost doesn't matter. Between the shock and pain of what she's endured, the emotional act has already happened..." He motioned to his partner. "Let's get her moved before she wakes up."

They transferred her to a stretcher, quickly covering her from head to toe with a waterproof sheet, and then he carried her through the downpour to the waiting ambulance, leaving the police to process the scene.

Carson stood in the doorway, watching as the taillights of the ambulance disappeared in the darkness, then dug Jack Michaels's business card out of his pocket.

****

Jack jumped when his phone rang then fumbled it, trying to get it out of his pocket.

"This is Michaels."

"I don't have Grayson March's number," Carson said. "Is he there?"

"Yes, do you want—?"

"Just inform him we have his daughter."

"Oh, thank the Lord! Is she okay?" Jack said and turned and gave everyone in the room a thumbs up, which brought Brendan to his feet.

"She's alive. They're taking her to Touro Infirmary," Carson said. "Tell Brendan Poe she asked for him first."

The hair suddenly crawled on the back of Jack's neck. The cop didn't say she was okay, just alive.

"Yes, yes, I will do that," Jack said. "And thank you."

"All of you need to thank Brendan Poe. Another five minutes and we would've been too late."

"I will tell them," he said.

Grayson was standing now, afraid to ask for details.

Jack saved him the effort. "I asked if she was okay. Carson said she was alive."

Lana March moaned then started to weep. Grayson had a hand on her shoulder, still waiting for the rest of the verdict.

Brendan grabbed Jack's arm. "What else?"

Jack purposefully raised his voice, intent that Grayson and his wife understand the extent of their betrayal.

"Carson said another five minutes and they would've been too late. He said she's alive only because of you, Brendan, and he also said that you are the first person she asked for."

Brendan grabbed Jack's arm as he swallowed back tears. "Where are they taking her?"

"Touro Infirmary," Jack said, then cupped the back of Brendan's head and gave him a brief hug.

When Brendan walked out of the room, the other employees of The Black Garter went with him.

"Where's he going? What did you tell him?" Grayson asked, as he grabbed Jack by the shoulders.

Jack wiped a shaky hand across his face. "He asked me where they were taking her so I told him."

"Where is she?" Lana cried. "Where are they taking my baby?"

"Touro Infirmary," Jack said and walked out.

Like Brendan, he was going to the hospital. He needed to know the extent of her injuries before he closed his eyes on this night.

Grayson turned to his wife. "Get your purse and raincoat. We've got to get to the hospital now."

Lana was still weeping as she began to gather up her things.

He took the purse from her hands, slung it over his shoulder, and led her from the room. He wanted to run. He needed to see Julie's face to reassure himself she was really alive, but Lana had finally come undone.

****

Brendan beat the ambulance transporting Julie to the hospital and then stood in the breezeway beneath the entrance to ER, anxiously awaiting the arrival. Some people came and went with injuries related to the fire, another came in on his own with a knife wound, while a young gunshot victim was brought in by family members.

He heard an ambulance coming through the city long before he saw it, but had no way of knowing if it would be the one with Julie on board. Then he saw it coming in hot with lights, sirens, and a police escort. It had to be her.

He waited as the ambulance backed up into the bay and moved closer as the EMTs opened up the doors. When he saw them pulling the patient out on the gurney, his heart sank. It wasn't Julie. It couldn't be. It wasn't until he heard her voice that the ground tilted beneath his feet.

God in heaven, Juliette! What did he do to you?

He grabbed hold of the gurney as they pushed it toward the entrance and ran beside it, calling out her name.

"Julie! It's Brendan. I'm here, baby. I'm here."

"Bren... can't see you!"

"I'm here, Julie. I'm right beside you."

He grabbed her hand as they rolled into ER, and all the while, she kept screaming, "With me... Stay with me. I can't see! Don't leave!"

He squeezed her fingers. "I'm here, Julie. Don't be afraid. You're safe now."

Once they were inside, staff took over and began trying to separate Brendan from the gurney.

"Sir, you can't go any farther. You have to wait—"

Julie screamed. The shriek was ear-splitting and frantic, and brought a doctor running out of another room.

"No! With me. He stays with me! I can't see. I don't know these voices. He stays with me—with me!"

Brendan turned to the doctor, begging him to intercede.

"Please! Her name is Juliette March. She was kidnapped less than two hours ago and they just rescued her from the abductor's home. I'll stay out of the way, but I need to be close enough that she can hear my voice. She needs to know that she's with someone she trusts."

"Related to Grayson March?" the doctor asked.

"His daughter."

It was the magic connection needed to turn the tide.

The doctor nodded. "But stay out of the way in the corner, okay?"

"Absolutely, and thank you," Brendan said, and then he hurried into the examining room, talking as he went. "Julie, I'm here in the room with you. I'm just staying out of the way so they can help you. Okay?"

She was moaning again, and from what he could tell, she was once again out of her head, reliving what had already happened. When they began to remove the sheet from her body, he knew he was right.

She moaned as she grabbed at the sheet, thinking she was fighting her abductor, instead.

"No more, no more! Oh God, please don't hit me again."

"Miss March, I'm Doctor George. You're safe. You're in a hospital."

Brendan added his voice, hoping to calm her.

"Julie! You're safe. You're in ER and the troll is gone for good. Chub Walton was his name and he's already in custody."

Her head rolled from side to side, searching for his location with sightless eyes.

"Brendan?"

"Yes. I'm here. Let go of the sheet, baby. They're trying to help you."

"Too late," she whispered, even as she let go.

Then he saw her body and nearly fainted. Besides the lash marks on her face, bloody stripes, oozing fluid and seeping blood, covered most of her torso and between her legs,. Even the hardened ER personnel seemed visibly shaken as the doctor quickly repeated his introduction.

"Juliette, my name is Doctor George. I'm going to be examining you now." He picked up her hands. "Feel my hands? These are my hands. Long skinny fingers, aren't they? I always wanted to play piano, but I have a tin ear. I'm going to put them on your legs, and on your stomach, as well. Is that okay?"

Julie ran her fingers over the doctor's hands. They didn't feel like the short stubby ones that had been hurting her.

"Brendan?"

"Yes, that's Doctor George and you're in Touro Infirmary. You know this place, right? Isn't this where your Nonny was last time she was in the hospital?"

Julie dropped her hands.

"Yes, Nonny was here. I'm sorry. I'll be still."

The doctor was all business. "Good for you. Now tell me, how did you get these cuts and contusions? What kind of weapon did this?"

She shuddered, started to speak but all she could do was sob. "Oh God." She licked her swollen lips and then took a breath. "A short whip with a bunch of leather strips."

"Like a cat-o'-nine-tails?" the doctor asked.

"Yes, that. He hit himself and then me over and over. He liked it. He liked pain. Are the cuts deep? Am I going to have stitches all over? Will there be scars?"

"No stitches at all. There are a few places where the skin finally broke, but they aren't deep. It appears he was quite skilled with inflicting pain without ripping the flesh. I venture to say the day will come when there will not be a mark left on your body as a reminder of what happened."

Her face crumpled. "I'll remember," she said, sobbing softly as they began tending her wounds.

Brendan could no longer see her for the tears in his eyes, but he wouldn't look away. If she had suffered it, he would endure it. Every few moments she called out his name, and every time she called, he answered.

The sounds in the room, even her gasps and moans of pain, became muted as the doctor and staff worked on her in perfect unison. They wheeled a portable X-ray machine in to make sure he hadn't cracked any ribs. When they did the rape kit, she nearly lost it, thinking the hands on her body were the troll's. It took Brendan standing beside her to keep her calm enough to finish it, and when they were done, her whole body was shaking.

The doctor tried to examine her eyes but they were too swollen for the eyelids to open.

"I want antibiotic ointment on her eyes and then bandaged," he ordered. "I'll have the pphthalmologist notified to check in on her tomorrow."

"Am I blind?" Julie asked, reaching toward her face.

A nurse caught her hand. "Don't touch, dear."

The doctor didn't know how to answer, so he hedged. "You're eyes are swollen, Julie. I'll have the specialist check them tomorrow after the swelling goes down."

"Okay," she said, and then just as swiftly cried Brendan's name.

"I'm still here. I won't leave you."

News of her ordeal was filtering through the ER as well as Brendan Poe's part in her rescue. Unknowingly, he'd become the hero of the hour.

They were just finishing applying the bandages on her eyes and were painting the wounds on her body with an antiseptic when a nurse stepped into the room.

"Doctor George, her parents are here."

"No!" Julie moaned. "I don't want them to see. Mama will say it's my fault."

"Tell them to wait," the doctor said.

Julie called out again. "Brendan?"

"Right here. Not going anywhere until you do, okay?

"Yes."

****

Grayson March was not a man accustomed to being told no. When the nurse came back informing him they would have to wait, he began to demand.

"She's my daughter! I have the right to —"

"I'm sorry, Mr. March, but your daughter is the one who asked you to wait. I'm sure you understand."

Lana moaned and clasped her hand against her heart. "Does she look bad? What did he do to her? Will she be scarred?"

Jack had been sitting quietly nearby and couldn't believe the first words out of Lana March's mouth had to do with physical appearance.

The nurse's eyes narrowed slightly, but she answered in a calm, professional manner.

"She has suffered greatly, but she will heal, Mrs. March. I'll let you know when they move her to a room."

"Where's Brendan Poe?" Grayson asked, frowning first at Jack who would no longer look at him, then back at the nurse.

"I'm sorry, I don't know anyone by that name," the nurse said.

All Grayson knew was that Poe had left the police station before they had, but he was nowhere in sight.

"Is there a man with her?"

The nurse frowned. "There are a lot of people with your daughter, sir, and they're taking very good care of her."

Grayson doubled his fists as the nurse left the waiting room. He turned on Jack in frustration.

"He's with her. I know he's with her. Why the hell will she see him and not us?"

Jack shrugged as he headed for the far end of the room to get a cup of coffee. He fumbled for change and dropped it in the vending machine, then blindly watched a thin stream of hot, dark brew dribble into a paper cup before taking a quick sip. It was not the best coffee he'd ever had, but it would suffice. He headed back to his seat.

"I'd like a cup of coffee," Lana said.

Jack kept walking without realizing she was speaking to him.

"Excuse me!" Lana said.

Jack stopped and looked back. "I'm sorry. I didn't realize you were speaking to me."

Lana sniffed. "Well, I was. I would like a cup of coffee, too."

"Yes, ma'am, but I'm sure you wouldn't want an unsavory sort like me getting it for you. Grayson, your wife wants coffee."

He walked back to his seat, ignoring the flush on Lana's face. He never would've imagined how freeing being unemployed could be.

Lana glared as Jack walked away and then tugged on her husband's arm.

"Did you hear the way he spoke to me? I don't think you should employ someone so rude."

Grayson glared at a spot on the floor. "He doesn't work for me anymore. He quit."

"So, what are you going to do about Poe and Julie?"

"There's not much I can do. Julie's of age, and Poe quit, too."

Lana frowned. "Really? What on earth did you—?"

Grayson sighed. "Look. When they first told me about Juliette's abduction, I handled it badly."

"How so?"

He shrugged. "I accused Anson of being behind it and Brendan of complicity."

Lana rolled her eyes. "Anson, I can understand, but why would you think the son would be complicit? As undesirable as his family is, he's treated her well, and while I hate to say it, it appears we also have him to thank for her life."

Grayson had always been Juliette's first hero and was not gracious about relinquishing the status.

"I already said I handled it poorly," he snapped and walked off to get their coffee.

****

By the time they moved Juliette to a room, she was exhausted and in so much pain she could barely stand it. She whimpered with every breath that she took and kept touching the bandages on her eyes.

"I hurt, Bren," she said softly.

"I know, baby. They just put something for pain in your IV and they put an antibiotic wash on your skin. It should all take effect soon."

"Brendan?"

"Right here."

She lifted her hand toward him as if begging forgiveness. "I wanted to die. I asked God to let me die."

He grabbed her hand, holding it to his cheek, unable to speak.

She felt his tears. He needed to know things. She just didn't know if she could speak the words. "I wanted to be dead before... before—"

"What he did to you will never change how much I love you," Brendan whispered.

"He didn't rape me."

Brendan sighed. He'd hoped she hadn't had to endure that, too.

"Thank God, but it wouldn't have changed me loving you."

"I know. But it would have made a difference to Mama and Daddy."

"Fuck Mama and Daddy," Brendan said shortly.

Julie started to laugh, then winced as the shift of facial muscles pulled at her swollen lips.

"Oh, Brendan, I can't believe I did that. I didn't think I would ever laugh again."

"You're a grown woman, Juliette. They're your parents

and you will love them for that, but they no longer steer the rudder in your life. You do. Remember that."

Julie could hear his disapproval and wished she could see his face.

"If I am sailing my own ship, then you're my North Star."

Brendan shuddered. "I will love you forever, but I'm not sure that being with me is the healthiest thing that can happen to you."

She clutched his hand in sudden panic. "What are you saying?"

"Knowing me could harm you. There was a time tonight when I wondered if Anson might've had something to do with your abduction. Even though we had the guilty man on security camera, I couldn't swear Anson hadn't hired him. God knows I wouldn't put it past him."

"But he didn't."

"We still don't know that. By sheer association, I've put you in harm's way."

Julie didn't answer, and Brendan thought she was finally falling asleep. And then her fingernails curled into the skin at his wrists.

"What did my father say to you?"

Brendan frowned. "What do you mean?"

"I know you. I can hear something in your voice you're not telling me, and don't lie to me. I've had enough drama to last a lifetime. What did he say?"

"I'm not going to tell you. If you want to know, you can ask him yourself. What I will tell you is that The Black Garter burned down along with a pretty wide swath of the Quarter and that I will never work for him again."

Julie's chin began to tremble. "Oh my God! What happened between you two?"

There was a shuffle of feet behind him. Brendan knew they were no longer alone.

"Like I said, you'll have to ask him. I have nothing to say except that I thank God you are alive, and I will love you forever."

When he stood up and turned loose of her hand, she cried out in sudden fear and confusion. "Brendan?"

He leaned over and kissed the spot closest to her mouth that wasn't hurt, and then he walked past her parents without a word.

Grayson knew he needed to say something and spoke quickly, hoping to catch him before he left. "Uh, Brendan, we—"

Brendan shut the door behind him.

Grayson frowned.

Lana sniffed. "That was rude."

Julie's hands were shaking. "Brendan?"

They hurried to her bedside to let her know they were there. "He's gone, Julie. Your mother and I are here beside you. We love you and are so thankful this whole ordeal is over."

"Yes, thankful," Lana echoed.

"Nothing is over," she muttered, as she pulled her hands away, curling them into fists and remembering the hurt she'd heard in Brendan's voice. "What did you do to him, Daddy? What the hell did you do?"

He didn't answer, but she felt her mother running a finger down the side of her cheek.

"Your poor little face," Lana said, patting her daughter's arm. "Don't worry, darling. We'll get the best plastic surgeons there are to make it pretty again."

Julie grabbed the sides of her face in sudden panic.

"Plastic surgeons? What's wrong with my face?

Brendan said the doctor told him everything would heal without scars."

"Oh my! I wouldn't think—" Lana began, then Grayson gripped her arm with such force that for a fraction of a second she forgot to breathe.

"Brendan was right!" Grayson said, trying to inject optimism in his voice. "There is nothing wrong with your face that time won't heal. Besides... you know your mother, always looking for what's wrong instead of seeing the beauty of what's right."

Julie felt sideswiped. She couldn't see either of their expressions, but she could tell by their tones there was so much more they weren't saying. She clutched the bedrails for stability as her socially acceptable world continued to unravel. She kept waiting for one of them to acknowledge the horror of what had happened to her, to say they loved her—to kiss her and hug her. When they didn't, she told herself it was because of the condition she was in, only to remember moments later that it hadn't deterred Brendan. She was getting scared. What was it they weren't saying? What awful thing was wrong that no one mentioned?

"Dad?"

"Yes, we're here."

"Neither one of you has asked what happened to me."

"That's because it doesn't matter," he said quickly, patting her hand. "You're here and safe and that's enough."

She gasped, unable to believe he'd just said that. "Doesn't matter? Are you fucking serious?"

He reached for her hand again, but this time she snatched it away. "I just meant that whatever bad things happened can be put behind you now," he said quickly.

Julie was trying to hold onto sanity and her parents

wanted her to forget. Brendan had seen and didn't back away. She needed to know they would do the same.

"Two hours ago, I was stripped naked and tied spread-eagle to the bed of the man I thought would kill me."

Grayson cursed beneath his breath as Lana covered her face. Neither of them wanted to know about the degrading things that had happened to her, but Julie kept talking.

"He stood at the foot of the bed, staring at my naked body while he whipped himself with a cat-o'-nine-tails. After a while, he began to whip me with it, too. He liked the pain. I'm alive because Brendan cared enough to chase down the man who took me. What were the rest of you doing besides pointing fingers and arguing? Jack is always the voice of reason. Where's Jack? Wasn't he there with you?"

"Yes, Jack was at the bar and with us at the police station while we waited for word of your rescue, and he was just out in the waiting room with us right up until we found out that you were being taken to your room. He said to tell you he loves you, and he'll see you tomorrow. Look, it was a bad time all the way around. You went missing and the fire was on top of us. The bar is gone," Grayson said.

"Was anyone hurt?"

"No, and we can rebuild."

"Brendan quit. Why did he quit?"

Grayson wanted this conversation over with. "He's not the only one. Jack quit, too."

Julie groaned. "What did you do?"

"That wasn't my fault. Your mother—"

"Oh my God! Shut up!" Julie winced and then ran her finger along her lower lip. She could taste blood, which meant it had split open again, another reminder of what she'd endured. "I thought I was going to die. I prayed to die so I wouldn't have to endure what I knew would be my fate. And then I'm saved, and all you two can do is quibble about who is to blame and fixing my imperfections with plastic surgery! I think both of you need to leave now, and I'd just as soon not see you again, at least until the bandages are off my eyes. I need to see you when we talk, and I'll know your lies when I see your faces."

Grayson felt sick. "Julie, I'm sorry. Truly. I never meant to hurt Brendan's feelings. I just got scared when I found out you were gone and blamed his father, and..."

"And what?" Julie snapped.

Grayson lifted his chin, refusing even now to admit he was wrong. "I insinuated that he might've known what his father was planning when I gave my statement to the police."

Julie couldn't believe it. "You actually told the police Brendan was responsible for my disappearance?" When he didn't deny it, she felt sick, imagining what Brendan must have thought—how betrayed he would have felt. "Get out."

"I said I was sorry," Grayson repeated.

"Get out, both of you," she repeated.

"Julie, darling, I didn't mean to hurt your feelings," Lana said.

Now that she couldn't see her mother's face, she heard all too clearly the wheedling tone of her mother's voice.

"Yes, you did," Julie said. "It's how you get your way. You whine like a baby until everybody caves in to your demands."

She began feeling along both sides of the bed, frantically slapping the sheets and feeling the sides of the bedrails.

"What do you need?" Grayson asked.

"The nurse's call button! I want you to go away! You think Brendan has a bloodline to live down? Mother cares more about appearances than people's feelings, and you, Daddy, are a jealous, selfish bastard. I don't need you to be the only man in my life. I just need you to be my father."

Grayson was stunned. "The nurse's button is just above the pinkie finger on your left hand. We'll be going now. I'm going to forget this ever happened and chalk it up to your emotional state. Lana, get your purse. We're leaving."

Julie was so mad she was shaking. "My emotional state! God in heaven, I won't forget you said that! I won't ever forget."

She heard their footsteps moving away, then the door opening and closing, and still couldn't tell if she was alone. She cocked her ear toward the door, listening, and thought she could hear someone breathing, which shocked her. She began fumbling for the call button until she found and pressed it. A voice came over the intercom.

"Yes, Miss March, how can I help you?"

"I need someone to come to my room and make sure I'm alone."

"We'll be right there."

Julie grabbed the bedrails, bracing herself against another assault. When she heard the near-silent sound of a door opening and closing, she leaned back against the pillow in mute defeat.

Even when she was at her most defenseless, they'd proved themselves untrustworthy.

Then the door opened again, but this time she heard the squeak of rubber soled shoes against the tile and knew one of the nurses was here.

"Miss March, I'm Fern. You wanted to know if you're alone?"

"Yes."

"You are now, honey. I just saw your father heading for the elevator. Do you want me to call him back?"

Julie was shaking and trying not to cry, but the misery was evident in her voice. "No, no, I don't want him here."

Fern touched Julie's arm to let her know her location. "It's okay. Is there anything you need?"

"Can you help me to the bathroom?"

"Absolutely," Fern said and let down the bedrail.

When the nurse left a few minutes later, Julie was finally alone and the quiet began to get to her. One image after another began flashing through her mind, all of which were of what she'd endured at Chub Walton's hands. She couldn't open her eyes and focus on something else to make the memories go away, because her eyes wouldn't open. It was like being in hell and stuck on rewind. When the meds began pulling her under, she went willingly, grateful for the oblivion that came with it.

Chapter Nine

It was close to 4:00 a.m. when Brendan pulled into the parking lot of his apartment complex. He killed the engine, then sat for a few moments, gathering himself before going inside. It seemed like a lifetime, but it had only been a few hours since he'd left here to go to work.

Anson's face slid through his mind like a bad memory, but he let that go, too. He was too exhausted to solve another problem. All he wanted to do was sleep the clock around, but that wasn't going to happen. It was already Sunday, and he'd promised Linny they'd go eat at the Crab Shack and get beignets. It wasn't easy being responsible, which was probably why Anson Poe had made such a sorry-ass man. If it wasn't easy, he wasn't interested.

The thunderstorm had passed while he was still at the hospital, and when he got out of his SUV, the rain-washed air was a welcome scent. If only a good hard rain could wash the ugly from his life this easy, he would be grateful.

His steps were dragging by the time he reached his apartment. He unlocked the door to find Claudette sitting on the sofa. She took one look at his face and stood.

"Tell me."

The solace of home enveloped him.

"We found her alive. She's in bad shape but will heal."

Claudette hugged him fiercely. "Praise the lord for the blessing," she said softly. "Do you want me to stay? I can if you need me?"

Brendan shook his head. "No. Take your much-needed time off. I promised Linny I'd take her and Mama out tomorrow."

Claudette frowned. "You need to rest."

"I'll rest when I'm dead," Brendan said and tried a smile that didn't quite make it.

Claudette's frown deepened. "Do not say that! So, I will go now and see you on Monday?"

"I begin looking for a new job on Monday, so yes."

"Oh no... The Black Garter burned, too?"

"Yes, but I quit Grayson March's employ tonight."

She didn't ask, but waited for him to say as much as he needed to say.

Brendan kept it brief. "All I will say is that Julie's father does not appreciate my ancestry."

Claudette sighed. "It isn't your ancestry. It's the present generation that's causing the trouble. The Poe name represented good people until that one was born. I think his mama made a pact with the devil. I think maybe she said, give me a beautiful boy and I'll give you his soul."

Brendan nodded. "You could be right."

"I will come earlier on Monday so you can get a start on job hunting."

"Thank you."

He took out his wallet to pay her for the past week.

She started to refuse it, and then she saw the look on his face and pocketed it instead. She understood a man needed to pay his own way to live easy in the world.

"Auntie, will you please let me call a cab for you?"

"No. I will call a friend to come get me."

Brendan wrapped his arms around her and gave her a quick hug. "You are a blessing to me and I love you."

She cupped the side of his face. "I love you, too and get some rest. You do your family no good if you are not well."

"I know. I will."

He locked the door as she left, savoring the silence. He wanted rid of his smoky clothes, a shower and a bed, but first, he needed to check on the other women in his life and headed down the hall.

Claudette had left a nightlight on, and when he looked in, saw Linny was asleep on her mother's bed.

He slipped quietly into the room to move her back to her pallet then paused at the foot of the bed. His mother had one arm flung out across the bed, and the other over her eyes, as if, even in sleep, the world was too ugly to face. He thought of all the times she'd comforted him through sickness and injury. She'd been his champion, no matter what. He'd taken a mental beating tonight, but nothing to what Juliette had endured. He could bear anything, as long as she was alive in the world.

"Good night, Mama," he said quietly and closed the door behind him.

****

Delle woke the moment Belinda was no longer in her arms. She got a glimpse of broad shoulders and Brendan's profile as he laid his little sister back on the pallet, then pretended to still be asleep when he paused at her bedside to whisper good night.

She listened as he crossed the hall, and a few moments later, she heard water running and knew he was in the shower. She tried to sleep, but wanted so desperately to know what had happened to Juliette. If he went to the kitchen instead of going to bed, she'd go talk to him. If not, it would have to wait until the morning.

****

The moment Brendan closed the door to his bedroom, he began taking off clothes, shedding the damp, smoky clothing as he went. As soon as he stepped beneath the hot steamy spray, he reached for the shampoo and started to scrub. A few minutes later, he switched shampoo for soap and began scrubbing his body until the scent of smoke was gone. It should've been enough, but he kept seeing the bloody welts on Juliette's body, and her eyes so swollen they wouldn't open, then began scrubbing again. He scrubbed until his skin was raw, but the memory was still there in his head—in his heart—jammed so deep in his soul that it hurt to breathe.

"Son of a bitch," he muttered, as he turned off the water and climbed out of the shower.

He was reaching for a towel when he caught a glimpse of himself in the mirror and for a split second saw her bloody face instead.

He spun toward the commode and threw up until there was nothing left but the bile, bitter as the image forever seared into his brain. The nausea slowly passed, leaving him emotionally gutted. He put on gym shorts to sleep in and crawled into bed.

The sheets were cool against his skin as he bunched the soft, floppy pillow beneath his neck. He took a deep breath and closed his eyes, waiting—praying for the silence to take him under. It never came. He kept hearing Julie's screams and being rocked by the shock of what she had endured. Rage swept through him, coupled with an agony so sharp he thought he would die. Tears came fast, hot and blinding.

****

Delle was almost asleep when she heard the first

choking sob. She was up and in the hall before she remembered to be cautious of her feet, but pain was nothing when one of her children was in need. She went into his room without knocking and was at his side without moments.

"Brendan... cher..."

Brendan covered his face, but there was no masking the thick, choking sobs.

She laid her hand on his chest. The heavy thud against her palm ripped through her mother's heart.

"There is no need to hide your tears, not from me."

"Oh God, Mama. My Julie..."

She grabbed his hand in panic, feeling the calluses and the strength—remembering when he was small how he would crawl out from beneath the covers and into her lap as she sang away the bad dream. But he was past songs and she didn't know how to make this go away.

"Did they find her?"

"Yes."

"Alive?"

He took a deep breath and wiped his face. "Yes."

"Talk to me, Brendan. Shared pain is a lighter load."

Brendan sat up. He could just see the outline of her face, but the tenderness in her voice was familiar and so dear.

He shoved a shaky hand through his still-damp hair. "Some man I am, crying in the dark so that his mama has to come tend him."

"What happened?"

"He tied her naked to a bed and whipped her with a cat-o'-nine-tails. I saw them pulling her out of the ambulance and didn't know her. Her eyes are swollen shut and her face and body are covered with lash marks. They found her before she was raped, but it almost doesn't matter. The mental act happened many times before they rescued her."

"Ah God," Delle whispered, remembering the tiny woman with the small, perfect body and wept quiet tears.

"Why do bad things happen to good people?" Brendan asked.

Delle shook her head. "You already know that answer. Bad things happen because of bad people."

The words cut to the core of who he was because he knew what she meant. He came from a bad man, as had all of her sons, and yet none had the manic tendencies that guided Anson's life.

Delle's grip was tight on his wrist, as if she could anchor his grief by will alone.

"I didn't have to know Juliette long to see she's a strong woman. She's suffering, but she'll be all the stronger for it once she's healed. You'll see. A woman can endure anything when she's loved."

"Like my sweet mama who is so very loved by her children," he said.

"And that's why I'm able to endure," she said quietly, then glanced at the clock. "It's almost morning. You sleep until noon. I'll keep Linny quiet until then, and when you wake, we will go on this outing she's talked about, and we'll pretend for just one day that we are a normal, happy family. Do you hear me?"

He smiled. "Yes, I hear you."

"So sleep now, my good son. I know there's more to be told, but not tonight. Just remember that the worst has passed, and everything after will be a day closer to perfect healing."

She leaned down and hugged him close.

"I'm ashamed to say this because a mother shouldn't

have favorites, but I think tonight you need to know that you're my favorite son."

He managed a half-hearted smile. "I thank you, Mama, but I think we'll keep that between us."

"Absolutely. Now go to sleep and remember what I said. No getting up before noon."

"Yes, ma'am. And you get off your feet."

Delle smiled. "Yes, sir."

She slipped across the hall, and after a brief check on her daughter, she crawled back into bed. But instead of trying to sleep, she began praying. She was still praying when the sun came over the horizon.

****

Anson woke at daybreak and turned on the television as he began dressing for the day. He was hoping to catch the latest on the fire from the local newscast.

Adelaine's had finally evacuated their restaurant and he'd been on his way home before midnight, well aware that March's guard dogs had followed a half mile behind.

He was dressed all but for his boots when he sat down on the side of the bed and began flipping channels before finally finding one broadcasting the event.

A wicked smile spread across his face when he heard the scope of the damage. Not only had Frenchie's burned to the ground, but so had The Black Garter. That was a two-for-the price-of-one deal he hadn't expected and wondered how the cocky bastard felt about the world this morning.

What he didn't know until now was that March's daughter had been kidnapped during the chaos, only to be rescued hours later. He scratched his groin and began putting on his boots, wondering how his high-and-mighty son was faring now. By the time he added his own brand of payback, there wouldn't be enough left of Brendan Poe to bury.

Anson eyed the remodeling still in progress as he headed downstairs. The house smelled of fresh paint and new flooring. Soon, there would be new curtains and draperies at the windows, and when that happened, he would be ready to reclaim his wife.

He was eating a piece of beef jerky and making coffee when his cell phone rang. It was Sam.

"You're late," he said shortly.

"Chance and I aren't coming out today," Sam said.

Anson frowned. "Like hell."

Sam wouldn't budge. "It rained four inches. We can't get into the fields, there's nothing to ship, and nothing to deliver. We are going to spend the day with Mama and Linny."

Anson's first instinct was to argue, and then he realized this played in perfectly with his plan.

"Yeah, okay. So tell them how pretty I'm fixing up the place for when they come home."

"I will," Sam said and disconnected.

Anson smiled. The day was starting off even better than he had hoped. He sat down to breakfast with a better attitude than he'd had in days, and it was still holding true when the Parish police rolled up in his front yard.

****

Anson was in the shed unpacking a shipment of new pots they used for the bamboo when he heard an engine. At first, he thought Sam and Chance must've changed their minds and come anyway. Then he stepped out, saw a police car driving up to the house, and went to meet them.

Seeing Detective Royal from the New Orleans P.D. behind the wheel somewhat eased his concerns. Royal was already in his pocket. The other cop with him was a different story.

"Hey! Are ya'll lost?" he asked.

"Morning, Poe," Royal said. "You know Detective Early."

Anson noticed a coffee stain on the front of Early's blue short-sleeved button-down as he nodded.

"What can I do for you?" Anson asked.

Royal loosened his tie and unbuttoned the top two buttons at the collar. "It sure is hot out here today."

"It's July. It's hot here every day," Anson said.

"I guess you'd be right about that," Royal said.

They stared at each other for a few seconds and then Royal shifted focus.

"Reckon you heard about the fire in the Quarter last night?"

"I was at Adelaine's eating dinner when it started, why?" Anson asked.

Royal frowned. He didn't want to have to arrest this man, considering the amount of money Poe paid him every month.

"So, you *were* in the city?"

Anson frowned. "Did I not just say that? What's the deal?"

"The report this morning is that it appears the fire at Frenchie's was arson."

Anson grinned. "Wow, wonder which one of the city bigwigs' wives finally figured out what was going on upstairs?"

A muscle twitched at the corner of Early's mouth, a small clue to the fact that he agreed with the comment.

Royal pulled out a handkerchief to wipe the sweat beading on his forehead. "Miss Branscum was questioned this morning as to that very thing."

Anson frowned. "Who's Miss Branscum?"

"Lisette," Early said.

Anson chuckled. "Well hell, all these years I been poking her and her girls and I never knew her last name."

Again, the fact that he readily admitted being a customer took them off guard.

"So you *were* a client?"

Anson's chuckle spread to a laugh. "So she's calling us clients? Damn, that's a good one."

Sweat was running down the middle of Early's back and into his pants. He wanted done with this follow-up and back in the air-conditioned car.

"Look. We're just going to come right out and say why we're here," Royal said. "Lisette named you as a possible suspect in the arson."

Anson offered a look of humorous disbelief.

"Man! She's been servicing big shots all around the state for nearly twenty years and running her girls along with it. She's bound to have pissed off a few people a lot more important than me in the process. Look, we parted company less than friends a few months back, but I can't imagine why on earth she'd think I'd do something like that? And why now, after our beef was so long ago?"

Early decided it was time he asked a couple of questions. "Miss Branscum said you were there only a week or so ago, and she turned you away at the door."

Anson sighed and then shook his head in sudden understanding. "Ah, so that's why she named me. To be honest I was testing the waters to see if all was forgiven yet, but she wouldn't let me in. Hell, I been turned down by women before and I haven't set one on fire yet. I can't imagine why she'd think I'd be all that hot under the collar since there are whores to be had all over the city. Besides, I already told you I was in Adelaine's eating dinner."

"When did you first get into the city?" Early asked.

Anson paused, as if considering the timeline. "I'd guess it was somewhere around 9:30 or something close to that. I checked in at the hostess stand, found out I'd have about a twenty minute wait, and was at the bar until they called my name. I'm sure the hostess can attest to when I went in, and plenty of others were at the bar who can verify that as well."

"You would still have had time to—"

Anson slapped his leg, as if he'd just remembered something. "Oh! Hey! I have some people you can talk to who probably know the exact time of my every move for the past several days."

"Like who?" Early asked.

"Go talk to Grayson March. We pissed each other off a while back, and he's had two of his boys tailing my every move since. They can verify everything I told you and then some."

Detective Royal's lips parted slightly, shocked Poe would even bandy a name like that around.

"Grayson March?"

Anson grinned. "Yeah. Surely you know the little son of a bitch? Short. Cocky. Rich as sin."

Early covered up a grin by coughing.

Royal dropped his notebook back into his pocket.

"We'll have to verify your alibi," he said.

"Yeah, I know how it goes. I watch TV," Anson said, and then he stuffed his hands in his pockets and waited for them to make the next move.

"So, thank you for your cooperation," Royal added.

"Happy to assist in any way that I can," he said and watched until their car disappeared from sight. "And that takes care of that," he added and went back into the shed.

****

It was just after 11:00 in the morning when someone knocked at Brendan's door. Linny jumped at the sound and glanced toward her mother. She had wanted her brother up hours ago, and this seemed like a good an excuse as any.

"Want me to go wake Bren?"

Delle shook her head. She had yet to mention anything about what had happened last night, but knew it wouldn't stay secret long.

"Go stand by the door and ask who it is."

Linny frowned. "What if it's Daddy?"

A little shiver of fear rolled across Delle's shoulders, but before she could answer, they heard someone call out with a hint of laughter in the voice.

"Hey, in there, I can hear you talking. Someone let us in."

Delle smiled. "It's Sam! Go unlock the door."

Linny flew across the room, giggling with every step. She hadn't seen her other brothers since her mama got burned, and the moment she let them in, Sam swooped down and picked her up, spun her over his head like a helicopter blade while she screeched her delight.

Chance came in behind him, shut the door, and headed for his mother.

"Hey, Mama," Chance said as he leaned over and kissed her cheek. "How ya'll doin?"

Delle couldn't quit smiling. They both looked so much like her daddy it made her homesick for the days when she'd been a child. They were tall like Anson, but both had reddish brown hair and square jaws, while Brendan had his father's black hair, finer features, and blue eyes.

"We're good, we're good. I'm so glad you came. I've been missing you both."

"Here," Sam said, handing Linny off to Chance.

Linny squealed all over again as Chance tucked her under his arm like a football and started galloping toward the kitchen.

Delle laughed as Sam sat down beside her.

"Such nonsense," she said.

He smiled. "How are your feet feeling, Mama? Are they healing up okay?"

"The bottoms are way better. I can walk around on them now if I don't stay up too long. The tops are not healing as fast."

Sam laid a hand on her head, noticing how much gray was in her hair now. He could remember a time when that would've bothered her.

"We would've been here sooner, but Daddy's been keeping us pretty busy. If it hadn't rained so hard last night, he would've sent us back to work today."

"Then I'm thankful for the rain," she said.

"Where's Brendan?" Chance asked as he dropped Linny down into Brendan's recliner on her head.

She was still giggling when Brendan walked into the room, scratching the whiskers on his jaw.

"I thought I heard an awful lot of fun going on in here without me," he said, pointing at Linny.

She stuffed her head underneath the throw pillow in the chair to smother the sound, but it was too late.

Delle frowned. "I'm sorry, son."

Sam laughed. "Don't be sorry. The lazy ass needs to be up. It's almost noon."

"He didn't get to bed until 5:00 this morning," Delle said.

Chance frowned. "Because of the fire?"

Linny came out from under the pillow. All she'd known was they had to be quiet to let Brendan sleep, but not why.

"What fire? What burned up?" she asked.

"A big part of the French Quarter," Delle said.

Linny gasped. "Did the place where you work burn up?"

"Yeah it did, among other things," he said briefly and gave his brothers a warning look not to push the issue in front of her.

They got the message.

"Hey, Mama, did you make extra coffee this morning?" Brendan asked.

"In the pot, honey. There's enough for all of you if you want."

"I'm in," Chance said and headed for the kitchen.

Brendan and Sam followed. Brendan heard their mother send Linny to the bedroom to play, which gave them time to talk.

Chance handed Brendan a cup of coffee, then leaned against the cabinet with his hands in his pockets, waiting for the caffeine to go down.

"What aren't you saying?" Chance finally asked.

Brendan took another drink then set it aside. "I take it you haven't watched any local news today."

"No, not really," Sam said.

"Neither did I," Chance added. "What did we miss?"

"While the Quarter was burning, someone kidnapped Juliette right out of the bar," Brendan said.

They both jerked like they'd been slapped.

Sam put a hand on his brother's shoulder. "Jesus, Bren. Have they gotten a call for ransom yet?"

"We already got her back," Brendan said and reached for the cookie jar.

"Who did it, one of her daddy's enemies?" Chance asked.

Brendan shook his head and returned the lid without a cookie, knowing his stomach wouldn't hold it.

"She had a stalker at the bar. We knew he was weird, but we didn't know he was crazy. While we were evacuating everyone out through the front of the bar, he took her out the back. Caught it all on the security camera."

"Don't make us ask you for every fucking detail," Sam snapped. "Talk to us, brother, because you look like you've been through hell."

Brendan shoved shaky hands through his hair, willing himself to maintain his dignity.

"The bastard had about a twenty-minute lead on us by the time we knew she was missing. We called the cops. It took a while for them to get there, so I went after her."

Chance looked at his brother with new respect. "After her?"

Brendan nodded. "I headed to the streets. We knew he'd taken her out the back, so I started asking questions, thinking someone had to have seen something. I ran all over the place, chasing down possible witnesses, and I finally found someone who saw someone, who saw someone else, and got a good lead. Cops found her."

Sam slapped the table with the flat of his hand in delight. "That's damn amazing. I'll bet her Daddy's patting you on the back. You'll be getting yourself a raise once they build the bar back."

"March blamed Daddy, then me when it happened. I quit."

Chance frowned. "What the fuck? Daddy, I can understand... but you? Why you?"

Brendan shrugged. "Blood tells, brother. You know the score. We've heard it all our lives."

"The son of a bitch," Sam said. "Well, at least your girl is safe."

A muscle jerked at corner of Brendan's mouth.

"No. She's alive, but I don't know if she'll ever feel safe again. The guy beat her near to death with a cat-o'-nine-tails before they found her. We don't know if she'll be able to see again. I need to call the hospital and check on her condition. Keep Linny occupied for me for a few minutes, okay?"

"Jesus wept," Chance whispered.

Brendan shrugged. "Probably. I know I did."

He downed the rest of the coffee and left them on their own.

Sam looked at Chance and then wiped a hand over his face as if trying to wipe away the shock of what they'd heard.

Chapter Ten

A nurse was settling Julie back into bed after a trip to the bathroom when the phone in her room began to ring.

"Want me to get that for you, hon?"

"Please, ask who it is first," Julie said as she tried to settle into a comfortable position. Every inch of skin on the front of her body felt like it was on fire.

"Hello, who's calling?" the nurse asked.

"Brendan Poe."

"One moment please," the nurse said and covered the phone. "Brendan Poe?"

Julie reached blindly for the receiver.

The nurse put it in her hand and left the room.

"Bren?"

He heard uncertainty and wondered what was going on. "Hello, sweetheart. How's it going?"

"I feel like I've been beat half to death."

He was surprised that she'd made a joke, however morbid. "That's because you were, but every day will be a day closer to being well, okay?"

It was the confidence in his voice that stayed her anxiety. "Okay."

"So what have they told you? Has that specialist been by to look at your eyes?"

"Yes, but I don't remember much. I know I could see light this morning, which he said was good, considering how swollen they still are."

"Oh, honey, that's wonderful. Best news today," he said softly. "So I want to come, but not while your parents are there."

"Come any time you want. They aren't allowed visitations."

He frowned. "Why not? What happened?"

"I'll tell you when you get here." Her voice was shaking again, and he wondered what else could've possibly gone wrong. She was alive. Surely that would have been enough for her parents.

"I will be there as soon as I shave and dress. Do you want me to bring you anything?"

"It hurts to eat. I tried breakfast and just made a mess."

"Can you drink through a straw?"

"Yes."

"I'll bring you a vanilla shake."

The gentleness in his voice when she'd been so certain she'd never see him again was all it took to start her crying again.

Brendan heard. Her despair broke his heart. "Don't cry, baby."

"Oh God, Bren! I can't seem to stop. Just when I think I have my act together and how blessed I am to still be alive, it falls in on me again."

"You'll get counseling and figure out how to deal, and we'll get through this together."

She choked. "I love you so much."

"I love you, too, sweetheart. See you soon."

He tossed his cell phone on the bed and changed his gym shorts for a pair of jeans. He was getting ready to shave when he heard someone knocking at the door and headed for the living room. He could hear his mother and Linny talking in her bedroom and knew they, too, were waiting for him to make good on a promise. He had too many responsibilities and not enough time. He walked into the living room just as Sam opened the door.

Detective Carson was on the threshold flashing his badge.

"I'm Detective Carson. Are you Brendan Poe?"

"No. I'm his brother, Sam."

Brendan walked up behind his brother. "I'm Brendan."

"May I come in?" Carson asked. "I won't keep you long."

"Yes, of course. Sorry I'm not dressed. Didn't get much sleep last night. These are my brothers, Chance and Sam Poe."

Carson nodded cordially.

"No apologies necessary. I have yet to go to bed, but it's on my agenda for today. I came to thank you personally for what you did last night. You acted quickly when the city was in a crisis situation, and it made the difference in Juliette March's survival."

"I'm the one who should be thanking you," Brendan said. "You found her alive. That's all that mattered to me."

"We were just doing our job," Carson said. "I also wanted to give you an update on your stalker. After several interesting revelations, it's beginning to look like the man we arrested is an active serial killer who'd never been identified. His real name is Conrad Walton, aka Chub Walton, and I'm guessing he's never lived in Louisiana before, or he would've known not to bury his bodies in the back yard. He had no idea that, since we're below sea level, bodies don't stay buried here. We were still processing the crime scene at sunrise when one of the officers came upon three fingers and the toe of a shoe poking up out of the ground behind the house, kinda like those fairy circles of toadstools that pop up after a rain.

"After last night's thunderstorm, it pretty much floated to the surface. We got to looking and found another right beside it. When we began questioning him about it, the bastard not only admitted to the murders, but bragged about them. He knows the death penalty is legal in our state and pitched a deal to the District Attorney, offering to give up the locations of his other victims if they'd trade the death penalty for a life sentence. So, we began checking the national data base for unsolved murders with similar M.O.s and a rather large number popped up."

"How large are you talking about?" Chance asked.

"Seventeen so far over a span of eleven years. Interesting side-note, the first one began in his hometown of San Francisco, two weeks after his mother's death. We're still checking details. We may not be able to connect him to all of them, but he'll most likely wind up doing life here in Louisiana for the crimes."

Brendan was stunned. He kept thinking of all those nights they'd watched him coming into the bar, completely unaware he was sizing up his next victim.

Carson kept eyeing Brendan closely. "How old are you?"

"Twenty-six. Why?"

Carson shrugged. "Your quick reaction to a dangerous situation was impressive. If you ever get an urge to change occupations, check out the police academy. I think you'd make a good cop."

Brendan was shocked. Not once in his entire life had anyone even hinted he had a future in anything.

"You know who my father is, right?"

Carson frowned. "One thing has nothing to do with the other. If you decide to follow through, give me a call and I'll write a letter of recommendation for you."

"Thank you," Brendan said, too stunned to elaborate.

Carson shook his hand. "You're welcome and I'm outta here."

"One more thing," Brendan said. "I cannot take all of the credit for the information I gave you. A lot of people helped me, but the turning point was Count LeGrande. He'd already identified the man who came and went as trouble before this ever happened and actually memorized his tag number. He's the real hero."

Carson frowned. "Are you talking about the old white guy in the frock coat and top hat who hangs around the Quarter?"

"Yes."

"Next time I'm down that way, I'll make a point of thanking him, too. Ya'll take care."

Chance eyed Brendan curiously as he closed the door behind the cop.

"So, what do you think about that police academy suggestion?" he asked.

Brendan shrugged. "I don't know what to think except that I *am* out of a job, and the women in my life need to get well."

"Speaking of the women," Sam said, as Delle and Linny came into the room.

"Linny's getting hungry," Delle said.

Chance grinned. "What a coincidence! So am I!"

"That's exactly why we're here," Sam said. "We came to take Mom and Linny out to dinner."

Linny sidled up to Brendan and leaned against him.

"Bren was taking us to eat at the Crab Shack and have beignets for dessert," she said.

Sam pretended to be surprised. "That's exactly what we were gonna do. How about that?"

Linny beamed.

Delle was happiest when she had all of her children together, but she kept watching Brendan's face. Yes, he'd promised to take them out, but she knew where his heart was today and needed to give him an easy out.

"Brendan, I just told Linny that Juliette got hurt last night and is in the hospital, so if you want to go see her instead of eat with us, we're fine with that. We've had the pleasure of your company every day since we've been here, and I think you need a break."

Sam quickly agreed. "She's right, Bren. We've got this. You stay with Julie as long as you want, and we'll stay here until you get back. Dad knows we aren't going to Wisteria Hill today. In fact, he has a little surprise he's working on for Mama and Linny back at the house."

"What kind of surprise?" Delle asked.

"He's remodeling Wisteria Hill. You won't recognize the place when you go home, Mama. It looks amazing."

Delle frowned. "You're kidding."

"No fooling, Mama," Chance added. "There's new tile in the kitchen, air conditioners all over the place. He's even painting inside and out, and I heard him on the phone the other day asking if the new curtains and drapes were ready."

Delle put a hand to her heart in disbelief. "Oh my!"

Linny frowned. "Did he do something in my room, too?"

"Painted the walls pink," Sam said. "New curtains for sure. Not sure about anything else."

"I love pink," Linny said, then gave her mama a quick glance to make sure she hadn't sounded too excited. When it came to things regarding her daddy, she was never sure how to react.

Brendan's heart sank. The scheming bastard did the one thing that would turn the tide in his favor, and he'd not only known what it was, but followed through.

"I'll be anxious to see it," Delle said.

She wouldn't look at Brendan. This was exactly what he didn't want, but she knew her place, and it wasn't mooching off her son's good graces.

Brendan wouldn't worry about this now. They weren't going home yet, and he had to make his peace with his little sister about breaking his promise.

He put a hand on his heart and then bowed from the waist as if he was in the presence of royalty.

"Good Queen Belinda, I pray you will excuse my presence at the dinner table today."

Linny giggled, then pointed at Brendan as if she was holding a jeweled scepter. "Of course, Sir Brendan. Please give your Juliette our regards."

Sam tugged her ponytail. "Regards? Regards? Where did you learn big words like that?"

Linny waved a hand in the air in a gesture of dismissal. "Queen Belinda knows stuff, that's where. So I am ready to leave anytime you are."

Delle glanced down at her feet and the sleeveless yellow shift she was wearing. It had an empire waist and a scoop neckline, which was comfortable for a Louisiana summer, but not exactly dress-up clothes. She had no choice as to shoes. It was flip-flops or barefoot. She still couldn't stand pressure on the healing burns.

"I don't have another dress to wear that looks any better than this one and these flip-flops are all the shoes I can tolerate."

Sam grinned. "We're going to the Crab Shack, Mama, not Delmonico's. Besides, you'll still be the prettiest woman in the place, except, of course, for the queen here. Nobody outshines Queen Belinda."

Linny threw her arms around Brendan's leg. "I'll bring you beignets."

Brendan tweaked her nose. "Thank you, pretty girl." He gave her ponytail a quick tug.

"We'll take care of them, Bren," Chance said. "Tell Julie we're thinking of her."

"I will," he said, then they were gone.

It had been so long since he'd been in the apartment alone that it felt too big and too quiet, but getting to Julie was uppermost in his mind as he headed to the bathroom to finish shaving.

****

Julie was drifting in and out of sleep when she heard a slight tap at the door. Without being able to see, all she could do was call out.

"Hello?"

Jack heard her before he saw her, and then he stopped mid-step, horrified by her appearance.

Julie was beginning to get nervous. "Hello? Hello? Who's there?"

When he realized his silence was frightening her, he quickly spoke up.

"Hey, sugar, it's me, Jack. Is it okay if I come in?"

"Jack! Yes, come in!"

He took the hand she held out and lifted it to his lips, struggling with the urge not to weep.

"Julie, honey, I'm so sorry this happened. I feel so guilty that I didn't know you were being threatened."

"That's my fault. I never said anything about it to you because I was never actually threatened. He was just creepy. I had no way of knowing this would happen, either."

He blinked back tears, doing everything he could to keep from sounding as devastated as he felt. "So, how do you feel, honey?"

Her shoulders slumped. "Pretty much like I look, I think."

"I'll be honest. I am guessing you hurt like hell, but at the same time, you also look like this should heal just fine."

Julie suddenly tightened her grip. "Really?"

He frowned. "Well yes, why would you be so surprised? I wouldn't lie to you about something like this."

"My mother mentioned plastic surgeons and—"

"She can use one if she wants, but you aren't gonna need that," he muttered. "I had a friend who looked far worse than you do from wrecking on his Harley, and he healed up. He wasn't wearing a helmet or leather, and after rolling across a good hundred feet of concrete, he looked like he'd been peeled."

Julie suddenly shivered, imagining what that man must have suffered.

"Thank you for that, and thank you for coming," she said.

Jack patted her hand. "You're welcome, and of course I would come. I wanted to see you before I left town."

"You're leaving New Orleans? Is it because of the fight you and Daddy had? What did he do?"

"It doesn't matter," Jack said. "The past is the past and I supposed it's time I retired, anyway. I'm not as young as I used to be."

"It does matter. You're like family to me," Julie said, trying not to cry.

"So, family stays in touch, right? I know how to email. You taught me, remember?"

"I also remember what a cussing fit you had until you figure it out. You're right. We'll email, but I'm still so sorry about Daddy."

Jack was in tears. He could hardly bear to look at her and what she'd endured, and yet she felt the need to apologize for her father's behavior.

"Nothing matters about this whole fucking mess but that you're still here with us. Understand?"

Now *that* sounded like the Jack she knew and loved. "Understood."

"Good, so be on the lookout for an email from me as soon as I get settled."

"Where are you going to go?" she asked.

"Inland. Anywhere a hurricane can't go... maybe Montana or Idaho. I always wanted to be a cowboy."

She tugged on his hand. "Hey, Jack, I want to tell you something."

"Yeah?"

"Remember those Karate moves you taught me when I was in high school?"

"Yeah, why?"

"I used them the night I was abducted and almost got away."

Jack's vision blurred all over again as he gave her hand a quick squeeze. He had to get out before he lost his composure. "That's my girl! Good for you, honey! Listen, I've been here long enough. You rest, heal, and I'll be in touch."

"I will. I love you," she added.

"I love you, too, kiddo."

She listened to the sound of his footsteps moving away from the bed and then out of the room. She felt sad, but at the same time accepting. Sooner or later, everything changed.

****

Portia March was nearly finished with her breakfast when her son and daughter-in-law arrived to take her to church. Or so she thought. Instead of apologizing for their early arrival, they informed her of her granddaughter's kidnapping. Her first comment was that they skip church and go see her. That's when she learned Julie had barred her parents from her hospital room. After that, she was so furious she could hardly think.

Grayson knew his mother was angry. He knew when her nostrils flared and her chin came up there would be hell to pay, and he was right. The tone of her voice was as cold as the look in her eyes.

"What do you mean, you are not permitted?"

Grayson tried to pass it off as something of no concern. "She got upset with us last night. She's under serious stress, as you can imagine, and we didn't handle it well."

Portia slapped her hands on the table so hard the crystal juice glasses rattled in place. She glared first at Grayson, then at Lana.

"Under stress? She was almost murdered! You are a fool for not recognizing the traumatic circumstances. God gave you one perfect child with a beautiful heart, so whatever has happened has to be your fault, not hers."

Lana frowned. She was just afraid enough of her mother-in-law not to talk back, but she didn't like the scolding.

"Well, Mother March, you weren't there and we were," she said primly.

Portia ignored her, mostly because she hated being called Mother March. It was a ridiculous title from a prissy-ass female who still acted as if she was in her debutante days, and she focused her attention on her son.

"Grayson, what did you do to cause this mess?"

He met her gaze without wavering. "I did everything

wrong and I'm the first to admit it, okay? Chalk it up to panic over finding out Juliette had been kidnapped, and my disapproval of her boyfriend's family."

Lana interjected. "I understand Grayson's disapproval of the boy. I mean, he's a Poe, and we all know what kind of a man his father is."

Portia arched an eyebrow. "A man kidnapped her. You don't like her boyfriend's family. I fail to see what one has to do with the other. And while you're discussing lineage, you both might be interested to know that's exactly what my mother said about Johnson March when we began to keep company. There hadn't been an honest generation in the March family before him, so none of you should be pointing fingers. The silver spoon Johnson was born with was probably a fake, and the only reason our family has finally garnered respect is because the people who knew the truth are all dead and long since gone."

"I said as much to Lana last night," Grayson said.

Portia frowned. "Then if you are that cognizant of your humble beginnings, how do you justify judging someone else by the accident of their birth?"

"I already said I made a mistake. I already told her I was sorry," Grayson snapped.

His mother glared. "Then what got you banned from her room?"

Grayson pointed at his wife. "Lana began talking about plastic surgery and needing to fix Julie's face."

Lana rolled her eyes. "And Grayson told her it didn't matter what had happened to her, and that we'd put it all behind us."

Portia had heard enough. "Oh dear God! Imbeciles! Both of you! Neither of you acknowledged what she endured, then add insult to injury by trying to whitewash it? No wonder she was upset. Grayson, you will take me to the hospital after church. I want to see my girl."

"But I told you, I'm not allowed in."

"That does not pertain to me," Portia said. "You can stand out in the hall for all I care until I'm ready to leave. Is that understood?"

"Yes, ma'am. Oh, and Mother..."

"Yes?"

"Happy birthday."

She rolled her eyes. "Unbelievable."

There wasn't anything happy about this day.

****

Julie began to feel jittery, even panicked, as the morning wore on. Being unable to see left her as helpless as she'd felt tied to Chub Walton's bed. When she learned the stiff clumps in her hair were dried blood, she'd had a small meltdown. A nurse solved the problem by helping her wash her hair, and Julie cried all the way through the process.

"Am I hurting you, honey?" the nurse asked.

"No, no, I'm sorry. I don't know why I'm crying. Don't stop. I appreciate this so much."

"You're very welcome, but if it does hurt, just say so."

"I will," Julie said, trying to gather her senses, but the symbolism of washing away the blood was too strong.

The first physical trace of her assault was going down a hospital drain. If only the rest of the trauma would be that easy to dispel. Once they had finished, the nurse towel-dried and combed her hair, then went to look for a hair dryer.

Julie ran her fingers lightly along the curve of her chin and then down her neck, tracing the length and shape of the welts left by the lashes. There were similar ones all over the front of her body and between her thighs. It hurt to walk. It hurt to breathe. But she was alive and grateful.

A few moments later, the nurse came back.

"Sorry, honey. I couldn't find a hair dryer. There had been one in our break room but it's not there now, so whoever it belonged to probably took it home."

"I don't care," Julie said. "I'm just thankful it's clean."

"Here's the comb. Maybe if you keep fluffing and combing, it'll dry quicker."

She handed the comb to Julie then raised the head of her bed a bit more for easier access to her hair.

"Do you need anything else?"

"No, thank you," Julie said.

Her hands were shaky, but she kept running the comb through her hair and fluffing it until her hair was almost dry. Emotionally and physically exhausted, she drifted off to sleep with the comb still in her hand.

****

Brendan came off the elevator carrying a sack with two vanilla milk shakes. When he saw the food trays in the halls and realized they were already serving lunch, he hoped he wasn't too late. Julie had already mentioned having a difficult time eating, so he went faster, anxious to get to her room.

The door was ajar. When he pushed it inward, it made a slight squeak, and as it did, he saw her turn her head toward the sound.

"It's me, baby."

She reached out without speaking, her hands trembling.

He hurried to her, then took her hand, put it on his cheek so she would know what he was doing, and leaned down to kiss her forehead. As he did, he smelled the shampoo.

Julie's panic subsided as soon as the scent of toothpaste and the warmth of Brendan's breath moved across her face, then his fingers were in her hair. She leaned against his caress and focused on the gentleness in his voice.

"Hey, honey, you washed your hair! I love it when you wear it down. It looks like sunshine and I'll bet it feels even better."

She took a deep shaky breath, trying to calm the level of increasing panic and made herself smile. "You have no idea. Come sit and talk to me. It's horrible not being able to see."

"It won't be for long," Brendan said. "Are you hungry? I saw food trays in the hall."

She wrinkled her nose and then tapped her finger against her bruised and swollen lips.

"The thought of food is not exciting, mostly because I don't want to chew."

"You want to try that vanilla shake? I brought one for you and one for me."

"Yes, I'll try. That sounds so good."

He put straws in the lids, handed her the cup, put the straw in her mouth, and then he watched to see if she could manage. Sucking the thick shake was more difficult that pulling water through the straw, and she had to quit.

She moaned. "I can't."

"Does it hurt?" he asked.

She nodded; too emotional to speak.

"Then I'll feed you," he said.

She waited, listening as paper rattled and a lid popped off the cup.

"Brendan?"

"Yeah?"

"Am I ugly?"

He frowned. "Hell no. What made you ask something like that?"

"Almost the first thing Mama said was that they'd hire a plastic surgeon to fix my face." Her hands began to tremble again as she reached toward her cheeks.

Anger hit him so fast he didn't temper his words. "What the fuck is wrong with her? Has she always been like that?"

"Like what?"

"Mean."

Julie froze. She'd never thought about the slight digs she'd heard all her life as being mean. That had just been Mama's way.

"I never thought of it that way."

"Well, it strikes me that way, and when it comes to you, I won't have anybody hurting you or your feelings. I don't care if it is your mama's way. So that explains why she's on your no-visit list. Why are you upset with your dad?"

"His comments leaned toward needing to whitewash the abduction so he doesn't have to face the unsavory facts. He wouldn't acknowledge what happened beyond saying it was over and we could all just forget about it."

When she suddenly crossed her arms over her breasts in a protective gesture, he suspected she was remembering the attack. What she'd gone through—what she was still going through was unimaginable.

"I'm sorry, Julie. I'm sorry they hurt you, but they're your parents. You know they love you, even if they got off on the wrong foot here. Maybe we could just chalk it up to the horrific shock of what happened to their child, and not knowing what the hell to say or do."

Julie sighed. "I don't know why you fell in love with me, but I am forever grateful that you did. I feel like the luckiest woman in the world."

"Ditto, darlin', now open wide. This shake is melting in my hot hands."

Julie did as he asked, and when the cold, sweet ice cream hit her tongue, she gave him a thumbs-up.

Moments later, one of the nursing staff came in with a tray. Brendan pointed to Julie's mouth and then waved it away. The nurse nodded and backed out of the room.

Chapter Eleven

Portia March wasn't in the mood for conversation as she and her son rode the elevator up to Juliette's room. She made it through the Sunday sermon without hearing a word, although she privately thought if the current pastor was more inspiring, it would have been easier to pay attention.

But the lackluster pastor was the least of her concerns. The truth was that she was scared, as scared as the day when they had come to tell her that her beloved Johnson was dead.

Juliette wasn't dead, but it was the unknown that was so frightening. What if Lana's comments had been warranted? What if her granddaughter was so disfigured that she would never be the same? It wouldn't matter to Portia, but it would to Juliette, and that's what hurt her.

She was still lost in thought when the elevator suddenly dinged, signaling they had reached their destination. She gripped the handle of her walking cane a little tighter as the doors opened, then allowed Grayson to take her elbow as they exited.

Grayson was anxious. His mother's color was too pale. He knew she was upset, and he willingly took his share of the blame. He loved all the women in his family and needed to straighten this mess out, no matter what it took.

"It's this room, Mother," Grayson said, as he paused outside 322.

Portia smoothed a hand down the front of her favorite summer dress, a pale lilac chiffon, and lifted her chin.

"I'm ready."

He pushed the door inward. The last thing he expected was to see Brendan Poe sitting on the side of his daughter's bed, patiently feeding her ice cream. Juliette's appearance was so horrifying—so shocking—and yet Poe's expression was one of love and devotion.

He felt shame he'd hadn't reacted that way for Juliette and envy that he'd never had that with Lana. She'd been chosen as a suitable match, but it was not a marriage of undying love. With Brendan and Julie, that was obviously not the case.

As a father, it should've eased his heart to know a man loved his daughter with that much passion. But, as her father, it scared him to death that the man was Brendan Poe. No matter how good Brendan might be, his father was just as evil.

****

Portia's first look at her granddaughter was one of horror. It sent her heartbeat into a flutter, imaging what Juliette had suffered, but then focus shifted as she gave thanks that she had survived. Today was Portia's birthday, and Juliette's rescue was the best present ever. She touched a hand lightly to her heart then stepped into the room, letting the door swing shut behind her.

Brendan heard the taping sound of a walking cane, turned to look, then stood abruptly. They'd never met, but in New Orleans, Portia March's face was just as familiar as her son, Grayson's.

"Julie, honey, your grandmother is here."

Julie wiped a drip of ice cream from the corner of her mouth. "Nonny?"

"Yes, darling, I'm here and I assume this very handsome man feeding you ice cream is your Brendan."

"Yes, Nonny, this is my Brendan. Brendan, this is my grandmother, Portia March."

Brendan set the milkshake aside and quickly shook her hand. "Mrs. March, it is a pleasure to meet you. Julie speaks of you with so much love."

Portia beamed as she patted Julie's hand. "And the love is returned."

"Happy birthday, Nonny," Julie said, and then all of a sudden her chin was trembling, remembering the reality of her situation. "Your present is at my apartment and now I'm going to miss your party."

"Nonsense! We are not having a party," Portia said. "I don't intend to celebrate until you're there to help me blow out the candles, just as you always do."

Julie stifled a sob as she clutched at her grandmother's hand. "Look at me, Nonny. I'm so ugly. I can feel all the marks. I know what he did to me."

Portia fought back tears, but this was no time to cry. She'd come for Juliette, to tell her what her parents should've said last night—what she needed to hear.

"I see you, but you are *not* ugly. You have been wounded, and you have been wronged. My heart is sick for what you went through, but I'm so proud of you, too. It is clear you have survived something horrific. Your body will heal long before your mind lets it go. You won't forget. Ever. But the day will come when it won't be *all* you think about, and when that happens, it will be the first day of the rest of your life."

Julie burst into sobs as Portia took her in her arms.

"Ah, cher... you *should* weep for what happened. Weep for the innocence that is lost. Weep for the pain that devil has caused. Your life will never be the same, but you have this beautiful man beside you. He will help you find your way."

Brendan was in tears. This was exactly what Julie had needed from her family—permission to grieve. He cupped the back of her head as she sobbed on her grandmother's shoulder.

"She's right, Juliette. I'm in awe of your strength. I'll always be beside you, but I need you far more than you'll ever need me."

With those few quiet words, Brendan Poe permanently sealed his place in Portia's heart.

****

Grayson heard his daughter crying, and then the soft murmur of his mother's voice, and that's when he got it. He'd been so elated when they'd found her alive that he'd expected her to feel the same elation. They had not acknowledged the true horror of what she'd suffered because they wanted the ugliness of what happened to go away. Even worse, they had not cried with her in her pain. In their own shock and awkwardness, they must have led her to believe they were ashamed. He knew she didn't want to see him, but now that he understood why, he couldn't spend another night with this awful thing between them. Despite the fact that he'd been banned, he entered the room.

Brendan's head came up like a wolf scenting prey.

Grayson held up his hand in a gesture of peace.

"Juliette, it's Dad. May I please talk to you?"

Julie felt the tension in Brendan's hand. All she had to do was say no and he would see that her father left. But she didn't like being on the outs with her family.

"I guess," she said softly, then took the tissue Portia handed her and blew her nose.

Grayson glanced at Brendan.

Brendan stared back. "If you're waiting for me to leave, don't waste your time because I'm not going anywhere. Say your piece, but you, by God, better not make her cry again."

"I don't want him to leave," Julie added.

Grayson didn't like being challenged, but accepted that he had Julie's best interests at heart.

"Julie, honey, I just wanted to tell you how sorry I am. Your mother and I handled everything badly. All I can say on our behalf is that we were in shock."

"Yes, well... so was I," Julie said. "I was the victim of an act of random violence and you both made me feel like I needed fixing before you could parade me out in public again. What happened to me had nothing to do with your elite status in the community, or for that matter, with Brendan's family. You don't just owe me an apology. You owe him one, as well."

"You're right, sweetheart. Please forgive us for hurting you. It was unintentional because you are our world."

Julie heard, but didn't completely believe him. Still, she wanted this ugliness behind them. "You're forgiven."

"Thank you," Grayson said and lifted her hand to his lips, but he could tell by the look on Brendan's face, he wasn't going to be as amenable, even though he owed it to him to try.

"Brendan, I used my disapproval of your father's lifestyle as a measure of the man you are, and I was vastly mistaken. I said harsh things to you and I'm sorry."

"So be it," Brendan said abruptly.

"Thank you," he said. "I'd also like to put all of this ugly business behind us and want you to know that when I rebuild, your job will be—"

"No."

Grayson flinched. When the cold glitter in Brendan's eyes suddenly reminded him of Anson, he knew that was that.

Julie suddenly lunged forward, grabbing the guardrail with one hand as she reached toward Brendan with the other.

He took her hand, surprised by how her muscles were trembling.

"What do you need, baby?"

"I need... I need... uh, Brendan, what time is it?"

Grayson glanced at his watch. "It's a quarter to—"

Brendan couldn't help frowning. She seemed distracted, like she'd lost focus in where she was. "Are you in pain?" he asked and was surprised when he felt her muscles jerking beneath his grip.

"Yes, pain. I hurt. I hurt, don't I? Why do I hurt?"

Grayson felt like a fifth wheel. Brendan knew what she'd meant by that question and he had not, more proof that he was out of step with the woman his daughter had become.

"I'll ring for the nurse," Brendan said as he helped her lie down.

Portia waited until Julie settled and then straightened her covers.

"We have talked enough, Juliette. It's time we leave so that you will sleep."

Julie wouldn't argue. The drama had, once again, worn her out.

"Nonny, I'm so glad you came."

"Of course I came. I'll be back off and on until you come home, too."

Brendan reached across the bed. "It was a pleasure to meet you, Mrs. March."

Portia shook his hand. "It was a pleasure to meet you,

too. God bless you, young man. We owe you the world for helping bring Julie home."

Grayson touched Julie's shoulder so she'd know where he was. "Rest well, honey. I'll bring Mother by later this evening and—"

Julie frowned. "Only if she doesn't talk about what I look like."

The request was a brutal reminder of how much they had hurt her feelings.

"I promise. And again, I am so sorry, sweetheart. Truly sorry."

He glanced at Brendan without getting a reaction, then escorted his mother out of the room just as the nurse came in with Julie's pain meds.

Brendan's milk shake was half-melted and Julie's was half-gone. He took a big drink from his as the nurse put the medicine into Julie's IV.

"Julie, is there anything else you need?" she asked.

Julie shook her head.

Brendan smoothed wisps of hair away from her forehead, careful not to touch the raw flesh as the nurse left.

"Are you okay, baby?"

"I hurt. I'm sorry. I think I keep saying that."

"Don't apologize. Always speak your truth."

"Will you stay with me a while?"

"Yes. I'll stay with you forever."

"I love you, Bren."

"Thank you, sweetheart. I love you, too."

"You're still mad at Dad, aren't you?"

"Yes."

She sighed again. "So am I. Maybe that bad feeling I have will heal when I do."

"Maybe so."

A few moments passed and he thought she was falling asleep.

"Bren?"

"Yeah?"

"Will you find Count LeGrande and tell him I said thank you?"

Brendan smiled. "That's already on my to-do list, but I will be sure that he knows you sent a special message."

She was holding his hand, but her fingers were beginning to lose their grip. When her breathing slowed, he knew she was out.

****

Delle and her sons were finishing off the last of their Po-boy sandwiches, while Linny, who'd quit hers some time ago, was coloring the paper place mat with the crayons provided at each table. Delle smiled absently as she watched the intense concentration on her little girl's face. Belinda was growing up so fast, a reminder of how swiftly time was passing. Because it was rare for them to have such a light-hearted meal together, she hated to break the mood, but her feet were beginning to throb, and staying much longer was not going to be an option.

Sam leaned over his little sister's shoulder to see what she was doing and was surprised by the scene she was producing with only four crayons. Not only was she coloring with a smooth, perfect stroke, but she was putting in shading and highlights.

"Hey, Linny, that's really good."

Delle smiled. "Amazing, isn't she? I wanted to get her in a summer art program, but your daddy said no."

Sam frowned. "Why not? He's got the money."

Delle shrugged. "Because I would've been leaving

Wisteria Hill every day to take her into town, and he didn't want to be inconvenienced."

Chance stifled a curse and looked away. He and Sam were just as guilty as their father. They'd been so used to Anson calling all the shots that they had looked away when he abused the power.

"Next summer for sure, okay, Belinda? And if Dad says no, I'll take you back and forth myself," he said.

Delle's eyes widened in surprise. "Why, Chance! That is the sweetest thing." She laid her hand on the top of Belinda's head. It was warm from the sunlight coming through the window, and there were bits of it coming down from the ponytail she'd put it in hours earlier. "Would you like that, Linny?"

"Ummhumm," Linny said.

"Then it's a deal," Chance said and tweaked her ear.

Linny blinked and then looked up to see everyone watching her. "What? Are we ready to get beignets now?"

They laughed, and the sound rolled across the little diner, turning more than one head toward the table with the happy family.

****

Anson paced the kitchen with his cell phone at his ear. He hated to be put on hold. Doing business face-to-face was always in his favor because no one ever made him wait when he turned on the charm. When his call was finally answered, he let them know by the tone of his voice he wasn't happy.

"Mr. Poe, what can I do for you?"

"Don't keep me waiting like this again."

There was a moment of silence that stretched to the point Anson thought the man was going to hang up, but then he finally answered, his voice low and restrained.

"Today is Sunday, a day of rest, and I was at the dinner table with my family when you called. Is there a problem?"

Anson frowned. "You need to know that the painters will be finished tomorrow. I expect you to hang draperies and curtains the next day."

"I already have another client scheduled for Tuesday. I can be there on Wednesday."

"I'm on a tight schedule here. I want this done—"

"I understand," Blakely said. "But I have my reputation to consider and breaking my word on an appointment is not the proper way to conduct business. I'm sure *you* understand."

Anson sighed. "Yes, all right, then Wednesday it is. And don't forget those matching bedspreads."

"Of course not, Mr. Poe. They're at the top of my list."

Anson hung up in the man's ear. No need swapping good-byes when neither one of them liked the other, but the appointment had been set. As soon as this last step in the renovation was finished, he was going after his wife and daughter.

When the grandfather clock in the hall began chiming, he decided to drive into New Orleans to get something to eat and began gathering up his keys and turning off the lights.

Lisette's good food crossed his mind, and he wondered if the one-eyed bitch and her upstairs whores had set up shop anywhere else. Damn shame about Frenchie's burning down or he might have been inclined to stop in for some of Chef Jean Luc's blackened sea bass, and a big side of red beans and rice.

Amused by his own humor, he was smiling as he got into the truck. But the smile disappeared when he caught a glimpse of himself in the rearview mirror. Sunlight was brutal, to both the ravages time and the hard living etched on his face. He wasn't as pretty as he used to be, but what the hell. He was on top and in charge, and the rest of it no longer mattered.

As he pulled out of his driveway, he caught the flash of sunlight on a windshield up in the trees across the road. So, March's men were still tailing him, which reminded him he should thank the sorry bastard next time they crossed paths. Their presence had been most beneficial in keeping his ass out of jail.

****

It was late afternoon. Julie had been awake and asleep a half-dozen times since her family's visit, and each time she woke, it was from reliving the nightmare of her attack. Every time she came to, gasping and crying, Brendan was reaching out and calming her fears. But this time when she woke, she woke up screaming.

He was so shaken by the terror in her voice that his heart was still pounding, even as a nurse came running.

"What's wrong? What happened?" she asked.

"She's dreaming again," Brendan said as Julie kept grabbing at his hand and sobbing.

The nurse put her hand on Julie's shoulder to let her know she was there.

"Good afternoon, Julie! I'm Kay. I'll be your nurse this evening." The nurse began checking Julie's IV and asking her questions.

Her voice was shaking as she tried to answer, but she couldn't focus for trying to get the bandages off her eyes.

"Take them off. Please take them off. I can't see him coming."

Brendan had been trying to stay out of the way, but when her comments began to sound confused, he couldn't stay quiet any longer. He moved to the side of her bed and took her hand.

"He's in jail, Julie. I promise you, he's in jail," Brendan said.

"No. He's in my head. I can't get him out. Take the bandages off my eyes."

"Can they come off?" Brendan asked.

Nurse Kay checked her watch. "Doctor is making rounds right now. I'll ask. In the meantime, do you need something for pain, Juliette?"

"I don't want to go back to sleep. That's when he comes, when I'm not looking."

Brendan frowned. She *was* talking out of her head. Nothing she said made sense, which was new. Maybe the bandages were causing some kind of paranoia. Before, Walton had tied her up so she couldn't move, so maybe she felt helpless all over again by not being able to see. When she kept pulling at the bandages and flailing her arms as if she needed to fight off something coming at her, it hit him.

"Is she taking any new meds?" Brendan asked.

Kay checked the records.

"No."

Julie kept picking at the bandages. "Brendan, I can't see. Am I blind? What's happening? Where is he? Where is the troll?"

"He's in jail, honey. You have bandages on your eyes. That's all it is... just bandages. Leave them alone, okay?"

She finally let go of the bandages, but he could tell her cognizance was impaired. She kept running her hands all over her body, marking the lashes she'd suffered by tracing them with her fingers, which amped Brendan's concern.

"She hasn't been acting like this. I think she's having a bad reaction to something."

Miranda headed for the door. "I'll find Doctor Ames."

Brendan was torn. Now was one of those times when she needed her family with her. He had no idea if this had ever happened before from a medication. He had no power to make a decision for her, and she was obviously in no position to be making them for herself. He was on the verge of calling her father when a doctor came in, followed by his nurse.

He eyed Brendan curiously as he introduced himself.

"I'm Doctor Ames. I was told she's behaving strangely. What's going on?"

Brendan began to explain. "I'm not sure why, but she's begun hallucinating, or suffering some kind of paranoia. You do know what happened to her, right?"

Ames frowned. "Yes. I'm aware of her abduction and the condition she was in when they brought her into ER. I spoke to Doctor George at length about it, but she had just been given a sedative when I examined her eyes this morning."

"And I left here a little before 4:30 this morning, right after her parents arrived. Your staff had just given her pain meds, but to my knowledge, no sedation. Then I was back here around noon. I didn't notice anything at first, but as the hours passed, her confusion has worsened."

As if on cue, Julie kicked at the sheets over her legs as if she was kicking at her abductor.

"Don't touch me! No! No! No!" she screamed, then reached for the bandages on her eyes again.

Brendan grabbed her hands.

"No, honey... easy! You're in the hospital. The bad guy is gone."

"No, he's here. I can tell. I can hear him breathing. I need to see. Take these bandages off my eyes. I need to see."

The doctor frowned. "What are the pain meds that she's on? That would have been prescribed and given to her down in ER

The nurse checked her records again.

"We have her on Demerol, Doctor, with no notation of allergies."

Ames glanced at Brendan.

"Can you confirm the 'no allergy' info with any of her family?"

"Yes, sir. Give me a couple of minutes," he said and stepped out into the hall, calling her father as he went.

He knew the call was going to scare Grayson and he was right. When Grayson answered on the second ring, his voice was shaking.

"Brendan?"

"Yes, it's me. The doctor needs to know if Julie is allergic to anything."

"What's wrong?"

"She seems to be having some kind of hallucinations, or suffering from a kind of paranoia. They have her on Demerol for pain. Is she allergic?"

"Not that I know of, but then she's never had to take anything like that before."

"I'll tell him. And I think you should come. I won't be able to stay much longer, and she shouldn't be alone."

"We'll be right there."

Brendan went back into the room.

"Her father said she's not allergic to anything they know of, but she's never had a reason to take this pain medicine before."

Ames nodded. "I think that may be what's causing this reaction. It's not a common occurrence, but some people do experience psychological problems when taking strong pain killers. I'm switching her pain meds to Tramadol. It's not as strong and hopefully this behavior will subside."

"In the meantime, is there anything you can give her to counteract this?"

Ames frowned. "I don't like adding fuel to the fire by mixing pain meds. She's already on an emotional roller coaster. It'll be out of her system soon enough. First, I want to see is how her eyes are progressing. She could see some light this morning. If we can get her some visual acuity, some of the paranoia might subside."

Brendan moved back to Julie's bedside so she'd know that he was there.

When Ames began removing her bandages she jerked then cried out.

"What's happening?"

Ames spoke quickly. "I'm removing your bandages. Just sit still for me, okay?"

Brendan put a hand on her shoulder. "I'm right here, Julie." She grabbed his hand, gripping his fingers so tightly they began to go numb. "Your dad is on the way."

The tone of her voice was barely an octave below a shriek. "I can't see. Am I blind?"

He squeezed her hand. "Doctor Ames is removing the bandages from your eyes right now, remember? You tell me if you can see when they're gone, okay?"

She choked on a sob. "Okay."

At that moment, Brendan hated Chub Walton about as much as he'd ever hated anyone in his life, even more than Anson Poe.

Doctor Ames took the last of the bandages away, then carefully wiped each eye clean.

"Okay, Miss March. Will you open your eyes for me, please?"

Her eyelids fluttered as she blinked several times in rapid succession. She began breathing rapidly, but Brendan couldn't tell if it was from excitement or fear. And then her lips parted, as if in surprise.

"How do your eyes feel?" Ames asked.

"They burn a little... and they feel weird."

"They're still swollen," Ames said.

Julie's voice began to shake.

"I'm in a hospital room. I thought I was still there with him." She looked up. "Brendan!"

He smiled. "Yes, baby, it's me."

"Doctor Ames?"

The short grey-haired doctor smiled. "In the flesh."

"I can see. I'm not blind." She put her hands over her face and started to weep. "I was so afraid I'd be blind." Then all of a sudden, she saw her arms and the panic on her face.

Ah shit. "You will heal, Juliette."

"Oh my God, oh my God," Julie shrieked and ripped the sheet off her legs.

When she saw the damaged flesh and the blood pooled beneath her skin, despair pulled her under. She had wanted to see so badly, and now wished it had never happened.

"Why didn't I die? Why didn't I die?"

"Julie, don't," Brendan said, but she shoved his hand away and tried to pull the IV out of her arm.

He grabbed her hand to stop her, and when he did, she hit his lower lip. He tasted blood and then had to grab both her wrists to keep her from tearing off her hospital gown. He was still trying to reason with her when Ames sent a nurse after meds to sedate her.

Julie kept sobbing and talking in a high-pitched manic

voice. "I'm ugly. I'm ruined. This is disgusting. I don't know how you can stand to look at me."

Brendan scooped her up into his arms, holding her close against his chest.

"I love you, Julie. I love you. I love you. Nothing will ever change that. You'll get well. We'll get through this together."

"I look ugly. I am ugly. Just like my mother said."

"You're not ugly. You're wounded. You'll heal," Brendan said and held her tighter, knowing he could be hurting her, but hurting her far less than she had tried to hurt herself.

Ames quickly added to Brendan's assurances. "He's right, Miss March. You will heal. The terrible thing is that you were brutally beaten. The positive aspect to it is that the man who did it was very skilled in causing pain without breaking the skin. The welts will heal. The blood beneath the skin surface is like a bruise. It will dissipate," Ames said. "It will take time, but I think you will heal without visible scars."

Julie kept moaning and weeping, and while Brendan was trying to console her, her eyes suddenly rolled back in her head and she went limp.

"What just happened?" Brendan asked, as he quickly laid her back down in the bed.

"That's part of the drug paranoia," Ames said. "Once the Demerol is out of her system, I predict this reaction will lessen considerably."

Brendan was helpless to fix her and sickened by the emotional shock she was suffering.

The nurse came back, injected the meds into Julie's IV, and then straightened her covers.

"We may need to restrain her," Ames said.

Brendan turned on the doctor with a look of shock that quickly morphed into fury.

"Hell no, you don't tie her down! That bastard tied her spread-eagle to a bed and nearly beat her to death. You do not fucking restrain her, do you understand?"

Ames paled. "Yes, I didn't think. But we can't have her hurting herself."

"Then keep her knocked out until that shit is out of her system, because you cannot tie her down."

And that's what Grayson and Lana March heard as they entered the room. They saw the blood on Brendan's lip and the hand he kept firmly on Julie's shoulder as if he was afraid she'd fly off the bed.

"What's happening here?" Grayson shouted as he strode into the room.

Ames introduced himself, then began to explain.

"She's suffering some psychological issues which are a side-effect of the Demerol she's been given. We've changed her meds, but until that's out of her system, she may still experience some delusions."

"He took the bandages off her eyes and she saw what Walton did to her," Brendan snapped. "Don't leave her alone. She tried to hurt herself."

Lana saw the cut and the blood on Brendan's lip.

"Did she do that?"

"She's out of her head. I just got in the way," he said.

Lana was upset. "What do we do, Grayson? Do you think we need to get some private nursing?"

Brendan stared. He didn't understand people like this and didn't care if he was overstepping his bounds. He turned on her like he had on the doctor.

"No, you do not hire a stranger to do your job. She needs family. If she gets upset again, one of you pick her the hell up and put her in your lap. Rock her like you rocked her when she was a baby. And if you can't do that, someone call me because I damn sure will."

He couldn't handle their lack of compassion any longer. Julie was unconscious, his mother and sister were waiting for him back home, and these people were clueless.

He felt like he'd just abandoned a baby to wolves as he walked out of the room.

Chapter Twelve

Brendan pulled into the parking lot and killed the engine, then sat staring blankly at the apartment building, wishing there was a way to change the last twenty-four hours of his life. He had been given a painful lesson in how fast it could go from near-perfect to nearly over. He didn't know what kind of a future he and Julie had left, of if they even had one. She was so hurt, and so messed up in her head she might never want a normal relationship with a man again. And the moment he thought it, he felt guilty. All that really mattered was for her body to heal and pray her spirit healed along with it. He was sick at heart and afraid of tomorrow, yet he made himself get out of the car, bracing himself for a barrage of questions.

The air was thick, almost too heavy to breathe. As he strode toward the entrance, he caught a faint scent of smoke from the fire that had burned through the Quarter, and an even stronger scent of charcoal. Someone was grilling nearby. It seemed like a lifetime since he'd considered something as ordinary as firing up his grill.

The old tomcat that haunted the Dumpsters behind the apartment was lying beneath the shrubs near the front door, licking a paw. The cat looked up at Brendan, hissed to show his displeasure at being disturbed, and slunk farther away into the bushes.

"Yeah, I know just how you feel," he said as he entered the building and took the elevator to the second floor.

As he neared the apartment, he could hear his little sister's laughter and guessed they must've had a good day. It was a happy sound. He hadn't heard her laugh like that since before Delle was burned.

He took a deep breath, bracing himself to face the family and was about to put the key in the door when it suddenly swung inward.

"You're home!" Linny crowed and threw herself into his arms. "We ate at the Crab Shack and brought food home for supper, and Sam bought beignets."

Sam sat at the end of the sofa, grinning. There was a deck of cards spread out on the coffee table. It appeared all the laughter had been because of the ongoing game of War.

Brendan tugged her ponytail. "How did you know I was out there? Are you psychic or something?"

She shrugged. "I just know stuff."

He let the comment slide. "Did you save me any beignets?"

"Yes. We have lots. Enough for breakfast even."

He glanced over at his brother. "So who's winning the card game?"

"She is," Sam said. "She cheats, but she's winning."

"I play like Daddy taught me," Linny said.

Sam's smile disappeared and Brendan frowned.

"And considering your daddy's negative attitude, do you think that is the smartest thing to do?" Brendan asked.

Linny looked up. "Did I do something bad?"

"Do you know how to play without cheating?" Brendan asked.

She nodded.

"They don't cheat again and it will be okay."

"All right," she said and began gathering up the cards to put away.

"Is Chance with Mama?" Brendan asked.

Sam nodded.

"I'll go tell him I'm back. You guys are probably more than ready to leave, but I really appreciate you helping out today."

"Yeah sure," Sam said. "Hey, I didn't even ask, how's Julie?"

Brendan couldn't speak the words. Instead, he shrugged. "She had a rough day."

Sam frowned. "I'm sorry. Look, anytime you need us, just call. Chance and I have copped-out on you long enough. We have just as much responsibility here as you do, okay?"

"Yeah, and thanks. Just give me a sec," he said and went down the hall. He interrupted their conversation as he walked into the bedroom where his mother and brother were visiting.

"Hey, you're back," Chance said.

"How is Julie?" Delle asked.

He was sticking with the same story for all concerned. "She had a bad day."

Delle started to say more and then stopped. There was a look on her youngest son's face she didn't like.

"I'm sorry to hear that."

Brendan nodded.

The brothers left soon afterward, and as soon as they were gone, Delle sent Linny to take a bath. She knew there was more to the story than Brendan was telling, and when she heard him banging cupboard doors in the kitchen, she got up.

Brendan saw her come in and stopped to pull out a chair out at the table. She sat gratefully.

"How are your feet, Mama? Was it hard on you to be up so long?"

"They're okay. I took another pain pill when I came home. I hate to keep taking them, but nothing else helps once they get bad."

"Did you all have a good day?" he asked.

She smiled. "We had a wonderful day. I can't remember when I've enjoyed myself so much."

He smiled. Her joy was lifting his dark mood.

"That's great. You both needed a day out. After living in a place the size of Wisteria Hill and then coming to an apartment in the middle of the city, you were probably feeling a bit caged."

"This place has been a godsend to both of us," Delle said. "Now sit down and tell me the rest of what's wrong."

"Want a beer?" he asked.

She smiled. "I don't mind if I do."

He got two longnecks out of the refrigerator, popped the tops, and handed her one. The first drink was cold and yeasty as it slid down his throat.

"That hit the spot," he said softly.

Delle took a sip of hers, then set it aside and waited.

Brendan kept staring at the ring of condensation left behind on the table and then set the bottle down, cupped it between his hands and looked up.

"She can see."

"Praise the Lord," Delle said.

He shook his head. "She saw what he'd done to her body and pretty much lost it."

"Oh Jesus, I didn't think..."

He kept talking. "She had a bad reaction to the pain meds. Caused hallucinations, paranoia and a whole host of things better left unsaid."

Delle hands curled into fists. "That will pass, right son?"

"They think so."

"What about her parents?"

A muscle jerked at the side of his mouth. "They're oblivious. Her mother started talking plastic surgery, and her father told her to forget what happened and put it behind her. It took a visit from her grandmother to set things right, but by that time, she was having trouble with the medicine. She's gone through so much and it's far from over."

Delle shook her head in disgust. "All that blue blood and money and that's the best they can do? I suddenly don't feel so guilty about the life I gave my children."

He frowned. "You gave us a great life, Mama. You loved us. You always had our back. Those are the things that matter most to a kid, okay?"

She shrugged. "Are you hungry?"

He thought about the milkshake he had abandoned hours ago. "I could eat."

"We brought home barbeque ribs and baked beans for supper. Heat them up now if you're hungry."

"Sounds good," he said and got up.

By the time Linny appeared, Brendan had finished eating and was making coffee. She sniffed the air.

"You ate barbeque."

He turned to acknowledge the slight accusation and instead, had a moment of pure clarity. The childish innocence of her face was already changing into true beauty. She was going to be a stunner when she was grown, but it hadn't happened yet. The long end of her ponytail was wet from her bath, and her clean T-shirt and gym shorts were sticking to her body, which meant she'd only half dried. He remembered doing the same thing at that age, always in a hurry.

"I did eat barbeque. I was hungry and I thank you for bringing it home."

"You're welcome," she said and slid under her mother's outstretched arm.

Delle nuzzled her nose under her little girl's ear.

"You smell good."

Linny beamed. "I used Bren's bubble bath."

Brendan started to tell her it was actually Julie's bubble bath, but then that would elicit an entire conversation about why Julie might be taking a bath in his apartment when hers was right down the hall, which wouldn't be a good idea.

Delle was still working on the beer when Brendan sat down with his coffee and the sack of leftover beignets.

Linny saw the sack and abandoned her mother's embrace as she slipped around the table to where Brendan was sitting.

"I suppose you want one of these, too," he said.

"Can I Mama?" she asked.

"May I, not can I," Delle corrected. "And yes, you may."

Linny happily bit into one of the sweet pastries, which sent a shower of sugar onto her bare legs and Brendan's knee.

Delle frowned. "Oh, Linny, you're getting sugar all over yourself and Bren."

"I don't mind," Brendan said, taking comfort in the feel of her warm little body leaning against him. She looked up with powdered sugar on her upper lip and joy in her eyes.

"I sure do love you, Brendan."

A lump rose in his throat. "I love you, too, baby."

She took another bite, talking with her mouth full. "We're going back home soon. You'll have to come see my new room."

He saw the truth in his mother's eyes and felt sick.

"So when did you decide this?"

She shrugged. "I always knew I would. I guess hearing Sam and Chance talking about what your Daddy was doing to the place reinforced my decision."

He was trying to quell a surge of panic. He had no way of protecting them once they were out of his sight, but at the same time, his mother was a grown woman. She had to live her life the way she saw fit, and it was his job to accept her decisions.

"Chance said Daddy painted my room pink. I like pink," Linny said, licking sugar off her fingers.

Brendan handed her a paper napkin. "I know you do. Queen Belinda is the queen of pink."

"When do I have to go back to the doctor again?" Delle asked.

"Wednesday."

"My feet are getting better."

Brendan knew she was saying this to reassure him she was ready. "I know, Mama."

She frowned, then reached across the table and patted his hand. "It will be all right."

He heard the words, but nothing about it felt right. Later, after everyone had gone to sleep, he got his laptop out and powered it up. He hadn't used it since he had gotten it back from the repair shop and decided to scan the job sites to see what was available in the area. He was confident he could get work, but without any marketable skills, he couldn't be picky. It occurred to him as he read through the listings, that he could go back to school. He had a couple of years of college under his belt. There were all kinds of possibilities, but at his age, he didn't just want a job. He had to think about the future.

****

Lisette Branscum walked out onto the second-floor

balcony of the room she was renting to look down onto the sight below.

Thanks to a customer who had dined regularly in her café, she had a roof over her head until she could figure out what to do next.

The streets were busy, and the air smelled of the bougainvillea blooming only a few feet above her head. There was the sweet smell of pralines made on site at the shop across the street and the faint fishy smell of the riverfront. But it was the smell of burned wood from the fire that had swept through the Quarter that made her shudder.

But for the grace of God, a whole lot of people could have died, including her. She took a deep breath and closed her eyes, letting the sounds of New Orleans wash over her. It was nearing sunset, for which she was grateful. At least it would be cooler when the sun went down.

She'd been leasing the building that burned, and the only insurance she'd had was on restaurant fixtures and personal property, not nearly enough to set up shop somewhere else on the same level. She'd given the high-end hookers her blessing to move on to other places, so she wouldn't be pimping girls anytime soon, either.

A mosquito buzzed about her head, then moved away. For whatever reason, they never bothered her. Something in her blood, her mama used to say. She shifted the patch over her eye to ease the pressure on a sore spot above her eyebrow. Sparks from the fire had blown onto her face and burned her skin before they'd burned out.

A loud crash suddenly echoed within the narrow street, then a loud string of curses. From where she was standing, she could see a homeless person digging through a Dumpster in the alley across the street as well as a man fighting with a woman up on the corner. There was a woman somewhere below her balcony cursing steadily without anyone responding, which left Lisette to assume the woman was either crazy-talking to herself, or giving hell to someone over the phone.

Lisette guessed that, in the grand scheme of things, her situation was no worse and no better than anyone else's, but it felt like it. Her biggest disappointment had come in finding out Anson Poe had an airtight alibi for the night of the fire. After learning it was arson, she'd been certain he was responsible, although she had to admit that the night her world went up in smoke, some woman in the crowd had been kind enough to point a finger in her face, call her a whore, and tell her she was getting what she deserved. If a total stranger could be that vicious, then there was no telling who was to blame.

She wasn't so naïve as to assume she hadn't made enemies in her business, and without anything but gut instinct to blame Anson Poe, she had to accept he would escape legal justice. However, there was another kind of justice she could enact all her own in case it was him. All she needed was to pay a trip to Mama Lou and get the voodoo priestess to cast a spell on Anson Poe that was foolproof from lies.

She'd always wanted to go to France. Maybe she needed to get herself a passport and, when her insurance money came through, plan an extended trip to Paris. She could speak the language, and she'd always heard French men appreciated women with certain sexual skills. If they didn't mind a one-eyed whore, she might just find a way to make herself at home.

****

New Orleans detectives Early and Royal were at a

standstill with the arson investigation. The info from the fire marshal had been useless as to pointing a finger in any one person's direction. They knew the fire started from something like a Molotov cocktail being tossed into Frenchie's basement; a basic firebug move. If there had been witnesses, none of them were coming forward.

When Lisette first mentioned Anson Poe as a possible suspect, Royal had panicked. Being in Poe's pocket was a risky move and having to arrest the man could have gotten tricky. No one was more relieved than Royal after interviewing Grayson March's men. As Poe had promised, they'd screwed the lid so tight on his alibi that it was never coming off, so unless some witness came forward, this was going to wind up a cold case.

They had just added their latest interviews to the report and saved to file on the computer when the lieutenant walked up and tossed an address down on Early's desk.

"They just pulled a body out of the river. There's the address."

Early frowned. "Why are we checking on a floater?"

"Because there's a bullet hole in his head."

Early nodded. "We're on it. Let's go, partner. "

Royal clipped a holstered pistol to his belt and followed his partner's exit. The arson investigation had just moved another notch down on the unsolved list and he was happy to work a case unconnected to his benefactor.

****

Chub Walton was close by. The sour sweat scent of him was in Julie's nose. She could hear the steady *whap, whap* sound of the leather straps against his leg. The keen of his high-pitched moan wasn't one of pain, but excitement. Any moment he would bring the leather straps down across her body instead of his.

Don't. Please don't.

When she heard the catch in his breath, she knew what was coming, and she threw back her head and screamed.

****

It was finally sundown, the end of one long, miserable ass day. Grayson had been watching his daughter sleep for over an hour. After tiring of Lana's running commentary about everything but Julie's situation, he'd sent her to get them some coffee. Lana's lack of emotion about what had happened was bugging him. Either she was shallower than he had believed, or she was in denial.

A few minutes later, Julie's sleep became restless. He got up to check on her. Her fingers were twitching and her eyelids were fluttering. He guessed she was dreaming. As she began to whimper, he leaned over the bed and said her name.

"Juliette. It's Daddy. You're safe."

She quieted.

He ran a finger lightly against her hair and sat back down, only to be caught off guard moments later by the scream. He bolted out of his chair, grabbing her by the shoulders just before she tried to leap out of bed.

"Julie! Open your eyes! You're not there anymore. You're in a hospital. You're safe!"

She responded to her father's command by digging her fingernails into his forearm, as if needing an anchor before she had the guts to look. But he hadn't lied. She *was* in a hospital. She *was* safe. She went limp.

"Dad?"

"Yes, sweetheart, it's me," he said, slowly easing his arm out of her grasp.

She'd drawn blood. He could feel the sting beneath his shirtsleeve as he lowered the bed rail, but he ignored it. He slid onto the mattress beside her and took her in his arms. She leaned against him, weak and exhausted by the emotional upheaval.

"You're okay, honey. I think you were dreaming."

Julie's nurse had heard the scream and came in to check on her patient. "Another dream?" she asked as she moved to the bed.

Grayson nodded.

The nurse eyed her patient's listless behavior and frowned.

"Okay, Julie, I need you lie back. Mr. March, would you please step out into the hall for a bit?"

"I'll be just outside the door, Julie."

As soon as they were alone, Kay pulled back the sheet and raised Julie's gown; checking the wounds on her upper torso.

"How do they feel? Are they still throbbing?"

"Yes, and I'm so hot. Why do I feel hot?" Julie asked.

"You have fever, dear, but the human body is an amazing creation. It's hot because it's fighting infection, and already setting itself into motion for the skin to begin re-growth. It hasn't quite been twenty-four hours since this happened, so the healing will take time."

"Are you going to put some more of that stuff on my skin?"

Kay nodded. "Yes. I know it hurts, but it will accelerate healing, which is what we need, right?"

"I'm not complaining, just bracing myself for the inevitable."

"Good girl. How is your anxiety level? Feeling any panic, or having any waking nightmares?"

"I don't feel panic once I wake up and see where I am, but until I do, it feels like my heart is going to jump out of my chest."

Julie watched the nurse making notes and then glanced toward the window. It was dark. Saturday afternoon she had done laundry, made a casserole, made love to Brendan, and later wrapped her grandmother's birthday present, looking forward to helping her celebrate the event. What a difference a day made.

She touched her fingers to her face, then to her eyelids. She could tell the swelling was going down, but the marks on her body were still the same. When the nurse began to apply the antibiotic onto her skin, she gritted her teeth to get through it.

The nurse was almost finished when the scent of food began to drift into the room.

"Did they already serve dinner?" Julie asked.

She nodded, eyeing Julie's swollen lips.

"We ordered a liquid diet for you. It's on hold."

Julie wrinkled her nose. "Brendan brought me ice cream. It was good. Do you think there will be ice cream?"

"If there's not, I'll get you some," Kay said.

"Thank you," Julie said, then closed her eyes. She hated this hopeless, helpless feeling. She hated that her life was so out of control.

As the nurse walked out, her father walked in.

"Are you okay?"

She combed shaky fingers through her hair, wishing for a band to make a ponytail.

"It was a dream. It's over for now."

"Is there anything I can get for you?"

"See if there's a ponytail band in my things. I want this hair up."

Happy to do something constructive, he opened the mini-closet, only to realize she didn't have any clothes. That's when he remembered they'd brought her in naked, and took a deep breath before shutting the door. He then searched through the drawer by her bed and found the one they'd taken from her hair in a small plastic tub with a brush and comb.

"Here's one."

"Thank you," she said, as she pulled the hair back and fastened it off. "That feels so much better."

"Anything else?"

"Where's Brendan?"

"He went home. Said his brothers had to leave and he needed to get back to his mother and sister."

Julie sighed. "Poor Bren. All the women in his life are suddenly helpless."

He frowned. He didn't like how Julie automatically included herself into Brendan's family circle.

"We're here for you," he said.

"Yes. I know." She hesitated and then added more forcefully. "I need to talk to Brendan."

Grayson sighed. "Do you want to use my phone?"

"I'll just use that one," she said.

He handed it to her then started to sit down when he realized she would be wanting some privacy.

"If you'll be okay for a few minutes, I'm going to go down the hall to the waiting room and get a Dr. Pepper. Would you like one, honey? It's your favorite."

"Yes, that would be great."

Julie waited until her father was gone, then got an outside line and dialed Brendan's number, waiting anxiously for the sound of his voice. She still felt tense inside and anxious—like someone was just out of sight, waiting to jump out of the shadows and grab her.

****

Brendan heated up the rest of the barbeque for the girls' supper and was nursing a cup of coffee as they ate. Linny was unusually quiet, and both Delle and Brendan noticed. He arched an eyebrow at his mother, who shrugged and took a quick sip of iced tea.

He slid the coffee cup off to the side and then tapped the table with his spoon. As soon as he did, Linny looked up.

"Queen Belinda, I am concerned by your silence. I pray you are not ill."

She shrugged. "I'm not sick," she said and swiped a French fry through ketchup.

"Do you have something you want to talk about?" he asked.

She nodded, but didn't follow through.

"So, you'll never get an answer until you ask. What's up, sugar?"

She took a quick breath then blurted it out without looking up from her plate. "What happened to Juliette?"

Delle quickly wiped her hands. "What do you mean, Linny? I told you she got hurt when the fire started."

Linny's frown deepened as she looked up. "Did she get burned?"

"No, no, nothing like that," Bren said. "The bar was empty before it caught fire."

Linny picked a piece of meat off a rib with her fingers and popped it in her mouth, then dropped a small bombshell as she chewed.

"I heard the news."

Brendan sighed. *Shit.*

Delle's expression stilled. Linny was too young for such ugliness, yet it was the world into which she'd been born.

"What did you hear?" Delle asked.

"A bad man kidnapped her and hurt her before she got saved."

Brendan scooted his chair closer to where she was sitting.

"The good news is that she's safe," he said and patted her arm.

"The news man said she was hurt bad."

Delle leaned forward. "Belinda, exactly what did you hear?"

"That she nearly died. Is that true?"

Delle sighed. She didn't lie to her children, but there were times when telling the whole truth wasn't necessary.

"No, they said that wrong. The truth is that she *could* have died if the police hadn't found her when they did. But she was talking to them and everything when they took her to the hospital, right, Bren?"

"That's true, Linny. I talked to her myself the whole time they were putting medicine on her arms and legs."

Linny looked up, tears welling in her eyes.

"Did she cry?"

"Yeah, baby, but then, so did I. It made me sad that someone had hurt her."

The tears in his little sister's eyes welled and rolled down her cheeks.

Brendan groaned. "Don't cry. It hurts my heart when you cry. Come here and hug my neck."

Linny shoved her plate aside and went from her chair to Brendan's lap.

He wrapped his arms around her as she crawled up on

her knees and wrapped her arms around his neck, hugging him hard.

"Now that's what I call a good hug," he said softly, patting her bony little back.

Delle got up and left the kitchen. When she came back, she was carrying Rabbit.

"You've had a really big day, honey. Why don't you and Rabbit go brush your teeth and get ready for bed? I'll come tuck you in later."

Brendan kissed her cheek and gave her backside a little pat.

"Good night, honey. Sleep tight and don't let the bed bugs bite."

Linny tuck Rabbit under her arm and slid off her brother's lap, giggling as she tried to dodge his hand.

And just like that, the trauma of what she'd overheard had passed. She'd think about it again, for sure, but in her mind, the worst was over because the people she trusted most has made it okay.

Brendan envied the naiveté of her youth and began cleaning up the kitchen as Delle put her to bed. He was washing the last of the dishes when his cell phone rang. When he saw the call was from the hospital, he had a moment of panic as he quickly dried his hands. What if Julie was worse? By the time he answered, his gut was in a knot.

"Hello?"

"Hey, Bren."

Relief washed through him. "Julie! Sweetheart! It's so good to hear your voice."

"I just wanted you to know I'm not feeling so crazy."

"Thank God. Are your parents there?"

"Dad is, but he's gone to get us something to drink."

"Everything okay between you two?"

"It's good enough. I'm going to be a long time getting past what was said to both of us."

"Don't make me a part of that relationship. You do what you have to do. You have to get right with your parents, but I don't care if they never like me."

"But I'll care, Bren. Every thought I have of growing old has you right there with me."

He was so touched by what she said that he had to make it a joke or start crying. "Growing old, huh? Am I old and fat in those thoughts?" He waited, then heard a slight giggle.

"And bald," she added.

Brendan laughed. "Now that's something to look forward to."

"I'll still love you, no matter what," she said softly.

"Now you know what I meant when I told you it didn't matter what you looked like. Do you get it now?"

She sighed. "I get it. So, what are you doing tomorrow?"

"Finding Count LeGrande. Job hunting. Going to see you. Staying busy so I won't think about the fact that Mom and Linny have decided to go back to Anson."

"Oh, honey, I'm sorry."

"It is what it is. It's not my place to tell Mom how to live her life, you know?"

"Yes, I know."

"I'm not sure of the time, but I'll be there with you tomorrow, okay?"

"It's always okay. I love you," Julie said.

"I love you, too. I'm so glad you called."

She hung up the phone and then lay back and closed her eyes, thinking of Brendan old and fat and bald. She was still smiling when her daddy came back.

"What's so funny?" he asked.

"Growing old," she said.

"What?"

"Never mind," she said and reached for the Dr. Pepper.

The can was cold and wet with condensation. She held it to her forehead and then her cheek, savoring the cold against her hot, achy flesh before taking a drink.

"It's good. Thank you, Daddy."

Thankful to be in her good graces again, Grayson beamed.

"You are so welcome."

Chapter Thirteen

Anson spent the whole afternoon making the rounds of his marijuana fields, then moved on to the bamboo in the shed and watered the ones already potted. They had a shipment ready to go out tomorrow to a wholesale flower market in Louisville, and that driver was always on time.

But the whole time he was working, he was thinking of his cash crop. Keeping thieves out of the marijuana patches was an ongoing problem. Someone was still helping themselves to a big armload of plants about once every six weeks, which pissed him off to no end. He'd already tried to get Sam and Chance to stand guard in order to catch them in the act, but they'd both refused point blank.

He kept on working with the bamboo, potting the new canes that were rooting and watering the order that was ready to go. He never noticed the evening coming to a close, or that the sun had already set. One minute, he'd been checking off an invoice and the next time he looked up, it was dusk. By the time he had everything packed, it was dark.

The swamp was alive with everything from crickets to the boom of bull gators—even the croak of tiny tree frogs were making their presence known. When the swamp suddenly went silent, he knew a bigger predator must be about.

The shriek of a panther a good distance away was followed by the howl of someone's dog, but it didn't faze him. He walked with his head up and his shoulders back, moving with the confidence of a man who was certain the world was more afraid of him than he was of the world.

He was almost to the back door when something on the doorstep caught his eye. He paused, wishing he had his flashlight, then remembered the penlight on his key ring. He aimed the weak beam toward the step and stopped, staring in disbelief at a tiny black coffin. The hair crawled on the back of his neck as he leaned down for a closer look. There was a picture of his face and a kitchen match on top of it.

Lisette's little visit to Mama Lou via the voodoo express had just arrived, and it never occurred to him she would be responsible. She had already spilled her guts about him to the cops and been told his alibi was airtight. Certainly, she would then have assumed any countless number of others could have caused the fire. So what was this about? No one knew a—

He stood abruptly as a dark scowl crossed his face.

One man knew.

Voltaire LeDeux.

His scowl deepened. This was something he would never have suspected from Voltaire. Although he lived under the radar of everyone and everything, it had to be him. There was no one else who could have fingered him. The question now was what did he do about it? He felt a little uneasy that he'd been cursed, but refused to let it get under his skin. He wouldn't accept that mere words, a fake coffin, and some chicken blood could make a man die. He kept staring down at the coffin, his mind racing, and then all of a sudden, it hit him. The scheme was so brilliant that he actually laughed out loud.

He picked up the coffin as casually as if it had been a jar of jelly someone left as a gift and carried it into the house, turning on lights as he went. He knew March's men would be watching for them to mark the time he'd come inside. He dropped his picture in the trash, put the match and coffin in a small plastic bag, and then made himself a sandwich and a beer as if nothing had happened.

With an eye on the clock, he went upstairs, returning a few minutes later wearing hunting boots and dressed completely in black. He'd smeared his face with chimney soot to hide his identity, even though he didn't plan on being seen, buckled on his holster and pistol, pocketed the baggie with the coffin, grabbed a flashlight, and slipped out the back door. If everything went according to plan, he'd be rid of every monkey on his back, including March's guards, before the night was over.

It was almost two miles as the crow flies from Wisteria Hill to Voltaire's hidey-hole in the bayou, and every bit of it rough going, but Anson didn't have enough sense to be scared. He was too focused on payback to worry about snakes and gators.

He slipped through the woods on the north side of his property and headed for the road. The first thing he needed was to eyeball March's guards. He knew where they parked and needed to make sure they were there.

He strode through the woods without worrying about being quiet, confident the city boys would be sitting with their windows rolled up and the air conditioner on. When he caught a glimmer of moonlight on the car they had backed up in the trees, he smiled. The first part of his plan was in place.

At that point, he took a sharp right and headed east at a trot, staying deep under cover. The mosquitoes were out in full force, swarming around his head, in his ears, even up his nose. He swiped them away and kept going, gaining confidence with every step. When he came to the first creek, he pulled out his flashlight and swept the area. No need asking for trouble by stepping on a snake, or even worse, walking up on some panther getting a drink. The creek was clear.

Even though the water was nearly up to his knees, he waded through it in four long strides and came out on the other side in a leap. Once he figured out how far he'd come, he shifted direction to the northeast and kept moving.

The undergrowth was thick, but timing was of the essence and kept his stride long and strong. He was about three-quarters of a mile from Voltaire's place when he heard a hound bay and then another answer farther south. Someone was hunting. He didn't want to run into them on the way back, and made note to change his return route.

Sweat was pouring from his hair and down through the soot he'd rubbed on his face, but he didn't dare wipe it off for fear of removing the disguise, so instead of a dark face, it was now striped. His clothes were sweat-soaked, as wet as the socks in his boots. It had been a long time since he'd done anything this physical.

He walked into a spider web and spent a few moments slapping at his head and clothes to make sure he wasn't crawling with spiders. Something swooped across his line of vision on soundless wings, most likely an owl. He heard the dogs again, signaling the fact they'd struck trail. They were closing in on their prey and so was he.

He came up on Voltaire's shanty almost before he knew it, then stopped short to survey the clearing. There was lamp light on the far side of the tiny house, which reminded him there was no electricity on the premises. Even better for what he intended.

He pulled the plastic bag out of his pocket and started moving toward the front door in a stealth-like stride. When an owl suddenly hooted from a nearby tree, Anson froze. Knowing Voltaire, he would read that as a warning and moved faster, needing to get the set-up in place before it was too late.

He was almost at the front door when he caught a glimpse of the lamp light moving through the house.

Son of a bitch.

He ran the rest of the way in an all-out lope. With only seconds between him and the lamp light, he set the tiny coffin and the match on the top step and then turned tail and ran as fast as he could into the trees.

He was already there when he heard the squeak of the hinges and watched as Voltaire opened the door. Anson saw the lamp and a vague silhouette of the man behind it and held his breath, waiting for Voltaire to step out.

To Anson's dismay, Voltaire came outside without seeing the coffin, then walked out into the yard just far enough to reassure himself there was no one there. It wasn't until he started to go back inside that he must have seen what was on the step.

The scream that came out of Voltaire's mouth was sheer panic. Anson watched him stumbling backward, tripping, and then dropping the lamp. Lamp oil spilled out onto the ground and took fire, highlighting the tiny coffin even more. Voltaire was on his knees throwing dirt onto the fire, when all of a sudden the match on the coffin that was a few feet away suddenly flared and caught fire, as well.

Voltaire began frantically throwing dirt onto the lamp fire, and then on the coffin, desperate to keep the fire from spreading to the tinder-dry wood of his little house.

Anson could hear him bawling and praying out loud as he vaulted over the smoking coffin and into his house, then slammed the door behind him.

Now it was Anson who took a nervous step back. That match was too far away from the fire to have started from the heat, so how did it catch fire all by itself?

Then he shook off the thought. It didn't matter. He'd done what he needed to do. The first phase of his plan had just been put in place, so he took off running.

****

Parker and Roberts were tired of chasing after Poe. It was their personal opinion that the man was way too smart to do anything that would get him caught. It was embarrassing that Poe had the balls to use them as his alibi when Frenchie's burned. But, March signed their paychecks and a job was a job. The worst part now was the all-night stakeouts. Nothing ever happened, which made them boring as hell.

They'd decided early on in the beginning to take turns sleeping, and tonight was Parker's turn to take first watch. He would wake Roberts at 1:00 a.m., then sack out in the back seat until daybreak. March had mentioned putting two other men on day watch and leaving the night shift to them, but it had yet to happen.

Parker downed the last of his coffee while watching a fat possum waddle across the road. They were weird-looking creatures, that when threatened, often played dead—unless, of course, someone got too close or tried to handle them and then they would bite—something like Anson Poe—lying low beneath the law's radar, but way mean enough to bite if messed with.

He glanced in the back seat at Roberts, who was snoring away, then quietly opened the door and got out to pee. The car needed airing out, too, because Roberts farted on a regular basis as he slept. They'd already disabled the dome light days ago, so he wasn't worried about being seen and was happily pissing away the three cups of coffee in his bladder when he thought he saw movement coming up the driveway from Wisteria Hill.

He watched, blinking several times to clear his vision before he realized it was a man in dark clothes, and before he got close enough to see his face, the man slipped into the trees.

Parker's thoughts were jumping from one scenario to another, wondering why the man was on foot and where he was going, but the bottom line was that if the man was coming from Wisteria Hill, chances are it was Poe. He didn't realize he was pissing on his own shoes until he heard the splatter and did a little shuffle step to get out of the way. The next time he looked up, the man was heading east and swiftly moving out of sight. He stifled a curse, reluctantly squeezed off the stream of urine, and jumped back in the car.

"Wake up, damn it! Poe is on the move!"

Roberts was out of the back seat and loading into the front as Parker started the engine.

"What's going on?" Parker asked.

"I don't know. I just saw a man dressed in black come up from Poe's place and then fade into the trees. He's heading east and moving fast."

"On foot?"

Parker nodded.

"So what makes you think it's Poe? He's got a truck. Why would he walk?" Roberts asked.

"Well he knows we're here, so I'd say he doesn't want us to know he's left the property," Parker said.

"Then how the hell are we going to tail him? It's not like we can drive up behind him without being seen."

"Shit," Parker muttered. He hadn't thought about that.

"Wait! There he is again on that rise, which means he's out of the trees and on the road. What the hell is he running from?"

"Follow him with the lights off," Roberts said.

"He'll hear the engine."

"Maybe not if he's running and breathing hard. Drive, damn it, or we're gonna lose him," Roberts yelled.

Parker put the car in gear and pulled out of the tree and into the road. The windows were down and the lights were off.

"Should we contact March?" Roberts asked.

Parker frowned. "I hate to wake him up at this time of night for nothing. What do I say... that a man we think might be Poe is running up a road in the dark?"

"And, Poe isn't going toward New Orleans. Whatever he's doing can't possibly involve anything to do with the boss or his family," Roberts muttered.

"Yeah, you're right, but we still better call the boss. If we don't and Poe pulls some kind of shit and we didn't tell him, we're fucked," Parker said.

Roberts made the call, unaware that March was not asleep, but at the hospital at his daughter's bedside.

Grayson answered, then went out into the hall to talk.

"Roberts? What's going on?"

"A few minutes ago Poe came up the driveway on foot. He disappeared into the trees, then jumped back out of them about a hundred or so yards up the hill and started running. Do you want us keeping track?"

"Hell yes. I want to know what the bastard does every waking moment. Stay with him and get back to me when you find out what's going on."

"Yes, sir," Roberts said and hung up. "Boss said stay with him."

"Then that's what we're going to do," Parker said, keeping his gaze on the swiftly disappearing figure.

****

Anson was damn tired. This was his second trip to Voltaire's place on foot, and it was going to be about a half-mile farther this way because he was not cutting through the swamp. But when he heard their engine start up, he knew they took the bait. Now he had pace himself so that they would be close enough to see where he went. He glanced over his shoulder and then took off in a long steady lope, ignoring the pain in his side.

****

"Do you still see him?" Roberts whispered.

"You don't have to whisper," Parker said. "The engine is making more noise than we are, and he's too far ahead to hear either one."

"Fine, then I'm talking loud and I still want to know if you see him," Roberts snapped.

"Yeah, I caught a glimpse of his silhouette when we topped the last rise."

"I don't think anyone lives around here. How much farther does this road go?" Roberts mumbled.

"Someone does because we followed Poe here once before, remember?"

Roberts frowned. "Oh yeah, but we never knew what he was doing."

"So maybe we're about to find out," Parker said and accelerated around the curve in the road.

"There he is, and you were right. He must be going to that same place."

"I see him!" Parker said.

"Are we gonna follow him down that road this time?" Roberts asked.

"We'll play it by ear," Parker said.

****

Anson knew they'd seen him. Now all he needed to do was issue the party invitations. Once again, he took to the trees as he ran toward Voltaire's house. There was a light shining through every window, which meant Voltaire was up and on edge.

He looked back toward the road, but didn't see the vehicle and had to wait until March's men got closer. He hunkered down in the shadows to watch for their car, and as soon as he saw them slip past the turnoff, he started running toward the house.

****

Voltaire was on his knees by his bed. His rifle was on the floor, his mother's bible on the bed and her rosary in his hands. He was shaking so hard he could barely stay upright. He hadn't prayed a day since his mother's funeral, but he hadn't stopped praying since he saw the coffin.

"Lord, Lord, if you will save me from this curse, I swear to never do another illegal thing again. I swear on my mother's soul this is so. Save me Lord, save me."

He buried his face against the mattress and began reciting every bible verse he could remember, then broke down, sobbing. He couldn't die this way... not from a voodoo curse. He didn't think God would let him into heaven if this happened, and if he didn't get to heaven, he would never see his sweet mother again.

The coffin was still on the front porch. He didn't know what he should do with it, but he didn't want to touch it.

He could hear rustling noises outside his windows and imagined the devil was out there, waiting to drag him to hell. God in heaven, if only he could go back and change the deal he'd made with Poe, he would.

And then it occurred to him that if he burned the money Poe gave him, it might put an end to the curse. If he didn't profit from the disaster, then maybe it would be okay. He didn't know if it would work, but he was willing to try. He pulled a lockbox out from under the bed and quickly removed his share of the money from the fire.

It was a solid wad of bills, more than he would make in a year selling crawfish and the occasional gator. But it wasn't worth a damn if he was dead. He ran into the kitchen, threw the money into the sink and then struck a match.

The paper was slow to catch. Anxious to put an end the curse, he shook the bills apart so they would catch fire faster, and within seconds, they were aflame. He watched the money burn until there was nothing left but ashes and then he threw up his hands and started talking.

"Look, God, look! I burned it. It's gone and I'm so sorry. Please make the devil take away the curse."

In a frantic need to remove even the remnants, he grabbed the handle on the hand pump and began pumping, drawing water up the pipe and into the sink. He pumped until every last bit of ash had washed down the drain, then threw his hands up in the air like he'd just scored a touchdown. Elation ended with a gunshot and the sound of breaking glass.

"No, God, no, I burned it all," he wailed.

But in the eyes of God, his repentance must have come too late. If someone was shooting at him, then none of it had worked.

It wasn't in him to go down without a fight. He grabbed

the rifle from his bedroom and headed for the door, unaware the shot he heard had not only broken a window, but also an oil lamp. The back of the house was already on fire.

****

The moment Anson fired the shot into Voltaire's house, he began running toward the road. He needed for March's men to see him running away before the next part of his plan could take effect. He was guessing they would have heard the first shot, but fired one more shot into the air to make sure.

And he'd been right.

The guards had just parked the SUV when they heard a gun go off.

Roberts jumped and then opened the door. "That was a gunshot!" he cried, as he drew his gun and jumped out then crouched down, using the open door for cover.

Parker followed suit. "We need to get across the road!" he yelled and started running.

They were in the middle of the road staring straight down the driveway when they heard another shot, this time much closer. Frantic to get out of sight before they were seen, they increased their stride, but it was too late. All of a sudden a man appeared, running toward them.

"There he comes!" Parker yelled.

Anson saw them, pretended to be startled at their appearance, then pivoted and started back toward the house at a frantic sprint, needing them to give chase. When he heard one of them yelling at him to stop, he lengthened his stride.

Ahead of him, he could see the front door opening and

Voltaire silhouetted against the lights behind him. One more step and then the rest was up to fate.

He fired one more shot, this time at Voltaire's house, taking care not to hit him, then looked back over his shoulder to make sure the men were already in sight before he dropped to the ground. He was crawling on his belly toward the trees when Voltaire opened fire.

Roberts and Parker lost sight of Poe for a few moments, and when they saw him again, he was silhouetted against a shack with a rifle in his hands. Before they could react, he opened fire.

"Look out!" Roberts yelled and fired off a shot toward the house as the shooter returned fire in rapid succession.

Parker was running for cover when he realized Roberts wasn't with him. Crouching down, he looked back. Roberts was face down in the dirt, unmoving. He spun, firing one shot after another as he went back for his partner. He was on his knees beside Roberts, still shooting, when he saw the man he thought was Poe beginning to stagger. Believing he was going down, he lost focus. By the time he realized it didn't happen, the shooter had emptied the rifle in his direction.

The last two bullets hit Parker; one in the chest; the last in the head. He was dead before he hit the ground.

Voltaire was swaying on his feet, still trying to shoot, but the gun was empty. He knew he needed to pray, but he couldn't make words for the bloody bubbles coming up his throat. The two men on the ground weren't moving. Maybe he'd broken the curse after all!

Then his heart skipped a beat. One more man came out of the shadows; moving toward him at a slow, steady pace. The rifle fell out of his hands as a terrible heat burned at his back. The sky was growing dark. He could feel the heat of hell as the devil came closer.

He took his last breath face down, sucking dirt up his nose and into his mouth; dying with the taste of Louisiana on his lips.

The moment Voltaire went down, Anson quickly moved from one body to the next to make sure they were all dead. As soon as he was satisfied, he grabbed a big handful of weeds and began sweeping the ground where he'd walked, wiping out just his shoe prints and destroying all the evidence that a fourth man had been there.

He knew there would be a bullet from his gun somewhere inside the burning house, so he wiped his gun down, stuck it back in the holster, and threw all of it into the fire, along with the empty cartridge from his first shot. The heat would discharge the bullets. The investigators would just assume it belonged to Voltaire because the gun had never been registered to Anson.

He backed into the trees, wiping his steps as he went, and when he was completely out of sight of the house and the road, he started running back home, this time without caution. He couldn't worry about snakes or panthers. The greater danger was being caught in the vicinity of the massacre.

He was past exhaustion and running with his second wind, glorying in the beauty of how perfectly the plan had worked and was about a half mile away when he heard the bullets in his pistol beginning to explode. He threw back his head and laughed.

****

Grayson March kept one eye on his watch and the other on his daughter, waiting for his men to call back. But the longer time passed, the more certain he was that something had gone wrong. After three long hours and no word, he called Roberts. Just when he thought the call was going to voice mail, a man answered, but it wasn't his employee.

"Hello? Who's speaking?"

Grayson frowned. "This is Grayson March. I'm calling one of my employees; a man named Roberts. You have his phone, so who the hell are you?"

"Parish Sheriff's department."

Grayson frowned. "Where's Roberts?"

"You need to speak to the sheriff. Hold please."

It was already obvious that something was wrong. Grayson was trying not to panic, but when another man answered, and it quickly went from bad to worse.

"Grayson, is that you?"

"Yes, who's speaking?"

"This is Sumter Henry."

"What's going on, Sheriff? Where's Carl Roberts?"

"What relation is he to you?" Henry asked.

"He works for me," Grayson said.

"I'm sorry to tell you that Carl Roberts is deceased. By any chance was Lonnie Parker also in your employ?"

"What do you mean, *was?*"

"They're both deceased."

Grayson was shocked. The last thing they told him was that they were going after Poe.

"What the hell happened? Where is Anson Poe?"

Henry frowned. "Anson Poe? Why did you ask about him?"

"Because the last time I talked to Roberts, he and Parker were trailing him, that's why. Again, what happened to my men?"

"We don't have any ballistic results to back this up, but at first look, it appears your two men had a shoot-out with a man named Voltaire LeDeux."

"Who?"

"Their bodies, along with his, are on his property, or what's left of it. His house also burned down."

Grayson couldn't believe it. "No! No, damn it, no! They were tailing Poe. Roberts told me, himself."

"In light of your information, we will definitely be interviewing him. If you would come in to the Parish precinct sometime tomorrow and give us an official statement to this effect, it would be appreciated."

"Hell yes, I'll be there," Grayson said. "Let me know when the bodies will be released from the morgue. They were working for me. I'll see to notifying their families."

"Yes, sir," Henry said and hung up.

****

Brendan woke up just before daylight, his heart pounding from a swiftly receding nightmare. By the time his feet hit the floor, he'd forgotten what he'd been dreaming. He glanced at the clock. It was almost seven. Time to get up and get moving. Claudette would be here in a couple of hours and he had a long list of things to get done in a short span of time.

After a quick trip to the bathroom, he headed to the kitchen to start coffee and then went back to shower.

He was in the kitchen frying sausage links and beating eggs when he heard voices and then a door slam. They were up and the day had officially begun.

****

Julie woke up needing to go to the bathroom and was surprised to see her mother asleep in a chair by her bed with a hospital blanket pulled up to her chin. She couldn't believe she'd actually inconvenienced herself enough to stay the night and reached for her buzzer to ring for a nurse.

A few moments later, her call was answered.

"Good morning, Julie. How can I help you?"

"I need to go to the bathroom."

"Someone will be right there," she said.

At the sound of voices, Lana roused, then groaned beneath her breath as she got up and stretched.

Her perfect coiffure was squashed on one side and there was a smear of mascara beneath her right eye. Julie knew she'd be horrified if she could see herself.

"Good morning, darling. How do you feel this morning?" Lana asked.

"I hurt, Mama... a lot. It's weird, but my body feels like I was burned instead of beaten."

Lana could barely bring herself to look at her daughter's condition and tried not to shudder. Her voice was trembling as she patted Julie's hand.

"I'm so very sorry I hurt your feelings. I can't begin to imagine your suffering, and I wish I could make it all better like I used to with a Cinderella Band-Aid and a kiss."

Julie was thankful for the honesty. It was the first really empathic thing her mother had said since this nightmare began.

"I wish that's all it would take, too," Julie said. "By the way, where's Dad?"

"I don't know. Something must have happened last night that had to do with work. He left before daylight to go home and clean up. Said he had some meetings he couldn't miss."

The news was nothing out of the ordinary, and Julie thought nothing of it.

The door opened and Fern, the day nurse, walked in

with a jaunty step. "Good morning, dear. Are you ready for your first walk of the day?"

Julie grimaced as she swung her legs over the side of the bed.

Fern patted her arm. "As soon as we get your skin treated again, this pain will ease.

"God, I hope so," Julie said, gritting her teeth with each step. She wanted this nightmare behind her and healing physically was the first step in making it happen.

Chapter Fourteen

Anson watched the sunrise from the kitchen window while waiting for his coffee to finish brewing. He had a blister on the back of one heel from running in wet socks last night, and a bruise on his shin from bumping into a dead log on the run home, but other than that, he felt fine—even satisfied—with a job well-done.

Today was the day the workers would finish the house, and a shipment of bamboo was going out, as well. He didn't know when the bodies would be found, but he knew the parish police would eventually come to see him, for the simple fact that those were the men who'd been assigned to guard *him* and now they were dead.

He turned away from the magnificent wash of pink and gold spreading across the early morning sky to pour his first cup of coffee. He wasn't moved by sunrises. They had come regularly every day for the last fifty years, and as long as he was still around to see the next one, he didn't care what they looked like.

When the grandfather clock in the hallway began to chime, he glanced at his watch, counting as it chimed seven times. It was five minutes fast, but what the hell. He didn't intend to live by it. He just liked the sound.

Sam and Chance would be here within the hour and most likely be surprised by the amount of work he'd done yesterday while they were gone. He sat down to eat a bowl of cereal and then put the dirty dish in the sink without bothering to rinse it. It would give Delle something to do when she came home.

At straight up 8:00 a.m., he heard Sam's truck pulling up in the back yard and looked out. Chance had ridden in with Sam, and there was a parish police car behind them.

And so it began. He shifted mental gears as he grabbed his gloves and his cell phone and walked out the back door.

****

Chance's truck was in the shop, so he'd hitched a ride to work with Sam. As always when they were together, they talked about the day they would quit working for Anson like a kid does counting down the days until he's old enough to drive. They longed for families and lives of their own, but neither one had the guts to confront him.

About halfway there, Sam glanced in the rearview mirror and realized a police car was behind them. He slowed down to give it room to pass, but when the driver made no move to accelerate, he frowned.

"Wonder what that's all about? There aren't any houses out this way but Wisteria Hill and LeDeux's place." Sam's fingers tightened on the steering wheel as he thought of the ramifications. "Man, I hope this isn't the day we finally all go to jail."

"Bite your tongue, bro," Chance muttered.

"If they turn off when we do, I'm officially freaked," Sam said.

A few minutes later, Sam signaled he was turning and so did the cop car.

"We're fucked," Chance said.

"Not until they handcuff us," Sam said, as he pulled up in the shade and got out.

"There comes Dad, and the son of a bitch is smiling," Chance muttered.

Sam recognized Anson's strut as one of satisfaction.

"So, we may not be fucked after all."

****

Sumter Henry, the Parish Sheriff, was bothered by the bind he now found himself in. He'd known from the start that taking money from Anson Poe could complicate his life, but he'd never imagined murder would be in the mix. He was pissed at himself, but at the same time, fairly certain no tie between him and Poe could ever be proven.

As they neared Poe's property, he recognized the truck ahead of them and realized they were following Anson's sons. At least he'd have them all together when he started questioning.

They drove in and parked behind Sam Poe's truck, then saw Anson coming out of the house.

"And there comes our man. Let's see what he has to say," Henry said.

Both officers got out, but they didn't have to go far because Anson came to meet them.

"Good morning, Sheriff. So what have my boys done now?"

Sam and Chance were immediately pissed that he would point a guilty finger at them, even in jest.

"We haven't done a damn thing," Sam said. "What do you want us to do first?"

Anson laughed. "Easy, Sam, it was a joke. So, what's up, Sheriff?"

Henry frowned. "We need to ask you some questions, and I'd like for your sons to stay."

"I don't mind. So what's going on?" Anson asked.

"Where were you last night?" Henry asked.

"Here, why?"

"Is there anyone who can verify that?"

"No, I was by myself all day and... Oh wait. I did have a caller last night."

"I need a name," Henry said.

"My neighbor, Voltaire LeDeux."

Henry was surprised, but kept a straight face. "Voltaire LeDeux was here?"

Anson nodded. "Yeah, for a little while. If he's in need of something only money can buy, he brings something to trade. Sometimes he brings me crawfish, which I will buy, but I'm not real fond of gator and he knows it."

"What time was he here?" Henry asked.

Anson frowned. He knew exactly the time frame to mention, but he didn't want to sound too positive.

"I'm thinking it must have been around 10:30. I was watching one of those late night shows when he came to the door."

"What did he want?" Henry asked.

Anson shrugged. "He said, he needed a new pair of shoes and would I want to trade for crawfish. Hell, boys, why don't you go ask him yourself? He'll tell you."

"Did you trade for crawfish?"

"Not right then," Anson said. "But I gave him the money. Told him to bring me crawfish once a week for a month and we'd be even."

Henry frowned. "You boys ever know this to happen?"

Sam shrugged. "The man hasn't worked a day in his life. He trades for everything. Everyone in the bayou knows that."

"Look, Chief, what's going on?" Anson asked. "Why are you asking me all this? Go ask him."

"He's dead," Henry said.

Anson knew the look of shock on his face was a good one because he'd practiced.

"The hell you say! What happened?"

"Someone shot him."

Sam frowned. "That's sick. Who would shoot Voltaire? He didn't bother anyone."

Henry wasn't here to give information. He was here to get it. He kept pushing Anson for answers. "How do you know Carl Roberts?"

Anson shrugged. "I don't."

"What about Lonnie Parker?"

Anson shook his head. "I don't know him either. Boys, do ya'll know 'em?"

"No sir," Chance said.

"Me, either," Sam said.

Henry's smile looked more like a grimace, but he thought Anson might have gotten himself into a bind with this claim.

"Well that's strange you don't know them, seeing as how you named them as witnesses to back up your alibi the night Frenchie's burned."

Anson's eyes widened. "Are you telling me those are the guys who work for March... the ones who follow me around all the time?"

Henry frowned. "Yes, you—"

"Well, hell, Chief. I didn't know their names. It's not like we've ever been introduced. I just knew March had put two of his watchdogs on me. I mean it wasn't a secret. Where I went, they went. So what the fuck do March's men have to do with Voltaire?"

"According to Grayson March, those men were following you last night as you left Wisteria Hill, and they were on your tail. His claim is that, if his men were on LeDeux's property, it's because they followed you there."

Anson shook his head, as if confused by the whole scenario.

"No, I didn't go there last night, but they've followed me there before. I was there not too long ago and got a bucket of crawfish, but that was in the daytime. They saw me go in. They saw me come out, and they followed me back home."

Henry frowned. "Well, March claims the men saw you coming up your driveway on foot, then slip into some trees all secret like."

Anson jerked as if he'd been slapped.

"On foot? No, I didn't... oh hell!"

Henry frowned. "What?"

Anson flung his gloves to the ground as his face turned red in sudden anger.

"Damn Grayson March to hell and back for ever putting his guards on my tail. If he hadn't, none of this would have happened. They must have seen Voltaire leaving here last night and thought it was me. Voltaire doesn't drive. He doesn't even own a car. He was the one afoot."

"But they'd know soon enough when they drove up and talked to him, it was not," Henry said.

"They don't drive up and chit chat with me, damn it. They just stay behind me in lurk mode. And Voltaire was afoot, so if he saw them following him, it would've scared him. He would've been running hell-bent for leather to get home. If they actually set foot on his property after scaring him like that, he would shoot first and ask questions later. Ask my boys. Ask anyone in the parish. You don't go to Voltaire's house at night unless he knows ahead of time that you're coming.

Henry had heard of the man, but had no knowledge of

his habits. He glanced at Poe's sons, trying to get a read on what they were thinking.

"Is this so?" he asked.

Sam nodded. "Yes, sir. Ask anyone."

Henry wasn't satisfied. "So how do I know it still wasn't you walking to this Voltaire LeDeux's house?"

Anson threw up his hands. "Maybe because I have a goddamn truck to drive? Why would I take to foot and go two and a half miles up a road in the dark after working all day? Answer me that, damn it."

Henry sighed. He'd ask around, but something told him this was as far as he would get with Poe, and without a witness to state otherwise, this might come down to March's men being the ones in the wrong and not Poe.

"Well then," Henry said.

"This is terrible," Anson said, then picked up his gloves and slapped them on the side of his jeans to shake off the dust. "So who's claiming Voltaire's body?"

Henry was surprised. "I can't say as I know, why?"

"Because if he wound up dead because of this disagreement between me and March, I feel somewhat obligated to lay him to rest. He doesn't have any family, and anyone who knows him, knows he would want to be buried beside his mama. If you would tell the mortuary who winds up with his body to send the bill for his funeral to me, I would be obliged."

The chief didn't quite know how to react. He'd come here thinking he might wind up arresting Poe, only to have the slick bastard slide out from under the accusation and wind up looking like a Good Samaritan.

Anson was waiting for a reply, but it never came. "Is there anything else I can do for you? I ask, because we have a truck coming after a load of bamboo this morning, and I have things to do."

Henry didn't like being the one to be dismissed.

"If we have other questions, I know where to find you," he said.

Anson couldn't resist one last parting shot. "I hope you know that when word gets out of this tragedy, people are going to be blaming March for throwing his weight around, putting hired guns in the midst of innocent people."

Henry didn't comment as they got back in the patrol car and drove away.

Sam looked at his father. "Was Voltaire really here last night?"

Anson turned on him like a rabid dog, spewing words in short angry bursts. "Hell yes, and don't you ever question me like that again. What the fuck would I have to gain by hurting Voltaire LeDeux?"

Sam didn't budge. "I don't know, Daddy. What the fuck did you have to gain by hurting Mama?"

Chance didn't want in on the explosion he knew was coming and took off to the shed without looking back.

Sam waited with his hands curled into fists, expecting the worst. Instead, Anson seemed to blow it off. "Go help your brother. There's work to do."

And that was the moment Sam knew his father *was* to blame.

****

Claudette arrived early Monday morning, for which Brendan was extremely grateful. She came in carrying a tote bag full of playthings for Linny and a small sack of makeup for Delle. As soon as she distributed her gifts, she got Brendan alone in the kitchen and handed him a gift, as well.

"This is from Mama Lou," she said and placed it in his hand.

Brendan looked down at the small pink cell phone and frowned.

"What am I supposed to do with this?"

"Mama Lou said, 'tell Brendan to put his phone number in it, put it on speed dial, then teach your little sister how to use it. It will be her SOS to you. Her 911 call. Tell her to use it only if she is afraid for her life.'"

Brendan's stomach rolled. The phone felt more like a ticking time bomb than a lifeline. What did Mama Lou know that he didn't?

"Did she say why?" he asked.

"Danger comes," Claudette said, then shrugged. "That is all."

"Well damn it," Brendan said softly.

Claudette cupped the side of his cheek. "Life is a series of highs and lows. This time in your life is a low for you and for those you love."

He palmed the phone and put it in his pocket.

"Thank you, Auntie. I will show her tonight when I come home."

Claudette nodded. "You will go see Juliette today?"

"Yes."

"Good. I have one more thing Mama Lou sent that is for her alone." She went back to her tote bag and pulled out a pint-sized cotton pouch. Inside was a pretty glass bottle with a pale amber liquid inside.

"What is it?" he asked.

"It will take away her pain and help heal the skin without leaving scars."

He frowned. "I'm not sure the hospital will let them use a medicine other than what they prescribe," he said.

Her eyes narrowed. "So don't let them know, just use it. Think about it, Brendan. If anyone knows how to heal the marks left from whippings and floggings, it would be the ancestors of slaves."

Brendan's eyes widened. "Damn, Auntie, that's cold."

She shrugged. "It is nothing but the truth."

He couldn't deny it. "You tell Mama Lou thank you for everything and I will do as she says."

Claudette smiled. "So, tell your family good-bye and do what you must. We will be fine."

"Will do," he said, gathered up the things she'd given him, and headed for his room.

He glanced in at the girls as he passed. They were head to head on the bed, digging through the tote bag Claudette brought. He put the pink phone in a drawer, got his wallet, car keys, and the medicine, and then went to tell them good-bye.

"Hey, Mama, I'm leaving now. If you need me, all you have to do is call. I'll be down in the Quarter for a while and then I'm going to see Julie. I'm picking up some groceries before I come home. Is there anything you need?"

Linny held up her hand like she would have in school, as if asking permission to speak.

Brendan laughed. "And what, pray tell, does Queen Belinda have need of today?"

"The queen would appreciate some candy," she said, and then she giggled when her mother poked her in the ribs.

"Linny, don't beg for things," she said.

Linny sat up with a perfectly serious expression on her face. "But I didn't beg, Mama. I asked."

Brendan chuckled. "She's right, Mama. She asked quite nicely, too."

Delle shook her head. "You're both hopeless. I don't need anything, son. We'll be going home soon and no longer spending your money. You need to take care of it now, especially since you don't have a job."

"I have money to get you whatever you need," he said shortly. "I've been checking the websites for available jobs and will have one soon enough, so don't worry. So, candy for the queen, it is. I'll see you both later, and if I'm going to be delayed, I'll call."

"Give Juliette our love," Delle said.

"I will," he said, and moments later, he was gone.

****

The burn swath through the Quarter was painful to see. Buildings that had been there for centuries had been reduced to piles of rubble. Locals were in clean-up mode, sifting through the remnants. A large portion of the area was still roped off, causing Brendan to have to park over a half-mile away.

He started out on foot, and although the day was still early, the sun was already hot on his face with a promise of greater heat yet to come. The sky, a washed-out blue, was cloudless. It made the soaring gulls appear as but tiny specks, trapped between horizon and heaven.

The area was full of history from the old brick streets laid centuries before to the elaborate ironwork framing balconies, to towering trees draped with Spanish moss hanging low on ancient limbs. He thought of the medicine Mama Lou made for Juliette. Time changed many things, but the evil in men's hearts was still the same.

By the time he reached the place where The Black Garter once stood, he began finding a few shop owners open for business. The bar was the last building to burn on the block, and from what he could see, March had wasted no time with clean-up.

From there, the streets began to slope slightly downward toward the river. He kept an eye out for LeGrande as he went, but he was nowhere in sight, so he headed for his apartment. He'd gone only a couple of blocks farther before he saw him sitting alone at the river's edge, watching a paddleboat coming toward shore. A few yards farther down, a line of people were at a dock, part of a day tour waiting to board. He jogged down to where LeGrande was sitting.

"Good morning, sir."

The old man looked up, squinting slightly against the light and then smiled. "Brendan Poe. Will you sit with me?"

"Yes sir, thank you," he said and sat down.

"It's a beautiful day, isn't it?" LeGrande asked.

"Yes it is," Brendan said.

"So you found your lady."

Brendan nodded. "Thanks to you. It's why I came. I had to thank you again, and Juliette asked me to thank you, as well. I don't know if you are aware of how close we came to losing her, but another five minutes and the police would've been too late."

The old man shook his head. "I heard the news. They found other bodies on the property, so the man was certainly a bad one."

Brendan nodded. "Yes, and he has confessed to other murders."

LeGrande gasped. "Indeed?"

"He has been killing women all across the country and no one had identified him as a serial killer. If you hadn't been so diligent, things would be very different."

LeGrande frowned as he shook his head. "I have lived too long, I think. This world has become a very ugly, very dangerous place to be."

Brendan couldn't argue. "Yes, sir, that it has."

"Is Juliette going to heal?"

Brendan hesitated briefly. "With time."

LeGrande turned until he was looking at Brendan face-to-face. "You won't let it matter?"

"No sir. Never!"

"Then you have a good day," LeGrande said. "And give your lady my best wishes."

He'd been dismissed, and that was fine. He'd said all he came to say.

"Yes, sir, I will," Brendan said, but LeGrande had already turned his gaze back to the wide expanse of water.

He wondered what it was that the old man saw, then let it go. Everyone had things they wanted to remember, and things they were trying to forget.

Chapter Fifteen

Grayson was on his way to the hospital when his phone rang. When he saw the sheriff's number on caller ID, he quickly answered. Finally, he'd get some good news.

"Hello."

"Mr. March, this is Sheriff Henry. I wonder if you could find time to drop by this morning. There are some things we need to discuss."

"I can be there in ten minutes," March said.

"Good. See you soon."

March hit the brakes, taking the next right with a surge of righteous indignation. He assumed they were going to tell him Anson Poe was in custody. He couldn't have been more wrong.

****

Grayson March leaped from his chair, slamming his hands on the sheriff's desk in sudden anger. "What the hell do you mean my men were in the wrong? I told you exactly what was reported to me. There could be no other explanation for what happened out there and you know it. What the fuck! Are you one of the cops on his payroll?

Sheriff Henry's face turned a dark, angry red as he eased up from his chair and leaned across his desk until he and March were practically nose-to-nose. He was so pissed he could hardly think for wanting to put a fist right in the middle of March's face.

"Sit. Down." Henry said shortly.

Grayson glared as he dropped back into his chair.

Henry delivered his words standing up. "This is my office, not yours. You do not speak to me in such a slanderous manner. I will, however, do you a favor and chalk it up to frustration and regret over the loss of two of your employees."

Grayson was still reeling from the knowledge that Anson Poe wasn't in jail.

Henry sat back down.

"Now, with regard to what our investigation has turned up, unless some witness unknown to us at this time comes forward, this is what's going in the report. Do you want to hear it or not?"

"I'm listening."

"Sometime after ten o'clock last night, Anson Poe said his neighbor, Voltaire LeDeux showed up at his house wanting to make a deal. We have since verified that bartering was the man's only way of doing business. He was something of a hermit, having lived in the bayou all his life and it's also been confirmed that everyone around seemed to know and accept his oddities. Poe said LeDeux needed a new pair of shoes and wanted to know if they could make a trade. Poe claims he gave Voltaire money and told him to bring him a bucket of crawfish once a week for a month and they'd be even. Shortly thereafter, LeDeux took his leave... in the dark... on foot... the same way he'd come in."

"What does that have to do with—?"

Henry held up his hand. "I'm not finished. Now, without the verification of your guards to back this up, the rest has to be conjecture, because all interested parties are now deceased. But according to Poe, and everyone else we have interviewed since, LeDeux did not like strangers, did not allow people on his property he didn't know, especially after dark. And even more important to the story, if he felt threatened, he would shoot first and ask questions later. So, enter your two men who are on stakeout. They see a man coming up the road from Wisteria Hill in the dark, and now this is where your statement plays into what happens next. You stated your men called you, said Poe was afoot, and had ducked into some trees along the road. Then you stated the men told you he came out of the trees farther up and started running."

"Yes, I did, and that's exactly what Carl Parker said."

"The only problem is that it appears your men didn't see Anson Poe. They saw Voltaire LeDeux, and I'm guessing the reason he was running was because he saw them too and got scared when he saw strangers parked up in the trees all secret-like. Since there wasn't any moonlight to speak of last night, your men assumed they were following Poe just because he came away from Wisteria Hill. But they made the mistake of following another man who was trying to get home to safety. Without any witnesses to say otherwise, the facts show that those men shot and killed each other. Ballistic tests aren't in yet, but I'll know soon enough if it all matches up."

"But how do you know it wasn't Poe doing all of that to get back at me?" Grayson asked.

"I'm sorry, but he could hardly plan something like that since LeDeux's appearance at Wisteria Hill was unexpected. Poe also stated your men have followed him to LeDeux's location before, which backs up Poe's claim of a neighborly relationship. He also denied having any kind of reason to walk to neighbor's house in the dark when he could have driven, and he would never go at night because Voltaire would most likely shoot him.

"For the record, a good number of other people

interviewed said the same thing about the man. They claimed he was distrustful of strangers and would not have willingly allowed anyone on his property after dark. So that's how this situation has played out. Your men made a mistake. It got them killed, and it cost an innocent man his life."

Grayson was stunned. He kept trying to find a way out of the tangled web of facts, but the only way out still implicated him and his men, and it hurt.

"I never told them to go onto anyone else's property," Grayson said.

Henry shrugged. "Yet they were there."

"So what happens now?"

Henry's eyes narrowed thoughtfully. "Do you mean, what happens to you?"

Grayson didn't respond.

Henry shrugged. "Legally, two of your employees went rogue and killed an innocent man. You'll have to deal with the public fall-out, but there will be no charges filed against you, if that's what you're asking."

Grayson felt numb. "Are we through here?"

"Unless something else comes to light," Henry said, shuffling a file from one side of his desk to the other. When March walked out, he got up to refill his coffee cup.

Outside, the sun was still shining, and the gull that had been sitting on a light pole was still there as Grayson got back into his car. He took a few moments to gather his thoughts. He was numb from the shock, and he knew when the media got hold of this news, he would catch hell. Still, he had somewhere to be and headed back to the hospital, anxious to see Julie before the day got any older.

****

Brendan got off the hospital elevator with a sack in one hand and a stuffed teddy bear in the other. He trusted Mama Lou enough to deliver the medicine she'd made up for Julie and hoped he could talk her into trusting him enough to try it. He paused outside her door, wondering which parent he'd be facing, then pushed the door inward.

****

Julie had been alone for almost two hours. Her mother had gone home to clean up and get some rest. She hadn't heard from her father, but it didn't matter. Their presence exhausted her. She was emotionally numb, coping with too many distraught glances from them in her direction—too many questions that sounded more like accusations. She knew what it would take to make it stop, but she was not giving up her apartment and moving home, and she wasn't dumping Brendan just to satisfy their social consciences.

Doctor Ames had made rounds while Lana was still here, but the news that Julie's eyes had escaped injury and she would suffer no adverse effects to her sight didn't seem to be all that newsworthy to Lana. All her mother seemed interested in knowing was if there would be scars. Once again, it sent the same message to Julie that her survival alone wasn't enough.

She leaned back and closed her eyes, wishing she and Brendan could just get in a car and start driving. Destination didn't matter. If they found a place that looked promising, they would stop. If not, there was always the open road and new possibilities.

In the back of her mind, she was honest enough to admit her daydream was no different from her mother's need to pretend this never happened. They were both ignoring the bottom line. There was no way to go back to what was. What she had was a huge knot in her stomach. Would she ever feel normal again?

She was almost asleep when she heard a tapping at the window. She opened her eyes to a pigeon on the ledge outside the window. He was fluffing his feathers and flapping his wings, and every few seconds he would give the window a sharp peck. It took her a few moments to realize the bird had mistaken his own reflection for another bird and was trying to chase it away.

She was still watching when she heard a knock. She looked up as Brendan walked in, and waved him over.

"Brendan, you have to see this." She pointed at the window, just as the pigeon did it again. "He thinks there's another bird in his space and doesn't realize he's seeing his reflection."

Brendan leaned down and kissed her. "Guys can be pretty dim sometimes, but not me. I come bearing gifts." He handed her a chocolate-colored teddy bear with shiny black eyes.

"Oh, Brendan! I love him."

"And I love you. So, I named him Merlin because he's going to make magic for you. Any time you get scared or feel sad, just tell him your troubles and he'll make them go away, like magic."

Julie hugged the bear beneath her chin. "You, Brendan Poe, are the magic in my life, but thank you for always thinking of me."

He smoothed the hair back away from her face and then set the sack on the table by her bed.

"There's more."

"Like what?" she asked.

"Mama Lou sent you something."

Julie's eyes widened. She leaned forward, whispering. "The voodoo Mama Lou?"

He nodded.

"Oh my God, I keep forgetting you two have a history. I don't know whether to be nervous or impressed. So what did she send me?"

Brendan pulled the glass jar out of the sack. "It's to put on your skin to make you heal faster."

Julie eyed the pale amber liquid a little nervously. "The hospital personnel would have a fit if I use this."

He sighed. "I know. I certainly can't make you try it, but here's the deal. Claudette said this is some secret concoction the slaves once used to heal themselves after they were whipped by their owners. The fact that Mama Lou is even sharing it is a big freaking deal, honey."

Julie pointed. "Can I smell it?"

He unscrewed the lid and held it beneath her nose. "It doesn't smell bad at all. Is it greasy?"

Brendan let a little bit drip into the palm of her hand. She rubbed it lightly across the lash marks on her forearm.

"It's not greasy at all, in fact, it's... Oh wow!"

"What?" Brendan asked, suddenly anxious.

Julie looked up. "It's numbing. It's taking away that hot, stinging sensation."

She threw back the sheet and then held out her hand for more.

He poured a little more in the palm of her hand then watched as she rubbed it on both legs.

"Oh, this is wonderful," Julie whispered. "It's really numbing the pain."

"What about putting it on the rest of you?" Brendan asked.

She untied the hospital gown and let it drop to her waist, unashamedly baring her body as she proceeded to rub it on every place a lash had struck. The last place she put it was on her cheeks and chin.

"I wouldn't put it anywhere around your eyes," Brendan said.

"Agreed," she said, then looked up at him and grinned.

"What?" he asked.

"Look at us. I'm sitting her bare-ass naked, rubbing some voodoo concoction all over myself while you hold the bottle. I wonder how long it would take Mama to pitch a fit if she walked in on this?"

"Oh hell, I never thought. Just hurry," he said and looked nervously over his shoulder.

She slipped her arms back through the sleeves of the gown and re-tied it.

"There now... all doctored and decent and no one's the wiser."

Brendan screwed the lid back on the bottle and slipped it into the cotton pouch.

"I'm going to put this in the bottom drawer of this table, okay?"

Julie watched him tuck it toward the back of the drawer behind the small plastic tub.

"Is there any rule to how often I can use it?" she asked.

"Claudette just said to use it as you felt the need. I think you should wash it off the palms of your hands, though." He gave her a wet, soapy washcloth to clean up.

As soon as she finished, she lay back down, tucked the bear beneath her arm and let out a long, shaky breath.

"Tell Mama Lou thank you from the bottom of my heart. This is the first time since it happened that I almost feel normal again."

"I will. Oh. I found LeGrande this morning and told him you sent your thanks for his help."

"What did he say?" she asked.

"He was pleased, I think. He told me to take care of you. I told him that was a given."

She smiled, but her thoughts were in free fall. "They're going to dismiss me in a day or so."

"That's wonderful," he said.

"As much as I hate to go there, I'll probably finish recuperating at my parents' home, but only because it will be easier until I can be mobile on my own."

"I guessed as much."

"You'll come see me, won't you?"

"I'll call you every day," he said.

"But you won't come there?"

Their gazes locked. Finally, it was Brendan who looked away.

She sighed. "I'm sorry. I shouldn't have asked."

Before he could explain, the door opened and Grayson March strode in. His face was flushed, and there was a glitter in his eyes that Julie recognized as fury. She didn't know what was wrong, but she knew her father was about to make the current situation worse, and he did when he glared at Brendan.

"This is the last damn person I want to see right now."

Brendan lifted his chin, as if bracing for a blow.

Julie was horrified. "Daddy! How dare you—"

Grayson was so angry he was shaking. "I can't prove it, but I know your father was responsible for—"

Brendan was fed up and pointed a finger in Grayson's face.

"That's enough, damn it! I'm sick and tired of being the punching bag for what's going on between you and Anson Poe. You two grew up together. You have known him a hell of a lot longer than I have. I haven't lived at home since I was nineteen years old and there is a reason for that. You're a grown man. Try acting like one."

Grayson flinched. The put-down was hard to hear, and

he could tell by the look on Julie's face she was going to be mad at him all over again.

Brendan lifted Julie's hand to his lips. "I'm sorry, Julie. I love you. I will always love you, but you have to go home to get well, and I wouldn't set foot there if my life depended on it."

Julie was crying. "I'm sorry. I'm so sorry."

"You are no more responsible for your father's actions than I am for mine. I'll call you."

"You don't understand," Grayson snapped. "Two of my men are dead and—"

Brendan's expression went blank. "Are you accusing me of murder?"

"No, but—"

"Then shut the fuck up," he said softly and walked out of the room without looking back.

Julie pointed at the door. "Get out."

Grayson sighed. "Look, you don't know what's been happening."

"I won't ask you again," Julie said.

He pivoted angrily and strode out of the room, blaming everything that was going wrong in his life on the argument he had with Poe at the apartment building. He was convinced that none of this would ever have happened had it not been for his daughter's infatuation with Anson's son.

****

Lisette Branscum finally made a decision. Knowing she had been burned out on purpose had destroyed any interest she might have had in rebuilding her life in New Orleans. Without knowing who her enemy was, she'd be living the rest of her life looking over her shoulder. She had applied for a passport and as soon as her insurance money and the passport arrived, she was going to Paris—maybe for good. In the meantime, she'd decided to make the rounds of the city where she'd been born, saying good-bye to her friends without tears or angst.

It was during one of her visits that she heard the latest local gossip about Anson Poe and wondered if the voodoo curse she'd asked Mama Lou to put on him had taken a wrong turn. If it was working, Anson should've been the one going down for murder, not giving a statement that pointed the finger at Grayson March's hired guns.

She feared she had misjudged him and made a mistake by having him cursed, then wondered what would happen to her for having a curse put on an innocent man. The only way she'd know for sure was pay another visit to Mama Lou.

****

Mama Lou had come by her name honestly. She'd birthed nine children in her life, seven of whom were still living. Those children had given her twenty-eight grandchildren, twelve great-grandchildren, and to date, one great-great-grandchild. She'd outlived two husbands and three lovers, and swore to this day that they all died with smiles on their faces. While her lust for life was unmistakable, it was her religion for which she was known.

Voodoo was as much a part of Mama Lou as the children she'd carried in her womb. Unlike some of the other practitioners who also catered to tourists, she lived under the radar, dealing only with locals and true believers. She saw her clients in her home and had one due at any moment, so when she heard the knock at her door, it was not Lisette Branscum she expected to see.

Lisette eyed the tiny little woman nervously, afraid her arrival would be viewed as a lack of faith.

"Mama Lou, I know you didn't expect me, but I need to ask you a question."

"You may ask."

The tiny row house, common to the area where Mama Lou had lived for the past seventy-nine years, was only feet away from the houses on either side. Lisette looked over her shoulder to make sure they were alone, then leaned down to whisper the question.

"What I asked you to do was because I believed a man was guilty of a crime. What happens if he is innocent? Does the curse still work or does it come back on me for cursing an innocent man?"

Mama Lou's gaze shifted to a spot just over Lisette Branscum's shoulder. At first, her eyes widened, and then they narrowed as if focusing in on a sight only she could see.

"The man is innocent of nothing. It will work as it is meant to work. When you leave here, take nothing with you of your past."

Lisette shrugged. "I have nothing left of my past. It all burned up."

"You have your ways. Do not practice them again or it will come to no good."

A shiver ran up Lisette's spin. "I understand."

"You go now," Mama Lou said.

Lisette left the stoop, moving at a fast clip down the sidewalk and never looked back.

****

Anson sat on the tailgate of his truck watching a cottonmouth slither across the ground only a couple of yards from where Chance was standing.

His boys had just finished loading up the bamboo pots in the wholesaler's truck and were cleaning up the workstations as the wholesaler drove away.

Anson was counting out his money while watching the snake and making silent bets with himself as to what was going to happen next. He was so into the game that he didn't realize he'd been made.

Sam happened to look up, noticed the odd expression on his father's face, which led him to follow Anson's line of sight right to the deadly snake only a few feet from the back of Chance's leg.

Sam grabbed a machete from the worktable, pushing Chance aside with one hand as he swung the knife with the other, swiftly cutting off the snake's head. Blood spurted on the back of Chance's pants as the snake's body began writhing in death throes.

"What the hell?" Chance yelled, then looked down and shuddered. "Oh hell! Thanks brother."

Sam turned to face Anson, the machete gripped tightly in his hand.

"You son of a bitch."

Anson frowned. "Watch your tongue, boy."

Sam pointed the machete at him to punctuate the question. "How long were you going to watch before you said something?"

Chance looked at his brother in confusion. "What do you mean?"

Sam was still staring at his father, stunned by the smirk on his face. "He knew the snake was there. He watched it getting closer and never said a word."

Chance turned on his father in disbelief. "Is that true?"

"You weren't in any danger," Anson said.

Chance took a step back, his voice sudden shaking.

"You were betting my life that the snake wouldn't strike? Is that all we are to you... a little entertainment at the end of a day?"

Anson laughed. "What are you gonna do? Cry about it?"

Chance doubled up his fists, but then seemed to think better of it and strode out of the shed without a word.

Anson arched an eyebrow. "By damn I think he *is* gonna cry."

Sam was so angry he was shaking, but what frightened him more was how easy it would be to behead their snake-of-a-father as he'd beheaded the one on the ground. Instead of acting on the thought, he laid the machete on the table and walked out, followed by the sound of his father's laughter.

"Get here early tomorrow," Anson yelled. "We got a crop to harvest."

Sam just kept walking.

Chance was waiting for him in the truck.

He got in without saying a word, started the engine and drove away.

Chance hands were fisted against his knees, his voice thick with tears. "What the fuck are we doing?"

Guilt weighed heavily on Sam's shoulders. He was the oldest. If he'd taken a stand, neither one of them would be in this position today.

"We're keeping Mama and Linny safe, that's what we're doing."

Chance shuddered. "If that's what you tell yourself to make this work, then so be it, brother. But I'm telling you now that no one is safe around him. He's always been wild, but now he's getting mean, crazy mean."

"So what do you want me to do?" Sam muttered. "If we quit, that leaves Mama and Belinda at his mercy."

Chance hit the seat with his fist. "Why do good people die, and people like him still keep living?"

Sam shook his head. "That's not for us to know or to judge. That's between them and God, little brother."

"I'm gonna make him sorry," Chance said.

"By doing what?" Sam asked.

"I'm not telling you, so you won't try and talk me out of it. But you'll know when it happens."

Sam frowned. "Don't go and do something stupid."

Chance laughed, but there wasn't a shred of humor in the sound. "Fuck it, Sam. We're already doing something stupid every time we set foot on Wisteria Hill. Every time we cut his fucking weed. Every time we do business with a man like Wes Riordan. We both heard Riordan talk about what kind of money he could get for selling Linny, and neither one of us said a thing. He was talking about pimping out our little sister to some sick perverts and we just stood there. Stood there! I still have nightmares about it!"

Sam's gut knotted. "And what do you think would happen to her if we weren't there anymore?"

And just like that, all of Chance's rage was gone. He scrubbed his hands over his face and leaned back against the seat in quiet defeat.

"I know you're right. But it's not going to keep me from wishing the bastard dead, and don't preach at me. That sin will be between *me* and God."

Sam shrugged. "I'm not throwing stones or preaching at anyone. We're both guilty of plenty on our own."

Chance changed the subject. "My truck will be ready tomorrow so I'll drive out on my own."

Sam eyed the jut of his brother's jaw. "What are you going to do tonight? Are you still seeing that pretty little hostess at the steak house?"

"No."

"Why not?" Sam asked.

"Because I don't want Daddy to know I like her. He'd find a way to fuck with her, that's why."

Sam couldn't deny he'd made similar decisions in the past. "This is a hell of a way to live, isn't it, brother?"

Chance shook his head. "I don't call this living. We're just going through the motions."

Sam sighed. "Look, I know you're right about everything. I'll think on this some myself. Maybe we can come up with a way to work this out and keep Mama and Linny safe, too. Okay?"

Chance hunched his shoulders and stared down at his boots. "Brendan was the smart one. He left before Daddy could get his hooks into him."

"That's not how I saw it," Sam said. "Didn't you ever stop to wonder why Daddy let him go?"

"Let him?"

"Think about it," Sam said. "Daddy's mean, but he's also smart. Brendan has bucked him from the time he knew how to talk back, and Daddy let it happen. He let Brendan leave home without a word because he knew if he didn't, the day would come when Brendan would challenge him and win. Daddy isn't afraid of anyone or anything, but he knows the only person he's never been able to scare or control is Brendan, and in a sick way, he respects Brendan for it."

"I don't want his fucking respect," Chance muttered.

"None of us do, least of all Brendan," Sam said. "I'm just saying that Brendan is also the most like Daddy. He's just as single-minded and hard-headed, but in a good way."

Chance shrugged. "I know, but it doesn't change the

fact that I wish Anson Poe would drop off the face of the earth."

"I'll add an Amen to that and buy you a beer before you go home."

"Done," Chance said.

Sam smiled. "As long as we stick together, we'll get through this. You'll see."

****

Brendan entered his apartment with his arms full of groceries, plus the candy Belinda had requested.

"Look at all this!" Claudette said as she began putting things away. "Are you planning a siege?"

Brendan shrugged. "I don't like to shop much, so I usually pack in enough stuff to last a while."

Claudette caught a tone in his voice and turned to look at him. His expression wasn't any better.

"You are not happy."

"It doesn't matter. It will either work out or it won't," he muttered.

Claudette decided to try another subject. She brushed flour from the front of her red sundress then continued to empty the sacks.

"Did your Juliette use Mama Lou's gift?"

"Yes, and was very grateful. She said it numbed the pain."

"Good. She will heal much faster. Is she coming home soon?"

Brendan didn't crack a smile. "She's going to her parents until she's better," he said and slid a six-pack of beer into the refrigerator.

"Will you visit her there?" Claudette asked.

Brendan looked up. "No, and she knows it."

"Was she angry with you?"

"Not with me."

Claudette shrugged. "Then it is all good."

Brendan shook his head. "No, Auntie, it's not good. It'll never be good between us again. Anson made an enemy out of Grayson March, and I'm the closest whipping boy. I need to call Sam. March was ranting about two people dead and said Anson was to blame and I didn't know what he was talking about."

"You can call your brother if you want, but I know the answers to your questions. It was on the local news at noon."

Brendan frowned. "On the news? What the hell has he done now?"

Claudette proceeded to tell him, right down to the last detail.

Brendan was stunned. "So March's hired guns were on LeDeux's property and thought it was Anson who was shooting at them?"

She nodded.

"And they're all dead?"

"Yes, both of March's men and LeDeux. His little house burned down in the shoot-out."

"Are they going to charge March in any way?" Brendan asked.

"They didn't say anything about it," Claudette said.

Brendan shoved a hand through his hair in frustration. "No wonder he was pissed. This isn't going to look good for him."

"This is what happens when armed men have a disagreement. Someone always gets hurt, and quite often killed."

Brendan heard footsteps and turned around just as Linny entered the kitchen.

"I thought I heard you talking," she said.

He shifted mental gears quickly as she sidled up beside him. "I brought candy," he said.

"Yay! What kind did you get?"

"Those little miniature chocolate candy bars you like." He handed her the bag. "Here you go, and don't forget to share."

"Thank you, Brendan, thank you!"

"You're welcome. Now you have to do something for me."

She was immediately curious. "Like what?"

"Bring your candy to my room and you'll see."

She grabbed the bag and followed him out of the kitchen. As soon as they reached his room, she crawled up onto the bed and waited, watching as he got something out of the dresser on the other side of the room. When she saw it was a phone, she squealed with delight.

"I get my own phone?"

Brendan sat down beside her, his expression grave. "It's a special phone, and I need to show you how to use it."

"I already know how," Linny said. "Sam lets me play games on his."

"This one isn't for play," Brendan said. "It's for emergencies only. Do you know what an emergency is?"

When her smile slipped sideways, Brendan was overwhelmed. No child should have to live like this. She nodded. "An emergency is when you have to call an ambulance, right?"

"Yes, or when you're in danger. Do you know what danger is?"

Her shoulders slumped, and then she leaned in against him. "Daddy is dangerous."

Brendan frowned. "Who told you that?"

"No one. I just know."

He was almost afraid to ask, and yet he had to. "Has he ever hurt you?"

She nodded.

Brendan pulled her onto his lap and then wrapped his arms around her. "Tell me," he said softly.

"I can't. He said if I told, he would hurt Mama."

The terror Brendan was feeling was almost more than he could handle. "Then this can be just our secret. You'll tell me and I won't tell anybody else, not even Anson, okay?"

She leaned back against his arm, searching the expression on his face. Something she saw satisfied her concerns. Once again, she leaned into him, resting her head against his chest.

"Once, he got really mad at me and squeezed my throat too hard. I couldn't breathe and went to sleep. When I woke up, he was throwing water in my face. He said if I told anyone, he would make sure Mama never woke up again."

"Oh Linny... baby... I'm sorry," he whispered and hugged her to him. "Why did he do that?"

"I used one of his coffee cups to clean my watercolor brush."

"Are you afraid to go home?"

"Not anymore."

"Why?"

"Cause Daddy is fixing the house all pretty and it will be better. Everything will be better. Mama said."

Brendan was so scared he couldn't focus. The walls were closing in around him and he was helpless to stop it.

"What would you say if I asked you to stay here with me?"

She sat up, suddenly uneasy. "No, Bren. I have to go

home with Mama, okay? Don't be mad at me. I have to go home."

"I'm not mad, honey. I could never be mad at you. I just asked. That's all."

She was visibly relieved. "Okay then."

"Right, so let's talk about this phone. It's only for when you feel like you and Mama are in danger, and all you have to do is just push this button. It will call my phone. You won't have to talk. You won't have to do anything, because I'll know if you make that call that you need me, understand?"

"Yes, Bren. I understand."

"Okay, let's practice. You go down to the end of the hall, press that button and then hide it in your pocket or somewhere in your clothes. Don't hang up. Ever. Because I can find you if the phone is still on... understand?"

"Yes, like leaving the television on even if you leave the room."

"Exactly," he said. "So which button are you gonna press?"

"This one," she said and put her finger on it.

"Go hide and call me."

She ran out, clutching the phone against her chest.

He hated this was happening—that it was even necessary—but he wasn't stupid. If Mama Lou said do it, then this was serious business.

All of a sudden, his cell phone began to ring.

He looked down at the Caller ID. The pre-programmed message he'd put in it was working. It read 911. He got up and walked out into the hall.

Linny was hunkered down in the darkest corner with her head down on her knees and the phone held tight within her hand.

"You did good," he said. "Do you know how to hang up?"

She punched another button and the 911 message disappeared.

"Good job," he said, as he squatted down beside her and handed her the cord to charge it. "You'll have to charge it every night. Do you know how?"

She took the cord, plugged it into the right spot on the phone, and then held up the end that went in the socket.

"This plugs into the wall, right?"

"That's right. Good girl," he said.

She stared down at the phone. "Hey, Bren?"

"What, honey?"

"What do I do after I punch the button?" she asked.

"You wait for me to come get you and Mama."

She leaned forward, her voice just above a whisper. "Sir Brendan will come to Queen Belinda's rescue?"

"Yes, I will," he said.

Her voice began to shake, as if she already felt the danger. "You'll come fast? You'll have to come fast."

"I'll come so fast you won't believe it."

When her shoulders slumped, he pulled her closer. "Remember, Linny. This is our secret. You can't tell anyone about this phone... not even Mama."

"I can keep a secret."

"Where are you going to hide it?" Brendan asked.

"I can't tell you," she whispered. "I'm the only one who'll know."

"Good girl," he said, then kissed the top of her head. "Go hide your phone and then come to the kitchen. We're gonna make cookies."

"Can I tell Mama that?"

"Yeah, you can tell Mama about the cookies."

He stood up as she left, then followed to see what she was doing. His mother was still asleep and Linny was on the pallet with Rabbit in her lap. He remembered seeing a small rip in the seam at the rabbit's back and realized she was putting the phone inside it.

"Fucking brilliant," he muttered, then headed for the kitchen.

Chapter Sixteen

Anson Poe's naked body was slick with sweat, as was the whore going down on him. The paper-thin sheet on the motel mattress was bunched up beneath him like a handful of used tissues, but he didn't care. He liked the discomfort of being too hot almost as much as the brain-freeze of holding onto a climax until it hurt.

When he finally turned loose to ride the blood rush, he had both hands in her hair, her face mashed up against his groin, completely oblivious of the fact that she was choking. She finally landed a blow to his balls to get his attention.

"What the hell?" he yelled as he pushed her back and sat up.

She fell backward off the bed and made a grab for her clothes and shoes as she bolted for the bathroom.

He leaped up from the bed to follow her and got the door slammed in his face for the effort. He could hear her inside, slamming doors, and crying and cursing. The toilet flushed. He stepped back, ready to grab her for round two, then heard the sound of a window opening.

"What the fuck?"

He began looking around for his clothes to chase her down, and he was putting on his jeans when he heard her yell.

"You owe me one hundred dollars, you crazy bastard, and I'm sending T-Boy to collect."

He cursed. Now her pimp would be bugging the shit out of him for the money.

"I'm not paying for something you didn't earn!" he yelled back.

"You wanted a blow job. You got a blow job. The end."

"Then open the door and I'll give you your money!" Anson shouted.

"Shove it under the door or wait for T-Boy. And just so you know, he charges interest."

"Bitch!" he said softly, then pulled out a handful of twenties and shoved them under the door.

He saw one red-tipped fingernail snake out from under the door and watched the money disappear.

There was more shuffling and then silence. The whore was gone.

What pissed him off was that she'd bested him. That never happened. He thought about enacting a little payback of his own, then reminded himself she wasn't worth the trouble it would take to break her nasty neck. Only now, he needed the bathroom and the door was locked, but it gave easily when he threw his weight against it, and the problem was solved.

He strode in, slammed the window shut and locked it, then kicked off the blue jeans hanging down his butt and turned on the water. He wasn't leaving until he'd washed every aspect of the bitch from his skin.

****

Julie's life had been out of control ever since Chub Walton dragged her out of The Black Garter, but not anymore. She'd made the decision to take it back during the early morning hours, and she was sitting on the side of the bed, waiting for the doctor to make his morning rounds.

When Doctor Ames finally came in, he was unprepared for her attitude and appearance. In the last twenty-four hours, she'd gone from manic and being hobbled by pain to sanity and a decent mobility. He examined the lash marks and was pleased her temperature was almost normal.

"These are healing quite well," he said. "They are no longer suppurating. Some of them are even beginning to granulize. I'm quite pleased by—"

"I want to leave now."

Doctor Ames was a bit taken aback, but not firmly opposed to her request.

"I suppose you could continue bed rest at your parents' home. I can recommend a private duty—"

"I'm not going there. I don't need a nurse either. I can take myself to the bathroom. I can apply the necessary medicine."

He frowned, convinced she was missing the bigger picture. "You do know that we've been keeping the media away, but you're setting yourself up for a deluge of reporters once they know you're free."

She shrugged. "I know what's going on and I know what happened to me is news. But once they've seen me, it will be old news, and unlike my parents, I have nothing to be ashamed of. I didn't commit a crime. I was a victim and I'm a survivor." Her voice started shaking. "Maybe the people of New Orleans would like to know what a survivor looks like. Maybe I'll wind up on Oprah." She slapped her hands against the side of the bed as her vision began to blur. "Maybe they'll make a fucking movie about me. Who knows?"

Ames sighed. He'd been waiting for this stage. Anger

was part of the grieving process, and she had plenty to be angry about.

"You shouldn't be alone," he said gently.

"I need to be alone," Julie said.

"But what if—?"

"Are you going to dismiss me or not?"

He sighed. "I will, but I'm noting in the record that it's against my better judgment."

"I don't care what your record says. Just sign me out, please."

He touched the top of her head in a gesture meant to be comforting, but she ducked away from contact.

"I'll send a nurse in with some instructions for your care."

Julie pulled at the hem of her gown. "They brought me here naked. May I have some scrubs to wear to get me home?"

He nodded. "I expect you to see your family doctor on a regular basis to make sure you don't develop any infections."

She nodded.

"I'm very sorry for what happened to you," Doctor Ames said.

"So am I," she said.

As soon as the doctor left, she reached for the phone, got an outside line, and called her grandmother. As soon as she heard her grandmother's voice, she started talking.

"Nonny, it's me, Julie."

"Julie! Darling! You're sounding much better."

"I'm feeling better, too. In fact, I'm leaving the hospital this morning, and I was wondering if I could stay with you while I finish recuperating."

"Of course you can stay. I will treasure your company,

but it bears the question, what's wrong between you and your parents?"

Julie burst into tears. "Oh, Nonny, it would be easier to tell you what's not wrong. Daddy is doing everything he can to drive Brendan away from me. I'm scared to death that he will get enough of it and leave me just to get rid of Daddy."

"You don't give your man enough credit. From what I saw, you couldn't drive him away. However, you stay with me and we'll fix this mess together."

"Thank you, Nonny. I don't know what I'd do without you."

"You're welcome, darling. Are you coming now?"

"Yes, as soon as the doctor finishes signing the release papers."

"I'll have Janie make up the bed in the guest room. What about clothes?"

"They are all at my apartment. I'll ask Brendan to bring some tomorrow."

"Then we're good to go. I'll see you soon, darling, and don't worry. I'll shake some sense into Grayson or know the reason why."

"There's one more thing, Nonny."

"What's that, darling?"

"My presence at your home may bring unwanted media attention."

"I didn't think of that, but we'll handle it as well. You come when you're ready, and the rest will take care of itself."

When the connection ended, Julie grabbed a tissue and blew her nose before making the next call, this time to her old boss. It rang three times and then she heard a click.

"Hello?"

"Jack, it's me, Julie. I was hoping you were still in town."

Jack Michaels beamed. "Well hello, honey! It's good to hear your voice."

"I need a favor."

"All you have to do is ask."

"I'm leaving the hospital and I need a ride."

"Now?"

"Yes."

"Is something wrong between you and Brendan?"

"Yes."

"Oh damn, honey, I'm sorry. What happened?"

"My father happened, that's what. He's ruining everything and I've got to get away from my parents before I lose Brendan altogether."

Jack frowned. "Don't tell me he's still riding that old horse about blaming Brendan for what happened to you?"

"He's lost his mind, Uncle Jack. He hates Anson Poe so much and keeps putting Brendan in the middle."

"Well hell. I'll be right there. You can tell me the rest when I take you... Oh wait. Where am I taking you?"

"To Nonny's. She's the only one who can keep Mother and Daddy in line."

"Good choice, sugar. Just give me a few minutes. I need to gas up before I come get you, okay?"

"Yes. I'll have them take me down to the emergency room entrance, just in case there are any reporters lurking about out front. That way all you have to do is just drive up and they'll bring me out."

"Sure thing. I'll see you soon."

She hung up. One more call—the most important one of all. When she heard Brendan's voice, despite her best intentions she started crying again.

First, it startled him, and then it made him angry. "What's wrong? Talk to me, sweetheart."

"I'm just heart-sick about what Daddy is doing to you. I hate him for it. I'm scared you'll leave me just to be rid of him and-"

"Julie, stop talking a minute, okay?"

"Okay," she said, then grabbed a handful of tissues and blew her nose.

"I will never quit loving you. I will never leave you. Do you hear me?"

"Yes."

"Then don't insult me by thinking that again. We're not the sum total of our parents, thank God, because mine is fucking crazy, and yours has a God complex. Other than that, they're just fine."

She laughed through tears. "Don't hold back, honey. Tell me what you really think."

He shoved a hand through his hair in frustration and then grinned. "Yeah, well, I'm pretty fed up with the both of them, myself."

"So am I, which is why I'm going to Nonny's to recuperate instead of going home."

He grinned. He and her grandmother had hit it off. "This is great!"

"I think so, too," Julie said. "I was wondering if you wouldn't mind packing up some stuff from my apartment and bringing it to her house sometime tomorrow."

"I would be happy to do that for you."

"Bring my toiletries, some clothes that are soft, and also loose or baggy, and my fuzzy house shoes."

He grinned. "Those purple things?"

"Yes, those purple things. I love them and they're soft, which, at this moment in my life, takes precedence over style."

"Will do," he said.

"Do you know where Nonny lives?"

"No. Hang on a sec and let me get a pen."

Julie could hear him shuffling through a drawer, then his voice in her ear.

"I'm ready. Go ahead."

She gave him the address. "So I'll see you tomorrow?"

"Count on it."

"Be aware of reporters who might bug you if they see you arrive."

"I lived nineteen years with Anson Poe. Reporters do not scare me, okay?"

She closed her eyes, letting the sound of his voice wash through her. "You are my world, Brendan Poe. I always count on you."

"Ah, Juliette... there you go turning my head," he said softly.

She closed her eyes, feeling every nuance of the love in his words. They would get through this hell together.

****

Two days later

Anson was ready to make a call to LaDelle and play nice. The remodeling was finished, the new curtains and drapes were up, and the pink bedspread to match the walls in Linny's bedroom was in place. It was the most expensive trap he'd ever set, but once it was sprung, the satisfaction he would get would be worth it.

He'd been up since daybreak, ready to get the day in gear, but time began to drag when his sons had yet to show.

Ever since their little dust-up with the snake, they'd

developed an attitude he didn't like. He'd gotten a call from Wes Riordan last night, and he wanted another load of marijuana and they didn't have one ready. Riordan would show up in five days and they didn't have any time to waste.

When nine o'clock came and went and they were still missing, Anson got pissed. He called Sam, but didn't get an answer. The day was already hot—the sky was cloudless and a blue so pale it looked white.

Anson walked off the back porch out into the yard, and as he did, he immediately smelled something burning. He sniffed the air to see which way the smell was coming from, but Wisteria Hill was surrounded on all sides by a heavy growth of trees and it was impossible to tell. He glanced at his watch again, then walked back into the house and all the way up to the second floor. If there was visible smoke, he should be able to see it from there.

He went into Linny's bedroom and looked out the window toward the front yard, but the sky above the tree line was clear. He crossed the hall to the spare bedroom on the opposite side of the house. The view from that window was toward the bamboo grove and the land beyond. He saw a plume of smoke rising above the treetops to the southwest, a second larger and darker one straight west, and an enormous plume of smoke to the northwest.

He couldn't tell how far away it was, but whatever it was, it was burning up fast. The smoke was thick and billowing, and without wind, hung heavily in the sky. He was trying to picture the layout of the land and what might be burning, when all of a sudden it hit him. He grabbed onto the windowsill to keep from staggering, watching in disbelief.

He was still looking out the window when he saw Sam drive into the yard and park. He watched him wiping sweat from his forehead as he got out and headed for the house, then watched him pause to sniff the wind, just as he'd done.

Seconds later, Anson watched his last truant son arrive, but at a frantic pace. Chance jumped out of the truck on the run, and from the window, Anson saw him shouting and pointing, and then saw Sam's reaction. When Sam broke into a run toward the house, and Chance headed for the packing shed, Anson decided it was time to make an appearance.

****

Sam's face was still numb from the shot the dentist had given him to fix his broken tooth. He was already sick to his stomach, and thinking about fighting fire in this heat seemed impossible, yet it appeared that's what was about to happen. He ran into the house, yelling as he went.

"Dad! Dad! Are you in here?"

Haste would change nothing. Anson came down the stairs at a methodical pace. The moment Sam heard the footsteps, he ran into the entry hall.

"Dad! I think the fields are on fire! Chance said he saw the smoke from the highway and tried to call you but you didn't answer."

Anson frowned and patted his pocket. The cell phone wasn't there.

"What the fuck?" he muttered, trying to remember when he'd had it last, and headed for the kitchen. It was lying on the counter next to the coffee pot. He checked his calls. He'd missed one—from Chance.

Fuck.

Sam ran right past him and out the door.

Anson pocketed the phone and followed as Sam pointed toward the packing shed.

"Chance went to get the little tractor. It still has the dozer blade on it. Maybe we can—"

Anson was still in shock, but it was swiftly turning to rage.

"I saw the smoke. It's too late. You're late. You're both late. Where the fuck have you been?"

Sam pointed to his swollen jaw. "I told you yesterday evening I had a dentist appointment this morning to fix that broken tooth."

Anson shifted from one foot to another, wanting to hit something, or someone.

"I didn't hear you say that. I fucking did not hear you say that."

Sam straightened. He could already see where this was going. "You laughed when it broke yesterday. Do you fucking remember that?"

Anson frowned. He didn't like to be wrong, but he did remember that. What the hell was happening to him?

Chance came out from behind the packing shed on the tractor, waving to indicate he was ready.

Sam glared. "If you're not interested in fighting fire, I'm damn sure not, either."

Anson knew they had to put it out or someone would eventually call the fire department, then one thing would lead to another and the secret pot fields would be a thing of the past. He pointed at Sam.

"You drive," he muttered and got in Sam's truck.

Sam got behind the wheel, stopped at the shed to throw in a couple of shovels, and followed Chance up through the bayou to the first of the marijuana patches. By the time they arrived, it was gone and the foot-high flames were burning toward the underbrush.

Chance headed for the fire line, lowered the dozer blade and plowed right through it, smothering out most of it, while Anson and Sam put out the rest by shoveling dirt onto the wild spots.

The heat from the fire was intense, adding to the heat of the day, and they were deep inside the backcountry without a breath of moving air to cool them off.

Mosquitoes buzzed their ears, making jerky forays to their bare arms and the backs of their necks as they slung dirt and tamped out the hot spots. Snakes slithered through the grass ahead of the flames while rabbits darted out of the smoking underbrush. Today, no one was happy in the bayou.

They moved to the second fire at a hasty pace, anxious to get it out as well, and repeated the process. But this fire was farther along than the first, and there were some anxious moments before they finally stopped the fire at the trees.

By the time they got to the last fire, it had pretty much burned out on its own. There was nothing left but smoke and ash, which was fortunate because all three men were so high on the pot-laced smoke they were staggering.

Anson sat down on the tailgate of the truck before he fell down, and Sam was bent over at the waist, trying not to puke. Chance got off the tractor and headed for the bayou, staggering and stumbling as he went.

"Where the hell are you going?" Anson yelled.

"In the water!"

Anson cursed. "Sam, go get your brother. He's so fucking stoned he'll probably crawl in beside a gator and wonder what the hell happened when his legs come up missing."

Sam pushed himself upright and headed toward the water as fast as he could move, yelling at Chance all the way. He caught him just inside the woods, clinging to a tree trunk to get his breath.

"I'm so fucked," Chance muttered, then looked up at Sam and laughed.

Sam frowned. "Are you crazy? If Daddy hears you laughing he'll kill you where you stand. If he wasn't so high, he'd already be shooting at something."

Chance's smile shifted to a smirk. "He laughed at me when that snake nearly crawled up my pant leg, and now I'm the one laughing."

Sam gasped. "Oh man... oh hell... you didn't?"

Chance's eyes narrowed angrily. "I told you I'd get even."

Sam looked over his shoulder then lowered his voice. "You set the fires?"

"I'm just sorry he wasn't tied to a stake in the middle of it."

Sam grabbed his brother's arm. "Listen, get that attitude out of your system and do it now. You do not want him to know this. Ever."

Chance shoved Sam's hand away. "You don't know what I want," he said, then staggered back toward the tractor. "I'm going to the house, and then, I'm going home. Our jobs here are over."

He walked off, leaving Sam to follow. By the time Sam got back to his truck, Chance was on the tractor and driving out of the field.

"Where's he going?" Anson asked. "I wanted to talk to him, too."

"I didn't know that. I told him to go home and sleep it off."

Anson swiped a hand across his face and then looked out at the blackened area, trying to figure out what happened.

"Cops didn't do this. They'd still be out here gloating and waiting to arrest me."

Sam's mind was racing, trying to come up with a story that would get Anson off their case.

"What about that thief? The one who kept stealing a little of your stuff? What if he got greedy, came in and cut down a whole bunch of it, and then set the fire to hide the theft?"

Anson looked again, trying to imagine something like that happening, and realized it was a damn good theory.

"You may be on to something, son. So we'll keep an ear to the ground, and if we hear of someone new with a big load to sell, I'll be paying him a visit."

Sam nodded.

"Take me back to the house," Anson said. "I need to call Riordan."

"Oh man, was he coming?" Sam asked.

Anson nodded as he got into the truck and then glanced out the window one last time. "This couldn't have happened at a worse time. I spent a lot of money fixing up the place, and I'm low on ready cash."

"So we'll replant," Sam said.

Anson didn't comment, and Sam had no idea what was going through his mind except that he was too damned quiet. He started toward home with a heavy heart, still worried that Anson would find out what Chance had done.

As for Anson, he hadn't been this high since before he was married, and he was having trouble focusing his thoughts. He liked Sam's theory that they'd been robbed, although something like this had never happened before. Before today, he would've sworn there wasn't a man living with the guts to steal from him. But there was that thing with the whore who'd gotten the best of him, and he'd never been tricked like that, either.

So when did things begin to change? He thought back to the day he'd poured coffee on Delle's feet. Brendan had knocked him on his ass and then shot that gun in his face, something he would've sworn could never happen. He'd planned a revenge that would gut Brendan's life. But maybe he should've done something sooner. Maybe he'd let the negative stay with him too long and it was affecting everything that happened after.

He thought about the coffin on the doorstep and what he'd done with it. Everything he'd planned on that caper had worked like a charm. But the voodoo hadn't been meant for Voltaire. It had been sent to him. What if there *was* something to that voodoo? What if he really had been cursed? And if he had, how did he get rid of it?

By the time they got home, Chance was long gone and the tractor was parked in the middle of the back yard. Anson frowned.

"Why did he leave that tractor out?"

Anxious to make sure Anson didn't view Chance's behavior as vengeful, he answered quickly. "He's just as high as we are, Daddy. Probably didn't know what he was doing."

Anson reached for the door handle. "I'm going to bed," he said, then almost fell on his face when he got out.

Sam heard him curse, then waited until he was all the way inside the house before he backed up and started home. So far, the only good thing about this day was that he'd gotten so high that the pain from the dentist visit was gone.

Chapter Seventeen

Brendan had been on his laptop most of the morning, scanning for jobs in his area. It was just after lunch before he got enough free time to take another bag of Julie's clothes to her grandmother's house.

He exited the apartment building with a suitcase in one hand and his car keys in the other, then dropped them on the sidewalk. The clink woke the old tomcat asleep under the shrubs, and when he bent down to pick them up, he got an angry hiss for his trouble.

"Sorry, dude."

The cat slunk away into the shadows as Brendan hurried to his truck. Moments later, he was on his way across town. He had just braked for a red light when his cell phone rang. When he saw it was Sam, his heart skipped a beat.

Sam rarely called, and never in the daytime when he was with Anson.

"Sam? What's wrong?"

"Everything. All three of the fields are gone. Burned to the ground."

"You're kidding! What happened? Did the DEA finally find them? Are you guys in trouble?"

"No, and this is what you can't tell. Chance and Daddy got into it the other day and this is the result."

"Holy shit! What set Chance off?"

"There was a water moccasin coming through the grass

toward Chance, and Daddy just set there watching it without bothering to warn him. I happened to see it just in time, killed the snake, then called Daddy on it. When Chance found out, he tore into Daddy then headed for the house. He told me on the way home that he'd make him sorry, and this is the result."

Brendan knew he should've been shocked, but he wasn't. Anson was crazy mean, and playing Russian roulette with a deadly snake was right down his alley.

"My hat's off to Chance. He knew exactly how to make him sorry."

"Daddy thinks someone just stole it all and then set the place on fire to cover up the theft."

"How did he come to that conclusion?" Brendan asked.

"Someone's been stealing a little here and there for over a year. When Chance told me what he'd done, I had to think fast to make sure Daddy didn't start blaming one of us, and that's what I came up with."

"Not bad," Brendan said, "but how's Anson taking it? Has he turned into a raving maniac yet?"

"No, but I think it's because we're all three stoned out of our minds. The fields were all engulfed by the time we got there. We fought fire all morning to put it out and smelling burning pot is just as bad as smoking it."

Brendan sighed. The light turned green. He accelerated through the intersection.

"And that's not all," Sam said. "Chance quit. Daddy doesn't know it. He just thinks he went home to sleep it off. When he finds out, he's not only going to be pissed, but he'll start thinking, and when he does that, he might figure out what happened."

"So, Chance finally quit. What about you?"

"I don't know. I can't think right now. I'm going to sleep this shit off and then go to confession. I haven't been to church in a long time, but I feel like things are beginning to come undone, and I'm scared."

Brendan frowned. "I'm sorry, Sam. You know I'll help you any way I can."

Sam laughed softly. "Thank you, little brother, but I don't think there's much anyone can do. Right now, I'm between a rock and a hard place. I don't want to alienate myself in case Mama and Linny come home."

"Oh, they're going home, all right. I just don't know when. Mama is already talking about it," Brendan said.

"Then I for sure need to stay on his good side. As long as I'm around, Daddy has to stay accountable for his actions. So, I'll talk to you later. Take care, little brother. I've got to lie down."

"Yeah, thanks for calling," Brendan said, but the line was already dead. "God in heaven," he said softly, then dropped the phone in the console.

Like Sam, he was scared, too. So much of their lives were based on secrets and lies, and now there were more lies—bigger lies—lies that could get his brother killed. By the time he pulled up at Portia March's house, he'd shifted mental gears. He had to put a good face on the day for Julie and began looking around for the reporters she'd been worried about, but didn't see anything out of the ordinary. As for Julie, she already had enough to deal with, and the less she knew about his family, the better.

Portia's home was in the Garden District of New Orleans, and from all appearances the narrow, three-story brick house was a very old one. Completely enclosed with a tall, wrought-iron fence that gave the place an austere appearance, it was the iron gates with their elaborate filigree designs that turned the iron into elegance.

With the addition of the live oaks and the hanging Spanish moss, the array of perfectly manicured grass, flowers beds and bougainvillea hanging from the west eaves of the porch, it looked like something out of a magazine.

He could imagine Julie playing here as a child, hiding in the bushes, ducking through the flowering archways, chasing after butterflies, and dodging all the bees. When he got to the front gate with the suitcase, he rang the bell.

Within moments, he saw her push aside the curtains at the front windows and wave. Her pretty face, still bearing the stripes from her kidnapper, was wreathed in smiles. Standing there in the shade of the live oak with a hot breeze blowing through his hair, it hit him. But for a few minutes and the grace of God, she would've already been dead and buried. Overwhelmed by that harsh reality, he blinked back tears and waved.

The front door opened. A thin, middle-aged woman emerged, wearing a neat, blue uniform with a crisp white apron over it. She came down the steps, then walked hastily toward the gate. Brendan smiled and waved at her. He and Portia's maid were becoming well acquainted.

"Good afternoon, sir," she said as she let him in.

"Good afternoon, Janie."

Julie was wearing a loose, oversized housecoat that he suspected belonged to her grandmother, and her feet were bare. It was still daunting to see the red and swollen marks on her skin and know she had the fortitude to smile through it.

"Hello, my darlin'," he said softly.

"I'm so glad to see you!" Julie said and lifted her face for the kiss she knew was coming. It was short but sweet and very polite. Considering they were in view of the street and her Nonny's maid, it was also very proper.

The maid pointed at the suitcase Brendan was holding.

"If those are some more of Miss Julie's things, I'll take that for you."

"That they are," Brendan said and handed them over.

"Come into the living room," Julie said. "Would you like something cold to drink? We have lemonade and iced tea."

"Maybe later," he said as he sat down beside her.

"Nonny is getting her hair done. She sends her regrets."

He ran a finger lightly down the side of her neck.

"Tell her I was devastated."

Julie giggled. "She'll love that."

"You look amazing," he said softly.

Her eyes widened. "Mama Lou is the amazing one. I swear the stuff she sent me is magic. I know I still look like a zebra, but the pain has lessened dramatically. Even more, I'm finally beginning to believe my skin will heal just as the doctors said it would."

"So how is the fall-out since you came here instead of going to your parents' house?"

She rolled her eyes. "The same. They aren't happy, but they never argue with Nonny."

"Good. You deserve some peace and quiet to recuperate. Oh, and I notice the reporters have yet to find you here."

Julie grinned. "Oh, they found out I was here, all right, but they are absent because Nonny made a few phone calls before I arrived. I don't know who she called or what she said, but as far as the media is concerned, I have dropped off the face of the earth."

"And more power to her," he added.

Julie threaded her fingers through his hand. "I feel like I've lost touch with you. Tell me what you've been doing."

"I've picked up some applications and filled out a

couple on site, but right now, no one's hiring, at least with my skill-sets. However, I'm not stressing about it since everything is still up in the air with my family. I would hate to begin a new job and then be needed elsewhere."

She nodded in agreement. "There will be time for job hunting later. Right now your family has to come first."

"And you. You're part of that for me."

Julie took a moment to appreciate the beautiful man before her. He had the appearance of an elegant dilettante, but the calluses on his hands and his chin-up, don't-fuck-with-me look was a giveaway to the real man behind the pretty face.

"You bless me, Bren."

He shook his head. "And, you bless me. I won't live without you in my life, and the dynamics of our families can't matter."

"Agreed, and because you are not only beautiful but also so sweet, I had Janie make cherry cheesecake just for you."

He grinned. "Any man worth his salt should reject the fact that someone just called him beautiful, but because it's you, I'll restrain myself, do the polite thing, and have a piece of that cheesecake. A big piece, if you please."

She giggled as she reached for a tiny bell on the end table and rang it.

Moments later, Janie appeared.

"We sold him, Janie. He requests a big piece of your cheesecake."

The maid beamed. "Coffee, too, Miss Julie?"

"Yes, coffee too," she said and eased herself into a more comfortable position.

"Are you hurting?" Brendan asked.

"Not like before. Clothes are still uncomfortable, but I'm not complaining."

Brendan leaned back, listening to her talking while wondering what tomorrow would bring. There was a knot in his gut that wouldn't go away. Anson was bound to come off that marijuana high fit to be tied, and he was about to return Delle and Linny to the ensuing chaos.

****

Anson had gone to bed and passed out, then woke up a few hours later in a state of shock. He'd been put out of the drug business in one fell swoop, and had no idea who the hell had done it. He needed to recoup the money he'd paid out on renovations and had nothing to sell.

It worried him that Riordan had been oddly non-committal when Anson told him what happened. He didn't want to lose the connection he'd worked so hard to foster, then edited the thought. What he really wanted was his life back, the way it had been before he threw the coffee on Delle's feet.

In a weak marijuana-infused moment, he regretted the act, but what was done was done. However, he could be proactive in one aspect, and that was to start making nice with his wife.

He rolled over in bed and reached for the phone, and as he did, remembered a bit of a nursery rhyme from his youth.

Come into my parlor said the spider to the fly.

It was time to sweet talk his woman back into his web.

****

LaDelle had just finished putting antibiotic ointment on the tops of her feet. Pleased with how well they were healing, she went to the bathroom to wash her hands and was rinsing off the soap when her phone began ringing.

"Linny! Answer my phone, please and tell whoever it is that I'll be right there."

Linny was coming down the hallway with Rabbit under her arm and when she heard the order, bolted for the bedroom.

"Hello, this is Belinda Poe speaking."

Anson hesitated. He'd had an opening comment prepared for his wife, not his daughter.

"Hey, Linny, it's me. Where's your mama?"

And just that fast, the smile on Linny's face was gone. "Mama said she'll be right here." Then she threw the phone down on the bed.

"Okay. How have you—"

Anson heard the soft thump as the phone hit the mattress and frowned. She'd abandoned him as fast as Brendan had. It appeared his daughter had been away from home a little too long.

He was still frowning when he heard footsteps, and then his wife's voice was in his ear. She sounded uncertain—even afraid, exactly how he liked his women.

"Hello?"

"Hey, sweetheart, it's me."

"Linny said it was you. What do you want?"

"I want you, Delle. I miss you. I want you to come home. I know I messed up, but I've been working long and hard to make it up to you. Everything you ever wanted done in the house has been done and more."

He heard her sigh and threw in another question. "How are your feet? Are they healing up okay? I'm really sorry about that."

"I know about the remodeling. The boys told me what you were doing and yes, my feet are healing."

He softened his voice and added a touch of dismay to the question. "Don't you want to come home?"

"Yes, but I don't know if I can trust you."

He laughed. "Darlin' Delle, you've never trusted me, and it didn't stop us from making some damn fine kids and a life together."

She smiled in spite of herself. He was right. She had never felt safe—not really—and that had always been the draw.

"You know what I mean," she said.

He shifted gears quickly. "Yes, of course I know what you mean. Just come home. You'll see what I did just for you. Will you? Will you come home?"

He waited, and when he heard her sigh, he knew he was getting to her.

"I want to," Delle said. "I think I have to. I don't really belong anywhere else."

He chuckled. "That's my girl. When do you want me to come get you?"

"Brendan will bring us home."

It wasn't what he wanted to hear, but he wasn't going to argue when everything was beginning to fall back in place.

"Okay, so when are you coming? I ask because I want to restock the groceries."

"Tomorrow. I'll ask him to bring us home tomorrow."

"That's fabulous! I can't wait to get my woman home and back in my bed."

"I'll be home. We'll talk about the bed. My feet are still very tender."

"Yeah sure, I understand. I love you, Delle, and I'm sorry." He waited, listening for another sigh, and when it came, he knew he had her.

"I love you, too," she said and ended the call.

Anson hung up the phone and then rolled over and laughed out loud.

Unaware of how she was being played, Delle looked down at the baby-pink skin on her feet and thought about what she was doing. It wasn't an easy decision, but it was right. It was time to let Brendan get back to his own life and quit worrying about theirs.

****

Brendan was at the kitchen table on his laptop, still scanning job sites when he heard his mama's phone ring. Claudette was changing loads of laundry, and the gumbo she'd started earlier was an aromatic promise of things to come. A few moments later, Linny came wandering up the hall and into the kitchen, dragging Rabbit by one arm. Brendan saw the expression on her face and closed his laptop.

"What's wrong, sugar?"

She went limp against his shoulder as she tucked Rabbit under her chin.

"Mama told me to answer her phone. It was Daddy. He's going to tell her to come home, and he's going to lie about being good to her."

He thought about how she's phrased that, as if she knew the future before it happened. "I thought you were ready to go home."

When she looked up, Brendan saw past the child to the old soul beneath. "Mama's ready, and I go with Mama," she said.

"Are you scared?"

She shrugged again. "I don't want them to fight."

He thought of all the nights when he and his brothers were little, and how they had huddled under their covers listening to battles that often went on until daybreak. They'd lived through it and she would, too. Still, it hurt him to think of the years of turmoil ahead of her.

"How about we get a cold pop and some cookies?"

Linny smiled. "Can I have two cookies?"

He laughed. "Queen Belinda, ever the negotiator. Yeah sure, why not? You get the cookies and I'll get the pop."

She headed for the cookie jar, her mood seemingly forgotten, but Brendan hadn't forgotten. He could hear his mother's voice, although he couldn't hear the actual conversation. It didn't take a genius to assume Anson was turning on the charm. The bastard was still the puppet master, making sure everybody danced to his tunes.

"What's going on in here?" Claudette said, when she saw them eating so close to lunchtime.

"Mama's talking to Daddy. I think we're going home," Linny said.

Claudette frowned. "Maybe I will have one of those cookies, too."

They were all working on their second cookie when Delle walked into the kitchen with her head up and her shoulders square to the world. There was a swagger in her step and a smile on her face. Brendan didn't like it, but he understood. She loved Anson Poe—despite every bad thing he'd ever done—despite the ongoing war between them—even when she knew it was wrong.

Claudette saw the look and recognized it for what it was. Just like the day LaDelle had defied her whole family to marry Anson, it appeared she was willing to risk her life all over again.

"Hey! I hope you saved me a cookie," Delle said.

Linny gave her one, then giggled when Delle pretended to bite her fingers and the cookie at the same time.

Brendan remembered her doing the same thing to him and his brothers when they were little. Despite the blind spot she had for Anson, she was an amazing mother.

Claudette stood up. "Want a Pepsi, sister?"

Delle smiled. "Don't mind if I do."

Claudette got another cold bottle from the refrigerator, unscrewed the cap, and handed it to her.

"When do you want to go home?" Brendan asked.

Delle looked a little taken aback that they'd already figured out her news, and then smiled shyly.

"I told Anson you'd bring us home tomorrow. I hope that's all right. If it's not, I can call him back and tell him to come get us."

Brendan frowned. "No. I'm the one who took you away. I'll be the one to bring you back."

Her smile slipped. "I'm sorry, Bren."

"Don't be sorry, Mama. I'm glad you're feet are getting better, and that you'll have a nice place to go home to."

"I think I'll be happiest about the air conditioning. I swear to my time, there's nothing worse than cooking in a hot kitchen."

Every nerve in Claudette's body was firing. Hot kitchens were a misery, but despite the added air conditioning, her sister was still returning to the heat of hell, and that made her sad on a level she couldn't explain.

As for Brendan, he just kept nodding and listening to his mother's voice, while the knot in his belly grew tighter with every word.

****

Sam woke up to an alarm clock going off, only to realize he'd slept from yesterday's nap all the way through to morning. He'd gone from a pot high to a hangover low and groaned loudly as he got out of bed. His head was throbbing as he staggered into the kitchen to turn on the coffeemaker, then back to the bathroom to shower.

By the time he was finished, the coffee was done. He

ate breakfast standing in the kitchen, wearing nothing but a frown and a towel around his waist, wondering what this day would bring.

When he went back to the bedroom to get dressed, he thought of Chance and what was on the horizon and wondered if he'd changed his mind. But when he tried to call, the fact that he didn't answer made him nervous. He left him a message, but even as he was hanging up, wondered what the hell to tell Daddy when Chance didn't show. He dressed with his gut in a knot, and when he stopped at the mirror for a last-minute check, all he could see on his face was the fear.

****

Chance woke up with a hangover of massive proportions. His drug of choice was the occasional beer, and he had never messed with anything else. Yesterday's events had been an unasked-for high.

He couldn't tell if this so-sick-he-had-to-get-better-to-die feeling was a physical reaction from the drug-laced smoke, or an emotional illness from the facts of his life. All he knew was that he felt dirty and he wanted it to go away.

For the first time, he thought he understood—really understood—what had driven Brendan away at such an early age. Despite the recent renovations to Wisteria Hill, it was rotting from the inside out, and taking everyone down with it.

Making the break as he had felt like taking the coward's way out, but he wasn't ready to die. He wasn't certain what came next, but it would be something of his own choosing.

When his phone rang and he saw Sam's name on caller ID, guilt hit him all over again. He sat staring at the name, refusing to answer because he was afraid he would cry. Only two years separated them in age, but Sam was the father he'd never had. Still, Sam made his choice and Chance was making his. Eventually, every child left home, it had just taken him longer than most to make that happen.

****

The day dawned cloudy with a chance of rain. The weather mirrored Brendan's mood. His mother and Linny had packed last night, and he could hear them chattering in their room down the hall as he made breakfast.

Claudette had said her good-byes to Delle last night. Both of them ended up crying because they knew this wouldn't happen again. When Delle made her choice to go home, it meant giving up contact with her sister again.

They made promises to keep in touch, but Claudette knew it wouldn't happen. Like before, Delle had chosen the devil over her own blood.

Brendan, on the other hand, had been just as adamant that his new Auntie would be a permanent part of his life. In a way, he would be the bridge between them.

Linny was going home with far more than what she'd brought. She had the doll and doll clothes Claudette had given her, Brendan's Xbox and games, and Rabbit with the secret phone hidden inside.

When Brendan called them to breakfast, they entered the kitchen chattering like two schoolgirls heading back after summer vacation.

Linny was talking about going back to see Sir Snapper and her kingdom in the bayou, and Delle was enamored of renovations to her home she had yet to see.

Brendan couldn't bring himself to swallow more than a few bites of the pancakes he'd made, but he kept his attitude positive. It wasn't like they were leaving the state. He would stay in touch as he'd always done, only this time more often. He couldn't help but wonder what would happen when Chance was a no-show, but that was out of his control. Maybe Delle and Linny's arrival would put Anson in a good mood and it would go unnoticed, at least for a while.

****

It was just after 10:00 a.m. when Brendan left the city. Storm clouds continued to build but the air was still. Even the weather was on hold, waiting to see what the homecoming would be like.

The closer they got to Wisteria Hill, the quieter Delle became. She was all but holding her breath as she waited for the first sight of the old mansion, and when he finally took the turn down the driveway, she scooted to the edge of the seat and then smiled.

"Oh, Brendan! Look! Just look how pretty! It looks amazing and the yard looks like a park! I can't wait to see the inside."

Linny was bouncing up and down in the back seat, excited because her mama was excited.

Brendan was stunned. This was way more than he'd expected and it made him nervous. By the time he pulled up and parked, his belly was in knots. When Anson came striding out the back door with a smile on his face, he felt like throwing up.

They all got out at the same time, but Anson had eyes for only Delle. He threw his arms around his wife and gave her a welcome-home kiss that was completely inappropriate anywhere but behind closed doors. Delle was so taken with the welcome she obviously forgot there were onlookers.

Brendan had Delle's suitcase in one hand and Linny's hand in the other. He looked away as they headed for the house, but he could tell his little sister was upset. Her steps were dragging as she held Rabbit tightly beneath her chin.

"You okay, honey?" Brendan whispered.

Her chin quivered. "Daddy didn't even say hello."

"Yeah, I know, but so what? Let's go see your new room."

Before she could answer, Anson and Delle were suddenly right behind them, and then Anson ran ahead. When they got to the porch, he was standing between Brendan and the door with his hands on his hips.

"No you don't, boy. This is as far as you go."

Brendan's head came up, and then a look passed between them. So, this was the payback for knocking Anson on his ass, taking his wife, and putting a gun in his face.

Linny started to shake. On the verge of tears, she hid her face against Brendan's leg, and then Delle walked up beside Brendan, put a hand on her daughter's head, and stared her husband down.

"The day will never come when you bar a child of mine from this door."

Anson felt the porch move beneath him, like the world had shifted a little bit off center, and once again, felt his power slipping away. He tried to play it down, but inside he was raging.

"It's your call, Delle honey, but I would have thought you'd at least be more understanding of my feelings. He put a gun in my face."

"After you hurt his mother," she countered.

At that moment, Anson hated the people before him with a rage he could barely contain. He'd misjudged Brendan's power-hold, but it wouldn't happen again. He made himself smile.

"You're right. You're totally right, honey girl. My bad. So ya'll come on in and take a look at how pretty I made it for you."

But the moment had broken Delle's euphoria. She glanced at Linny. The fear was back on her baby's face, and she already doubted her decision. What the hell had she done? The word *wait* was on the tip of her tongue when Anson pulled her inside, and then it was too late.

The tour through the house left Brendan stunned and Delle in awe. She was so fascinated by the elegance and new furnishings that her earlier anxiety faded.

As for Linny, she did what she always did and disappeared.

Sam came up from the packing shed in the middle of the tour to welcome his mother home. When Brendan caught his eye, Sam managed a smile.

"Where's Chance?" Delle asked.

"Oh, we had a bad day yesterday," Anson said. "I think he's just taking a little time off."

Delle frowned. "What kind of a bad day?"

"I thought Anson would have mentioned that last night when he called you," Brendan said.

Anson frowned. "How the hell did you find out?"

"I told him, Daddy," Sam said quickly.

Anson cut an angry look at his eldest, but didn't say more.

Brendan was happy to drop the bomb. "You're out of the drug business, Mama, although temporarily, I'm sure."

Delle spun. "What happened?"

Anson's eyes narrowed and his lips thinned, turning his picture-perfect face into an unflattering caricature.

"Someone stole the crops and burned us out."

Delle wanted to cheer. This was the break they needed to get back on track, but she had to take this slowly.

She put a hand on Anson's arm. "Maybe it was God's way of telling us that time is done," she said softly.

Brendan shook his head. "God doesn't make deals with criminals, Mama. Call if you need me." He kissed her cheek and walked away.

When the screen door slammed, Sam flinched. He had never felt so alone in his life.

Delle wanted to cry. She had no one to blame but herself and looked around for her daughter.

"Where's Linny? I don't think she ever came up to see her new room."

"I saw her running into the woods as I came up. You know how she is. She probably went to play," Sam said.

Everything was going wrong. Near tears, all Delle could think about was the storm.

"But it's going to rain."

Sam was more concerned about the storm building inside the house, but was thankful for an excuse to leave.

"I'll go find her, Mama."

Delle's anxiety eased as Sam hurried away.

The moment they were alone, Anson walked up behind her, put one hand on her breast and the other between her legs.

"I've been missing you, Delle. Come to bed."

She turned to face him, saw the same expression in his eyes she'd seen the day he burned her feet, and in that moment, what was left of her spirit died. She dropped her head and walked ahead of him up the stairs.

Chapter Eighteen

Sam found Linny sitting on a big rock by the water. Her head was on her knees, her shoulders shaking. His heart sank. She was crying and he felt helpless to make it better. A twig snapped beneath his shoe as he started toward her, and when her head came up and he saw the look of terror on her face, it only made him feel worse.

"It's just me, sugar. Why are you crying?"

She stood up slowly, rising tall on the knobby rock, her head up despite the tears.

"My kingdom is at war and my army is gone."

Sam stopped. He knew the game and realized her need to escape into an alternate world.

"I'm still here, My Queen. What would you have me do?"

Thunder rumbled overhead, a sign that the storm was about to break.

Linny looked up into the dark swirl of gathering clouds, then back at Sam. "The Evil Overlord is back in control. Dark times have come upon the land and I need a plan."

"How can I help?" he asked again.

She pointed her finger at him as if it was a scepter.

"Make a list of every bad thing the Evil Overlord has done. Make another list of all the bad people he knows. Write down everything you know about both of them."

Sam was stunned. Not only was the wisdom was sound, but it was something he would never have thought to do.

"What are you going to do with this information, My Queen?"

She was silent for a moment, and then she pointed into the storm. "There will come a day when you will use it to destroy him."

"Sounds like a plan to me," Sam said, wishing it could be true.

Lightning cracked somewhere nearby.

Linny leaped from the rock into Sam's arms. The queen was gone, leaving behind a frightened child. Sam held her firmly.

"Mama sent me to find you. It's going to storm."

"Take me home, Sammy."

He took her by the hand as they headed for home, trying not to think about how fragile she felt, and how easily she could break.

****

Anson strutted from his bed to the bathroom, satisfied that he was, once again king of his castle. He paid no mind to the fact that Delle had neither moved nor spoken through the entire sexual act. He didn't care. He'd just as soon fuck a corpse as a whining woman.

Delle's heart was broken. She'd finally accepted the fact that the man she loved existed only in her mind, and the one she was married to was a madman. She'd escaped once, but he wouldn't let it happen again. Her chance for redemption had come and gone.

The moment he shut the bathroom door, she leaped out of bed, grabbed her clothes, and made a run for the door. He would most certainly want a repeat performance when he returned, and she had no intention of being available. She dressed in an empty bedroom with her hands shaking and her heart pounding. As soon as she was decent, she bolted for the stairs in her bare feet, carrying her slippers.

The rumbling thunder sounded as disgruntled as she felt. The first drops of rain were beginning to blow against the windows as she reached the first floor and she didn't know where her daughter was. And then the moment she thought it, the kitchen door flew open, slamming against the wall with a bang. When she heard her children's voices, she sighed with relief. Sam had found her.

"There you are!" Delle cried and opened her arms.

Linny ran to her mother and buried her face against her breast.

Delle brushed the flyaway wisps of hair from her daughter's eyes and then tilted her chin until they were looking eye-to-eye.

"You shouldn't have run away with the storm so close," Delle said, then watched her daughter's eyes well with unshed tears.

"Daddy didn't even say hello."

"I know. I'm sorry," Delle said.

Linny shrugged. At the early age of nine, she already knew it wasn't wise to show a weakness. "It's okay. He's just the Evil Overlord, and I don't want to talk to him, either."

Delle frowned. "Don't talk like that. Your daddy wouldn't like it."

Linny's chin jutted. "And I don't like how he treated me. Like Bren says, things go both ways."

Delle had no answer for the truth. "Your clothes are wet. Go change into something dry, okay?"

"Is *he* upstairs?" Linny whispered.

Delle frowned. "Don't be so dramatic. Go change your clothes."

Linny glanced up at Sam.

"I'm not going anywhere, sugar. Go do what Mama said."

Linny feet were flying as she ran out of the kitchen and up the stairs.

****

When Anson came out of the bathroom, he was pissed that Delle was gone. But his mood quickly shifted as a clap of thunder rolled overhead, followed by a shaft of lightning so loud he thought it had struck the house. When he heard footsteps in the hall and then a door slam, he began to dress. By the time he came out, whomever he'd heard was gone. Once again, he felt abandoned and didn't like it.

He was walking toward the stairs when he heard footsteps behind him, but when he turned, there was no one there. He looked down. There was something on the floor only a few feet away.

It was a match.

"What the fuck?"

Before he could move, thunder rumbled again, this time closer.

Linny came flying out of her bedroom and ran past him without acknowledging his presence.

When he looked back down, the match was gone. He frowned. Had he just imagined it? He must have. It couldn't just appear and disappear on a whim. Then he heard the sound of distant drumbeats, and then closer, he heard the sound of rattles. He turned abruptly, fearing a rattlesnake had gotten into the house and was at his heels, but there was nothing to be seen.

Sweat beaded on his upper lip. He flashed back to the little black coffin on his doorstep, the same coffin he'd taken to Voltaire LeDeux's.

Was this part of what happened when someone was cursed? Refusing to believe it, he started toward the stairs.

The rattle sounded again and he moved faster.

"No way," he said, but he lengthened his stride.

The rattle was louder now, encircling him—then it was in his head, drowning out the sounds of the storm.

"NO!" he shouted, and all but threw himself down the stairs in an effort to escape, but there was nowhere to run. Not when the enemy dwelled within.

****

Two weeks later

Even though Juliette's nights were stuck on a rewind of waking up in Chub Walton's arms and the ensuing events, her body was healing at a steady pace. Portia March continued to run interference with Grayson and Lana, giving Julie time to regroup. As she began to heal, the ability to cope with her parents constant pressure became easier. The bottom line was obvious. They didn't want to be associated with the name Poe, no matter who wore it, and she wasn't going to leave Brendan to suit their social status.

Brendan visited daily, sometimes to bring cupcakes from Julie's favorite bakery or cold, smooth vanilla shakes for both Julie and her grandmother, and always to bring her mail.

Today, when he rang the bell at the gate to Portia's house, Julie was the one who came bouncing out, eyeing the mail tucked under his arm.

"Neither rain not sleet nor dark of night," she said as she unlocked the gate to let him in.

When he swooped down for his hello kiss, she resisted

the urge to throw her arms around his neck. It wouldn't do to make out on Portia March's front lawn.

"Come in," she said.

"Only for a minute," he said. "I'm going for an interview in less than an hour, and don't want to be late."

"Ooh, come tell me about it," she said, then led him into the house.

Portia came out of the library, delighted with their guest's arrival.

"Welcome, Brendan. Will you stay and have lunch with us?"

"No, ma'am, I have an interview shortly, but thank you for the invitation."

"Another time then," she said sweetly. "I'll leave you two to visit. If you need me, I'll be in the kitchen with Janie."

"Yes, ma'am," Brendan said.

Portia was still smiling as she walked away.

"Nonny adores you," Julie said as she led him into the living room.

"Can't ever have too many people loving on you," he said.

"As long as I'm at the head of the list, I'll share," Julie said.

He leaned in for a long, hungry kiss, then caught himself, shortened it to a quick kiss, and quickly backed off.

Julie frowned. "What's wrong?"

"What do you mean?"

"You kiss me and then act like I taste bad."

Brendan was quiet long enough that it made Julie nervous. She scooted closer.

"Talk to me, Bren."

"I don't want to push you into something that makes you uncomfortable."

Her frown deepened. "What do you mean? We've been naked together too many times to suddenly get weird here."

Brendan's head came up and the look on his face startled her.

"Yes, but that was before you were kidnapped and beat half to death. We haven't talked about any of this because I didn't want it to seem like I was in some big-ass hurry to get in your pants after all you'd endured. For all I knew, you would be disgusted with the thought of ever having a man touch you again, and I would gladly spend the rest of my life doing without, as long as you didn't stop loving me."

"Oh, Brendan." Julie's vision blurred.

He wrapped his arms around her.

"I do want to be with you again, but not until I can look at myself without cringing," she said.

"Duly noted, and totally agree," he countered.

"We'll seal this deal with a kiss, please."

He happily obliged.

And now that the moment of crisis had passed, Julie was back to the question at hand.

"So where are you going to interview?"

He shrugged. "It's at a car dealership. Just grunt work that will keep my bills paid and food on the table until I finish what I really want to do."

Julie slid off his lap. The certainty in his voice was a new facet.

"What's that?"

"I made a decision the other day that came from something Detective Carson told me the night you were rescued."

"What did he say?"

"He said I had good cop instincts, and that if I was interested in going to the police academy, he'd put in a good word for me."

Julie's eyes widened, and then she threw her arms around his neck all over again.

"I think that's wonderful, and I support you one hundred percent."

"You wouldn't mind being married to a cop?" he asked, then watched her eyes widen.

"We never used the word marry before."

His heart sank. "Sorry, I just—"

"No, you misunderstand," she said quickly. "After all the crap my dad has put you through, I was afraid you'd write me off as too much trouble."

He laughed. "Oh, you'll always be trouble, but not too much for me."

And just like that, her fear that he would leave her was gone. She grinned.

"I'll make you pay for that."

He grinned. "And I'll hold you to it, but not today. I need to leave. The interview is on the other side of town and I don't want to be late."

"Will you call me later and let me know how it went?"

"Absolutely," he said.

A few minutes later, he was back in his vehicle and heading across town. It felt good to be making plans for a real future. The Black Garter burning down had forced him out of a comfort zone to nowhere. For the first time in his life, he was thinking long-term, and part of it had to do with his mom and sister. If he ever got out of his apartment into a real house, he firmly believed Delle and Linny would leave Anson and stay with him on a permanent basis.

****

Sam had been potting bamboo plants for so many years that he could do it without thinking. Now that Chance had quit, it was strange working alone. Anson had always issued orders and they'd done the work, but lately Anson was as off-center as Sam felt, and as the days passed, he was forced to admit that something else was happening to his father—something he'd never seen before.

Anson spent days in the family library digging through old books on voodoo and spells. If he wasn't screaming at Linny for being underfoot or ordering Delle around like a slave, he was talking to himself. He was a man living on the edge of insanity and they didn't know why. Even stranger, he began making everyone else take the first bites of the food Delle made as if he believed she was trying to poison him. For the first time in his life, Anson Poe looked old and didn't seem to mind he wasn't pretty anymore. No one knew why, but they all felt it was only a matter of time before he reached a crisis.

****

Chance had the first legal job of his life working as a parts man at an auto supply. It was somewhat boring, but the fact he didn't have to look over his shoulder for the cops every day was a plus. When he talked to his brothers, he refused to discuss anything that had to do with Anson. He'd only called his mother once since he quit, and when Anson caught her talking to him, Anson ripped the phone out of her hands and started screaming at him for running out on them like a coward. Chance disconnected and hadn't called back. He didn't know how to fix what was wrong with his family, and was too sick at heart to even try.

****

Linny was a ghost in the house, slipping from room to room like a little mouse, staying in the shadows, never making noise, never looking up. Her theory was that if she couldn't see Daddy, he couldn't see her.

Rabbit had become her talisman. The secret phone inside the stuffed toy was her connection to Sir Brendan, her most brave and faithful knight. At night, she slipped the cord to the phone charger into the rabbit and plugged it in, then tucked Rabbit beneath her arm. Each morning, she hid the cord so as not to give away the phone's existence and kept Rabbit within arm's reach everywhere she went.

She knew something bad was wrong with Daddy and Mama. Mama cried when she thought no one was looking, and Daddy threw things and screamed. She said prayers each night for God to protect them, but was afraid to talk too loud. All she could do was hope He was listening.

****

Anson couldn't sleep. Everywhere he looked, things burst into flames, and then he'd look again and the fire would be gone. In a moment of desperation, he went into New Orleans and knocked on Mama Lou's door for help. As soon as she saw who was there, she shut it in his face.

Anson went wild. First he cursed her, then remembered why he'd come and begged her to let him in, offering her large amounts of money for her help, but nothing happened. She was the one person he knew who might be able to remove a curse, unaware she was the one who had created it.

He went home in a rage that carried well over into the evening, and then just before bedtime, his cell phone rang.

He answered without looking at Caller ID then frowned when he recognized Wes Riordan's voice.

"Hey, Anson, it's me. I'm checking in to see if you've located any new product."

Anson thought about the million dollars' worth of pot that had gone up in smoke, then rattled the ice cubes in his whiskey and took a quick drink before answering.

"Not yet. The law's tightening down around here on growers, and I was the only one paying for protection."

There was a long silence afterward that left Anson in fear his ass was about to get dumped, but he was wrong.

"Well, anytime you have something else to sell, will you let me know?" Riordan said.

There was a noise out in the hall that made Anson jump, and when he got a glimpse of Linny darting past the doorway, he frowned.

"What was that you said?" he asked.

"I said, anytime you have something else to sell, let me know."

And just like that, he remembered Riordan mentioning what a kid Linny's age would bring on the open market. The moment he let himself consider the notion, he realized he'd rather have the money than her. It would be what he needed to get back on top, and at the same time get Belinda out of his hair. But he'd have to figure out a way to make it happen so no one would suspect.

"Yes, I'll definitely let you know," Anson said, and then put down the phone and walked out into the hall, but Linny was gone again. The little bitch was like a firefly, here one moment, gone the next.

Delle came out of the library carrying a dust mop and a can of furniture polish. She saw Anson too late to turn back and moved the dust mop from her left hand to her right in a subconscious need for self-defense.

To her surprise, Anson made no move to grab at her breasts as he usually did or pull her into a room and take her standing up without care for who might see. Grateful for small favors, she put her head down and kept on walking, unaware of what was going through his head.

****

Four days later

The sun was barely above the horizon when Anson locked himself in the library and then opened the wall safe to count the cash. There was a difference between the money on hand and the money in the bank. The one in the bank was for their legal business, the one on hand had been from the marijuana, and it was dwindling at a scary rate. They had another shipment of potted bamboo nearly ready to go, but it would never bring in what he wanted.

A couple of days earlier, Sam had come up with the idea of delivering the bamboo themselves to flower wholesalers, rather than wait for buyers to come get it. Even though they would be renting a truck to deliver, they would be the ones going to market. No more short sales to others.

Anson had been hesitant to put out the money for a rental, but had to admit it was a good idea. His daddy always said you had to spend money to make money, and he was still toying with the idea of making a deal with Riordan.

Before the fire, he had coldly planned to kill Delle to get back at Brendan and conceal her body in the attic in the crawl space. He knew she regretted coming back, and it would have been a kick to know she would never leave Wisteria Hill, not even in death.

But after spending time out here on his own, he'd come to realize he liked his food hot and ready and a hot and ready woman in his bed. So, killing her was out because it would impact his comfort. The bigger revenge would be getting rid of the kid, a loss that would affect all of them, and get him back on his feet at the same time. He would make a deal with Riordan, and when Sam left to deliver the bamboo, he'd snatch the kid and make the sale off-site. When Belinda didn't show up for supper, he'd make sure they believed she'd become a victim to the dangers in the swamp. It was a beautiful plan—just like the night he'd set up Grayson March's guards to self-destruct. He loved it when a good plan came together, and it was time to make this one happen.

He scanned the contacts in his cell phone and when he came to Wes's name, hit call. Riordan answered on the second ring.

"I figured you'd be calling me," Wes said.

Anson frowned. "Why?"

Wes chuckled. "Because we have a good working relationship I assume you don't want to lose. Did you find some new stuff?"

"Something better."

Wes quickly countered. "Like what?"

"You said you were in the market for prime females of a certain age," Anson said, and when he heard a slight gasp, he knew he had Riordan's attention. "Well? Are you or aren't you?"

"Who are we talking about?" Wes asked.

"Mine."

There was another moment of silence and then a hesitant question. "You're offering your own kid up for sale?"

Anson was immediately defensive. "This is no different

than what my ancestors did. They fucked their slaves and sold their by-blows. The kid is a commodity. Are you interested or not?"

"Hell yes, I'm interested. I'll give you seventy-five—"

"No. You'll give me a hundred thousand, which is the amount you mentioned the first time it came out of your mouth."

"Done. When can I expect delivery?"

"Two days. I'll let you know where later."

"I'll be waiting for the call," Riordan said.

Anson hung up, then sat for a moment, savoring the silence before getting up to pour himself a stiff shot of whiskey. He'd had booze for breakfast plenty of times and this was a moment of celebration. Within days, his cash flow problem would be over. He tossed back the whiskey like it was medicine, savoring the burn as it rolled down his throat.

His stride was long and sure as he headed for the door, until a loud, sudden drumbeat stopped him mid-step, followed by the warning rattles of the snakes he feared. He broke out into a cold sweat, and when his heart began to beat in a rapid rhythm with the rattle, he bolted from the room.

****

Sam drove in with the rental truck before daylight and began loading up the pots of bamboo. It was the first time he'd taken a lead in the business and it made him feel good. If these were picked up at market as he hoped they would be and the money was good, it would be the beginning of a new facet of the bamboo trade. He was already loading the truck when Anson showed up in the packing shed.

"Everything all set?" Anson asked.

Sam nodded. "Yes. I have a contact at the flower market and should be unloaded and back before noon. If there are any delays, I'll call."

"Good, good, so, I'll talk to you later," Anson said, and walked out.

Sam thought nothing of the abruptness of the visit. Anson never wanted anything to do with the dirty work. As soon as he was loaded, he drove out without bothering to stop at the house. It was early and he would check on them later when he got back.

Anson was standing at the window, watching Sam drive away. He could hear footsteps on the floor above him, which meant Delle and Linny were up. He also knew that as soon as his daughter ate, she would be out of the house like a rocket and headed to the swamp. That's when he would make his move and no one would be the wiser.

He left his dirty coffee cup on the counter so Delle would know he'd finished breakfast, then got in his truck and took off toward the burned pot fields. But instead of taking a left turn at the packing shed, he pulled his pickup up inside it and parked. He was safely out of sight of the house, but only feet from the path Linny took to go play. The moment he got out, he called Riordan.

Riordan answered quickly. "It's me. Is this still on?"

Anson frowned. "You know me better than that. I'm calling to make sure you're where you said you'd be."

"I'm here and waiting."

"You don't get anything until I get my money," Anson said.

"Don't threaten me, Poe." There was a long moment of silence, and then Riordan heard Anson make what sounded like a growl. He shivered in spite of himself. He worked with lots of bad people, but there was something about Anson Poe that gave him the creeps. "Fine. Whatever," Riordan muttered.

"I'll call when I'm on the way," Anson said.

As soon as he hung up, he looked around the corner of the shed to see if Linny was on the way, but she was nowhere in sight. He got a rag and the bottle of chloroform he bought yesterday from beneath the seat of his truck, and then took a stance at one of two very dusty windows so he could see the house and settled down to wait.

****

Delle entered the kitchen with a tentative step then saw the dirty cup on the counter. When she looked out the window and saw that Anson's pickup was nowhere in sight, her relief grew. He'd either gone off to work or was in town fooling around. Either way suited her just fine.

In a better frame of mind, she began making scrambled eggs. The room was cool and the floor beneath her feet was smooth. There were so many things that had been made beautiful, but she couldn't appreciate them properly for wishing the man responsible would do them all a favor and drop dead.

A few minutes later, she heard Linny coming down the stairs.

"Linny! Breakfast is ready. Come eat!"

Linny poked her head around the doorway with Rabbit clutched in one hand. "Where's Daddy?"

"Already gone to work," Delle said. "Sit down while your eggs are still warm."

Happy that the Evil Overlord was nowhere in sight, Linny moved to the table with a bounce in her step. She laid Rabbit on the table and dug into her food with gusto.

Delle eyed her daughter, taking note of the haphazard

ponytail and the old T-shirt and shorts she was wearing and then decided it didn't matter. She was a little surprised that Linny had begun to carry the stuffed toy around as she had when she was a toddler, then decided it had to do with how she was dealing with the trauma of her life. She felt guilty enough without telling Linny she should leave the toy behind, but thought it prudent to give her some rules for the day.

"I need you home in time for lunch, so don't come dawdling in hours later telling me you lost track of time. You know when the sun is directly overhead that it's time to check in, okay?"

Linny nodded. "Yes, Mama, I know. I will."

Delle frowned. "What do you do out there, anyway? There's no one to play with."

Linny shrugged. "I just play, Mama."

Delle smiled. She remembered the days when imagination was far better than any computer game, and was glad her daughter hadn't succumbed.

"Okay, but pay attention to stuff around you. I don't want you getting hurt."

"I always pay attention," Linny said.

Anxious to be out of the house, Linny finished her eggs, washed them down with the last of her milk, and grabbed Rabbit.

"I'm through. That was good. Thank you, Mama. See you later."

She was out of the house before Delle could even ask for a kiss.

The sun felt good on Linny's face as she moved with a bouncy step through the back yard and to the woods beyond. Birds dropped from tree limbs into the grass to feed, then hopped just out of her reach as she passed by. Butterflies flitted from flower to flower in the wild honeysuckle that had overtaken the old fencerow off to her right. The vines were in full bloom, and the scent was so strong and so sweet, but she knew from experience, also deceiving.

Once when she was little, she'd picked a bunch of honeysuckle blossoms and put them in her mouth, thinking they would be as sweet to eat as they smelled. Between the bitter pollen on the stamens, and the honeybee she'd almost swallowed in the process, it hadn't taken her long to spit them out. But she was older and smarter now, and her thoughts were already on gathering berries for Sir Snapper and ruling over the denizens that passed by her throne. Anxious to get there, she tightened her grip on Rabbit and lengthened her stride.

****

When Anson saw her coming, he doused the rag with chloroform and moved as close to the side of the shed as he could get without giving himself away. He planned to grab her from behind as she walked past.

As he waited, he heard a rustling on the other side of the shed and saw a rat slip out from under of a stack of pallets and disappear in the heavy grass beyond the shed. Seconds later, a big bull snake came out from behind the same pallets and slithered off into the grass. Survival of the fittest was always at play in the bayou and today was no different.

A bead of sweat came out of his hairline and ran down the back of his neck. When he heard her humming, he gripped the chloroformed rag a little tighter and watched the lengthening shadow of her approach. When she finally walked past him, she was farther off the path than he'd expected. Anxious not to let her get too far, he leaped out of the shadows.

Linny heard the sound of running feet, and before she could turn around, she saw a huge shadow overtaking her own and she screamed. She was already running as she thrust her hand inside Rabbit. She'd practiced this moment so many times she instantly found the right number and pressed it. She didn't look back to see who was chasing her. She didn't have to. She'd known in her heart the day would come when the Evil Overlord would try to destroy her and this was the day.

Anson was stunned by how swiftly she moved, and when she screamed, he lengthened his stride, desperate to stop her before Delle was alerted that something was wrong. He took Linny down in a flying tackle, heard her grunt as they hit the ground together, and then she was silent.

He got up quickly, brushed the dirt off the front of his clothes and grabbed the rag to put her out, then realized she wasn't moving. His heart skipped a beat as he reached down to feel for a pulse. It was there, but it was faint. What the hell?

He picked her up, then turned her over his forearm and thumped her back to get oxygen into her lungs. When she coughed and began to struggle to get free, he breathed a quick sigh of relief. He'd just knocked the wind out of her. He picked up the chloroform-soaked rag as she struggled against his grasp.

"Stand still," he ordered and shook her so hard it hurt.

"No, Daddy, no! I'll be good. I'll be quiet. Don't do this! Don't hurt me!"

He shoved the rag over her face.

Chapter Nineteen

Wes Riordan ate when he was nervous, and today he was nervous. He'd already gone through a bag of salted cashews, a thirty-two ounce Pepsi, and a package of powdered sugar doughnuts while waiting for Anson Poe to show. He was too tall to stand up comfortably in the motor home, which forced him to sit listening to Thorpe, his armed guard, and Marty, his driver, arguing about racehorses. He was thinking about getting another snack when Marty suddenly yelled out.

"Hey, boss, here comes Poe."

Wes stooped over to look out the front windshield. It *was* Poe's truck, and with the recognition came excitement. He'd done nothing but think about Belinda Poe since Anson's call. She was beyond stunning, a lean, leggy filly with a long black mane of hair and the clean, classic features of a thoroughbred. The fact that she was still a child was what brought the big bucks. Even though he was paying a hundred thousand dollars to get her, he already had the names of three men willing to pay upwards of half a million to get their hands on something this fine. Putting the girl on the market was going to be one hell of an auction before it over.

"When he stops, Marty, you pull up beside him. When I get out, Thorpe, you bring the money. I want this transfer to be as seamless and quiet as possible."

Marty started the engine and Thorpe grabbed the briefcase. When Anson came to a stop, the driver inched a little closer, keeping just enough room between the motor home and the pickup for Riordan to get out.

****

Anson drove fast while keeping a careful eye on the kid. It occurred to him that he'd never really studied her features close-up before, and he had a misplaced sense of pride that she got her looks from him. When he took the turn into the last curve and saw the motor home parked up ahead, he breathed a sigh of relief. A few moments later, he was out and circling his truck to make the trade. Belinda was still unconscious, but her pulse and color were good.

Wes saw her, and he frowned. "She's unconscious and there's a red streak on her chin. What the hell happened to her?"

"She fell," Anson said. "She's fine."

Wes wasn't satisfied. "Why is she unconscious?"

Anson looked at him with disdain for even asking such a stupid question.

"I took her down with chloroform, you dumb ass. Surely you didn't think she would come willingly?"

Wes felt for a pulse. It was strong. He slapped the side of her face lightly a couple of times in an effort to wake her up, and as he did, her eyelids began to flutter. She was regaining consciousness.

"Yeah, okay," Wes said, then fingered the edge of her T-shirt. "Is she as perfect beneath those clothes as she is like this?"

Anson frowned. "She's perfect, but I'm not gonna stand here while you strip her to see. I gotta get back. Where's my money?"

"Thorpe has it," he said.

The man opened the briefcase so Anson could see the money.

"Put it in the seat of my truck," Anson said.

Thorpe did as he was told, and when the briefcase hit the seat, Wes held out his arms.

Anson handed Linny over like an unwanted sack of potatoes and headed back to his truck.

Wes couldn't believe his good fortune. He saw nothing but money beneath the old clothes and dirt.

"When you've got a new crop, let me know," he shouted.

"Yeah, right," Anson said, and jumped back in the truck, made a U-turn in the road, and headed for home.

Wes carried her inside, and moments later, Marty drove off in the opposite direction. Belinda Poe's future had never been good, but at this point in her life, it was seriously shaky.

Wes had a cot set up against the wall, and once he laid her down, he began assessing her as he would a new car. He didn't like the red mark on her chin and the dirt on her face and hands, but that was easily rectified. He grabbed a handful of peanuts from a nearby bowl and popped them in his mouth as he began planning how he'd dress her the day of the auction.

"Turn the air conditioning up on high," Wes yelled.

Marty waved to indicate he'd heard him.

Wes began to pace, ticking off things on a mental list that would have to be done before he unloaded her. Still bothered by the dirt on her face and arms, he went after a wet washcloth, pulled up a chair beside the cot, and began polishing his prize.

****

Linny felt something wet on her skin. Someone was washing her face.

Mama?

When she became aware of the sound of wheels against pavement, she felt a little panicked.

What's moving? I'm moving. Why am I in a car?

She struggled harder to wake up. Something wasn't right. Then she became aware of the muted voices—the voices of strangers—and someone talking about how much money she was worth—and everything came rushing back. Her kingdom was crashing. She was being banished to a lonely tower, and the Evil Overlord was on her throne.

"Hey, I think she's awake," Thorpe said.

Wes leaned over and peered closely at her face. "I think you're right," he said and poked her on the shoulder. "Wake up, kid."

Linny's eyes flew open, followed by a loud and piercing scream.

The sound was startling enough that Thorpe fell backward off his seat.

Wes stood up abruptly and then bumped his head on the ceiling.

As for Linny, all she could think about was getting away. Within seconds, she was off the cot and running toward the only exit. That it was in a motor home, moving at a rapid clip down a long, busy highway didn't matter. She just wanted out.

"Grab her!" Wes yelled as Thorpe lurched to his feet.

Marty was already braking and steering toward the shoulder.

Linny's hand was on the doorknob when Thorpe grabbed her by the arm and yanked her backward, pulling her hard against his chest.

"Let me go! Let me go!" Linny screamed, kicking and flailing against his grip.

Her heel caught Thorpe in the crotch. He groaned and cursed as he dropped to his knees. But before she could move, Wes grabbed her by the shoulders and spun her around to face him.

"Stop this shit!" he yelled, then slapped her face and shook her so hard that the room began spinning around her.

Furious they'd been bested, even temporarily, by a mere kid, he all but threw her back onto the bed.

"Tie her up and make it tight!" he yelled, and Thorpe, still hobbling with his hands at his crotch, hastened to obey.

Linny could taste blood, and her face hurt where she'd been slapped. The room was still spinning from behind shaken so hard, and when Thorpe began tying her feet and arms, he yanked the rope too tight.

"That hurts," she cried.

"It's your own fault, isn't it?" Wes yelled, and then kicked the bed she was lying on to get her attention.

Her face was wet with tears when she realized she knew her abductors. At that moment, she felt the first stirrings of an emotion she would later come to know as hate.

Wes Riordan saw the look and grinned. "She's a Poe all right. Look at those eyes. If looks could kill, we'd all be dead. I should've known she'd be a spitfire. Don't be scared, kid. We're not gonna hurt you."

Fear was all mixed up now with rage. Even though her voice was shaking, she spit words as if they had a bad taste.

"I'm not stupid. I heard you talking about men who want to buy me."

Wes shrugged. "It's business, kid. They'll treat you good."

"Brendan will kill you."

Riordan was a little taken aback by her vehemence, but he wasn't worried. "Sorry, little sister, but your brother is never going to know what happened to you."

Linny lifted her chin like the queen she was, and stared straight into Wes Riordan's eyes.

"Yes, he will, and when he finds you, he will slay you, just as he slays all of the dragons who threaten my kingdom."

Wes frowned. "Crazy kid," he muttered, then dragged his chair between her and the door and sat back down.

****

Brendan was on his way out of the apartment when his cell phone rang. He glanced down at it absently and then stumbled and stopped. It was Linny's SOS.

He bolted toward his SUV, scared to death and immediately sick to his stomach. There was no way to know what was happening or if he'd be too late. He immediately called his mother's phone, but it rang and rang and then went to voice mail. He called Sam's number, hoping his brother was already out there, and then spun out of the parking lot and headed out of town as it began to ring.

"Hello, little brother, what's up?" Sam said, as he answered the call, and then he heard the panic in Brendan's voice.

"Where are you?" Brendan yelled.

"I'm in New Orleans on my way to deliver a load of bamboo to the flower market. Why?"

"I just got an SOS call from Linny. Something's wrong."

Sam hit the brakes and quickly pulled off into a parking lot. "What the hell are you talking about?"

"Weeks ago, Mama Lou told me Linny would be in danger. I gave her a phone in secret that she was never to use unless she or Mama was in trouble. I just got the call."

"Oh shit," Sam mumbled. "What did she say?"

"Nothing. All she had to do was punch a number. I would know it was from her and that she needed help. I'm already on my way."

"Daddy's been acting crazy as hell for days now. I should've known he would snap. I'll call Chance," Sam added.

"Just so you know... if Anson has hurt either one of them again, I'll kill him."

"Wait, Brendan! Don't do anything crazy. We're coming and—"

The line went dead in Sam's ear. He groaned, made a call to Chance, and then pulled out of the parking lot and headed home.

Chance answered quickly, and from the tone of his voice, Sam could tell he was obviously bothered.

"Hey, Sam, I can't talk now. I'm—"

"Brendan got an SOS call from Linny. He's on his way out there threatening to kill Daddy, and I'm in the city in a delivery truck. I won't get home in time to stop him."

Chance lowered his voice. "Damn it all to hell, Sam. I could lose my job over this if I leave."

"You can get another job, but we can't replace our family."

Chance sighed. "I'll see what I can do."

Sam hung up. He'd done all he could from here. One of them had to get to Brendan before he did something they'd all regret.

****

As soon as Brendan passed the city limits sign, he made one more call—to Julie.

"Bren! Good morning, sweetheart! Are you on your way here?"

"No. I can't talk long. Just needed to let you know something's wrong at home. Got an SOS call from Linny. I'm on my way there now."

Julie's heart sank. "Oh no! Oh, Brendan, I'm so sorry. Is there anything I can do from here?"

"Say prayers," Brendan said.

"Don't do anything rash," she begged.

"I'll call you later," he said and disconnected.

Julie sat down, shaking in every fiber of her being. If anything happened to Brendan, she'd die.

****

Delle came in from outside where she'd been watering the flowers in the big pots on the front of the house, and set to mopping the kitchen floor. She'd just finished mopping when she heard a vehicle and looked out. It was Brendan. She started to smile, then saw the look on his face as he got out and her heart skipped a beat. Brendan was running when he hit the back porch. He came inside without knocking.

"Brendan, what on earth is—?"

He grabbed her by the shoulders. "I tried to call you, but you didn't answer."

"Sorry. I was outside for a bit and—"

"Never mind. Where's Linny?"

Breath caught in the back of Delle's throat. "Why...? She's out playing in the bayou. Why?"

He shook his head and asked another question. "Where's Anson?"

Delle flinched. "Damn it, Brendan, stop this. You're scaring me!"

"Linny is in trouble, and I need to know where to start looking."

Delle staggered backward as her heart began to pound. "How do you know this?"

"I gave her a phone. She was never to use it unless one or both of you were in danger, and less than fifteen minutes ago she called me."

Delle felt like throwing up. "She left the house to go play. I told her to be home by noon."

"Did she go toward the swamp?"

"Yes."

Brendan pivoted quickly and ran out the door as fast as he'd come in. Delle came to her senses and followed.

The sun was hot on the back of his neck as Brendan came down off the porch. A red bird flew across his line of vision as he ran along the well-worn path his little sister always took. Red meant stop. Was it a warning from Mother Nature to beware? He kept imagining all the terrible things that could happen to a person in the swamp, wondering why in hell they'd ever let her play there, and then wondered where Anson was.

He started past the packing shed, then stopped and ducked in long enough to make sure she wasn't there. It was empty of everything but the bamboo cuttings being rooted in water and the dozens and dozens of empty pots. He stepped over a rag on the ground, then without thinking, went back to pick it up. The smell was still strong enough it was staggering.

"Son of a bitch!" he muttered, and tossed it on the counter.

Delle caught up with him there, breathing hard and already limping.

"What's wrong?" she cried.

Brendan glanced down at her feet. "Your feet are bleeding."

"I don't care. She's *my* baby and I'm going to the swamp after her."

"Damn it, Mama, she's not lost. Someone took her."

"No, that can't be. No one was here but us."

He was already pulling the phone out of his pocket to call the police when he saw something in the grass a few yards away. He ran over to get it, and when he stood up, he was holding Linny's stuffed toy.

When Delle saw it, she gasped. "What on earth? Why would she leave Rabbit here when she's been carrying it with her everywhere?"

Brendan thrust his hand into the back of the rabbit and pulled out the phone. She'd done exactly what he said and hadn't hung up. Unfortunately, it appears she didn't have the option of taking Rabbit with her.

"She carried it because it was where she'd hidden the phone," he said. His hands were shaking as he handed it to his mother. "There's blood on the fur and that rag inside the shed reeks of chloroform. She didn't leave here willingly."

Delle let out a wail that sent the birds in flight as she clutched the toy to her breast.

Before Brendan could think what to do next, he saw Anson's pickup coming down the driveway. He grabbed his mother and ducked inside the shed.

Delle was still wailing when Brendan clamped a hand over her mouth and shook his head. "Anson is home," he said softly, watching him as he hurried inside the house.

Delle grabbed his arm. "We need to tell him what happened. We need to call the Parish police. We need—"

"The only person who would've been in this shed was Sam or Anson, and I already talked to Sam. He's in New Orleans."

Delle shook her head in disbelief. "You can't mean you suspect your own father of hurting Linny? She's his daughter. He—"

"Linny's missing, Anson was gone, and he just came back alone. He doesn't love anyone but himself and we both know it. Now I'm going into the house. Don't mention one word of Belinda's absence and let me do the talking."

Panicked by what was happening, all she could to was nod.

"Give me the rabbit," he said.

She handed it to him then had to run to keep up as Brendan loped toward the house.

****

When Anson saw Brendan's vehicle, he debated with the notion of leaving the briefcase full of money in his truck until the bastard was gone, then changed his mind. He was a business man. He could carry a briefcase any damn time he wanted.

He got out with his head up and his shoulders back, striding toward the house with it swinging against his leg, thinking what a high it was going to be to carry all that money in beneath their noses without them suspecting a thing.

But his bubble quickly burst when he walked inside. He could tell from the silence that the house was empty, although he called out to make sure.

"Hey, Delle, I'm home! Where are you?"

When no one answered, he strode swiftly toward the library and then straight to the safe.

****

The quiet was unsettling as Brendan entered. He put a finger to his lips and then pointed at his mother to be quiet. She slipped out of her floppy shoes and followed him through the house in her bare feet.

Brendan heard a scuff of boot to floor, and the sound of rustling paper in the library and quietly slipped inside to see what Anson was doing. When he saw the open briefcase and all that money, it startled him. He didn't have any pot to sell. Where the hell had that come from?

But then Delle walked in behind him, saw all that money and gasped.

And that was the sound that Anson heard. He spun around, his body crouched and ready to fight and then saw then in the doorway and straightened up.

"Damn it all to hell, what's the matter with you people sneaking up on a man like that?"

Seconds later, Brendan was in his face. "What the hell did you do to Linny?" he asked and thrust the bloody rabbit in his face.

Anson was taken aback by the question and surprised that they'd already found the rabbit.

"I didn't do anything," he said and shoved him back.

"There's blood on Linny's rabbit and she's missing," Brendan snapped.

Anson's heart skipped a beat when he saw the blood, but then quickly recovered.

"So maybe she had a nosebleed. How should I know where she is?"

Brendan grabbed Anson by the shoulders, pushing

harder and talking faster. "Did she get the nosebleed before or after you chloroformed her?"

Anson heard drums, and then the rattlesnake. "You're crazy," he muttered and began trying to get free of Brendan's grasp.

"Belinda is in danger, and don't say she's not because I already know it. She called me for help, so start talking or I'll beat it out of you."

Anson frowned. "You're lying. She didn't call—"

Brendan grunted as if he'd been punched. "How do you know what she did or didn't do?"

Delle had been standing quietly aside, unable to grasp the full meaning of what was happening until she heard Anson give himself away.

"Noooo!" she screamed and launched herself at him like a mad woman, digging her fingernails into his cheeks and clawing them down his face. "I put up with you for years so you would leave my children alone! You lied! You lied!"

Before Brendan could separate them, Anson retaliated. Roaring in pain, he backhanded her so hard she fell against the desk, her head striking the sharp edge of the leg before slumping lifelessly to the floor. When a small pool of blood began to spread beneath her head, Brendan lost it.

"You killed her!" he screamed and hit Anson so hard his head popped back against the wall safe. Brendan grabbed him again, slamming him up against the wall. "Did you kill Linny, too?"

Anson tried to take a swing that Brendan blocked. "You sorry bastard," Anson shouted and swung again, but Brendan blocked it, then punched him in the face.

"Where's Belinda?" Brendan yelled.

Anson moaned. The drums were louder, and so were the rattles.

Brendan hit him again. "I can't hear you. What did you do with my sister?"

He was about to hit him again when Chance ran in, grabbed Brendan's arm. Anson slid to the floor, unconscious.

"You won't get any information if you kill him," Chance shouted.

Brendan shook his head, then staggered and dropped to his knees beside his mother's body to feel for a pulse. When he felt the thump beneath his fingertips, he breathed a shaky sigh of relief.

"She's alive, but we need to call an ambulance. Belinda's missing. There's blood on Rabbit, and Anson just came home with a briefcase full of money."

Chance stared at the money, and then suddenly jerked as if he'd been hit.

"Oh shit! Oh no! He wouldn't! God in heaven, tell me he didn't!"

But Anson was still out and had nothing to offer.

Brendan's panic increased as he jumped to his feet. "What's happening? What do you know that I don't?"

Chance pushed past his brother to where Anson was lying. "I need his phone. Help me find his phone."

"You call an ambulance for Mama. I'll look," Brendan said and began digging through Anson's pockets as Chance made the call to emergency services.

"I don't see it," Brendan said, then saw the phone beneath the desk where it must have fallen out of his pocket. "Oh wait! Here it is."

Chance yanked it from his brother's hand and quickly pulled up the call record.

"Oh dear God," Chance whispered, then stared down at his father in disbelief.

"What the hell's going on?" Brendan yelled.

Before Chance could answer, they heard the back door slam and then running footsteps coming through the house.

"Where is everyone?" Sam yelled.

"In here!" Chance shouted.

Sam stopped in the doorway, saw his mother unmoving in a pool of blood and his daddy on the floor and panicked. Were they too late?

"Dear God, are they dead?"

"Mama's hurt. Anson knocked her down after she scratched his face. Chance called an ambulance," Brendan said.

Sam dropped to his knees beside his mother's body.

"What happened? Where's Linny?"

"I'll tell you what happened," Chance said. "Linny is missing. Daddy has a briefcase full of money. And the last three calls on his phone are to Wes Riordan."

Sam paled. "No."

"He fucking did it," Chance said.

Brendan grabbed the phone out of his brother's hand, his voice shaking. "Somebody talk to me. What do you know that I don't?"

"Wes Riordan told Daddy weeks ago that Linny was worth a hundred thousand dollars to the right buyer, and the last three calls on Daddy's phone were to Riordan, one less than an hour ago."

Brendan stared at Anson in disbelief, then ran to the wet bar, filled a decanter with water and dumped it in his face.

Anson was sputtering and groaning as Brendan

yanked him to his feet and slammed him backward into a chair.

Chance grabbed an arm of the chair and spun it around until he was staring down into his daddy's face.

"You sold Linny to Wes Riordan and you're going to jail. I'll testify against you myself that I heard the two of you talking about it weeks ago."

Anson spit blood, then looked up at his sons and smiled.

Sam's mind was racing. "I have evidence against him," he said abruptly.

"Against Daddy?" Chance asked.

Sam nodded his head. "Against Daddy and Riordan. Linny told me days ago to make a list of the Evil Overlord's friends and bad deeds and we would use it to destroy him."

"Sweet Jesus," Chance said.

Delle moaned.

Chance dropped to her side and started weeping. "I'm sorry, Mama. I shouldn't have run away. I'm sorry."

"You defied me and this is what you get," Anson said, then laughed.

"Somebody gag him," Brendan said, and then grabbed Anson's phone, pulled up Riordan's name, and hit Call as Sam pulled off his belt, jammed it between Anson's teeth and pulled it tight against the back of his head.

Anson was grunting and kicking when Brendan turned around and hit him again, knocking him out.

"What the fuck are you doing?" Sam asked.

"Getting Belinda back," Brendan said, and the moment the call was answered, he put it on speaker so all three of them could hear.

"Hells bells, Anson. What do you want now? Got another kid you want to sell?"

"I'm not Anson. I'm Brendan. Anson's indisposed."

Wes was a little startled, but not enough to panic. "So, the pup calls, but I'm not—"

Brendan interrupted angrily. "Shut the hell up and listen, because you're only going to have one chance to make this right before I bring your world down around your fucking ears. I know you have my sister, and I have the money you paid for her, with your fingerprints and your DNA all over it. I also have Anson's cell phone. The last three calls he made were to you. He disappears. My sister disappears, and he comes back with a briefcase full of money.

"So here's the deal. I don't know how far away you've gotten, but you have less than an hour to get back to Wisteria Hill with my sister safe and unharmed, or I start making phone calls to the local police, the state police, the DEA for dealing drugs, the FBI for child endangerment, kidnapping, and trafficking children into prostitution. Bring her back and you get your money back. We get our sister, and we both call it quits. You know our background. We don't want the cops involved in our business any more than you do, but if you keep going, know that I will happily give you up and take the consequences. And just so you know, I will find you, and when I do, I will kill you."

Riordan shuddered. The young Poe was unknown to him and he didn't know how much of that was bluff, and how much of it was as ruthless as his daddy. He glanced at the girl. She'd said Brendan would kill him. It sounded like he might be the kind to make good on her threat.

Wes covered the phone to talk to his driver. "Hey, Marty, pull over and stop."

The driver began slowing down.

Sam picked up the conversation.

"Riordan, this is Sam. You know me. You also need to

know I have all of the contact information you and my Daddy have traded over the past six years. I know where you live. I know who works for you. I know where you bank your money, and a hundred other little details you or Thorpe have let slip over the years while my brother and I were loading you up with drugs."

"You heard him," Brendan said. "If you're not back here within the hour with my sister, we will destroy you and everything you own."

Riordan heard the call disconnect, and then palmed his phone as he walked over to where the girl was lying. She was watching his every move without making a sound. He thought of the money she would bring, and then of the threats they'd made. This was his fault for getting too friendly.

He glanced at Thorpe. "How many weapons do we have on board?"

Thorpe went to the back to check. "Four semi-automatics, an AK47, and a rifle with a scope."

Riordan's eyes narrowed. "Hey, Marty, turn this bus around."

Thorpe stared. "We're going back?"

Wes nodded.

"Why?" Thorpe asked.

"To get my money and get rid of some witnesses."

"I'll get ready," Thorpe said.

Wes looked at the girl again. She was still staring at him. He didn't like the blank stare and tried to ignore it, but he could feel her eyes on him every time he made a move.

Thorpe walked past her and caught the same stare. "What are you looking at?" he snapped.

"A dead man," Linny whispered, then closed her eyes.

****

As soon as Brendan disconnected, he dropped down to his mother's side.

"Hang on, Mama. Help's coming," he said, and then reached for his phone.

"What are you doing?" Sam asked.

"Calling the Parish sheriff's office."

Chance frowned. "You told Riordan you wouldn't call the police if he brought Linny back."

"I lied," Brendan said. "I hear the ambulance. Someone go walk them in. We gotta get Mama out of here before Riordan shows back up."

"What about Daddy?" Sam asked, eyeing Anson's swollen eyes and the bloody gouges Delle had put on his face.

"He's hurt himself worse than that getting drunk and falling down the stairs. He's not going anywhere but to jail," Brendan said and pulled up the number to the office of the Sheriff of Orleans Parish.

****

Sumter Henry was in shock and trying to hide it as he and his deputy, Blakely, led the way to Wisteria Hill with four parish cruisers behind him. He was still trying to wrap his head around the fact Anson Poe had actually sold his daughter to a drug dealer, and that Brendan Poe swore that after some threats they'd made, the man was bringing her back. If this was the case, they didn't have much time to get in place and set a trap.

They met an ambulance on the way out, and supposed it was the one with Anson's wife, who'd been hurt during the fight. When they reached the property, they saw

Brendan standing at the side of the driveway near the house. They braked as Brendan ran to meet them.

"You need to hide the cruisers! You can put three behind the packing shed behind the house. Drive the other two back across the road and up in the trees. When the motor home comes down the driveway, they can follow it in."

"You do know this could precipitate a hostage situation and set yourself up as a target?" Henry warned.

"I'll take my chances. Linny's life depends on it," Brendan said.

Henry quickly dispersed the cruisers, then positioned each of his remaining officers in positions of defense.

Brendan led the way inside with Sheriff Henry behind him.

"Where's Anson?" the sheriff asked.

"Tied up in the library. Chance is with him."

Henry shook his head. "He really sold his little girl?"

"For a hundred thousand dollars," Sam said.

"Lord have mercy," Henry whispered. "How long has she been missing?"

"Less than two hours," Brendan said.

"How on earth did you figure this out so fast?" Henry asked.

"It's a long story," Brendan said. "As soon as we get Linny back, we'll gladly explain everything in detail."

Henry hesitated to comment for fear of giving away the fact that he had taken money from Anson, but he was curious to know.

"That's a hell of a lot of money all right, but gossip is that your daddy wasn't exactly hard up for money."

Brendan shrugged. He was past telling lies.

"Someone burned him out."

Henry's eyes widened. "Really? Who did it?"

"I did," Chance said as he walked into the room.

Henry stared. "You? Why?"

"Why the hell not?" Chance muttered.

"Where's Anson at?" Henry asked.

"In the library. I'll take you there," Sam said.

"Make it quick," Brendan said. "We have to be ready the minute they drive up."

Sam frowned. "You don't think they're going to give her back?"

"I think Riordan is too smart and been in business too long to cave so easily. They're coming back to get their money all right, but I'll lay odds he plans to get rid of us, too."

The sheriff eyed Brendan curiously. "That's pretty sound reasoning."

Brendan shrugged. "If you're going to pay your respects to Anson, make it fast."

Henry paused, then shook his head. "I changed my mind. I can talk to him later." He got on his hand-held, verifying that his men were all in place and signed off. "I'm going to stay here at the front of the house for a view of the road."

Brendan took off up the stairs, leaving the sheriff with his brothers. He would have a bird's-eye view of the main road *and* the driveway from his old bedroom upstairs.

Chapter Twenty

Brendan was sick about what had happened to his mama, but blamed part of it on her for coming back. Still, they'd sent her off to the hospital with strangers and no one to speak for her—no one she knew would be there when she woke up—if she woke up.

He thought of Claudette. Too bad his mama didn't have some of her sister's good sense. She'd come through for them before, maybe she would again.

He scanned contacts in his cell phone, then called. The phone began to ring and he waited. Just when he thought it would go to voice mail, she answered.

"Hello?"

"Auntie, it's me, Brendan. Mama is on her way to the hospital. The same one Julie was in."

Claudette moaned. "Oh no... Did Anson hurt her again?"

"Yes. It's a long ugly story, which I'll explain in depth later. Once again I'm asking for your help."

"Of course. What can I do?"

"She's unconscious. If you could be there and answer any questions they might have, we would be grateful."

"Where are your brothers? What about Belinda?"

Brendan's voice started to shake. "Worse, Auntie, much worse. She's gone. Anson sold her. We're here at the house with the police."

There was a moment of silence, and then Claudette's shock was echoed in her voice. "What? Say that again!"

"Anson fucking sold her to a drug dealer for a hundred thousand dollars and we're trying to get her back."

"Oh dear lord, no! Not that sweet baby!"

"Say prayers, Auntie. I've got to go."

"Call me," Claudette said. "I'm leaving for the hospital now."

Brendan heard her disconnect and then turned back to the window. The first thing that went through his mind was what Linny might be enduring. The little queen had summoned her favorite knight and he had failed to protect her. He felt like throwing up.

****

Riordan was getting nervous. They were cutting it close getting back to Wisteria Hill within the hour they'd been given. He had confidence he would be able to disappear should the authorities be notified, but it would destroy a set-up he'd spent years creating. The optimum ending to this farce would be completely eradicating the rest of the Poe family, then taking his money and the girl and moving on.

"Hey, Marty! How much farther?" he yelled.

"Another five minutes and we're there," the driver said.

Wes checked his watch. That would put them right on the hour. He glanced at the kid to make sure she was still securely tied. She should've been crying for her mama or begging them to let her go. But she just lay there, continuing to watch his every move without saying a word. For a little kid, she had one hell of a stare.

Linny was afraid, but she wouldn't show it because she knew what was going to happen. She knew there would be shooting and someone was going to die. She'd tried and tried to work her hands free but to no avail. Her arms ached and her hands were almost numb. They'd tied her wrists and ankles too tight. Even if she got free, she had nowhere to run.

When she realized they were slowing down, her heart began to hammer. Before, she'd been afraid of going home because of Daddy. Now, it was Daddy's friends who brought the fear.

****

When Brendan saw the motor home turn off the road and come down the driveway, a wash of relief went through him. Secretly, he'd been afraid Riordan would call his challenge and keep on driving.

He'd confiscated one of Anson's guns earlier, and grabbed it off the bed as he ran from the room. By the time he got downstairs, the others were on their way to the kitchen.

Sam clapped Brendan on the back. "Good call, brother. You got them back."

Brendan frowned. "That was the easy part. The hard part is yet to come. Is Anson still tied up good?"

"He's tied and I cuffed him, too," Henry said.

Brendan ran into the library to grab the briefcase full of money.

When Anson saw him take it, he began grunting and squealing behind the gag in his mouth, but Brendan got the message.

"Kiss my ass," he said.

He eyed the bloody gouges in Anson's face as he took a bottle of whiskey from the wet bar, then ran out of the library and headed back to the kitchen.

"What are you doing with the money?" Sam asked as Brendan walked past him.

"Just cover me," Brendan said as he dug through the cabinets.

"What the hell are you looking for? And you're not going out there on your own," Chance said.

Brendan kept digging. "Where's that chef's torch Mama uses to make crème brulee?"

"It's here," Chance said as he opened another cabinet. "What the fuck are you going to do with it? Set them on fire?"

"Just the money," he said.

"Then let me make sure this thing fires up," Chance said and got the lighter. Moments later, the butane torch shot a blast of blue fire a good three feet away.

"That'll work," Chance said. "I'm coming with you."

Sam came into the kitchen with one of Anson's rifles. "So am I," he said.

Brendan shook his head. "I'm going alone. If they only focus on one target, it might give the rest of you an edge. Linny's safety is all that matters."

Sam shook his head. "Belinda belongs to all of us, Bren. We'll do this together or not at all." He gave the sheriff a hard look. "Now's the time to redeem yourself, Henry, so don't fuck this up."

Henry frowned as he realized Sam knew he'd been on the take, but he got the message.

"I've got your back," Henry said.

Chance opened the door and the brothers walked out, ready to put their lives on the line for the child caught in the middle of hell.

****

Marty had just pulled the motor home up behind the

house and braked when the back door opened. When Wes saw the three brothers emerge, he frowned. One was armed, one had the briefcase, and one was carrying some kind of torch. He hadn't expected all three of them, but it didn't matter. He had the greater firepower *and* the kid.

He cut the ties from her ankles and grabbed her by the hair as he yanked her to her feet.

"You make one wrong move and I'll break your neck," he said and yanked hard again to prove his point.

Linny was so scared she was shaking, and when he yanked her hair, she cried.

"You're hurting me. Stop hurting me."

Wes frowned. "You make one wrong move and I'll kill your brothers."

She could already see the blood on the ground even though it had not been shed and willingly let him drag her out of the motor home. But then she saw her brothers and all of her bravado was gone. She started crying.

Brendan's gut knotted the moment he saw her. One side of her face was swollen and there was blood on the front of her shirt, but he couldn't lose focus. He swung the briefcase to call attention to it, flipped the latch, and dropped it, knowing it would fall open and the stacks of bills would spill out.

Wes frowned as they tumbled out onto the ground.

"What the hell, Poe? Is this supposed to be your sign of good will?"

Brendan unscrewed the cap on the bottle of whiskey and began pouring it all over the money at his feet.

"What the fuck made you think there was any good will between us? You stole our little sister. There's no good will here... none at all."

Wes was shocked that he was soaking the money with

booze. It made no sense. He didn't know what was going on, but he didn't like it.

"Thorpe, if they make one wrong move, kill them all," he said loudly.

Thorpe swung the AK47 toward them. All he had to do was pull the trigger and the spray would take them all down.

At that point, Sam shouldered his rifle and pointed it squarely at Wes Riordan's head.

"If you turn Thorpe loose on us, you need to know I'll get off one shot before I die. And that shot is aimed at you, so I'd be real careful about starting something you can't finish," Sam said.

"Let Linny go," Brendan said.

"Not without my money," Wes muttered.

Brendan toed the briefcase forward. "Send your hired dog to pick it up."

Wes turned back toward the motor home and yelled. "Marty!"

The driver jumped out on the run. "Yeah, boss?"

"Pick up that money."

"Sure thing," he said and started forward.

"Stop right there," Brendan said.

At that point, Chance fired up the chef's torch. The blue flame shot across the space between them, punctuating the order.

Marty hesitated, unwilling to approach the blaze.

Brendan pointed at Linny. "Turn her loose first or my brother is going to start the most expensive bonfire you've ever seen."

"God damn it!" Riordan yelled and twisted Linny's hair even tighter.

She shrieked again, this time begging Riordan to stop.

Chance's reaction was instantaneous. "Stop hurting her, damn it, or your money is history!"

He waved the lit torch over the top of the money to punctuate the threat. The air above it was full of the alcohol fumes and instantly flamed. It went out just as quickly as it had caught, but the warning was there.

Riordan stared at the money, then the men, and slowly loosened the grip.

"You think I won't do it?" Chance yelled. "I burned down over a million dollars' worth of marijuana. Torching a hundred thou is nothing to me."

"You burned the fields?" Wes cried. "What the fuck made you do something like that?"

Chance locked gazes with Riordan. "Daddy made me mad. You don't want to make me mad, too."

Wes stared at the flame. It was far too close to the whiskey-soaked money for his state of mind. He eyed Poe's sons with new respect. It was painfully obvious that, even if he had a dozen more men and an army of weapons, these three would still do exactly what they said.

One wrong move—the money would be in flames—and he'd have a bullet in his head.

"Ah, what the hell," he said, cut the ties on Linny's wrists, and gave her a shove.

Linny didn't need a second invitation. She fixed her gaze on Brendan and started running.

Brendan dropped the empty whiskey bottle at his feet, pulled the handgun from the back of his waistband and aimed it at Riordan, too.

"Just in case my brother misses," he said softly.

His gun was still trained on Riordan as Belinda leaped into his arms, sobbing.

All of a sudden, police cars appeared around the corner of the house, pulling up behind the motor home with lights flashing. Three other cruisers shot out from behind the packing shed and headed toward the house with lights flashing and sirens blaring.

Other deputies came out from the woods where they'd been hiding with their guns drawn, shouting for the men to drop their weapons.

Enraged that they'd been caught in a trap, Wes started screaming at Thorpe, "Shoot them, shoot them all!"

Brendan dropped, shielding Linny with his body as the shooting began, and even though it was just a matter of seconds, it felt like forever.

There was a roar in his ears he later realized were Linny's screams. He could see a ladybug crawling in the dust by her arm. The scent of her sweaty little body was up his nose, and the faint smell of marijuana was in her hair. He kept praying they wouldn't die.

The shooting stopped as abruptly as it had begun. The police were in control, and Riordan's crew was on the ground.

Brendan rolled off Linny, then picked her up into his arms as she continued to sob.

"It's over, baby. It's over," Brendan said as she threw her arms around his neck.

Sam came running with Chance right behind him. "Is she okay?" he yelled.

Brendan nodded.

"Jesus wept," Sam muttered, then put his arms around them as Chance did the same.

They couldn't change what had happened to Belinda, but she was alive, and that's all that mattered.

Sheriff Henry was standing on the porch with Anson Poe in his grip. For once, Poe was speechless, eyeing the number of police on his property and more that kept coming.

Thorpe was flat on his back, the AK47 at his feet and a bullet hole in his head.

Marty, the driver, stood out like a parrot in a cage full of wrens wearing a red and green floral shirt and green shorts. His ensemble went well with his new handcuffs.

Wes Riordan was facedown on the ground with a deputy on top of him, locking handcuffs on him as well.

Linny was sobbing helplessly as Brendan headed for the house with her in his arms. "You're okay, baby girl. You're okay."

"You're safe, honey, and the bad guys are going to jail," Sam added.

"I want my Mama," she whispered.

Brendan frowned. More bad news she wasn't going to like. "Mama is at the hospital, but we'll go see her."

Linny's demeanor shifted. "What happened to her? Did she get shot?"

"No. She got hurt before you even got here."

Disbelief was on her face. "Did Daddy hurt her again?"

"Yes," he said and kept walking to the house.

Sheriff Henry had Anson by the arm and was walking him toward a police car.

Anson gave his daughter an angry glare as they passed. "I should've dropped you in the Mississippi the day you were born," he growled.

Linny looked up from her brother's shoulder, her eyes and cheek red and swollen, her face streaked with tears.

"You are going to die," she whispered.

Anson started to laugh, then choked instead as a thin spiral of smoke suddenly appeared on the ground in front of him. He lurched backward, crying out.

"Look! Look at that smoke! Do you see that?"

Henry yanked him back into place. "Stand still. You're not going anywhere."

Anson was in a panic as he struggled against his restraints. The smoke had turned into a flame. It kept getting bigger and moving toward him at a steady pace.

He began scream. "Can't you see it? It's burning! We have to get away! Get me out of here now!"

Brendan just kept walking.

"Daddy's going to die," Linny said as the deputies began shoving him into the backseat of a cruiser.

"Whatever happens to him has nothing to do with you," Brendan said as he entered the house. "Let's get your hands and face washed, and then we need to get you to a doctor."

Linny face crumpled. "I don't want to see a doctor. I want to see Mama."

"But they're in the same place, sugar," Sam said.

"Why do I have to see a doctor? I'm not sick," Linny wailed.

The brothers looked at each other at a loss as to how to explain the need to make sure she hadn't been raped. Then she surprised them by saying it for them.

"They didn't touch me. Not anywhere, Brendan. I'd tell you if they did."

Brendan set her on the kitchen counter and then wrapped his arms around her, his voice shaking. "You were so brave. You did everything right, and I was so afraid I had failed you."

Linny hugged him. "You came just like you said you would." She looked up at Sam and then Chance, giving them both a shaky smile. "I have the best brothers ever."

Chance ran into the library and came back with Rabbit. "Here, sugar. You won't want to go without Rabbit."

Linny turned her head and wouldn't look at it. "Rabbit is all bloody," she whispered. "I think he died."

It was all Chance could do not to cry. "Yeah, maybe you're right. We'll leave him here for now."

Linny kept her face hidden on Brendan's shoulder. "You need to bury him. That's what happens to things that die," she whispered.

"I'll bury him for you, baby. I promise," Sam said.

She wouldn't look back as they carried her away.

****

LaDelle woke up in ER as a nurse was shaving the hair from her head. All she could feel was a pounding pain at the back of her head before she passed out again. After that, she kept drifting in and out of consciousness, once as an X-ray machine was being moved over her head, and again as they were putting staples in her head. She kept trying to remember what had happened.

The next time she woke up, Claudette was at her bedside praying, and Delle wondered if she was going to die. It wasn't until Brendan and Linny arrived that her pain went from bad to worse, only it wasn't her head that hurt then. It was her heart.

****

Delle began coming around after they'd moved her to a regular hospital room. She'd talked briefly to Claudette, but it was awkward. The accusation was in her sister's eyes. She'd knowingly gone back into a place that had not been safe, and she had to accept that she was mostly responsible for the situation she found herself in now.

She knew Linny had been rescued, but it wasn't until she saw her for herself that she began to feel easier.

Brendan came in holding Linny's hand as firmly as if

she'd been a toddler trying to walk. And when Delle saw the bruise on her daughter's cheek and the cut on her lip, even though she knew they would heal, she felt guilty all over again.

"Oh, Linny! Sweetheart! My prayers have been answered. I'm so glad you're safe," Delle said and held out her arms, but Linny leaned backward against Brendan instead.

"Your hair is all gone."

Delle was shocked by her daughter's reticence, and sensed it had to do with much more than her lack of hair.

"I have a lot of staples in my head. They had to take it off to fix what got hurt. Will you come let me hold your hand? I need to touch my baby girl to know she's really okay."

Linny laid her hand in her mother's palm, but looked out the window rather than in her mother's eyes.

Delle squeezed the slender fingers gently. "Look at me, honey."

Linny's gaze shifted.

Delle sighed. "I'm so sorry about what happened to you. I would never have believed your daddy could have been that bad."

"I told you he was the Evil Overlord and you didn't believe me... even when he was mean to you, too."

"I know. I made a mistake and you paid for it. I'm sorry. I'm so sorry," Delle said and started to weep.

Brendan frowned. This wasn't what Linny needed. Not now.

"We have to go, Mama. Sheriff Henry wants Linny to be examined so they'll know exactly what charges to file."

Shock swept over Delle again as she realized what this meant. Dear God, they were going to do a rape kit. The invasive exam would most likely scare her all over again, and she wasn't able to be there with her. She covered her face and started to sob.

Claudette sighed. LaDelle was a strong woman, but with a single weakness that had nearly destroyed them all.

"Brendan, do you want me to go with you?" she asked.

He glanced at Linny and then shook his head. "We'll be fine, Auntie, won't we little sister?"

Linny nodded, but tightened her grip just in case. "When we're done, I want to go home with you, Bren. Can I go home with you?"

"Yes, honey. Once we're done here at the hospital, you are going home with me."

****

Brendan was still reeling from what Linny had to go through. The person who'd done the rape kit had been very gentle, speaking to her in a very slow, quiet voice explaining everything she did ahead of time.

Brendan stood beside the exam table, holding his sister's hand with his gaze firmly fixed on the red imprint on her cheek and the bloody split on her lip where Riordan had slapped her. He wanted to throw up. In the middle of all that, Julie sent him a text.

Is everyone okay?

He sent one back.

We're alive. For now, it is enough.

Sending you my love. If you need me, all you have to do is call.

Love you, but stay away. I don't want you dragged into the chaos that surrounds me.

She sent him back one last message. No words. Just a heart. It was enough.

****

The arrest of Wesley Riordan for child trafficking and kidnapping was shocking, but nothing to the uproar that hit when people began learning that Anson Poe had actually sold his nine-year-old daughter into prostitution.

But it wasn't the sale of a child that was garnering the most attention. It was how her three brothers had pulled off her rescue. One of the cops had captured the whole thing on a cell phone and even though it had been filmed from a distance, the graphic nature of it had been shocking. Once the video showed up at police headquarters, it wasn't long before it was leaked. It showed up on YouTube, and before night, it went viral. They became instant heroes as the media swarmed the city of New Orleans vying for interviews, and no one was prouder than Juliette March. Once again, the man she loved had proven himself worthy of so much more than the name he bore.

She'd caught part of a news report earlier the following morning, showing Brendan coming out of the hospital holding Linny's hand, then another of the news conference Sumter Henry held praising Brendan Poe's quick actions, the brothers' bravery, and his department's swift response, and she went to find her grandmother.

****

Portia March was in the back garden, sitting in a white wicker glider with an open magazine in her lap. Every so often she would toe the ground to give the glider a slight push, just enough to keep it in motion as she gazed off into the distance. When she heard footsteps approaching, she saw her granddaughter and smiled.

"Good morning, darling. I was just out here enjoying the sun. Come sit with me."

Julie slid onto the seat beside her and then took her by the hand. "Nonny, it's time for me to go home."

Portia eyed the fading marks on Julie's face and arms.

"You know I've loved having you here, but it's your call."

"I couldn't have gotten through these past weeks without you," she said and kissed her grandmother's cheek.

Portia snorted lightly. "Of course you could and would have if the need had arisen. You are a March, and you are a survivor. So are you going back to your apartment?"

"Thank you for the vote of confidence, Nonny, and yes, I'm going back. Brendan needs help, and I need to feel useful again. In the grand scheme of things, who would ever have imagined that my abduction would actually become a useful experience? I can relate to what his little sister is going through better than anyone."

Portia eyed her granddaughter thoughtfully. "You are a very special young woman. I would never have thought to look at it from that point of view."

Julie's smile slipped. She struggled not to fall back into that dark place where she'd put Chub Walton and his whip.

"I'm ready to live my life again, whatever that means... whatever it brings."

"You are a brave girl, and I'm very proud of you."

"Thank you, Nonny. I'm going to go pack and I'll leave after lunch."

"Call your father. Make him take you home."

Julie frowned. "I'll call a cab. I'm not in the mood to put up with him today."

Portia shook her head. "Call him. Do it for me."

Julie relented. "All right, I will, but only because you asked."

Portia patted her hand. "That's my girl. Now go tell Janie we'll have an early lunch today in honor of your departure."

"Yes, ma'am," Julie said and hurried back into the house.

****

Grayson March was as chastened as a man could be and not be groveling. Like the rest of the world, he'd watched the rescue take place while acknowledging to himself that he wouldn't have had the guts.

Twice in the space of just weeks, Brendan Poe had shown not only remarkable courage, but sharp foresight in coping with two equally dire situations. The media was all over the event and how it had played out, right down to the harrowing showdown.

Grayson was still finding it hard to believe what Anson had done. Grayson loved his daughter so deeply he couldn't imagine ever doing something as cold and callus as what Poe had done.

He was coming out of an early morning meeting when his cell phone rang. When he saw it was from Julie, he stepped aside into a foyer to take the call.

"Good morning, darling."

"Hope I didn't catch you at a bad time."

"No, it is the perfect time. Are you okay? Do you need something?"

"I'm fine. In fact, that's the reason I'm calling. I told Nonny this morning that I'm ready to go home, and she insisted I call you for a ride."

He frowned. "I'm sorry you wouldn't have thought that for yourself."

"Look, Daddy, every time we're together, I get the third degree from you and Mother about my personal business, and frankly, it hurts my feelings. Surely you can understand why I wouldn't immediately want to thrust myself right back into that environment."

"Yes, I'm sorry about that, and we need to talk."

Julie groaned. "No. We do not need to talk. In fact, never mind. I'll call a cab to take me back to my apartment."

Grayson flinched. "No, no, you misunderstood me. I want to apologize."

"You've apologized before and it didn't take. Why would this be any different?"

He winced. Truth was hard to take.

"Look, I can be hard-headed and resistant to change as much as the next man, but when faced with an impeachable truth, I like to think I'm man enough to back down. Once again, your Brendan has proven himself to be a most remarkable, even heroic man. I get it. I get him. And honestly, I think it was his looks that made it so hard for me to separate him from his father. Maybe because they looked so much alike, I kept thinking they would be alike in personality as well."

"Well, they're not," Julie said.

"And I finally see that. I'm sorry. I'll tell him the same thing. And, yes, I will happily take you home. Just tell me when to come pick you up."

"Has Mother reached the same understanding?"

Grayson paused. "You know your Mother."

Julie frowned. "Then don't bring her with you."

"I won't. I promise. I'll be there about half-past one. Is that okay?"

"Yes and thank you."

"You're very welcome, Juliette."

Grayson dropped his cell phone back in his pocket and then headed back to his office with a new mantra—one thing, one day at a time.

He went home for lunch, purposefully to speak to Lana about his revelations, and he was in the dining room reading his newspaper while waiting for her to arrive.

Lana came in minutes later, pleased that Grayson had come home to have lunch with her, and greeted him with a perfunctory kiss, then looked over his shoulder to see what he was reading.

"So, isn't that just shameful about that Poe family?"

Grayson looked up, frowning at Lana as the maid came in with two servings of crab salad and a basket of hot croissants and served them at their seats.

Grayson nodded his thanks, and the moment they were alone, responded. "On the contrary, Lana, the family isn't shameful. Anson is the only degenerate in the bunch."

She arched an eyebrow then forked a bite of the crab salad into her mouth, talking as she chewed, a trait that irked Grayson to no end.

"Now, Grayson, you know what I mean. They are a disreputable lot, to say the least."

"I don't agree."

She frowned. "But they were growing and selling marijuana, then Anson sold that poor little girl. Why, she'll never be able to hold her head up as long as she lives. People will—"

Grayson felt his gorge rise. It was people like Lana who would ostracize that child, if for no other reason than the belief in their own superiority.

"Damn it! That's enough!" Grayson said and slapped the table so hard it made Lana jump.

She frowned, then laid her fork across her plate and dabbed her mouth with a napkin.

"I won't be yelled at, at my own table," she said. "You don't—"

"No, *you* don't, Lana. Don't ever let me hear you say a bad word about Belinda Poe again. She's an innocent, beautiful nine-year-old child, and-"

Lana sniffed. "How do you know she's so innocent now? I mean, those men—"

Grayson's eyes narrowed angrily. "You heard me. Not a fucking word, and if you do, I will make you sorry."

She started to snap back at him and then something in his eyes made her stop.

"Whatever," she said and broke off a piece of croissant, popping it into her mouth as well. "I have Garden Club this afternoon."

"And I'm taking Julie home. She called me this morning and asked for a ride back to her apartment."

Lana frowned. "I can't believe you're doing that. She needs to come home where she belongs."

"Actually, Lana, she's a grown woman capable of making her own decisions. I've also come to the conclusion that Brendan Poe is a remarkable and honorable young man, and that she's lucky to have him."

Lana gasped. "That's ridiculous."

"Well, no it's not. Don't you pay attention to anything but the gossip in your social circles? It's because of him that we still have our daughter, and now he and his brothers have pulled off what some considered an impossible rescue. He's an impressive man, and I'm sorry it's taken me so long to see that."

Lana was pouting now and he could see through the ruse. He stifled a grin. He might as well ruin the rest of her day while he was at it.

"I'm going to get a lawyer for LaDelle and her boys. The

DEA is already involved, and they don't deserve to be dragged into anymore of Anson's hell."

She looked up, horror etched on her face. "You're going to get a lawyer for them? Why on earth would you involve us in such a disgusting situation?"

"Because your daughter will likely marry Brendan Poe, which will make them our in-laws, that's why."

"No!" Lana cried and clutched her heart as if it was about to leap from her chest. "I won't have it. Did she tell you this? When did she tell you? We have to do something!"

"She didn't tell me, but I know it. I knew it when I saw them together at the hospital and I wouldn't acknowledge it. He saw her at her worst and loved her anyway. He didn't turn away in disgust. He didn't even ask if she'd been raped because it wouldn't change the way he felt about her. He's better than both of us, my dear wife, and after what he did to save Julie, and then the brilliance in the way he helped rescue his little sister, he should be lauded, not shamed."

Lana's face was flushed with anger. "Our friends will laugh at us behind our backs."

"Then they won't be our friends, will they?"

"It's all so simple for you," Lana said. "You don't have to deal with the evil, back-stabbing bitches of this city. They can break hearts and reputations without blinking an eye."

"Be careful how you describe your friends and yourself. From the way you were talking about an innocent child moments ago, I thought I was married to one of them."

She glared.

"And, Lana dear, you must remember that if you say that about one child, what do you think people will say to you about yours? It's the same situation, my dear. They were two innocent people who got caught up in something not of their making."

The flush on Lana's face slowly disappeared as the truth of what he'd said soaked in.

They finished their lunch in silence. Grayson had done what he could to foster good feelings between mother and daughter. The rest was up to them.

****

DEA agents Faro and White came on the scene within two hours of Anson and Riordan's arrest. Faro was a tall, skinny redhead. White was a tall, skinny blond. Their features were Nordic but their Boston accents gave them away. They looked enough alike to pass for brothers, which they were not.

Anson asked for his lawyer upon arrival at the jail, which ended an early attempt to interrogate him, and then, in the words of the jailer, Anson Poe began to unravel.

They issued his prison garb, which he managed to set on fire, and when they issued the second set of clothing, he refused to put it on. The agents had been given to understand he was in his cell, naked and raving about curses and God.

They moved on to Wesley Riordan, at which point he politely asked for his lawyer, and again, their attempts at interrogation came to a swift halt.

The next morning, the three sons were brought in for questioning. They came in together and were immediately taken into separate rooms for interrogation.

After a quick conversation with each of the three, they quickly learned Brendan Poe had never been a part of his father's lifestyle and that he and Anson were actually enemies—a statement which was backed up by the older brothers. But when they confronted Brendan as to why he hadn't turned his family in to the authorities, since he was aware his father's illegal business dealings, his words came out in short, angry bursts.

"Because the damn courts would have bonded him out before nightfall, and everyone involved in turning him in would've been dead before morning. As for why he'd never been arrested for his illegal activities, you might want to start looking at the local cops. He had plenty in his pocket, making sure that didn't happen."

"Do you have any names you could give us?" Faro asked.

"I haven't lived there for over seven years. I didn't witness anything. I never saw any money change hands. Without true knowledge of who he did and didn't pay to look the other way, I'm not commenting. I believe it's the law's stance that gossip doesn't hold up in court, so you do the digging. I'm staying out of that, just like I did everything else connected to Anson Poe. So either arrest me, or I'm leaving. My mother is in the hospital with sixteen staples in her head, and I have a little sister who's afraid to close her eyes now because her daddy sold her for some pervert to fuck."

"We might need to—"

Brendan stood up. "I promised Belinda I'd be back and it's about damn time someone keeps a promise to her. I'd just as soon it was me. Am I under arrest?"

Faro hated to lose control, but since both of the other brothers had willingly admitted Brendan had nothing to do with anything at Wisteria Hill, they watched him walk out, and directed their attention to Anson's older sons.

Both Sam and Chance freely admitted to working the drug crops at their father's bidding, claiming it was his daily threats and ruthless personality as well as their fear of what he'd do to their mother and sister that kept them under his thumb. They both denied knowledge of which cops Anson might have paid off, although they both agreed that they believed it was so.

The agents' questioning was long and exhausting, but both of the brothers stayed true to their stories without wavering.

Faro kept pushing at Chance, trying to get him to admit they were willing participants in their father's business until Chance finally lost his cool.

"Look, I already said this every way I know how, and I'll say it until the day I die. I hated my father and everything he stood for. He is a mean, heartless bastard with a pretty face. I put up with him and his behavior because as long as Sam and I continued to show up at Wisteria Hill, our mother and sister stayed in one piece."

Faro smiled. "That's real noble of you, padding your pockets with easy money, and justifying it by calling yourselves babysitters."

Chance reeled as if he'd been slapped. "There wasn't anything noble about it. It was hell on earth and our pockets weren't padded. I have a note on my truck, and rent due on an apartment in town. So does Sam. Daddy pocketed the money. We got a salary from the bamboo business, which is perfectly legal, and that's it! I hated his fucking weed patches, and I hated him, and I finally grew some balls and burned him out. He still doesn't know it, and I don't care. I should have done it a long time ago."

Faro's surprise showed. "You burned him out? Why?"

Chance smiled. "One of those final-straw moments."

The interrogation went on up into the night before they let them go.

Sam was fatalistic, and Chance was angry at himself

for waiting so long to make his break. They left discussing the need to hire lawyers.

Chapter Twenty-One

When LaDelle was informed the DEA agents were coming to talk to her, she was scared to death they were going to arrest her for abetting in Anson's trade.

Claudette knew Delle was nervous, but she had a plan. Instead of putting makeup on her sister to face the agents, she had her scrub her face clean. Now Delle waited for their arrival with a newly shorn head, sporting sixteen metal staples instead of a part in her hair, and a completely unadorned face. It made her look younger, even tragic, a victim rather than a co-conspirator. To add to the drama, she'd left LaDelle's feet uncovered, knowing they would also see the painfully pink and healing skin.

Just before 3:00 p.m., there was a knock at the door. Delle braced herself, gripping Claudette's fingers tighter as the door opened. But it wasn't the agents. It was Grayson March, accompanied by a stranger.

Grayson was taken aback by LaDelle's appearance and knew his instinct for coming here had been a good one.

"LaDelle, I apologize for coming without calling, but may we come in?"

Delle frowned. "If you've come to visit, I'm not much in the mood. I'm expecting some agents from the DEA."

"After speaking to my daughter today, I gathered as much. But now to the reason we're here. LaDelle Poe, this is my lawyer, Armen Bales. He's going to represent you until all this is ironed out."

Delle blushed. "I can't pay a lawyer, and I sure can't afford Mr. Bales."

"No, no, you misunderstood," Grayson said. "He's at your disposal and I'm picking up the bill."

Delle was stunned. "That's very kind, Grayson, but I can't let you do that."

Grayson sighed. "Well, actually you can. In fact, you probably should, considering the fact that we're most likely going to be in-laws one of these days."

"Let him help," Claudette whispered.

Delle clutched her sister's hand. "I'm sure you remember my sister, Claudette DuVeau. She's been a rock for us throughout this whole ugly mess."

Grayson smiled. "Of course I remember you. It's great to see you again. Claudette, my lawyer, Armen Bales. Armen, this is LaDelle's sister, Claudette DuVeau."

The lawyer nodded and smiled, then turned his attention to Delle.

"So, Mrs. Poe, Mr. March told me part of what's happened, but I need to ask some questions before the agents show up."

"Ask away," Delle said.

The lawyer moved closer to her bed as they began to talk.

When Claudette stepped away, Grayson followed, still eyeing the majestic woman and the gray dreadlocks hanging halfway down her back.

"You look amazing," he told her. "And you definitely outgrew me," he added.

Claudette smiled. "Do not feel bad. At my height, I look down on a lot of people."

Grayson nodded. "Brendan is very tall, too."

"All of Delle's children are tall, even Linny."

And just like that, the mood shifted. "Is she okay?" he asked.

Claudette shrugged. "She will be. The blessing is that they did not have her long enough to do anything but scare her."

Grayson sighed. "Thank the Lord. I kept remembering how terrified I was when Juliette was kidnapped, and she was a grown woman who understood what was happening. There's no way to imagine what horrors a child would make out of all that."

"Yes, this is true. We are blessed."

"We're both blessed, and a good portion of that belongs to Brendan. Once again he has surprised and amazed me," Grayson said.

Claudette eyes narrowed thoughtfully. "I understood you were not so pleased about your daughter's friendship with my nephew."

"I wasn't, but I'm man enough to admit when I'm wrong," Grayson said.

"Detective Carson is helping him get into the police academy," Claudette added.

Grayson was sincerely happy to hear this. It would go a long way in making Brendan Poe socially acceptable for Lana.

"That's wonderful news, and in light of the recent events, it seems he has a knack for doing the right thing," Grayson said.

"We think so," Claudette said.

"And I concur."

Claudette smiled. "It is good when families get along."

He returned the smile. "Yes, ma'am, that it is."

At that point, there was another knock on the door and then two men entered.

"LaDelle Poe?"

"Yes, I'm LaDelle," she said as they flashed their badges.

"Agent Faro, DEA, and my partner, Agent White. We need to speak with you."

"I'll be leaving now," Grayson said and nodded to the men as he passed them on the way out the door.

Grayson's lawyer introduced himself.

"Armen Bales, attorney at law. I'll be representing Mrs. Poe."

The agents were taken aback as they spoke to LaDelle.

"Does this mean you're not going to cooperate?" Faro asked.

"I'm happy to answer any question you ask, but Mr. Bales is going to make sure I don't wind up being railroaded into jail for being married to the devil," she said.

"Then let's get down to business. For the record, we'll be recording this," Agent White said.

Bales pulled out a similar device. "As will I," he countered.

The questioning began.

When did they begin growing marijuana?

What part did she play in it?

Did she ever entertain drug dealers in her home?

And with every question answered, Delle's opinion of herself grew smaller and smaller. Even when Bales interjected to make sure she didn't incriminate herself, she continued to feel shame. Her eyes were swimming with tears—her chin trembling with every word she spoke, but she'd didn't falter, not even when the nurse came in to check her wound and inject pain meds in her IV. At that point, the agents stopped and stepped back.

The nurse administered the meds, filled her water pitcher, then paused at the bedside.

"Is there anything you need, honey?"

Delle pointed toward her bare feet.

"My feet are really hurting. I scratched them up when my son and I were searching the property for my daughter, and I don't want them to get infected just as they've finally begun to heal."

The nurse moved down to the foot of the bed to get a closer look at Delle's feet. It was obvious that the new skin on the healing burns was scratched, and in some places completely gone.

"This isn't good," the nurse said. "I'll need to call the doctor to get orders, but we'll get something on this. Be right back."

Delle leaned back against the pillow as the nurse left the room.

Faro had been empathetic to a point, but he'd seen far too many family members wrapped up in the drug trade to buy the hopelessness of their situation. However, now that attention had been called to her feet, he was curious.

"What happened there?" he said.

"Anson poured hot coffee on my feet a few weeks ago. They were just beginning to heal."

Faro frowned. "Poured it on purpose?"

"Yes."

"What for?" he asked.

Delle looked up at him. "Because it amused him, that's why."

Agent White shifted uneasily then glanced at his partner.

Faro frowned. "You and your two oldest sons are adults. Why would you continue to stay with someone like this if you disagreed so strongly with how he behaved? Why didn't you turn him in for spousal abuse, or for the drug trade, if you so violently disapproved?"

"My sons stayed to protect me and my daughter, and that's my burden to bear for staying with him."

"Well, obviously that didn't work, considering what just happened to your daughter. But why *did* you stay? Why didn't you turn him in?"

She gestured at her body. "Look at me. I have broken bones that healed without ever being set. I've been raped and beaten so many times I've lost count. You don't know him. You don't know how vicious he could be. I had to stay. As for turning him in, that's a joke. He would have been out on bond within hours, and the moment he laid eyes on me for what I'd done, my children and I would've been killed in retribution."

Agent Faro remembered Brendan Poe making a similar statement and ended the recording.

"I think we have enough for now."

The lawyer turned his recorder off, as well.

"Have you spoken to Anson Poe?" Armen Bales asked.

"He lawyered up. We'll be talking to both him and Riordan tomorrow."

Armen Bales eyed the agents, aware they didn't have the power to make deals, but it was time to offer one up.

"I've been told that Samuel Poe has documentation that will incriminate both his father and Wesley Riordan, not only for the growth and sale of marijuana, but also the sale of LaDelle's daughter, Belinda. And remember Chance Poe was personally responsible for burning the fields that put his father out of the drug business. While Mrs. Poe cannot be forced to testify against her husband, she is more than willing to do so. It might be in your best interests to give my client, and her sons, complete immunity in return for testimony that would assure convictions on both men, putting them behind bars for a long, long time."

Faro shrugged. "We don't have the authority to offer or discuss any of that."

Bales smiled. "But you have access to people who do. I think Mrs. Poe has been forthcoming enough for one day, and since it appears she's in need of more medical treatment, we need to be finished here."

"Agreed," Faro said.

Bales shook Delle's hand. "Mrs. Poe, I hope you are able to get some rest. I'll be in touch." He gestured toward the door. "Gentlemen, after you."

Moments later, they were gone.

Delle looked at Claudette, her eyes brimming with tears.

"I've never felt so worthless in my entire life," she whispered.

Claudette scooted onto the side of the bed and took her sister in her arms. "You are not worthless, and after hearing what you said to those men, it has become obvious to me that you are a battered woman. Being abused and controlled as you have been all these years, it is actually amazing that you are still alive."

Delle started to weep. "I let my children down. I got all of them in trouble. I would gladly go to prison if they would be set free."

"Grayson March has done you a great favor, my sister. That lawyer is a very smart man, and I'm thinking you will all come out of this just fine."

"I sure hope so," Delle said and reached for a tissue to wipe her eyes.

By the time the nurse came back with medicine and bandages for her feet, Delle had her emotions in control. She sent her sister home with much gratitude and a hug, then closed her eyes and went to sleep, too exhausted to dwell on the future.

****

Anson Poe was causing trouble in lockup. Within hours of being jailed, the clothes he'd been issued caught fire, and he'd barely gotten out of them before being burned. The jailer hadn't been able to find any kind of matches or lighters to have caused it, and Anson kept telling them it was voodoo. They issued a second set of clothing, but he refused to wear anything combustible again, and it was still folded and lying on the corner of his cot. His face was on fire from the scratches left behind from Delle's fingernails, and he spent the entire night naked and screaming for help, claiming the place was about to catch fire. The jailer's threats had done nothing to silence him, and neither had the other prisoners' complaints.

****

After a night of pure terror, Anson was sitting in a corner of the jail, his head was down and his shoulders trembling as he continued to wail. Every time he closed his eyes, he saw a coffin with the lid ajar, his charred body inside, burned black as a piece of coal.

He had never believed in God.

He had never believed in voodoo.

But every breath he took now was spent begging a God he didn't know to save him from a curse that didn't exist.

Just before noon, his lawyer showed up. When the jailer came to get him and saw the shape he was in, he frowned.

"Hey, Poe! Get up and get dressed. Your lawyer's here."

Anson put his hands over his ears and began shaking his head in denial. "Nope, nope, can't get dressed. No clothes. They'll burn. I'll die. Not moving. Can't go."

The jailer shrugged. "It's your funeral," he muttered, but Anson heard it and began screaming.

"NO! It's not my funeral. It's not. I can't die. It's not fair. I'm saying prayers. Make it go away."

The jailer left, but came back shortly with the lawyer.

The lawyer took one look at his client, and his heart sank. "Mr. Poe, It's me, Larry Feinstein. We need to talk."

Anson shook his head wildly, waving his arms at the man to go away. "Can't talk. Can't look. I'll burn. Tell God I'm sorry. Tell Him I won't do it again."

"Do what?" Feinstein asked.

"Set any more fires. Tell God I'm sorry about Frenchie's, and the Quarter, and Voltaire. Tell God I'm sorry. I'm sorry. I'm sorry."

Feinstein stared in disbelief. "Are you saying that you're responsible for burning down Frenchie's, as well as the ensuing fires that burned through the French Quarter?"

Anson rolled over onto his side and curled up in a fetal position with his hands over his head, his gaze fixed.

"Yes, yes, sorry. Voltaire knew. Had to keep him quiet. Tell God I'm sorry, sorry, sorry. Make Him take away the curse."

Feinstein's lips parted, but for the life of him, he had no response. His client had just confessed to arson and murder, as well as to the rest of the mess he was in, which left him wondering how to proceed.

"What do you want to do?" the jailer asked.

"He needs a psych evaluation before anything else transpires. I'm through here for now," Feinstein said.

The jailer escorted him out with Poe's screams following his retreat.

"Tell God I'm sorry, I'm sorry, I'm sorry. Make Him take away the curse."

****

Brendan had a sack of groceries in one hand, and his door key in the other. His little sister walked beside him, as always, with her finger hooked in the waistband of his jeans. But this time, she had a new stuffed toy tucked under her arm. After nine years of Linny and Rabbit, Rabbit had been left behind and buried.

Brendan had seen the sadness on Linny's face and had known the loss of Rabbit was as real to her as a death. And in an effort to make it better, they'd spent the better part of an hour down in the French Quarter at Michelle's Candy Basket looking over her assortment of stuffed animals.

He'd stood by silently, watching Linny pick up the stuffed toys one by one, look at the face, feel of the fur, and then tuck it under her chin and close her eyes. She repeated the steps over and over until it became apparent it wasn't just looks that she was going for. She was searching for one that gave her a good feeling as well. He was sick for the loss of her innocence. Her trust was gone, and she was looking for courage from a toy made in China.

They'd been there for more than thirty minutes, and during that time, she kept moving along the shelves without making a choice. The toys were all soft and cute, but Brendan surmised they must not feel right.

****

Linny looked over her shoulder to make sure Brendan was not running out of patience, then caught his wink and relaxed as she began looking through another row.

Like before, she started at the bottom, but this time, she saw there was a second row of stuffed animals behind the ones in front and sat down for a better view. Within moments, she saw a fuzzy little face looking back at her from between two white Teddy bears. She leaned closer and felt its gaze.

"I see you, too," she whispered, then pulled it out, tucked it beneath her neck, and closed her eyes.

Almost immediately, the tension in her body dissipated. It felt right, too.

She looked up at Brendan and smiled.

He looked past the healing cut on her lip to the light in her eyes.

"Is he the one?"

She nodded.

"That's a fine-looking little hound you've got there. Do you know what kind he is?"

She nodded. "A bloodhound. One of the boys in my class brought a picture of his daddy's bloodhounds to show-and-tell once. They help find people who are lost."

Her reasoning hurt his heart. Even her toy needed to be a form of protection. *Damn Anson Poe to hell a thousand times.*

"What are you going to name him?"

"Tracker. I'm going to call him Tracker."

"That's a perfect name for the perfect friend. So let's go pay Michelle, and maybe we should pick out some candy to take home while we're at it."

She almost smiled. "We could get some chocolate-covered raisins. Those are our favorite, right?"

Brendan put his hand on the top of her head and then brushed a stray lock of hair back into place.

"Yep, they are our favorite, which means we should probably get extra."

Her little smile came and went all too quickly, but knowing it wasn't completely lost made this trip worthwhile.

And so they'd come home with a little brown dog named Tracker and a sack full of chocolate-covered raisins.

He headed to the kitchen to put up the groceries as she went to the extra bedroom and kicked off her shoes. She came back barefoot with the little dog still under her arm.

"What are we having for supper, Bren?"

"We have a couple of choices," he said. "We can either have hamburgers and fries or chicken strips and fries."

"Do we have ranch dressing?" she asked.

"Yep."

"Then I choose chicken!"

He grinned. "Do you dip *everything* in ranch?"

She frowned. "I don't dip breakfast stuff in ranch... Oh, except for when Mama makes little sausages with my eggs."

He laughed and was still laughing when someone knocked at the door.

Linny grabbed the dog and slunk back against the wall.

"It's okay, baby. All the bad guys are in jail, remember?"

She nodded, but she didn't move as he left the room.

Brendan opened the door and just like that, all of his sadness and exhaustion was gone.

"Julie!"

She smiled. "Surprise. I moved home."

"This home?"

She laughed. "Yes, this home. Couldn't stay away from you any longer. Is Linny here?"

He nodded.

"Do you think she can handle this?" she asked, indicating her healing wounds.

"Let's find out, okay?"

She grimaced. "I'm a little scared."

He cupped her cheek. "Honey, I've been scared ever since the both of you disappeared, and I'm still not over it."

He led her into the kitchen.

Linny was still standing against the wall.

"Hey, little sister, you have a visitor. I'm gonna put the chicken in the oven while you two catch up."

Linny's eyes widened. Her lips parted, and then closed again.

Julie opened her arms.

"You better come give me a hug. I haven't seen you since I got hurt. Is that little dog new? He's so cute."

"His name is Tracker. He's going to keep me safe," Linny said, but stopped short of a hug and pointed to Julie's arms instead.

"Does that hurt?"

"No much anymore, but it hurt a lot at first."

Linny's voice was soft, muffled, and verging on tears. "I'm sorry you were hurt."

"And I'm sorry you were, too. We are really two lucky girls, aren't we?"

Linny frowned. "What do you mean?"

Julie pointed at Brendan. "He saved our lives, didn't he?"

Linny cut her eyes over at her brother, then nodded. "Sir Brendan is my bravest knight."

"And a good cook, too," Julie said and tweaked Linny's ear. "Is there enough chicken for me if I promise not to eat too much?"

"I'll share," she quickly offered.

"We have plenty," Brendan said. "Who wants something cold to drink while the chicken cooks?"

"Me, me," Linny said, and for a few moments, she was a light-hearted child again.

Julie moved up to the counter beside Brendan as Linny dug through the choices of soft drinks.

"How's your mother?" Julie asked.

"She looks like hell, but she's going to be okay. The big worry right now is if she and my brothers get charged along with Anson."

Julie frowned. "I'm so sorry."

He shrugged. "They knew the risks a long time ago. It's all up to the authorities now."

She leaned in and whispered, "Does Linny know all this?"

He shook his head.

Unable to speak her mind, she just made a sad face.

"Hey, Julie, do you want something, too?" Linny asked.

"Yes. You choose one for me, okay?"

Linny got busy all over again.

"Thank you," Brendan said.

Julie shrugged. "Our experiences were horribly similar. Maybe we can help each other get through this."

He dumped some French fries on one end of the big cookie sheet and chicken strips on the other end, then popped it in the oven.

"It feels so good to be home," Julie said.

Brendan paused, then leaned down and stole a quick kiss. "It's good to have you home, too," he said softly.

Linny had three glasses of Pepsi, iced down, on the table and ready to drink.

"Come and get it," she said.

Brendan laid his hand on her head. "Thank you, honey. That looks good."

Linny pointed at the glass in front of him. "I made sure your ice didn't float, just like you like it, Bren."

He grinned. "That's my girl!" He took a quick sip and then set it aside.

"So what's on the agenda later?" Julie asked.

He shrugged. "Just hanging out, probably. Why?"

"I thought if you had things you needed to do, Linny might like to come back to my apartment with me and we'd have a little girl time. I have new nail polish and bubble bath."

Linny gasped, then looked up at her brother. "Could I?"

He laughed. "Who am I to interfere with nail polish and bubbles?"

"Yay!" Julie said.

"Yeah... yay!" Linny echoed and then remembered Tracker. "Can my dog come, too?"

"Absolutely!" Julie said.

And just like that, what started out as a tense, anxious day was mellowing out into a better evening. It gave Brendan time to check his messages regarding job applications and do laundry at the same time.

Chapter Twenty-Two

The DEA agents, Faro and White, received a phone call from Poe's lawyer just before noon the next day. Anson Poe wanted a priest, and he wanted to confess. They grabbed their recording equipment and headed for the jail.

The lawyer and the priest met them in the parking lot, and quickly introduced themselves.

"Thank you for coming. I'm Larry Feinstein, Poe's lawyer, and this is Father Patrick."

Faro eyed the pair, one in a white summer suit, the other in black, both of a similar height and on similar paths. One dedicated to saving lives, the other to saving souls.

Faro nodded. "I'm Agent Faro, and this is my partner, Agent White. So Poe wants to confess?"

Feinstein shrugged. "Against my advice, I might add. I wanted to petition the court for a psych evaluation, but he has refused it, so that's why we're here."

"Why the psych evaluation?" Agent White asked.

Feinstein shrugged. "You'll see. Follow me."

White carried the recording equipment, and Faro had a briefcase and the tripod. They entered the precinct without conversation, but instead of giving them an interrogation room in which to set up, they soon learned they were being led straight into the jail.

Faro stopped. "Why aren't we going to an interrogation room?"

"Again, you'll see," Feinstein said.

When they began to hear crying and screaming, even before they entered the cellblock, White paused.

"What is that all about?" he asked.

"That's Poe," Feinstein said.

By the time the jailer led them to Poe's cell, Faro's first thought was that Poe was setting up an insanity defense. He was curled up in a corner of the cell, as naked as the day he'd been born.

"What the hell?" Faro said.

The jailer moved toward the bars. "Poe! Your lawyer is here."

Anson was still moaning and wailing, praying the words of the rosary so fast the words were nearly unintelligible.

Feinstein took a step closer.

"Mr. Poe! Mr. Poe! The authorities are here as you requested."

Anson looked up, took a shaky breath, then rolled over onto his knees and eased upright against the wall. His pupils were dilated, his body trembling. He had yet to focus on either one of the agents.

"Do you see it?" Anson cried, pointing at the floor in front of him.

"See what?" Feinstein asked.

"The fire! The fire! It's there, waiting to burn me. I need to confess. I need to make it go away."

"Let's get set up," Faro said and unfolded the tripod as White readied the camera.

Within a couple of minutes, they were ready to go.

"We're ready, Mr. Poe."

Anson seemed to have forgotten they were there and had begun slapping at his arms and the back of his legs.

"Burning me... It's burning me," he mumbled, then crouched in the corner. "Where's the priest? I need the priest."

"I'm right here, Anson. My name is Father Patrick."

When Anson saw the face behind the voice and realized he knew him, he started to weep.

"Bless me, Father, for I have sinned. It's been many, many years since my last confession."

The priest turned around. "If he confesses to me, it's privileged. You can't be a witness."

Anson screamed, "No, no, I need everyone to hear! It's the only way the curse will go away!"

Father Patrick's fingers curled around the cross hanging from his neck as he watched Anson shove his hands through his hair over and over until the sides were standing up in a caricature of fright. Between the crazy hair and the gouges in his face that were beginning to scab over, he finally looked like the monster that he was.

"What kind of curse?" the priest asked.

"Voodoo," Anson whispered, then looked all around as if speaking the word would actually summon the demons. "Someone put a curse on me because of what I did. I have to confess or I'm going to die."

Faro interrupted. "Look, Father. You can stay or you can go, but either way we're going to film this."

The priest frowned. "This is highly irregular and I'll not consider it an actual confession. I will simply be another witness to what he says, but that is all. Is that understood?"

"Whatever," Faro said. "So, let's get this started." He signaled White to begin filming. "Mr. Poe, for the record, look up at the camera, state your name and age, and why you were arrested."

Still squatting in the corner, Anson curled his fingers

over his knees and focused on the camera like it was the face of God.

"Anson Poe. I'm fifty years old and I was arrested for human trafficking and drug charges. I am making this statement because I need to confess all my sins or I'm going to die."

Faro frowned. "Why do you think a confession will save your life?"

He moaned and then slapped his cheeks as if he'd done a bad thing.

"I didn't believe in God and I didn't believe in voodoo, then someone had a curse put on me. I thought it was a joke and used it against someone else and caused their death. I'm going to die if I don't make amends. I'm going to burn just like the fire I had set at Frenchie's."

Faro frowned. "What's Frenchie's?" he whispered as Anson kept talking.

Feinstein already knew his client was responsible for the fire that swept through the French Quarter.

"It's a long story. Just let him keep talking, and I'll explain later."

The agent tuned back in to what Anson was saying.

"...payback for not letting me fuck her whore. It burned The Black Garter, too, which was next on my list. Then the little coffin showed up on my doorstep. It had a match and my picture on it. That's voodoo. Someone had a curse put on me. I tried to make Mama Lou take it off, but she shut the door in my face. I have to confess to God or I'm gonna die."

White shook his head. He was not a believer of anything paranormal and certainly not voodoo.

Anson suddenly shrieked and rolled sideways. "Fire between my feet," he screamed, then started talking faster.

"Grayson March set his guards on me. It pissed me off. I wanted payback and needed to get rid of the loose ends. The guards were my payback. Voltaire LeDeux was the loose end. I tricked all of them. They took each other out and there was no one left to tie me to the fires. It was a bad thing I did. I lied. I lied. I lied so many times and I'm sorry. I'm so sorry. Forgive me. Somebody has to forgive me."

Father Patrick was praying quietly, his lips barely moving, his words purposefully muted.

"Why did you sell your daughter?" Faro asked.

Anson shuddered, then again grabbed his hair with both hands, pulling fistfuls of it up and away from his head, as if trying to alleviate some kind of weight.

"Things were going wrong. I needed money and none was coming in. Family was getting away from me. I was losing control. I always had control. Had to get it back."

"How did you maintain control before?" Faro asked.

Anson crawled back into the corner then curled himself up as small as he could get. "Pain and fear. Pain and fear. That's power. That's how you maintain control."

"You hurt your family?"

Anson sat up and laughed and then slapped himself violently, as if in remorse for the sacrilege.

"Sorry, sorry. Not funny. Bad. I did bad things. They were afraid to disobey. That's control."

Faro glanced at his partner and mouthed the word, *wife*. They'd just gotten confirmation as to what the whole family kept claiming. LaDelle Poe said she was afraid to leave. He'd just confirmed it without knowing anything about what she'd said to them.

"Your sons worked with you growing and selling marijuana," Faro said.

Anson slapped his knee with the flat of his hand, punctuating every word with a slap.

"Those fields were mine, not theirs. They did the bamboo. I did the pot. I made them work it, but the money was mine—all mine. They did what I said to keep their mama safe. She was the pawn in my games. Always the pawn. Always the goody-two-shoes trying to change me. Fuck her!"

And then the moment those two words were spoken he threw his head back and screamed. "Make it stop. The fire is hot. Make it stop. I take it back. I'm sorry."

The priest's pallor was as white as the collar around his neck.

"Dear Jesus," he whispered and prayed harder and faster.

White frowned. "What's the matter?"

The priest shook his head and kept praying.

Faro moved closer to the cell. "Anson Poe, why would you want to sell your little girl into a life of prostitution? She's just a child."

"Someone stole my marijuana and set the fields on fire. I needed money."

"Your son, Chance, confessed to burning the fields," Faro said.

Anson gasped. His face contorted into an angry grimace as he jumped upright. "The bastard! I should've cut this throat a long time ago."

The vehemence in Anson's voice was so strong that White shuddered, and seeing the man upright, muscles flexed and fists doubled, punctuated the strength of the statement.

"So you sold your daughter to Riordan because you needed money. Is that right?" Faro said.

Anson started toward the cell bars, then stopped and very quickly backed up, pointing at the floor in front of him until he could go no farther.

"It's smoking. Can't you see it? I'm sorry. God has to forgive me. I'm sorry."

"Why did you choose Riordan?" Faro asked.

Anson's hands were cupped over his genitals, his eyes wide and glassy.

"He always bought my pot. He said he would buy my kid, too. I didn't want her. Easy decision," Anson whispered.

Faro felt sick to his stomach. He'd heard plenty of confessions coming out of the mouths of criminals, and probably just as many lies, but he'd never heard anyone speak of his crimes in such a cold, emotionless manner before.

"Is there anything else you want to confess?" Faro asked.

Anson wiped his face with both hands, stared straight into the camera, and spoke without a trace of emotion.

"I planned to kill my wife, LaDelle, for revenge. It would have been payback to my son Brendan for challenging me. He knocked me down. He shot the hat off my head in my own house. By God, nobody does that to me. But, I decided she was worth more to me alive than the revenge I would've gotten. I like to fuck and I like good cooking. That's what she was for. So selling the kid hurt all of them. I showed them it wasn't smart to go against me."

There was a bitter taste in Faro's mouth, and White's hands were trembling.

The priest made the sign of the cross.

Feinstein swallowed past a knot in his throat then breathed a quick sigh of relief. He didn't want to be this man's lawyer, and he damn sure didn't want to try this case in a court of law. The confession had just relieved him of a jury trial. Poe would be convicted according to the laws of the state for each separate charge against him, which basically meant he would never live as a free man again.

Anson leaned back against the wall, his shoulders slumping. He was as relieved as his lawyer, but for a different reason.

"I told it all. I confessed to my crimes. I admitted to my sins. This means God has to take away the curse, right, Father?"

The priest hardly knew where to begin. "God doesn't make deals, Mr. Poe. He is the Almighty and his ways are not always clear to us, although you have done right to ask His forgiveness."

Anson looked like he'd just been slapped. "But I told the truth."

"That's how you should have been living all along, not a thing to be rewarded," the priest said.

Anson shook his head and began counting things off on his fingers. "No, I confessed my sins. I confessed my crimes. I confessed to what I planned to do, even though I didn't do it. I am now guilt-free, right? God has to fix the curse."

Father Patrick clutched his cross as he moved a little closer to the cell. "God may forgive you, but the law will not. You're still guilty. The lies you told were harmful and caused people to die."

"I'm not lying anymore," Anson shrieked.

The priest took a step forward. "So you say, but you have lived your life on lies, have you not? And the longer truth is buried, the more powerful lies become."

Anson started to argue and then dropped to his knees and pointed at the floor. "I didn't lie to you today and the fire still burns. I told my secrets, but it didn't go away."

"He's crazy," Faro muttered.

"What happens if a judge sees this and decides he

needs to be hospitalized, instead of incarcerated?" Feinstein mumbled.

"Hell if I know," White said. "It's our job to catch them. It's the court's job to put them away."

All of a sudden, Anson began moaning and pointing at the concrete floor.

They all turned and then stared in disbelief at the curls of smoke that appeared out of nowhere and began moving toward the man in the corner.

"Do you see that?" Faro cried.

White's belly rolled. He felt like he was going to be sick.

Anson was as far back in the corner of the cell as he could get, and yet it continued to move toward him.

"Do something!" Feinstein shrieked.

The jailer jerked as if he'd been slapped, then ran for the fire extinguisher at the far end of the hall.

Anson began weeping, shaking his head in mute denial and trying to climb the walls, but this time there was no stopping the smoke.

"Wait, wait, I forgot the cops. I paid off the cops, too," he screamed.

The priest dropped to his knees and began praying in earnest.

The prisoner directly across from Anson's cell saw the smoke and started yelling, "Fire!"

It started a chain reaction of panic from the prisoners in the other cells, until the whole place was alive with shouts and screams.

"Who were the cops you paid off?" Faro asked.

Anson couldn't hear the question. His focus was on the smoke at his feet. When it began to curl around his ankles, he began screaming as if he already felt the heat. Then the smoke went higher, wrapping around his legs and his body, then crawling along the lengths of his arms and up his neck. His cry was one continuous shriek as the smoke reached his head. When his hair began to smoke, he threw up his arms in supplication and burst into flames.

"Oh my God!" Faro shouted and jumped back.

White was in shock, still standing beside the camera, unaware that it was still filming.

By the time the jailer reached the cell with the fire extinguisher, Anson was dead, his body curled up on the floor, his limbs contorting as the skin on his body bubbled and burst.

Father Patrick was sobbing now, prostrate on the floor in front of the cell, praying loudly to his God for protection.

The jailer dropped the fire extinguisher and threw up.

Word quickly spread from cell to cell what had happened. The men inside them were silent. Some curled up on their cots with their faces to the wall. Some were on their knees in prayer when the door to the cellblock opened and police began pouring into the area. Unfortunately, it was a case of too little, too late.

White finally realized the camera was still running and reached up with shaking hands to turn it off.

Faro seemed to be in shock and hadn't moved since Poe went down.

Feinstein helped the priest to his feet as Sumter Henry pushed his way through the crowd.

"What happened? What the hell happened here?" the sheriff yelled, and then he saw the blackened corpse in the corner of the cell. "Who is that?"

"My client," Feinstein muttered.

Henry gasped. "Poe? Is that Anson Poe?"

"Yes, sir," Feinstein said.

Henry kept staring. "Who did this? How did that happen?"

Faro shoved a hand through his hair. "I'd tell you, but you wouldn't believe it."

"We were filming his confession when he burst into flames," Agent White said.

"What do you mean, 'burst into flames?'"

"Spontaneous combustion. I saw it with my own eyes," Father Patrick said.

"There's no such thing," Henry muttered.

"He said he was cursed," Feinstein said. "He said it was voodoo."

Henry flinched. "Like hell." Then he took out his handkerchief and covered his face against the stench of burned flesh. "Get the crime scene crew in here, ASAP. The rest of you, out! I want statements from everyone here and—"

White held up his hand. "Like I said, we were taping his confession. You can see it for yourself."

"In my office," Henry said. "All of you! Now! And bring that camera."

****

Linny was sitting on the sofa watching Juliette paint her toenails. She had Tracker in her lap; Julie's bear, Merlin, tucked under one arm; and a bowl of popcorn near the other. She was fascinated by the fact Julie had a bear named Merlin. She knew all about Merlin. He was the powerful magician who helped King Arthur and his knights. Just knowing *her* faithful knight, Sir Brendan, had given him to Julie made the bear more special, and she liked the pale green color Julie was putting on her toenails. It was almost the same color as the grass down by her throne in the swamp.

"When you're done, are we doing my fingernails, next?"

Julie paused and looked up. "I think we should, don't you?"

Linny eyed the assortment of nail polish on the coffee table. "I like pink, too. It's my favorite color."

Julie paused and looked up. "Well, then we should use pink on your fingernails, I think. What do you say?"

"I say yes," Linny said and leaned over Tracker for a closer look, then reached for the popcorn, chewing thoughtfully as she eyed the healing wounds on Julie's skin.

"Can I ask you something?" Linny asked.

"You can ask me anything," Julie said.

"You said the marks don't hurt, but are they going to go away?"

"They did hurt but not so much anymore, and yes, the doctor said they'll go away. Mama Lou gave me some special medicine to make them heal faster."

Linny gasped. "She gave Brendan the telephone I used to call Brendan when... when Daddy..."

Julie's heart hurt for the child. She didn't even have the words in her vocabulary to explain she'd been sold into sexual slavery by her own father. She patted Linny on the knee.

"Then that makes us twins all over again, doesn't it? First we both get kidnapped, and Mama Lou helps save both of us, and Brendan buys us very special stuffed animals to help us get well. What are the odds of that ever happening?"

Linny eyes were suddenly shiny with fresh tears. "I'll bet we made Brendan worry a lot."

"We didn't cause it, but I know he was worried. He's a very good man. You know that, don't you?"

"He's not afraid of Daddy," she said.

"No one should ever be afraid of their father. I'm sorry that you are."

Linny shrugged. "I'm not afraid anymore."

Julie finished the last toenail on Linny's little foot, then screwed the brush back into the bottle.

"Because he's in jail now, right?"

"No, because he's dead now," Linny said.

Julie frowned. "No, he's not dead, honey. He's in jail."

"Yes, but he's dead now, too."

Julie was shocked. She didn't know if this was a break from reality because of what she'd gone through or if something more was going on.

"How do you know he's dead?" she asked.

Linny shrugged. "I just do."

"Okay," Julie said. "So, are you ready for something to drink? Popcorn makes me thirsty. Are you thirsty? I have lemonade."

"Yes, and I like lemonade."

"Good. You sit really still so your nails will dry without getting messed up, and I'll go get the lemonade. We can do your fingernails later. Here, you can watch TV while I'm gone. My cable works the same way Brendan's does."

She left the remote with Linny and headed for the kitchen, but instead of pouring the lemonade, she called Brendan.

****

LaDelle was catching Brendan up on her interrogation as well as Grayson March's generosity in getting them a lawyer. Brendan didn't know how he felt about that personally, but was grateful for anything that kept the rest of his family out of jail.

"Grayson said you were amazing, and that he'd seriously misjudged you," Delle said.

"He talks out of both sides of his mouth," Brendan said.

Delle frowned. "He said since we were going to be in-laws, and that it would be good to get along."

Brendan's eyes widened. "He said that?"

She nodded, but before she could say more, there was a knock at the door and then Sheriff Henry walked in.

Brendan took one look at his face, then stood and reached for his mother's hand.

"I'm sorry to intrude, but I need to talk to you," Henry said.

Delle's voice began to shake. "Are we in trouble? Is the DEA going to charge us?"

Brendan's phone rang. He started not to answer it, and then saw it was from Julie. "Hang on a minute before you say anything. I need to take this. Hey, Julie. Everything okay?"

"You tell me," she said. "I was about to get Belinda some lemonade when, out of the blue, she told me her daddy was dead. Has she ever said or done anything like this before?"

Brendan frowned. "She said that?"

"Yes, and without any emotion. Just stated it as a fact."

"Look, I'll call you back in a few minutes, okay? Sheriff Henry just walked in and we need to talk to him."

"Yes, okay."

Brendan disconnected and looked at the sheriff. "By any chance are you here to tell us Anson is dead?"

Henry frowned. "How did you know? I gave specific orders for nothing to be released until all the family was notified."

Delle gasped. "What do you mean? Brendan, what's going on?"

"That was Julie calling. She said Linny just told her Daddy was dead."

"What? No," Delle muttered.

Henry sighed. "I'm sorry, Mrs. Poe, but that's why I'm here. I'm sorry to tell you that your husband passed away about an hour ago."

Delle gasped. "No... why... how? Oh, my God."

Brendan's first reaction was relief. "What happened?"

Henry started to answer, then wiped a hand over his face and started over. "He actually burned to death."

Delle moaned beneath her breath, and then curled up on her side and covered her face.

"Burned? What the hell?" Brendan asked.

"It was witnessed by the jailer, a priest, and two DEA agents. In fact, they were taping his confession. He has... uh, had confessed to everything from causing the fire at Frenchie's to tricking March's men into killing Voltaire LeDeux because LeDeux was a loose end to the arson. He kept saying someone had put a voodoo curse on him." Henry was still unnerved by how close he came to being outed for being on Anson's payroll. He glanced at Delle, then back at Brendan. "He also revealed how he controlled his family with pain and fear, and that he planned to kill your mother but then decided to get rid of your sister instead, knowing it would hurt all of you for defying him."

Brendan's stomach rolled. "God in heaven."

Henry kept talking. "He seemed to think that if he confessed his crimes... his sins, so to speak, it would save his life. But as soon as he finished the confession, smoke came out of nowhere and he pretty much burst into flames. I'm sorry. They ran to get help, but it was too late."

Brendan shuddered. "Someone cursed him for sure."

"That's what he kept saying. Do you have any idea who it might have been?" Henry asked.

Brendan shook his head. "It could have been anyone. He made his share of enemies outside the family, too. So what happens to Mama and my brothers?"

"It's not my call, but after what he said, and what the agents witnessed, I'd be shocked if anyone besides Riordan is ever charged."

"Thank God," Brendan said.

"Hey, sorry that leaked out before we got a chance to notify everyone," Henry added.

Brendan shook his head. "It didn't get leaked. Sometimes Belinda just knows stuff."

Before today, Henry would've said he didn't believe in psychics, fortune tellers, or voodoo, but what he'd seen had seriously given him pause for thought.

"After what I saw, I may never sleep again. I'm sorry to be the bearer of bad news."

"His death is not bad news to me," Brendan said.

Delle didn't answer because she was crying and was still crying after Henry was gone.

Brendan was not only puzzled, but somewhat angry that she could grieve for a man so evil.

"Damn it, Mama, why are you sad? I would have thought you would be relieved."

Delle took the tissues he gave her and blew her nose. "I'm not sad. I guess it's a combination of relief and guilt. I prayed that he would die and he did. What does that make me?"

"It makes you human. Do you want me to call Sam and Chance, or do you want to do it?"

"You," she said.

"Okay, and by the way, we need to start paying attention to the stuff Belinda says. She's got a gift, Mama, whether you want to face it or not."

LaDelle sighed. "I know. She's just like Mama and Claudette."

Brendan stared. "You never mentioned any of this before. Why now?"

She shrugged. "It was always easier to ignore it than deal with it."

He frowned. "No more ignoring shit, Mama. Not ever again. I'm going to call the guys, then go home and check on Linny."

"Godspeed," Delle said.

"From your lips to God's ears," he said, kissed her good-bye and left the room to make the calls.

****

Brendan set up a mini-conference call so he wouldn't have to tell the whole thing twice, then broke the news to his brothers about Anson's death. The silence that came afterward was odd.

"So, either one of you have anything to say?" Brendan asked.

"Don't expect me to say, I'm sorry," Chance muttered.

"Me, either," Sam added.

"There's something else," Brendan said and told them about Linny's call. "She's always saying stuff and we ignore it. I think it's time we start paying attention. She told me after he burned Mama's feet that something bad was going to happen to her. I attributed it to the shock of what happened to Mama and ignored it."

"Yeah, and remember she told me to make that list of bad people Daddy knew, and all of the things that he'd done to destroy him," Sam added. "It wound up being part of what rattled Riordan enough to bring her back."

"And now knowing Daddy died before anyone told us,"

Chance said. "We're not only going to have to pay attention to what she says, but also what we say to her."

"For sure. No more lies," Brendan added.

"No more lies," they echoed.

****

Grayson March was waiting in the parking lot of Brendan's apartment when he saw him drive up. Grayson was prepared for rejection, although it was no more than he deserved, considering how many times he'd rejected Brendan.

Brendan saw him get out of his car and stopped.

Grayson kept walking. "Have you got a minute?" Grayson asked.

"Start talking," Brendan said.

Grayson held out his hand.

Brendan hesitated so long Grayson thought he wasn't going to shake it, and then he finally relented.

"I'm sorry," Grayson said, "for everything I ever said or insinuated about you."

Brendan waited without comment as Grayson continued.

"I got a call from the Parish sheriff that your father confessed and cleared the names of my employees who were blamed for Voltaire LeDeux's murder. It will be a blessing for their families."

"He's dead, you know."

Grayson's mouth opened, but nothing came out.

"It's a long story, but suffice it to say, he brought it on himself," Brendan said. "My little sister is with Julie. They're painting toenails. Want to come up?"

Grayson was surprised, but pleased by the invitation. "Yes. I would like that."

"I'm going to marry your daughter," Brendan said.

Grayson nodded. "I guessed as much."

"I suppose you think I should have asked your permission," Brendan said as they headed toward the building.

Grayson shrugged. "I think I lost any expectations of having that honor right after I accused you of being part of her kidnapping."

"I'm glad we understand each other," Brendan said.

Grayson laughed. "We might butt heads along the way, but I'd say we *definitely* understand each other."

"I'll make Juliette proud of me, and I'll never let her down."

Grayson sighed. "I know that, and I thank you."

"I'm going to the police academy in the fall."

"An honorable profession," Grayson said.

"Not all of the time," Brendan said, thinking of the men his father had paid to look the other way. "I plan to be one of the good guys."

Grayson nodded. "I have no doubt."

They walked the rest of the way in silence, and when Brendan knocked on Julie's door, the look on her face when she opened it was priceless.

"Brendan! Daddy! Are you—?"

"We're fine," Brendan said. "Is Linny okay?"

She nodded. "It's weird, but she actually seems relieved. Was it true?"

"Yeah. I'll tell you later. Did you save us some lemonade?"

"We drank it. I have sweet tea."

"Even better," Grayson said.

Linny came bounding into the room with Tracker under her arm.

"Brendan! You're back! Did you know Daddy was dead?"

He arched an eyebrow. "So I heard. Are you okay?"

She nodded. "The Evil Overlord has been defeated. All is well in my kingdom, thanks to my best and most faithful knight."

Brendan laid his hand on her head as she leaned against him.

Grayson smiled at her. "Who's the knight?"

"Why that would be me," Brendan said. "I can't believe you had to ask."

"And when Sir Brendan and Juliette get married, she will be his Lady," Linny added.

Brendan winked at Julie, then tugged on Linny's hair. "Who said anything to you about us getting married?"

Linny shrugged. "I just know stuff."

"Yes, you do," he said softly, then tugged her ponytail again. "Julie is going to talk to her daddy for a bit. I want to talk to you."

"He burned up. I saw it, Bren. It's okay. Bad people burn in hell."

Brendan sighed. "Maybe we can skip that talk after all."

"Don't be upset. I just know stuff, Brendan. Remember?"

"Well hell," Brendan said softly.

Grayson looked a little pale. Dead was one thing. Incinerated was another. "Juliette, do you happen to have anything stronger than sweet tea in this place?" he asked.

Julie pointed to the sofa. "You boys sit. We'll do the honors, won't we, sugar?"

Linny nodded. "Yes, I'm getting big enough to carry lots of stuff now, even the stuff that spills."

"Definitely, big enough," Brendan said, watching her walk away with her head up, her shoulders back, and keeping up with every step Julie made. Life had kicked his little sister in the teeth and caused her to grow up too fast for his liking, but it was what it was.

"Two damn fine women, if I say so myself," Grayson said.

Brendan shoved his hands in his pockets so no one would know they were shaking, thinking to himself how quickly things began to right themselves once Anson Poe was no longer of this world.

Chapter Twenty-Three

Grayson went home shortly after his arrival, and Brendan and Linny were on their way out of Julie's apartment as well.

Brendan handed his little sister the keys to his apartment, knowing she liked being the one to unlock the door and then watched her skipping as she headed down the hall with Tracker tucked under her arm. He stayed behind just long enough for one last hug from Juliette.

"We love. We'll make love. Soon," she whispered.

Brendan cupped her face in his hands, rubbing a thumb across her lower lip.

"I told your father I was going to marry you."

Julie blinked.

He sighed. "I know. I should have probably asked you first."

She grinned. "You think?"

"Forgive me?"

"Only if you promise to do it right next time."

"Brendan! Are you coming?"

"Gotta go," he said. "Remember, the answer should be yes."

He hurried up the hall, leaving Julie smiling as she shut the door.

As soon as they were inside the apartment, Linny put Tracker down and then followed Brendan to his room.

"Can I call Mama?" Linny asked.

Brendan was relieved she was ready to talk to her. "Sure. I'll get her on the phone, okay?"

She sat quietly, watching Brendan's face as he made the call. He spoke briefly, then handed her the phone and went into the living room to give her some space.

He turned on the television for something to do and was lost in thought and ignoring the show, when he felt two small hands slipping around his neck and then warm breath on his ear.

"Thank you, Bren."

"You're welcome, sugar. Is everything okay between you and Mama?"

"Yes."

"Come, sit down, and talk to me," he said.

"I can't right now. Company's coming."

There was a knock at the door.

"It's for me," she said and ran to answer.

"Wait! What the hell, Linny? You know better than to do that? It's not safe."

"This time it is," she said and opened the door.

"Auntie!" Linny said.

Claudette leaned down and gave her niece a kiss on the cheek. "I have someone who wants to talk to you."

Brendan saw her and smiled. "Hey, Auntie, come in. I was-" He saw the tiny woman who stepped out from behind Claudette and his smile widened. "Mama Lou!"

"I would speak with your sister," the old woman said and took Linny by the hand.

When Brendan started to follow, Claudette stopped him with a touch, then a look.

"It is time this happens," Claudette said. "The trauma of what happened to Belinda has triggered what was already there in her. She needs to know how to control it."

Brendan frowned. "Is this going to make her life more difficult?"

"Life is always difficult, Brendan. You of all people should already know that. This is who she is. Let it be."

Long minutes passed, then turned into half an hour before they returned. It took Brendan a few moments to realize the panic was gone from Linny's face. When they stopped at the sofa, Mama Lou put a hand on his shoulder.

"The liar is gone and so are the lies," she said. "There are no lingering spirits at Wisteria Hill of which you should be concerned." She laid a hand on Belinda's head. "The Queen of the Bayou has abdicated the throne. There is no longer a need to live in a make-believe land. Soon you will change the armor of a knight for a uniform, a badge, and a gun."

"And will I live happily ever after?" Brendan asked.

Mama Lou smiled. "If you so choose."

Claudette stood. "Are you ready to leave now?"

"Yes. I have done all that was needed for now. She knows I will be there for her in the future as well."

They were gone as abruptly as they'd come, leaving Brendan a little uneasy. He didn't know what to do or say to Linny now.

"Is there anything you want to tell me?"

She frowned. "Like what?"

"I don't know. All this talk about being someone different made me wonder, that's all."

"I'm not different, Brendan. I just quit pretending to be something I'm not. When Mama goes home, it'll be okay this time. Sam loves Wisteria Hill so much. He'll make it a good place again. You'll see."

"You are one brave girl," Brendan said.

Linny crawled over the back of the sofa and onto the cushion beside him, then glanced up, her eyes narrowing as she studied his face.

"People can look alike without being alike," she said softly.

"You are right about that," he said.

He knew how much he looked like Anson, and what it must cost her to have feared one, loved the other, and had the strength of heart to know the difference.

"You know what, Bren? One lie is as bad as a thousand lies, but I think the lies in our family died with Daddy. I promise to never tell a lie as long as I live."

Brendan swallowed past the lump in his throat as he put his arm around her. She'd come so close to being lost to them forever, and he couldn't forget it.

"Do you know what a touchstone is?" he asked.

"No."

"It's the way someone might measure what is best in life, like the thing that keeps them focused and on the right path."

"Oh."

He pulled her closer. "So you, Belinda Poe, are my touchstone. You are the best of the Poes who have ever lived. You are everything God meant you to be, and will be. I am proud to share your name."

She leaned against him. "One day when you and Julie are married and have babies, I'll be the best auntie ever to them."

He laughed from the joy of knowing there was actually a "one day" on the horizon.

"From your lips to God's ears," he said.

Her brow furrowed. "No, Bren. We should always say 'from our lips to God's heart,' because that's where the love comes... from His heart."

Epilogue

Months later—Christmas Eve

Juliette Poe was pregnant and, according to the doctor, about five weeks along. She came home from the appointment, went straight to the bedroom and stripped, and was now standing in front of her full-length mirror, turning first one way and then the other, eyeing her naked self.

Unless you knew where to look, the lash marks from her abduction were barely visible, all except for one on her upper thigh that left a long, thin scar. She didn't mind that scar so much anymore, mostly because Brendan called it her badge of honor and because he often traced the length of it with his fingertip as they made love.

It was because of all that love-making that she was in this condition, and she was not only elated by the timing, but talk about the perfect Christmas gift for hubby, way better than a tool set from Sears.

But it wasn't just the joy of becoming parents that was so important. It was also because of what it was going to mean to them, personally. This child was going to be the final piece needed to end the lingering cold war between her mother and the Poes.

Julie's mother was polite to Brendan's family, but she wasn't friendly. She almost hated her mother for that faux pas, but she was trying to follow Brendan's path and take the high road in all of it. He'd reminded her only yesterday when he kissed her good-bye before going to work.

"They're our families, but they're not us. Whatever hitches they carry in their steps does not cripple you or me."

She'd put her hand on his chest so she could feel his heartbeat. "You're right, as always. Be safe, be smart, and come home to me."

It was something she'd said his first day on the job as a cop at the New Orleans P.D, and she'd said it every day since as her own kind of talisman.

She moved back a step from the mirror and turned to the right to check her belly. It was still flat, although not for long. But it wasn't just about the changes to her body that mattered. It was the changes within the families.

Out of all that had happened, LaDelle Poe had probably changed the most, not only outwardly, but from within. She'd gone home from the hospital with a shaven head, and when the hair began to grow back, it came in snow white. Trauma-based stress everyone said. But her daughter said different. She said it was because her mama was an angel on earth, and that God had changed her hair so that everyone could know.

No charges were ever filed against Delle or her sons. Wesley Riordan was in a federal prison and would most likely die there. Delle's relief that they'd escaped prison was boundless, and her joy in family continued to grow.

As Linny predicted, Sam moved home to take care of the family and the family business of bamboo. Under his care, both were thriving.

Chance joined the Louisiana National Guard. He still had something more he needed to prove to himself, and when he came home, got his job back at the auto supply. He was a regular guy through the weekdays, but two weekends a month, he turned into a warrior, confident he was finally doing something right with his life.

Once Anson was gone, Claudette regained her sister, for good this time. And now, with this baby, even more changes were to come.

Julie turned to face herself in the mirror and put a hand on her belly.

"You, my sweet baby, are going to have *the* best aunties ever. One is Claudette. The other is Belinda, and they will know your heart long before you know yourself."

She heard a door slam and her heart skipped a beat. Brendan was home.

She heard another door open and close and knew he'd just removed and stored his weapon.

Before she could get her clothes back on, he was standing in the doorway, still wearing the blue shirt and dark pants of the New Orleans P.D.

He grinned when he saw her naked.

"Now this is what I call a great welcome home."

She lifted her arms and did a neat pirouette. "Take a good look because this trim little body isn't going to last long. This isn't exactly how I planned to tell you, but Merry Christmas, Brendan Poe. You're going to be a father."

His smile slipped, his lips parted, and then he opened his arms and was at her side in three steps. He touched her face, her breast, then dropped to his knees and laid his cheek against her belly.

Julie laughed as she dug her fingers through his hair, but it wasn't until she felt his teardrops that she realized he was crying.

"Brendan! Honey?"

Unashamed of the tears, he stood up, taking her with him. Her feet were dangling against his knees as he started kissing her cheeks, her forehead, on both eyes and then the tip of her nose. By the time his mouth finally centered on her lips, they were both in tears. When he sat down on the side of the bed, she was in his arms.

She caressed his cheek and then ran the tip of her finger along his lower lip. "I take it you're okay with this?"

"Beyond okay," he said, then wrapped his arms around her. "You have no idea what this means to me. For twenty-six years, I've fought my way through life, mostly because of the social disgrace of my last name. This baby will be the beginning of a new generation to bring dignity and honor back to the family. I am so happy for us, but to you personally, I am grateful beyond words for making this possible."

"No, Bren. This baby isn't the beginning of a new generation. That honor goes to you. You were a hero twice over before you ever put on a badge, and wearing this uniform just makes it better. I was always proud *of* you, but being your wife adds a whole other level to my pride."

He kissed the palm of her hand and then pressed it against his heart. "I swear to you, I'll never do anything to make you ashamed of me. I would die for you, Julie, without thinking."

The steady thump of his heartbeat was strong against her palm.

"I don't want you to die for me. I need you, and this baby and all the babies to come will need you. Stay strong for us. Stay safe for us. That's all I ask."

"I'll do everything in my power to make that happen."

"You swear?"

He leaned forward until their faces were only inches

apart. "You know me better than anyone. Would I lie to you?

She saw her reflection in his eyes and shook her head. "Never in a million years."

The End

Made in the USA
Lexington, KY
28 September 2013